PLOUGHSHARES

Fall 1997 · Vol. 23, Nos. 2 & 3

GUEST EDITOR
Mary Gordon

EDITOR
Don Lee

POETRY EDITOR
David Daniel

ASSISTANT EDITOR
Susan Conley

ASSISTANT FICTION EDITOR
Maryanne O'Hara

FOUNDING EDITOR
DeWitt Henry

FOUNDING PUBLISHER
Peter O'Malley

PLOUGHSHARES, a journal of new writing, is guest-edited serially by prominent writers who explore different and personal visions, aesthetics, and literary circles. PLOUGHSHARES is published in April, August, and December at Emerson College, 100 Beacon Street, Boston, MA 02116-1596. Telephone: (617) 824-8753. Web address: http://www.emerson.edu/ploughshares/.

EDITORIAL ASSISTANTS: Thomas McNeely, Jessica Olin, Debra DeFord, and Tom Herd. FICTION READERS: Heidi Pitlor, Billie Lydia Porter, Emily Doherty, Michael Rainho, Leah Stewart, Tammy Zambo, Monique Hamzé, Craig Salters, Karen Wise, Ellen Tarlin, Holly LeCraw Howe, and David Rowell. POETRY READERS: Paul Berg, Richard Morris, Caroline Kim, Michael Henry, Renee Rooks, Jessica Purdy, Charlotte Pence, R. J. Lavallee, Tom Laughlin, Bethany Daniel, Lori Novick, and Ellen Scharfenberg.

SUBSCRIPTIONS (ISSN 0048-4474): $21 for one year (3 issues), $40 for two years (6 issues); $24 a year for institutions. Add $5 a year for international.

UPCOMING: Winter 1997–98, a fiction and poetry issue edited by Howard Norman & Jane Shore, will appear in December 1997. Spring 1998, a fiction and poetry issue edited by Stuart Dybek & Jane Hirshfield, will appear in April 1998. Fall 1998, a fiction issue edited by Lorrie Moore, will appear in August 1998.

SUBMISSIONS: Reading period is from August 1 to March 31 (postmark dates). Please see page 241 for detailed submission policies.

Classroom-adoption, back-issue, and bulk orders may be placed directly through PLOUGHSHARES. Microfilms of back issues may be obtained from University Microfilms. PLOUGHSHARES is also available as CD-ROM and full-text products from EBSCO, H.W. Wilson, Information Access, and UMI. Indexed in M.L.A. Bibliography, American Humanities Index, Index of American Periodical Verse, Book Review Index. Self-index through Volume 6 available from the publisher; annual supplements appear in the fourth number of each subsequent volume. The views and opinions expressed in this journal are solely those of the authors. All rights for individual works revert to the authors upon publication.

PLOUGHSHARES receives additional support from the Lannan Foundation and the Massachusetts Cultural Council. Marketing initiatives are funded by the Lila Wallace–Reader's Digest Literary Publishers Marketing Development Program, administered by the Council of Literary Magazines and Presses.

Distributed by Bernhard DeBoer (Nutley, NJ), Fine Print Distributors (Austin, TX), Ingram Periodicals (La Vergne, TN), and Koen Book Distributors (Moorestown, NJ).

Printed in the U.S.A. on recycled paper by Edwards Brothers.

© 1997 by Emerson College

CONTENTS

Fall 1997

INTRODUCTION
Mary Gordon   5

FICTION
Alice Adams, *The Visit*   7
E. M. Broner, *The Agenda of Love*   13
Bliss Broyard, *Mr. Sweetly Indecent*   32
Susan Daitch, *A Day in the Future*   46
Tim Gautreaux, *Resistance*   62
Patricia Hampl, *The Bill Collector's Vacation*   77
Ethan Hauser, *The Dream of Anonymous Hands*   86
Lucy Honig, *Police Chief's Daughter*   100
Carole Maso, *Votive: Vision*   119
Joyce Carol Oates, *The Wake*   124
Richard Panek, *Permanent*   140
David Plante, *The Tent in the Wind*   152
Helen Schulman, *My Best Friend*   159
Maxine Swann, *Flower Children*   176
Eileen Tobin, *Goodbye, Tinker Bell, Hello, God*   186
Nola Tully, from *What Mattered We Left Out*   195
Meg Wolitzer, *Tea at the House*   203

ABOUT MARY GORDON   *A Profile by Don Lee*   218

BOOKSHELF/EDITORS' SHELF   226

POSTSCRIPTS   *Cohen Awards*   234

CONTRIBUTORS' NOTES   239

Cover painting: *Still Life: Green and Red with Peaches* by Nola Tully
Oil on canvas, 26″ x 32″, 1991

Ploughshares
Patrons

This publication would not be possible without the support of
our readers and the generosity of the following individuals
and organizations. As a nonprofit enterprise,
we welcome donations of any amount.

COUNCIL
Denise and Mel Cohen
Eugenia Gladstone Vogel

PATRONS
Anonymous
John K. Dineen
Scott and Annette Turow
Marillyn Zacharis

ORGANIZATIONS
Emerson College
Lannan Foundation
Massachusetts Cultural Council

COUNCIL: $3,000 for two lifetime subscriptions,
acknowledgement in the journal for three years,
and votes on the Cohen and Zacharis Awards.
PATRON: $1,000 for a lifetime subscription and
acknowledgement in the journal for two years.
FRIEND: $500 for a lifetime subscription and
acknowledgement in the journal for one year.
All donations are tax-deductible.
Please make your check payable to
Ploughshares, Emerson College,
100 Beacon St., Boston, MA 02116.

Introduction

If the novel is the bastard child of two passionately but uneasily matched parents—poetry and journalism—then the short story seems clearly able to trace its descent from the distaff side. I grant poetry the female gender, for reasons that there should be no need to state. Or if there is a need, the meeting of it may be a task too impossible in its lineaments for this place and time. There are, of course, plot-driven stories; it is the more usual case that a story be plot-driven; but in its intensity of construction and its relationship to a central image or images, the short story is similar in its formation to the poem.

The short story is usually only about one thing; I am deliberate in my vague use of the words "thing" and "about." The thing can be an object, a character, a moment; the thing can be any number of things. And the about can shape itself in any number of ways. The relationship of the one thing to the other things that surround it is, precisely, the story's form. The short story is like a wagon wheel: the spokes must be connected to the hub, or graceful movement is impossible. Or, again, the short story is like a peacock's tail: at the center is a dense circle of color from which emanates the iridescent, resonant shades that spread out to dazzle and delight. But the source of every tone must be the center, and the story will succeed or fail on its relationship to its own center.

I like to think that this was my primary criterion for the stories I selected: did the story relate properly, that is to say beautifully, to its own center? Another way of saying this is: did the story do what it was trying to do in its own terms?

It pleases me to say that I think the terms presented in this issue of *Ploughshares* are quite various. Some of the stories follow a straight narrative line and some do not. Some draw richness from the evocation of exotic or unfamiliar times and places. Some reach back to the dreamy purity or cloudiness of childhood; some find themselves enmeshed in the complex process of discovering or inventing adult relationships in a world which seems to offer only

unsatisfying or unsatisfactory models. There are parents and siblings, lovers and enemies, strangers, deaths approached or avoided, embraced or run from. There are reflections on the process of
making art, and moments of violence, cruelty, and deceit.

Like poetry, short fiction is deeply dependent upon voice, and
as a reader I am always drawn to a voice whose texture is in itself a
pleasure to me. I rebel against any closing, or closing of possibilities of voice, and I was heartened that the legacy left to us by the
flattening hoof of Hemingway was only sporadically taken up by
these writers. Although they chose many different degrees of
embellishment, the writers of these stories weren't afraid of the
lyrical, weren't drawn to a mindless minimalism that automatically rejected the flourish or the furbelow, the jeweled surface, or
the embroidered one. Place, clothing, food, weather, light, find
their ways into these stories, reminding us of what it is sometimes
too easy to forget: that the writer, as well as the reader, has a body.

I was pleased, as well, to be able to include writers at diverse
stages of their careers. Some of the writers are well-known, and
have received many deserved laurels for their fiction. Some
appear here for the first time; to be able to say that you have given
a gifted writer her or his first public appearance is a particular joy.
In one case, a writer has published in this issue of *Ploughshares*
for the first time in over fifty years. All of these writers moved me
by the originality and acuteness of their vision, by the evidence
they give that the short story is lively, only waiting for the proper
abode to shelter and nourish its life.

The Visit

S he's just dying to see you, so excited, and you really can't refuse a ninety-two-year-old," said Miles Henry to his old friend Grace Lafferty, the famous actress, who was just passing through town, a very quick visit. Miles and Grace were getting on, too, but they were nowhere near the awesome age of ninety-two, the age of Miss Louise Dabney, she who was so very anxious to see Grace, "if only for a minute, over tea."

"I really don't remember her awfully well," Grace told Miles. "She was very pretty? But all Mother's friends were pretty. Which made her look even worse. Miles, do we really have to come for tea?"

"You really do." He laughed, as she had laughed, but they both understood what was meant. She and the friend whom she had brought along—Jonathan Hedding, a lawyer, retired, very tall, and a total enigma to everyone so far—must come to tea. As payment, really, for how well Miles had managed their visit: no parties, no pictures or interviews. He had been wonderfully firm, and since he and Grace had been friends forever, if somewhat mysteriously, it was conceded that he had a right to take charge. No one in town would have thought of challenging Miles; for one thing, he was too elusive.

The town was a fairly small one, in the Georgia hill country, not far from Atlanta—and almost everyone there was somewhat excited, interested in this visit; those who were not were simply too young to know who Grace Lafferty was, although their parents had told them: the very famous Broadway actress, then movie star, then occasional TV parts. Grace, who had been born and raised in this town but had barely been back at all. Just briefly, twice, for the funerals of her parents, and one other time when a movie was opening in Atlanta. And now she was here for this very short visit. Nothing to do with publicity or promotions; according to Miles, she just wanted to see it all again, and she had carefully picked this season, April, the first weeks of spring, as being the most beautiful that she remembered. Anywhere.

It was odd how she and Miles had stayed friends all these years. One rumor held that they had been lovers very long ago, in the time of Grace's turbulent girlhood, before she got so beautiful (dyed her hair blond) and famous. Miles had been studying architecture in Atlanta then, and certainly they had known each other, but the exact nature of their connection was a mystery, and Miles was far too old-time gentlemanly for anyone to ask. Any more than they would have asked about his two marriages, when he was living up north, and his daughter, whom he never seemed to see.

If Grace's later life from a distance had seemed blessed with fortune (although, four marriages, no children?), one had to admit that her early days were not; her parents, both of them, were difficult. Her father, a classic beau of his time, was handsome, and drank too much, and chased girls. Her mother, later also given to drink, was smart and snobbish (she was from South Carolina, and considered Georgia a considerable comedown). She tended to say exactly what she thought, and she wasn't one bit pretty. Neither one of them seemed like ordinary parents, a fact they made a point of—of being above and beyond most normal parental concerns, of not acting like "parents." "We appreciate Grace as a person, and not just because she's our daughter," Hortense, the mother, was fairly often heard to say, which may have accounted for the fact that Grace was a rather unchildlike child: precocious, impertinent, too smart for her own good. Rebellious, always. Unfairly, probably, no one cared a lot for poor, wronged Hortense, and almost everyone liked handsome, bad Buck Lafferty. Half the women in town had real big, serious crushes on him.

Certainly they made a striking threesome, tall Grace and those two tall men, during the short days of her visit, as they walked slowly, with a certain majesty, around the town. Grace's new friend, or whatever he was, Jonathan Hedding, the lawyer, was the tallest, with heavy, thick gray hair, worn a trifle long for these parts but still, enviably all his own. Miles and Grace were almost the exact same height, she in those heels she always wore, and, in the new spring sunlight, their hair seemed about the same color, his shining white, hers the palest blond. Grace wore the largest dark glasses that anyone had ever seen—in that way only did she look like a movie star; that and the hair; otherwise she was just tall and a little plump, and a good fifteen years older than she looked to be.

Several times in the course of that walking around, Miles asked her, "But was there something particular you wanted to see? I could take you—"

"Oh no." Her throaty voice hesitated. "Oh no, I just wanted to see—everything. The way we're doing. And of course I wanted Jon to see it, too."

Miles asked her, "How about the cemetery? These days I know more people there than I do downtown."

She laughed, but she told him, "Oh, great. Let's do go and see the cemetery."

Certainly Grace had been right about the season. The dogwood was just in bloom, white fountains spraying out against the darker evergreens, and fragrant white or lavender wisteria, across the roofs of porches, over garden trellises. Jonquils and narcissus, in their tidy plots, bricked off from the flowing lawns. As Grace several times remarked, the air simply smelled of April. There was nothing like it, anywhere.

"You should come back more often," Miles chided.

"I'm not sure I could stand it." She laughed, very lightly.

The cemetery was old, pre–Civil War; many of the stones were broken, worn, the inscriptions illegible. But there were new ones, too, that both Grace and Miles recognized, and remarked upon.

"Look at those Sloanes, they were always the tackiest people. Oh, the Berryhills, they must have struck it rich. And the Calvins, discreet and tasteful as always. Lord, how could there be so many Strouds?"

It was Jonathan who finally said, "Now I see the point of cemeteries. Future entertainment."

They all laughed. It was perhaps the high point of their afternoon, the moment at which they all liked each other best.

And then Grace pointed ahead of them, and she said, "Well, for God's sake, there they are. Why did I think I could miss them, totally?"

An imposing granite stone announced LAFFERTY, and underneath, in more discreet lettering, *Hortense* and *Thomas.* With dates.

Grace shuddered. "Well, they won't get me in there. Not with them. I'm going to be cremated and have the ashes scattered off Malibu. Or maybe in Central Park."

Five o'clock. Already they were a little late. It was time to go for tea, or rather to be there. Grace had taken even longer than usual with makeup, with general fussing, though Jonathan had reminded her, "At ninety-two she may not see too well, you know."

"Nevertheless." But she hadn't laughed.

Miles lived in a small house just across the street from Miss Dabney's much larger, grander house. It was thus that they knew each other. As Grace and Jonathan drove up, he was out in front poking at leaves, but actually just waiting for them, as they all knew.

"I'm sorry—" Grace began.

"It's all right, but why ever are you so nerved up?"

"Oh, I don't know—"

Inside Miss Dabney's entrance hall, to which they had been admitted by a white-aproned, very small black woman, where they were told to wait, Jonathan tried to exchange a complicitous look with Grace: after all, she was with him. But she seemed abstracted, apart.

The parlor into which they were at last led by the same small, silent maid was predictably crowded—with tiny tables and chairs, with silver frames and photographs, love seats and glassed-in bookcases. And, in the center of it all, Miss Dabney herself, yellowed white hair swathed about her head like a bandage, but held up stiff and high, as though the heavy pearl choker that she wore were a splint. Her eyes, shining out through folds of flesh, were tiny and black, and brilliant. She held out a gnarled, much-jeweled hand to Grace. (Was Grace supposed to kiss the rings? She did not.) The two women touched fingers.

When Miss Dabney spoke, her voice was amazingly clear, rather high, a little hoarse but distinct. "Grace Lafferty, you do look absolutely lovely," she said. "I'd know you anywhere, in a way you haven't changed a bit."

"Oh, well, but you look—" Grace started to say.

"Now, now, I'm much too old to be flattered. That's how come I don't have handsome men around me anymore." Her glance flicked out to take in Miles, and then Jonathan. "But of course no man was ever as handsome as your daddy."

"No, I guess—"

"Too bad your mother wasn't pretty, too. I think it would have improved her character."

"Probably—"

Miss Dabney leaned forward. "You know, we've always been so proud of you in this town. Just as proud as proud."

The effect of this on Grace was instant; something within her settled down, some set of nerves, perhaps. She almost relaxed. Miles with relief observed this, and Jonathan, too.

"Yes, indeed we have. For so many, many things," Miss Dabney continued.

A warm and pleasant small moment ensued, during which in an almost preening way, Grace glanced at Jonathan—before Miss Dabney took it up again.

"But do you know what you did that made us the very proudest of all?" Quite apparently wanting no answer, had one been possible, she seemed to savor the expectation her non-question had aroused.

"It was many, many years ago, and your parents were giving a dinner party," she began—as Miles thought, Oh dear God, oh Jesus.

"And you were just this adorable little two- or three-year-old. And somehow you got out of your crib and you came downstairs, and you crawled right under the big white linen tablecloth, it must have seemed like a circus tent to you—and you bit your mother right there on the ankle. Good and hard! She jumped and cried out, and Buck lifted up the tablecloth, and there you were. I don't remember quite how they punished you, but we all just laughed and laughed. Hortense was not the most popular lady in town, and I reckon one time or another we'd all had an urge to bite her. And you did it! We were all just so proud!"

"But—" Grace protested, or rather, she began to protest. She seemed then, though, to remember certain rules. One held that Southern ladies do not contradict other ladies, especially if the other one is very old. She also remembered a rule from her training as an actress: you do not exhibit uncontrolled emotion of your own.

Grace simply said, "It's funny, I don't remember that at all," and she smiled, beautifully.

Miles, though, who had known her for so very long, and who had always loved her, for the first time fully understood just what led her to become an actress, and also why she was so very good at what she did.

"Well, of course you don't," Miss Dabney was saying. "You were much too young. But it's a wonder no one ever told you, considering how famous—how famous that story was."

Jonathan, who felt that Grace was really too old for him, but whose fame he had enjoyed, up to a point, now told Miss Dabney, "It's a marvelous story. You really should write it, I think. Some magazine—"

Grace gave him the smallest but most decisive frown—as Miles, watching, thought, Oh, good.

And Grace now said, abandoning all rules, "I guess up to now no one ever told me so as not to make me feel small and bad. I guess they knew I'd have to get very old and really mean before I'd think that was funny."

As Miles thought, Ah, that's my girl!

The Agenda of Love

One of the few friends I have left asks the question. As a poet, you would expect him not only to ask but to answer.

"How do we know the agenda of love?" he asks and elaborates, "If you expose the heart, it can split wide open."

"So why do we love?" I ask him.

"For the danger of it," he says.

Care

My uncle is sibilant in the room. His slippers shuffle him in. He whispers, "What is it? There was a time—long ago—it was all there then."

He had been a brain scientist. He was all there then.

"Where did everyone go? Out of the door? Out of my life?"

"I'm here," says his wife. "Sit down and have tea."

"Tea and treat," he says.

"All right," his wife agrees.

He trips sitting himself down. His wife pulls out the chair to make more room as he tries again.

"I'll bring you a snack, my dear," she says, "and juice to go with the little pill."

He spills the glass of juice. The pill floats in the orange juice.

"I'll find a double-handled cup," she says. "Better to hold on to."

"Forget the cup." He's cranky. "Give me lox."

"No salt for you," she tells him regretfully.

"Herring!" His soft voice is raised.

"Salty," she says. "Toasted challah?"

He tries to push away from the table.

"A nice walk? A talk with your niece? The news on TV?"

He shakes his head.

"Where are you going, my beloved?" his wife asks.

"A few paces down the hall, a sharp right turn into the bedroom, and then I shut the door and lie down."

She laughs.

"Do everything but shut the door," she instructs.

"Once they were all here," we hear him say in the hallway.

"We're here, my dear," says Gertie.

"Once we laughed and played," he calls from the bedroom.

He stretches out. Even though it's warm in the apartment, he pulls the down quilt up over his jacket, sweater, shirt, and tie.

"Once we discussed the possibilities of mankind," he says and yawns, "the... endless... possibilities."

My aunt sits at the dining table planning amusements for her love: First thing in the morning she will order fresh cinnamon rolls delivered from the corner bakery. Then she will take him on an outing. He, leaning heavily on her arm, will walk the two blocks to the park and sit under the purple jacaranda trees. He may or may not notice the infants digging in the sandbox at his feet. If she takes him to a movie, he sleeps and awakens wondering about the looming images in the dark.

"The only problem is," she says, "that he sleeps twenty hours out of twenty-four. Those four hours have to count."

Attention

"Koochie-koo," says the eighty-five-year-old cousin. "Peek-a-boo."

The one-year-old, in his dragon pajamas, puts his fingers over his eyes and peeks out.

"Boo!" says the old cousin.

The baby boy dimples and runs around the apartment waiting to be found.

The cousin has just returned from chemotherapy. She cannot raise herself from the chair, but she peers around the side of the chair, over the top, while the baby shrieks with the excitement of being lost and found.

Words

A woman I once knew surprised me.

We had talked many times over breakfast, or afternoon tea. We had frequent meals at her home or mine. Our fingers interlocked as we spoke intimately of our days. I thought we would never untwine our hands. We spoke jokingly of being roommates in an old folks' home.

Now her gesture is forbidding, her eyes unfamiliar. She has pushed me away from her life.

"We're through."

So fast are people finished if they are in different places.

I had sinned, though it had felt like a triumph. I had climbed up the ladder in the world of literature. And she, older and heavier than I, was still struggling at a lower rung.

Silence

I see a friend across the street and wave. The wave is not returned, the hand stiffening at her side.

At a gathering, a friend has her back to me. I softly call. The back never turns towards me.

The word has gone forth.

I am to be shunned.

There are religions that practice this form of punishment.

Definitions

It is predictive that, within the agenda of love, the opposite emotion will come into play. The dangers are indicated in the etymology of *agenda: agitation, intransigency, ambiguity, litigation.* Even *navigation* and *transaction,* indicating separate paths, are causes for rejection. One must not differentiate one's self from others.

The Funeral

I paused at the door of the memorial. Her family and affinity groups were here—her writing group, her dreaming group, her antiwar group, her Monday night women's eating group.

There was a coolness in the air. Relationships were encoded. We addressed one another and awaited the reply before deciding how to respond: a small nod of the head to a hesitant remark, aggressing with gesture and speech to a larger effort on the part of others.

Going from "Hello" to "Hello there!"

A caste system was in effect.

If you had fallen into or remained in obscurity, you were avoided, bad luck to others who, after seeing you, would know they would have a harder time in the world of commerce. The Untouchables still had their dreams, their writing, art, acting selves were eagerly there, but not important to anyone else.

All of us, until the rentals were impossible in the city, tried to live where curators could visit our studios, or agents be consulted and writers' meetings attended. Some had to be up for early morning auditions. One trained in from Coney Island and had to spend the day wandering the city, between appointments, before she could return to the isolated apartment with the affordable rental.

A few still have a bit of luck: a painting in a group exhibition, a small part in an off-Broadway show, a story that wins a minor prize. That may be all that's left to some, and it's culled for the obits, which will not be too far off, for we have been together for forty years.

To the younger, the children of this group, the art magazines publish glamorous photos not of their work but of them. They are part of The In-Group of talented writers, hanging out, hanging around the theater, all going to the same analyst. Their words, still freshly lisped, are taken for wisdom. Those still in their teens put out zines, their own pubs.

The tougher, older group on the other side of the church pew were gathered nearer to the coffin.

Our last group photo was a few years ago, at a rally. Some recited poetry, read short pieces of fiction at that rally. For them, it was their last public performance.

When we looked across the church to the younger group, more than generation separated us. Success or lack of it were deeper.

The funeral was informal, as befits the passing of an activist, but also surprisingly stately, in a church with a choir singing and the Episcopalian priest leading services. The only curious thing was that the deceased had been Jewish.

Everyone was there, decades of everyone from the West Village. We had run the gamut from activism to idleness, Stalinism to capitalism, hippie on the commune to head of the PTA. The arts had also changed, the painters, once the Abstract Abstractionists of the early fifties, had gone back to the figure, the political writers had turned to romance.

She, the deceased, in the sixties had been humiliated publicly but later spoke proudly of that time. She had been arrested for protests, had borne a child and reared him alone, had lived in a cold-water flat. She lived a split life—innately elegant while radical; her hair coiffed, clothing fitted—as she learned to sew—while her voice shrilled at the police, or she picketed in front of City Hall or the downtown Federal Building.

Now, lying with hands folded, nothing was out of place in her appearance. Seeing her proper family behind the coffin, one realized that she had been out of place all of her life.

There were photographs in a collage: The young laughing girl, light hair blowing across her face. Stern activist. She was partly an underground figure: having driven cars of war protesters, escapees across the New York–Canadian border at Niagara or Buffalo. She lived largely a private life, almost underground, unless one read the early mimeographed magazines of the movement, or drank in the West Village bars. No one ever saw her lovers, for they visited her clandestinely while her child slept.

When she was not at a meeting, she visited her friends one at a time. One friend had a view of the Statue of Liberty from her apartment window. She began to think of herself as unstatuesque in contrast, full-bosomed but slight, narrow in the hips and ankles, thin nose, delicate arms incapable of holding up lanterns or torches.

But she was a lit-up person, the skin luminous, the hair richly white and wavy, an elegance of spirit. Even her grieving at close deaths in the family seemed of some fine material wrapped around her.

I spoke.

"I have heard a scientist speak of Niches of Sound, that he discovered every creature, mammal, insect, bird, has its own niche. When the scientist returned to record a second time, there were empty spaces on the scale where species had become extinct. Where our friend stood, there is now silence. She is an extinct species."

Enemies

Does one have more enemies in New York than in New Jersey or Massachusetts? I asked a famous writer.

She nodded.

The wrestling of the dinosaur egos, she said. The ground trembles as if all the subways were running on the same tracks.

A heavy-bodied woman with hair once black and now shoe-polished comes by giving us dirty looks, to me rather than to my more famous friend, for I can do her no harm and my friend could, if she wished.

A thin graying person comes by pressing close, brushing my shoulder, not speaking. She wants me to know she can brush against me.

In this society, the unforgivable is political—being an interventionist among pacifists—or, worse, being visible among the invisible.

Name-calling

"Villain!" said a former friend whom I had known for fifteen years. "You harmed my career."

But she was an artist. I could not possibly harm her career. Her own vision had harmed it long ago.

But here I stand, smiling tightly at some of the funeral-goers, turning carefully away from others, all of us mourning and reflecting and being part of a congregation in an Episcopalian church.

History

We had known each other from the early 1950's.

Some of my friends were at Atelier 17 on E. 8th Street, where Bill Hayter greeted Anais Nin and Dylan Thomas and, after the long hours of printing editions on the etching press, everyone went to The White Horse Tavern. There, we helped drink Dylan to his untimely death.

One friend, Anita, loomed over Dylan, blond and beautiful. His nose, by now, was pocked, his stomach bloated, and his eyes bleary, but he had a yen for Anita.

"Come to me, Anita!"

"Forget it," said Anita and turned her back on him.

"I have fucked bigger women than you," he shouted, "and flung them over the cliff."

I had never heard *fuck* before. It tasted salty in my mouth.

They both died soon afterward, Anita and Dylan, separately and of different causes, the sober Anita of leukemia, Dylan of the ravages of drink.

In those days we were strong. The artists had muscles from

grinding ink. We were, in that atelier in the postwar fifties, racially and sexually mixed: urban black woman and Southern gay guy who started a printing press; refugees from Hitler who returned to Europe with Hayter when the INS began investigating them for being "premature anti-fascists." Some of us were artistically rich but economically poor—living in cold-water flats but training or continuing in our careers. Others were middle-class, coming down from the Upper East Side. We were famous—our diaries bestsellers. Or not. We were the beginning of the people we were going to be.

Were there politics then? Mostly art politics. I was taking poetry classes at NYU at night with Allen Tate, the thin, elegant, elderly poet with a thing for young girls. I was so impressed by him that I could hardly believe it was he who said the words "niggers," "fags," "kikes."

None of those groups would win poetry awards from the committees on which our prestigious teacher served.

Still in Those Days

I watched Hayter helping a young artist, a fellow tall, gangly from no regular food, but gently handsome.

"How did you print this etching?" he asked the young man. "It's very pale."

"With a spoon," said the fellow. "There were no etching presses at my school."

"You son-of-a-gun!" Hayter took the large zinc plate, inked it, covered it with a printer's blanket, and put it through the rollers. "Don't you know an etching goes through an etching press?" He looked at the young man wearing cotton pants in winter. "Come join the shop."

The fellow had no money, no job.

"It so happens," said Hayter, "I know of a fellowship, if you want to be the super and clean up the place."

The fellowships at the atelier were out of Hayter's pocket, as were the steins of beer late at night, as were the stories.

Some went to the Cedars Bar—the Hans Hoffman people. But we were The White Horse Tavern crowd. Late one night, after printing, the group walked westward to the White Horse, only to find its owner, Ernie, with his teeth knocked out.

"Who did it?" asked Bill.

"A drunken cop," said Ernie.

We whistled. It was the fifties. Who ever heard of such a thing?

We writers and artists lived any way we could. Those in the Village, like a filmmaker, became the caretakers of the building. Some of us lived Midtown, in the shadow of Bellevue Hospital, still on DC current. We had a cold-water flat, the walls plastered so unevenly we painted them black. Above our heads was a metal molding ceiling that we painted lavender. The place was small. The oil paintings dried under the bed, and turpentine was our perfume.

If we went for a walk towards the East River, along Bellevue, when the mental wards were out getting the air, we were cursed until we fled. That was unusual in those days, to be raged off the street, though ordinary enough now to pass the fulminating person.

Time

The years went by.

First she was walking, then stumbling, then bedridden.

In the bed she was spoon-fed, sipped her liquid through a straw. Later she was fed through tubes.

She had been handsome, charismatic. Students came those first years, still bringing manuscripts for her comments. All but the firmest of friends were frightened by the later years—the unrecognizable, bloated face, the lumpy body, the voice that sounded palsied. But she could still point a finger at an offensive paragraph, an infelicitous expression. She could make a face when the work didn't work at all.

Her critical judgment lasted until the last day, when she blinked her eyes, looked deeply into those of her caretaker/lover. He helped her shut her lids. He removed all the tubes. To his surprise, she smiled and slept and slipped past him.

Appreciation

His shirt has just returned from the cleaner's, starched and pressed. He wears a tie this day. He wears soft leather loafers. Everything matches—the green-gray pants, the brown shirt, the brown and red tie, the cordovan loafers.

"You're so handsome!" she says.

He smiles. His smile is not so broad as once it was, before the illness.

He walks towards her, one side slower than the other.

She reaches out her hands. He is her great love.

Gender

The little golden-haired girl asks, "Do you love me more than the mountains? Do you love me more than the sun? Do you love me more than God?"

The grandmother is in the language of a fairy tale.

Her other grandchild, a raven-haired eight-year-old boy, informs her, "I won the spelling bee, spelling two words, s-c-i-e-n-c-e and m-a-t-h-e-m-a-t-i-c-s."

He is spelling out his future work.

Alone

The squares on the calendar are empty.

If the phone rings, sometimes she lets it ring.

The answering machine is broken.

"Why should I pay to fix it," she asks, "when it costs as much to fix as to buy a new one?"

But then, the dust piles on the table.

Her hair becomes dry, without conditioner or beauty salon.

When she's cold she wears the lining of old coats over her clothes.

She does not read the newspaper. She has forgotten to pay the delivery bill.

She has valuable artwork but has forgotten the names of the artists.

If you manage to reach her, she is delighted to hear from you.

"Where have you been?" she accuses.

But when you make an appointment to see her, she is not at home.

You wait in her lobby. Eventually she returns. You ask, "Where were you?" She pauses, then, "I don't remember."

No one asks her how she is anymore.

The professional organizations have dropped her from their mailings. The catalogues have ceased coming. Record companies do not send out their releases. Lincoln Center has dropped her from its list of prized subscribers.

Yet, she has plans.

"I will swim in Mexico. I will fly to Switzerland and then hear Mozart in Austria. I have friends around the world."

But the world has forgotten to befriend her.

"I can't afford my life!" she cries. "Who can live on Social Security? And the Austrian government has not paid indemnity and now the big shots tell us they're giving us each the same: $7,000. Big deal! As if it would break Austria. In the meantime, how do I live?"

Once she had respect, a house in the Hamptons, an apartment on Park Avenue, a large dog, and, every winter, with her partner, a spa in Mexico.

Even in her late middle years, she swam strongly. She built furniture for her summer house. She cooked for huge parties of theater people.

Her body is not swimming or cooking or walking the Labrador retriever. Her body bloats, her gait is unsteady. Her face and arms are swollen and discolored from banging into walls.

We bring flowers to help her forget the long winter.

Someone has already been there, presenting her with a cuddly plush toy dog.

She laughs delightedly.

"You adorable creature." She buries her face in it.

She is in love.

She dreams of feeding the cocker spaniel, of ringing for the elevator, the dog impatient as the car descended, and then, when the doors opened, straining, running at the end of its leash down the street, she in tow.

Memory

She spoke at his funeral. The coffin had been closed, and she remembered out loud.

She remembered his childhood, his short stature so that he determined to be a basketball player and run between the legs of the giants. She spoke of the accent he developed at home, so that he determined to go into theater and speak in many accents. She spoke of his dark coloring and how he had bleached his brilliant black hair a yellow-white.

"He was a person in opposition, to himself but in connection to others," she told the mourners.

She looked around. Former lovers were there, still resentful of her. A brother could not accept their having lived together for all those years. Her parents still wrote to her old separate address because they had never married.

But it was her duty to remember him with love.

"He found people on the street and invited them indoors and taught them how to work. He found people who were agoraphobic and never went outdoors, and he taught them to jog, bike, and skateboard indoors and, gradually, outside.

"He found children failing classes, and he talked to them until they were convinced that they could think. He found old people with no one to advocate for them, alone all day, and he made phone visits at the same time every Sunday. And then he told them to dress up for the phone call, that it was like a real visit. Then he told them to initiate the calls to him. Then he sent them an invitation on fine paper to visit him. And they did.

"He found himself, not nearly the man he wanted to be—a lover of music who could not sing on-key, a reader of poetry who could not memorize a line, an aficionado of literature who could not write a sentence. And he had to remake that unsatisfying person until the air sparkled around him when he talked and students wrote down his words, until he spoke so poetically that composers made music of his sayings."

She looked around the room. A little girl was crying, either from the stuffy room or because her father had tears on his cheeks.

The last thing she had to say was the hardest.

"I have to live."

The mail still came for him. The bills still had to be paid for his lingering illness. The phone rang from former patients who had not been informed.

And she could not separate herself from the connection. She touched the coffin lightly. He would soon be ashes, gathered in their bedroom in a Chinese urn. She would meditate, pray, speak to the vase. She knew the bits of bone would rattle, the ashes gradually would leak through. He would find a way to come to her.

Pastoral Visit

The minister of a large house of worship is besieged by requests for visits and consultations. This is in addition to scheduling weddings, funerals, and attendance at hospitals.

The loyal secretary is fielding phone calls. How many sore hearts can be eased? How many egos expanded? One must choose, she feels, which disconsolate or even desperate person can be uplifted?

Oh, says a minister, what does this have to do with God, with the Bible, with all the Commentaries?

But then the guest chair is filled, and the congregant makes herself/himself known from among those in the crowded pews. The person speaks hesitantly or in a monologue to describe a life with drama, melodrama, or even that is colorless.

The head of the minister is bent under the weight of the information.

One congregant speaks of caring for a severely disabled son into the teenage years, of being able to leave the house only for a few hours a week. A visitor is living with mental illness which uses all his energies to appear sane, to hold a job, to attend a class, and there is nothing left to give another. Or even one's self. A third visitor describes the slow decline of a loved person whose history has altered from energetic to wheelchair-confined, from charismatic to mute. There is even one who is heartbroken because decades-long friendships have ended in bitter quarreling and there is no way to recover one's past. And she is too advanced in years to make a new history of friendship.

Then the ministering person may touch the congregant's hand, or, if more restrained, holds on to the edge of the desk to stop from leaping up with emotion. The minister may press his or her hands together, as if piously, but chiefly to keep them from trembling with the force of the data confided.

What does one person do with another's life?

Where is God? Or does that not matter?

Even the congregants are unsure of what they want. Is it to be blessed? Forgiven? Understood?

At that point it helps if the ministering person remembers a story recorded by a Sage. He tells the parable:

"There is a singer whose soft voice cannot be heard. Another singer, with a more powerful voice, lifts the melody, and, between them, the song soars."

At the end of this pastoral call, our turmoil is calmed. That is, if our aria is heard.

Geography of Love

There are whole blocks in the Village that are dangerous. I have memories of restaurants where we met, of street corners where we gathered signatures for petitions, of markets where we shopped together or the greengrocer-farmers' stands at Grosvenor's Square on Saturday mornings where we selected our vegetables for near-wholesale prices.

There are sections of town where one collides with regrets.

Once there was the pleased smile, now turned to disappointment at suddenly meeting one another's eyes. There was the expectation of a good conversation over tea and canoli at the Italian restaurant where operas filled the air. Now I see her there, sitting near the window, toying with the salt and pepper shakers.

If we could only honor our past, hand each other on to the next era with good wishes, the heart would ease.

But there is no closure to separated friendship, for our lives go in parallel lines—she up Ninth Avenue, I down Sixth Avenue, the avenues never converging.

Funeral

We die before we die.

Someone near—our child, our lover—has gone and then we disappear a little. We reach out, trying to grab on to them but thin air greets us.

The stairs from her walk-up seem steeper, the weather chillier. She bundles up in a winter coat though it's spring.

Her will has become will o' the wisp.

Instead of walking to her appointed meeting, she begins to lag, arrives late, missing everyone. Soon no one expects her on time. No one expects her to participate in the latest protest, the most recent government's capitulation to capitalism.

She is still so neat in appearance, cutting her hair carefully, her skirts taken up or let down as style demands. Her nails are buffed, covered with Pearl, lipstick matching the subtle polish on the nails.

Inside her, there is a colorful growth, foreign cells inhabiting the organs. The only outward sign is a polite cough, her posture stooped.

From someone who inserted herself so seriously onto this earth, who proclaimed her stance from every podium, she breathed more pantingly until she quietly exhaled her last.

The death became a problem to some because of what was unfinished: the prologues to pamphlets, the ending of a piece of fiction, the pile of rejected manuscripts. Who could simply leave those manuscripts in their manila envelopes to gather dust or to be filed away? Who was the executor, in that non-hierarchical group? Which one would continue submitting her work, monitoring rejections, cross-indexing stories and magazines?

Would her voice, now interrupted, be totally stilled?

At the funeral is a reading. Each old friend reads a paragraph from one of her books, or a story, or recites a political manifesto. New friends, young women, reminisce about her beautiful white hair, her clothing French-seamed, the shoes she selected with care from the bargain stores. They spoke of her library visits, her memorizing poems, the eloquence of her speech. She taught them to live with elegance and an empty purse.

And around the coffin are the photographs of the group, some newspaper shots—all of us alive, and in front of a draft board protesting—thirty years ago. Most of us picketing Wall Street at an almost action. Some of us were doing passive resistance, carried onto a paddy wagon while the stockbrokers jeered.

Decades later, we have arms around one another in front of the Federal Building in solidarity with the one of us who was arrested in a D.C. march. The *Times* never put us or our beliefs on page one, but, deep inside the paper, we are shown in chilly winter, in that square in front of the massive building, unrecognizable within our caps, scarves, mittens, behind our signs.

Perhaps it was the pressure of the outside world that kept us together, this affinity group.

When that style of politics went out, we were, in a way, unemployed.

She, lying there on the bier, is an activist at rest.

We, from opposite sides of the room, are now in opposition to one another.

Marriage

I know about married love, the shared calendars, the separate weekly reminders.

I know about sitting on a love seat, the arm pieces carved like bookends.

I know about photo albums and seeing the pictures of my parents tipped in, from the time my father was a young man with thick hair, bushy brows, and horn-rimmed glasses. His photo is opposite my mother's, with her wavy brown hair primly in place. She is smiling self-consciously. I understand the self-consciousness of the pose. She is sitting, lap concealed behind a flowering bush. She is pregnant with me.

My husband and I share history: his mother with ebony hair and widely spaced black eyes, gypsy inheritance in that lineage where his father has a wide large jaw, light eyes, and light hair. Even in that black-and-white photo, his hair could have been red. He was a farmer who met the dark gypsy.

Our parents age in the photo album. It takes until her seventies for his mother's hair to whiten. The father's hair, for some time dyed red so he can appear younger as he applies for factory work, is no longer an issue. He has died younger than he or the family expected.

My father's bushy hair settles softly around his head, while my mother takes the pins out of her hair and shakes it loose. In the end, both are white-haloed, a deep wave of hair over my father's eyes. You can't really see his eyes because they have deepened in his head, hidden behind the glare of the glasses. Her eyes, once large and gray, have become hooded.

But when they sit together, they smile with closed lips, their eyes crinkling at each other. They are one another's wrinkles, crinkles, smiles, worried frowns, swollen knuckles.

So you see, long-lasting love is natural to me.

I know the physicality, the geometry of it.

He is on my wall in his sailor suit, four years old. I am next to him, framed, hand-colored yellow bow above long curls, hands primly together in the lap of the colored yellow dress.

These framed children will grow up and meet and each help the other grow older.

A Mother's Love

She tells him everything he needs to know as he grows: what to eat, the appropriate clothing of the seasonal weather. She teaches him behavior.

She tells him the meaning of words. She helps him build his blocks high on the carpet until they tumble. Then they rebuild together.

She tells him stories about the father he's never seen, an adventurous man, who traveled, entered every fray, and was killed in battle.

He wants to be just like his father.

But, in the meantime, he has eczema and asthma. His problems require a satchel full of medication wherever he travels.

He has trouble with building one thing atop of the other.

How can he possibly go into battle?

And which battles should he choose?

What the mother has not told her beloved, her only son, is that she has made up his father.

If she told him, the boy's dreams would have to alter. Instead of having the genes of a leader of men, he would be the son of the mother and an indifferent other. He would have to thank her politely for all the games they played, the lottos, the building blocks, the Erector Set—everything that helped him build himself.

He would have to adjust to being the son of monolithic love.

Parental Love

She came to them two decades ago, from birth a mistaken shape.

The eyes never opened properly. The tongue stayed twisted. The body could not raise or lower itself.

She had a way of laughing, of coughing, turning her head, banging it.

Her language was movement, a throat cleared, a bark, snuffle, cough.

For two decades they spoke to her, dressed her ("Which dress?" She turns her head. "This dress?" She smiles) and wheeled her chair into the sun.

In the courtyard, perhaps she would sprout or rise from the

chair or sing like the creatures among the leaves.

She turned her face upwards. She smiled. She coughed or laughed. That was her vocabulary.

They interpreted each sound into paragraphs of meaning. They wrote the stories she would have written.

And, thus blessed, what was broken was made whole.

Their heads bent above her, elicited sound, something like whistling or trilling, climbing up the scale of love.

They make stories of her sounds. It is the book they daily read.

Analytical Love

He was a different kind of therapist. He was on her side, all the way.

"What did your former friend do to you?" he asked.

"She stopped loving me."

"Anything else?"

"She spoke against me."

"I've seen her around," he said. "She lives in my building. I'll snarl at her in the elevator."

She grins. An advocate helps one to heal.

Loss

"Don't let your husband and children take advantage of you," her friend told her. "Don't let this friend or that get the better of you. You have to take care of yourself."

Her friend monitored the world around her.

"Don't take politics more seriously than people," her friend advised, "and look behind you all the time to see what people are doing."

Then, one day, she was behind me glaring, tramping on the back of my heels.

I was no longer to be cared for, or with her, to be a discussant on my life.

A seat was missing in the auditorium.

A card was absent at holiday times.

Someone was not there with the pot at potluck.

When the party photographs were taken—at birthdays, anniversaries, children's parties—she is not in the background, candles gleaming in her eyes.

She is not in love with me.

The Ologists

There is an assassinologist who founded an Assassin Museum in Texas.

My doctor for serious matters is a cardiologist. I love the cardiologist. He keeps my heart pumping, and I send him Valentine's Day cards. However, he can do nothing about a broken heart.

There are garbologists, such as the one who went through the garbage of Bob Dylan.

There are herbologists who will alter our skin tone and keep us tony.

This is the Giftologist, says the sign on a Broadway store.

From the assassin of the heart, from the heart's healer, from the mess of our lives and the savory herbs that disguise it, from our wrapped and unwrapped presents to one another, we compose our songs.

The Boyish Man

I love him.

Once there was a man who had been a boy and was still boyish. There was such tenderness in him that he went into Central Park to feed the homeless young people, to invite them to his room, to council them, to tutor them.

Sometimes he became one of the homeless, wandering without address, calling from a corner phone, blaming the past and those who bore him and who grew up with him.

When you speak to him there is such stimulation coming into the brain, colors that burn with intensity, sounds that startle like honking truck horns, that it seems as if you were speaking from a wind tunnel, roaring into his ears.

And yet, when he can quiet himself, he goes to the Library of Judaica and uses the computers. Like a Kabbalist he studies the mystical numbers of math and hopes for a spell that can cure pain and danger and homelessness.

He is aging and not aging, growing older and not going anywhere. And yet, like honey, his sweetness spreads among the innocents in the park.

Between

There is a man of strength and presence, a person of dignity and quiet demeanor. But when he raises his hand with his painting brush a wildness appears. On canvas, planes explode, people jettison into space. Or he sits before a glass table with his watercolor box. A choreography occurs as his creations, like feathers, float between heaven and earth, tumbling, crouching, separated or touching, hair spreading, hands reaching out, plunging. Do they fall into a hell or are they only birdlike on currents of air?

This man is between this time and another, like his people, floating, stumbling as his stance is less steady, trembling a bit, but steady in his life, blameless in his character.

And she, connected to him, what will she be, bound and unbound?

The Only Agenda

Her poet friend had told her it would be this way. You love until there is no breath left. You love until you pant with it.

"All that has breath loves you," we praise the One Above.

You love and breathe in that love, that life, that joy, that separation, that madness and illness. You breathe it in until you labor with breathing, you choke with asthma.

Somewhere in that parade of beloveds and enemies, of one's family and friends, one searches the self. There may be no love she has left for herself.

She is a writer. She knows she is. They tell her. But when her life becomes like a playground, full of fretful pullings and hittings, she forgets her plots.

She is between work and exhaustion; between imagination and dull fact.

When do the people return to the page? When do the angels surround her, soundproof her space, before her, behind her, so that her words, with no one else's accent, flow?

There is no room for tenderness or tiredness or playfulness. The only use for the sore heart is as reference.

The poet is partially wrong. A novelist could tell him that work is also on the agenda.

Mr. Sweetly Indecent

I meet my father in a restaurant. He knows why I have asked to meet him, but he swaggers in anyway. It's a place near his office, and he hands out hellos all around as he makes his way over to my table. "My daughter," he explains to the men who have begun to grin, and he can't resist a wink just to keep them guessing. "Daddy," I say; his arms are around me. He squeezes a beat too long, and I'm afraid I might cry. He kisses me on both cheeks, my forehead, and chin. "Saying my prayers," he has called these kisses ever since he used to tuck me into bed each night. They started as a joke on my mother, who is French and a practicing Catholic. Because my mother always kept her relationship with God to herself, the only prayer I knew is one my father taught me.

> Now I lay me down to sleep.
> I pray the Lord my soul to keep.
> If I should cry before I wake,
> I pray the Lord a cake to bake.

I only realized years later that he had changed the words of the real prayer so I wouldn't be scared by it.

My father orders a bottle of expensive red wine. He's had this wine here before. When it arrives, he insists that I taste it. He tells the waiter that I'm a connoisseur of wines. The truth is that I worked one summer as a hostess in a French restaurant where I attended some wine-tasting classes. We learned that a wine must be tasted even if it's from a well-known vineyard and made in a good year because there could be some bad bottles. I could never tell the good wines from the bad ones, but I picked up some of the vocabulary.

I make a big fuss, sniffing the cork, sloshing the wine around in my mouth. "Fruity. Ripe," I say.

The waiter and my father smile at my approval. I smack my lips after the waiter leaves. "But no staying power. Immature, overall."

My father gets a sour look on his face. He's taken a big sip so that his cheeks are puffed out with the liquid. After he gulps it down, he says, "It's fine." And then he adds, "You know, it's all right for you to like it. It costs forty dollars."

"I'll drink it, but I don't really like it."

He looks ready to argue with me and then thinks better of it, glancing instead around the restaurant to see if anyone else he knows has come in.

We don't say anything for a bit. I'm hesitating. I sip the wine, survey the room myself. I've recently begun to realize that my father's life exists outside the one in which I have a place. Rather than viewing this outside life as an extension of the part that I know, I choose to see it instead as a distant land. Some of its inhabitants are here. Mostly men, they chuckle over martini glasses; one raises his eyebrow. They all look as if they have learned something that I have yet to discover.

Finally, I put my glass down and smooth some wrinkles in the tablecloth. "Dad, what are we going to do?" I ask without looking up.

He takes my hand. "We don't need to do anything. We should just put it behind us. We can pretend that it didn't even happen, if that's what you want."

"That's what you want," I say. I'd caught him, after all, kissing a woman on the street outside his apartment.

As long as I can remember, my father has kept an apartment in this city where he works and I now live. In his profession, he needs to stay in touch, he has always said. That has meant spending every Monday night in the city having dinner with his associates. Occasionally, it had occurred to me that his apartment might be used for reasons other than a place to sleep after late business dinners. Then one night, while I still lived at home, my mother confided that a friend of my father's contributed $100 a month toward the rent to use it once in a while. I remember that my mother and I were eating cheese fondue for dinner. On those nights my father was away, my mother made special meals that he didn't like. She ripped off a piece of French bread from the loaf we were sharing and dipped it in the gooey mixture. "This friend brings his mistress there," she explained. "I hate that your father must be the one to supply him with a place to carry out his affair."

I didn't say anything, my suspicion relieved by this sudden confidence. My mother tilted back her head and dropped the coated bread into her open mouth. When she finished chewing, she closed the subject. "His wife should know what her husband is up to. I'm going to tell her one day."

When I was walking down my father's street early last Tuesday morning, it didn't even occur to me that my father would be at his apartment. I was on my way to the subway after leaving the apartment of a man with whom I had just spent the night. This man is a friend of a man at work with whom I have also spent the night. The man at work, call him Jack, is my friend now—he said that working together made things too complicated—and we sometimes go out for a drink at the end of the day. We bumped into his friend at the bar near our office. The friend asked me to dinner and then asked me to come up to his apartment for a drink and then asked if he could make love to me. After each question, I paused before answering, suspicious because of the directness of his invitations, and then when he would look away as if it didn't really matter, I would realize that, in fact, I had been waiting for these questions all night, and I would say yes.

When we walked into this man's living room, he flicked a row of switches at the entrance, turning on all the lights. He brought me a glass of wine and then excused himself to use the bathroom. I strolled over to the large picture window to admire the view. Looking out from the bright room, it was hard to make out anything on the street. The only movement was darting points of light. "It's like another world up here," I murmured under my breath. I heard the toilet flush and waited at the window. I was thinking how he could walk up behind me and drape his arm over my shoulder and say something about what he has seen out this window, and then he could take my chin and turn it toward him and we could kiss. When I didn't hear any movement behind me, I turned around. He was standing at the entrance of the room. "I'd like to make love to you," he said. "Would that be all right?" There was no music or TV, and it was so silent that I was afraid to speak. I smiled, took a sip of wine. He shifted his gaze from my face to the window behind me. I glanced out the window, too, then put my glass down on the sill and nodded yes.

"Why don't you take off your coat," he said. I slipped my trench coat off my shoulders and held it in front of me. He pointed to a chair in front of the window, and I draped the coat over its back. Then he asked me to take off the rest of my clothes.

Once I was naked, he just stood there staring at me. I wondered if he could see from where he was standing that I needed a bikini wax. I wanted to kiss him, we hadn't even kissed yet, and I took a small step forward and then stopped, one foot slightly in front of the other, unsteady, uncertain what to do next. "Beautiful," he finally whispered. And then he kept whispering beautiful, beautiful, beautiful...

I had just reached my father's block, though lost in my thoughts I didn't realize it, when from across the street, I heard a woman's voice. "Zachary!" the voice called out, the stress on the last syllable, the word rising in mock annoyance, the way my mother said my father's name when he teased her. All other times, she called him, as everyone else did, just Zach. I looked up, and there was my father pushing a woman up against the side of a building. His building, I realized.

My father's face was buried in her neck, and she was laughing. I recognized from her reaction that he was giving her the ticklish kind of blowing kisses that I hated. I had stopped walking and was staring at them. I caught the women's eye briefly, and then she looked away and whispered something in my father's ear. His head jerked up and whipped around. I looked down quickly and started walking away, as if I had been caught doing something wrong. If my father had run after me and asked what I was doing in this neighborhood so early in the morning, I wouldn't have known what to tell him. I glanced back, and the woman was walking down the street the other way, and my father was standing at the entrance of his building. He was watching the woman. She was rather dressed up for so early in the morning, wearing a short black skirt, stockings, and high heels. She pulled her long blond hair out from the collar of her jacket and shook it down her back. Her gait looked slightly self-conscious, the way a woman's does when she knows she is being watched. Before I looked away, my father glanced in my direction. I avoided meeting his eyes and shook my head, a gesture I hoped he could appreciate from his distance. As I hurried to the subway, the only thought I had was fleeting: my man had not gotten up from bed to walk me out the door.

For the next few days, I waited for the phone to ring. Neither man called. I asked Jack, the man at work, if he had heard from his friend. "Sorry, not a peep," he said. He patted me on the knee and said that he was sure his friend enjoyed the time we spent together and that I would probably hear from him soon.

It was unusually warm that day, and I walked home rather than taking the subway. All the way home, I kept picturing myself back in the man's apartment. I saw us as someone would have if they had been floating nine stories high above the busy avenue that night and had picked out the man's lighted window to peer into: a young women, naked, moving slowly across a room to kiss the mouth of her clothed lover. It seemed that the moment was still continuing, encapsulated eternally in that bright box of space.

When I walked in the door that afternoon, my phone was ringing. I rushed to answer it before the machine picked it up. It was my mother. She had already left a message on my machine earlier in the week to call her about making plans to go home the following weekend. Whether I should tell her about my father was a question that had been gathering momentum behind me all week. My mother is a passionate, serious woman. My father met her when she was performing modern dance in a club in West Berlin. The act before her was two girls singing popular American show tunes, and after her, for the finale, there was a topless dancer. She didn't last there for very long. My father liked to describe how the audience of German men would look up at her with bemused faces. Her seriousness didn't translate, he would say, and the Germans would be left wondering if her modern dancing was another French joke that they didn't get. After the shows, all the women who worked there had to *"faire la salle,"* which meant dancing with the male customers. At this point in the story I would ask questions, hoping that a bit of scandal in my mother's past would be revealed, or at least to find out that she had to resist some indecent propositions at one time. But my mother always jumped in to say that she had learned that if you don't invite that kind of behavior, then you won't receive it. Such things never happen by accident. My father married my mother, he would explain, because she was one of the last women left who could really believe in marriage. He said she had enough belief for the both of them. I hadn't called my mother back.

"Oh, sweetie, I'm glad I caught you," she said. "You're still going to take the 9:05 train Saturday morning, right?"

"Uh-huh."

"Okay, Daddy will have to pick you up after he drops me off at the hairdresser's. I'm trying to schedule an appointment to get a perm."

"Ahh."

"I feel like it's been forever since I've seen you. Daddy and I were just saying last night how we still can't get used to you not being around all the time."

I tried to picture myself back in my parents' house. I couldn't place myself there again. I couldn't remember where in the house we spent our time, where we talked to each other: around the dining room table, on the couch in the den, in the hallways; I couldn't remember what we talked about.

"Is everything okay, honey? You sound tired."

"Hmmm."

"All right. I can take a hint. I'll let you go."

After we hung up, I said to my empty apartment, "I caught Daddy with another woman." Once these words were out of my mouth, I couldn't get away from them. I went out for a drink.

When I woke up the next morning, I decided to cut off all of my hair. I have brown curly hair like my father's. It's quite long, and when I stood in that man's living room, I pulled it in front of my shoulders so that it covered my breasts. The man liked that, he told me afterward as he held me in his bed. He said that I had looked sweetly indecent. I lost my nerve in the hairdresser's chair and walked out with bangs instead. In the afternoon, I went to a psychic fair with a friend, and a fortune teller told me that she saw a man betraying me. "Tell me something I don't know," I said, but that would have cost another ten dollars.

I called my father Sunday morning at home. I knew when he answered the phone that he had gotten up from the breakfast table, leaving behind a stack of Sunday papers and my mother sipping coffee.

"We have to talk before I come home next weekend."

"Okay. Where would you like to meet?" He didn't say my name, and his voice was all business.

"Let's have dinner somewhere." He suggested a restaurant, and we agreed to meet the next evening after work.

"Tomorrow, then." I put a hint of warning in my voice.

"Yes. All right," he said and hung up. I wondered if my mother asked him who had called, and if she did, what he would have told her.

Next, I called up the man in whose living room I had stood naked. The phone rang many times. I was about to hang up, disappointed that there was not even a machine so I could hear his voice again, when a sleepy voice answered. I was caught by surprise and forgot my rehearsed line about meeting at a bakery I knew near his apartment for some sweetly indecent pastries. I hung up without saying anything.

The waiter takes our empty plates away. My father refills my glass. I have drunk two glasses of wine already and am starting to feel sleepy and complaisant. My father has already told me that he is not planning on seeing the woman again, and I am beginning to wonder what it is that I actually want my father to say.

He drums his fingers on the edge of the table. I can see that he is growing tired of being solicitous. He sought my opinion on the wine, he noticed that I had my bangs cut, he remembered the name of my friend at work who I was dating the last time we got together.

"I'm not with him anymore," I explain. "We thought it was a bad idea to date since we work together." I consider telling my father about the other man, to let him know that I understand more about this world of affairs than he thinks. He would be shocked, outraged. Or would he? I'm not sure of anything anymore.

I let myself float outside the man's window again, move closer to peer inside. But this time I can't quite picture his face. What color are his eyes? They're green, I decide. But then I wonder if I am confusing them with my father's eyes.

"Someday, honey, you'll meet a guy who'll realize what a treasure you are." My father pats my knee.

"Just because he thinks I'm a treasure doesn't mean that he won't take me for granted." I take another sip of wine and watch over the rim of my glass for my father's response. I remember watching him at another table, our dining room table, where he sat across from my mother. She had just made some remark that I couldn't hear from where I perched on our front stairs, spying, as they had a romantic dinner alone with candles and wine. Earlier, my father had set up the television and VCR in my room and sent me upstairs to watch a movie. My father put down his glass and got up out of his chair. He knelt at my mother's feet, and though I couldn't hear his words, either, I was sure that he was asking her to marry him again.

"Honey. Listen. It was nothing with that woman. It doesn't change the way I feel about your mother. I love your mother very much."

"But it makes everything such a lie," I say, my voice now catching with held-back tears. "What about our family, all the dinners, Sunday mornings around the breakfast table, the walks we love to take..." I falter and hold my hands out wide to him.

My father catches them and folds them closed in his own. "No. No. All of that is true. This doesn't change any of that." He is squeezing my hands hard. For the first time during this meal, I can see that I have upset him.

"But it didn't mean what I thought, did it?"

Right then the waiter appears with our check. My father lets go of my hands and reaches for his wallet. Neither of us says anything while we wait for the waiter to return with the credit card slip. I don't repeat my question because I am afraid that my father will say I'm right.

The next day at work, I ask my friend again about Mr. Sweetly Indecent.

"If you want to talk to him, call him up."

"Do you think I should?"

"It can't hurt."

"If we didn't work together, do you think things could have turned out differently with us?" We are in the photocopying room where, in the midst of our affair, my friend had once lifted my skirt and slid his fingers inside the elastic waist of my pantyhose.

"Oh, hell. You'll meet someone who'll appreciate you. You deserve that. You really do."

I call the man up that night. He doesn't say anything for a moment when I tell him my name. I imagine him reviewing a long line of naked women standing in his living room. "That one," he finally picks me out of the crowd. Or maybe it's just that he's surprised to hear from me.

"I had a really nice time that night," I say. "I thought maybe we could get together again sometime."

"Well, I had a good time, too," he says, sounding sincere, "but I think that we should just leave it at that."

"I'm not saying that I want to start dating. I just thought that we could do something again."

"It was the kind of night that's better not repeated. I know. I've tried it before. The second time is always a disappointment."

"But I thought we got along so well." We had talked over dinner about our families; he told me how he was always trying to live up to the kind of man he thought his father wanted him to be. He had talked in faltering sentences, as though this were something that he was saying for the first time.

"We did get along," he says. "God! And you were so beautiful." He pauses, and I know he's remembering that I really was beautiful. "I just want to preserve that memory of you standing in my living room, alone, without any other images cluttering it."

Yes, I want to tell him, I have preserved that image, too, but memories need refueling. I need to see you again to make sure that what I remembered is actually true. "Is this because I slept with you on the first night?"

"No. No. Nothing like that. Listen, it was a perfect night. Let's just both remember it that way."

As the train pulls into the station, I spot my father waiting on the platform. I take my time gathering my things so I'm one of the last to exit. He hugs me without hesitation, as though our dinner had never happened. As we separate he tries to take my suitcase from me. It's just a small weekend bag, and I resist, holding on to the shoulder strap. We have a tug of war.

"You're being ridiculous," my father says and yanks the strap from my grip. I trail behind him to the car and look out the window the whole way home.

That afternoon, I sit at the kitchen table and watch my mother and father prune the rose bushes dotting the fence that separates our yard from the street. My mother selects a branch and shows my father where to cut. They work down the row quickly, efficient with their confidence in the new growth these efforts will bring. Behind them trails a wake of bald, stunted bushes and their snipped limbs lying crisscross on the ground beneath.

After they have finished cleaning up the debris, my father brings the lawn chairs out of the garage—he brings one for me, too, but I have retreated upstairs to my bedroom by this time and watch them from that window—and my mother appears with a pitcher of lemonade and glasses. My mother reclines in her chair, with my father at her side, and admires their handiwork. Her confidence that the world will obey her expectations makes her seem so foolish to me, or perhaps it is because every time I look at her, I think of how she is being fooled.

On Sunday morning, my mother heads off to Mass, and I am left alone in the house with my father. He sits with me at the kitchen table for a while, both of us flipping through the Sunday papers. I keep turning the pages, unable to find anything that can hold my attention. He's not really reading, either. He is too busy waiting on me. He hands me the Magazine and Style sections without my even asking. He refills my coffee. When Georgie, our Labrador retriever, scratches at the door, he jumps up to let her out. When he sits back down, he gathers all the sections of the paper together, including the parts that I am looking at, and stacks them on one corner of the table. I look at him, breathe out a short note of exasperation.

"Are you ever going to forgive me?" he asks.

"Why aren't you going to see that woman again? Just because I caught you?"

He looks startled and answers slowly, as if he is just testing out this answer. "She didn't mean anything to me. It was like playing a game. It was fun, but now it's over."

"Do you think that she expected to see you again?"

"No. She knew what kind of a thing it was. And I'm sure that she prefers it this way, too. She has her own commitments to deal with."

"Maybe she does want to see you again. Maybe she felt like you had something really special together. Maybe she's hoping that you would leave Mom for her."

"Honey, when you get older, you'll understand that there are a lot of different things that you can feel for another person and how it's important not to confuse them. I love your mother, and I'm very devoted to her. Nothing is going to change that."

My father sits with me a few minutes more, and when there doesn't seem to be anything else to say, he stands up and wanders off. I realize that if I had told my father about the man during our dinner, he would have understood what kind of a thing that was before I even did.

When my mother gets back, she joins me at the kitchen table.

"Do you want to talk about something, honey? You seem so sad." I look at my mother, and the tears that have been welling in my eyes all weekend threaten to spill over.

"Daddy says you're having boy trouble."

I shake my head no, unable to speak.

My mother suggests that we take the dog out for a walk, just the two of us, so we can catch up. She gathers our coats, calls Georgie, and we head out the door. "I don't even know what's going on in your life since you've moved out. It's strange," she says. "I used to know what you did every evening, who you were going out with, what clothes you chose to wear each day. Now I have no idea how you spend your time. It was different when you were at college. I could imagine you in class, or at the library, or sitting around your dorm room with your roommate. Sometimes I used to stop whatever I was doing and think about you. She's probably just heading off to the cafeteria for breakfast right now, I would tell myself."

We are walking down our street toward the harbor.

"But you know that I go to work every day. You know what my apartment looks like. It's the same now."

"No, it's not," she says. "It's really all your own life. You support yourself, buy all your own clothes, decide if and when to have breakfast. And somehow, I don't feel right imagining what your day is like. It's not really my business anymore."

"I don't mind, Mom, if you want to know what I'm doing." We have reached the harbor, and my mother is bending over the dog to let her off the lead so I'm not sure if she hears me. She pulls a tennis ball out of her pocket, and Georgie begins to dance backward. My mother starts walking to the water. I stay where I am and look off across the harbor. On the opposite shore, some boats have been pulled up onto the beach just above the high-tide mark for the winter. They rest on the side of their hulls and look as if they've been forgotten, as if they will never be put back in the water again.

My mother turns back toward me, holding the tennis ball up high over her head. Georgie is prancing and barking in front of her. "You know what I love about dogs? It's so easy to make them happy. You just pet them or give them a biscuit or show them a ball, and they always wag their tails." She throws the ball into the water, and Georgie goes racing after it.

My mother's eagerness to oblige surprises me. I think of her dancing with men in that club in West Berlin. I had always imagined her as acting very primly, holding the men away from her with stiff, straight arms. Perhaps she wasn't that way at all. Maybe she leaned into these men, only drawing back to toss her head in laughter at the jokes they whispered in her ear.

"Mom, what made you go out with Dad when you worked in that club? You didn't go out with many of the men that you met there, did you?"

"Your father was the only one I accepted, though I certainly had many offers."

"Did he seem more respectable?"

"Oh, he came on like a playboy as much as the next one."

"Then why did you say yes?"

"Well, somehow he seemed like he didn't quite believe his whole act. Though he wouldn't say that if you asked him. I guess I felt I understood something about him that he didn't even know about himself. So he went about seducing me, all the while feeling like he had the upper hand, and I would go along, knowing that I had a trick up my sleeve, too."

She isn't looking at me as she says this. She is turned toward the water, though I know that she is not looking at that, either. She is watching herself as a young woman twirling around a room with my young father. They dance together well; I have seen them dance before, and this memory brings such a pleased private smile to her lips that I don't say anything that would contradict her.

I am quiet during dinner. My parents treat me like I am sick or have just suffered some great loss. My mother won't let me help her serve the food. My father pushes seconds on me, saying that I look too skinny. "Maybe I should take you out to dinner more often," he says.

I look up from my heaping plate of food, half expecting him to wink at me.

"That's right. You two met for dinner this week. See, honey, that's just the kind of thing I was talking about. It's nice that you and your father can meet and have dinner together. Like two friends."

My parents tell stories back and forth about me when I was young; many stories I have heard before. Usually I enjoy these conversations. I would listen to them describe this precocious girl and the things she had done that I couldn't even remember, only interrupting to ask in an incredulous and proud tone, "I really did that?" I was always willing to believe anything my parents told me, so curious was I to understand the continuum of how I came to be the woman I was. Tonight, while these memories seem to console my parents, I can only hear them as nostalgic, and they remind me of everything that has been recently forsaken.

After dinner I insist on doing the dishes. I splash around in the kitchen sink, clattering the plates dangerously in their porcelain bed. I pick up a serving platter, one from my mother's set of good china inherited from my grandmother, and consider dropping it to the floor. I have trouble picturing myself actually doing this. I can only imagine it as far as my fingers loosening from the edges of the platter and it sliding down their length, but then in my mind's eye, instead of the platter falling swiftly, it floats and hovers the way a feather would from one of the peacocks pictured on the china's face. I have no trouble picturing the aftermath once it lands: my mother rushing in at the noise with my father a few steps behind, not sure if he must concern himself, and she angry at my carelessness. I imagine yelling back at her. I would tell her that it's no use. Old china, manicured lawns, a happy dog: these things don't offer any guarantee.

I stand there holding the platter high above the kitchen floor, imagining the consequences with trepidation and relief, as if this is what the weekend had been leading up to, and with one brief burst of courage, I could put it behind me. I stand considering and strain to hear my parents' voices in the dining room, thinking their conversation might offer me some direction. I put the platter down and peak around the open kitchen door. A pantry separates me from the dining room. I can see them: they are talking, but I can't make out their words.

They are both leaning forward. My mother cradles her chin in the palm of her hand. Abruptly, she lifts her head, sits up tall, and points at my father. His arms are folded in front of him, and he looks down and shakes his head. I am reminded again of that dinner of my parents that I spied on years ago, but this time what I remember is the righteousness of my mother's posture as she sat across from my father and tossed off remarks, and the guilty urgency of my father's movements as he sank to his knees at her feet, and how there was something slightly orchestrated about their behavior, as though their exchange had a long history to it. And the next thing I remember makes me tiptoe away, as I did when I was a child, aware that I had witnessed a private moment between my parents not meant for my eyes. What I remember now is how many years ago my mother had reached down her hand and pulled my father up and kept pulling him in toward herself so that she could hold him close.

A Day in the Future

In the future, everyone will be someone else.
At her school, the future had been discussed as if it were a definite sort of business, with tangible boundaries like an island nation. It was a place you could rocket to or grope towards in a state of anticipation. But if thinking about your actual future seemed like an exercise in futility, you could, in a wish-upon-a-star kind of way, imagine an idealistic prospect in which the logic of gravity was suspended and anything was possible. Hands shot up against a map of Europe and waved with the anxiety of uncontainable ideas spilling over into a damp afternoon. Audrey had nothing to say. Bored with the easy-out of imagining miraculous surgeries, faster cars, Big Brother governments, she watched the clock, sometimes listening to the discussion, sometimes not. When the bell rang, she slammed out with everyone else, part of a wave headed towards buses and subways.

As she walked home, past a peeling blue kiosk, newspapers weighted down with leaden Yankees and Mets symbols, past a Mexican restaurant whose sign was a giant sequined sombrero, it all seemed permanent yet futureless. The sombrero might blow away and land on the head of the Statue of Liberty, the newspaper stand might be taken over by someone who knew of Yankees only as a kind of soldier. She stopped to look at magazines and videos in a shop near her apartment building. The shop was empty; the Russian clerk looked bored and drummed his fingers as if playing a piano, then, when he grew aware of Audrey's watching, he stopped only to nervously twirl the dial of a radio propped between a display of razor blades and boxes of water filters. His family ran the shop, and they spoke Russian to one another, arguing and shouting behind the counter. Today only the middle-aged son was in the shop, agitated and cracking his gum. He finally settled on a salsa station, and Audrey moved on. In another part of the store, far from his gaze, she eyed greeting cards, rows of aspirin bottles that were of no interest, so on she strolled to flip through magazines. These, at least, were entertaining. In pictures of women wearing expensive clothing in remote settings, the models looked terminally adult and inaccessible, able to have conversations with men who appeared in the margins or background of the photographs. They stretched their provocative legs over car seats, lay on beaches holding glasses of white wine the color of sand, pretended to run down rain-drenched streets in billowing black coats. Audrey turned the pages slowly. The clerk came around from behind the counter and told her to buy one or stop damaging his merchandise. In response she circled the aisles as if she had some purpose for being there, as if she were looking for something in particular, although all she was really doing was wasting time. He kept staring at her. Audrey wanted to say to him: *You're afraid I'm going to steal cough syrup used to produce a nauseating high, a model of the Empire State building, Godzilla attached, a Mars bar, anything.* She edged close to the back room. There in the back, one found videos mixed in with the magazines. She'd poked around in such remote shelves before. What she found was a source of curiosity and undefined mystery, if not danger. Audrey stopped in front of a row of video boxes featuring nearly naked men on their covers and picked one up. A photograph of a man holding the end of a towel between his legs looked the image of good health. Just as she was about to put it back, the clerk pushed his way past crates of unopened stock that lined the narrow aisles and approached her with the face of a demon, insulted and provoked by a mosquito he was determined to annihilate. Orange foil wrapping from discounted Halloween candy clung to his cuff. He grabbed the box from her as if she were two years old.

"No minors alone here," he said. "Curiosity kills the mouse."

Audrey looked down at the profile of a foil witch that had fallen to the floor and wished she could pretend to be an alien, unable to speak English. In a foreign vernacular whose vulgarities would make her sound sophisticated or at least really smart, she would tell him to leave her alone, but instead of uttering fake silent Italian, she turned her back on the magazine racks of half-naked men and women and muttered a few nonsense syllables that she imagined sounded like expletives in some kind of language.

"What?" the clerk asked, angry at her, at all children. "What did you say to me?"

She looked at him in mute horror, slouched up to the cashier at the front, paid for a juvenile magazine she didn't want, and, feeling acutely self-conscious, left the store.

She walked past a building that was partly bricked up. Squatters occupied a few of the floors. A girl in a devil costume looked out of a second-story window. A younger child—still, Audrey hadn't ever seen her in the neighborhood before. The girl wore red tights, a black cape, and had rubber horns attached to her head. She waved a pitchfork at Audrey, prongs covered in tin foil, then she disappeared into the building.

It hadn't been a friendly wave, and although Audrey didn't feel threatened by some junior loony tune acting tough, the little devil materialized in such a way so as to appear part and parcel of her crappy afternoon. Scripted to be stifling, a finger wagging oppressively as if someone were telling her that just when she thought she was judging her surroundings with a cool above-it-all eye, she couldn't even look at a magazine or a row of videos without being thrown out, accused of being a girl who transgressed, who looked where she was bound to suffer, to be bitten badly, to have her pretensions unmasked. Audrey rounded the corner of her street, inhaled the sugary smell of the twenty-four-hour Mexican bakery whose doughnuts and twists of fried dough offered some kind of comfort. She tossed the juvenile magazine in a trash can. A white girl in a chartreuse halter winked on its cover. No similar image of coyness and perkiness could be found on her street. The images from the videos danced in a crazy quilt of—what? terror? shock? What do women and men or men and men do? *Buy me,* they seemed to taunt. *Try me! What's the big deal? Are you a little devil, too? Kind of a half-assed one. You're so at sea!*

When she arrived at her building, the old woman who always sat by the stoop on a folding chair or a milk crate was waiting for her. Audrey's mother called the woman "the concierge" because she sat there day after day, watching whatever was going on in the street, secretly monitoring the kinds of people who visited Mr. Davis on the third floor or complaining about the way certain tenants slammed the front door when they came home early in the morning. Her stockings were rolled down, and she drank beer out of a coffee cup positioned near her feet. The woman made Audrey uneasy, and she tried to avoid her. She had once heard her complain about the late hour her mother left for work, and this from a woman who sat on her duff all day annoyed Audrey no end. Parked on the front steps, there was no way to avoid her, and her mother always told her to be nice to the old woman no matter what. *She doesn't know what she's saying. No, you're wrong, she knows exactly what she's saying.* The woman was reading a newsprint magazine, the headlines read, "Royal Monster, Close Relative of Queen Victoria Discovered at Last." On the cover was a picture of a wrinkled and deformed creature, a kind of E.T. in a suit, apparently a long-lost member of the Royal family.

"What are you reading about?"

"Prince X."

"Doesn't he have a name?"

"No, dummy, he was kept hidden away."

"Well, he's dead now, isn't he?"

"If he was found today, they could have fixed him with plastic surgery."

Audrey looked at the picture of the monster with interest; it gave her an opportunity to appear curious, and so keep the nosy concierge at a friendly distance.

"How did they know he was a man?"

"How do you think? Get lost!"

The grotesque prince reminded her of part of the class discussion. He could have had his brain put in another's body. The volunteer might then have been in line to the throne. Her neighbor found this an entertaining suggestion.

"Would they accept a woman's brain to go into a man? You could keep changing bodies, you could live forever." She took a drink from the beery paper cup as if it contained coffee.

Audrey jingled her keys and went upstairs, hoping the concierge hadn't pissed in the hall because she couldn't make it up to her apartment, a frequent occurrence. Although no one ever saw the old woman do this, it was assumed she was the only tenant capable of such audacity and weakness. As Audrey reached the first landing, unzipping her jacket, she hummed a song which had stuck in her head since lunch recess. She walked slowly. Her shoes felt as if they had lead in them. There was a dented triangular mirror placed over a corner near the ceiling so one could see whether anyone lurked down the hall. She thought she saw half a trouser leg and a foot disappear around a corner.

Her mother was already home.

"Brain transplants," Audrey said to her mother as she took off her shoes, "will be as easy as tonsillectomies, and all ethical questions will be suspended. The procedure will be done as a fairly routine outpatient operation. You think you recognize someone on the street, but you can't be sure. He's not the man you thought he was."

By a week after Halloween, the streetlights along Fourteenth Street were decorated with flat red and white furry Christmas bells. Ronnie hated them. She wanted to swing from bell to bell like Tarzan. She hoped they would float away on a strong wind and land somewhere out in the middle of the Atlantic to be washed ashore on a Senegalese beach. The wire and tinsel would be taken apart and woven into baskets, balanced on heads or incorporated into ceremonial objects that would glint more usefully in villages than they did in her city, where as fake bells they only served to remind people of shopping, or if you didn't have to buy anything, the decorations signified the rapid passing of time, one holiday slamming into the next. She stopped to buy a newspaper at a store which also sold greeting cards, toys, and party decorations. A woman with an ambulance-driver insignia on her sleeve stood ahead of her in line and bought cigarettes and a toy Road Runner. The plastic bird had legs which swiveled just as those of the cartoon character did, and blue-gray plastic dust was somehow attached to its body in artificial clouds. Ronnie wondered if the bird was intended for the ambulance dashboard and who the cigarettes were for. When would the driver herself have time to smoke? She had once seen an old movie in which Robert Benchley played a doctor who sat at his office desk, smoked cigarette after cigarette, and offered all kinds of health advice. The audience had laughed hysterically, not so much at the advice intended to be absurd, but at the image of a doctor chain-smoking. The idea of an ambulance careening around the city with a driver puffing away had the same comic cast to it.

Ronnie peeled some of the other characters off their Velcro backings: Batman, Daffy Duck, a pirate whose name she didn't know, then put them back. Audrey was too old for these small figures. There was nothing in the store Audrey would want, but Ronnie looked among the pens and calendars, read a few greeting cards and joke books, as if her daughter were a tyrant who demanded gifts. She knew this wasn't true, but somehow the ambulance driver, still wearing beepers and stethoscope, made her feel guilty, although she didn't know why. She finally left the store with her newspaper and a pocket-size Mickey Mouse.

The job was described to Ronnie when she answered an ad in the paper: she would have to call the people quoted in articles and verify what they had said by repeating attributed lines over the telephone. It required someone meticulous, someone who could throw him- or herself into the problem of tracking down speakers and verifying statements which were often controversial. It wasn't a magazine she read on a regular basis unless she was in a waiting room, but no one in the personnel office asked her what she read. The job required a clear speaking voice and persistence. Ronnie doubted she had either of these skills, but she was hired and sent on to another set of offices. The woman who was in charge of Ronnie's future department introduced herself as Mrs. Binder and looked over her forms sent from personnel.

"Place of birth: Berlin," Mrs. Binder read out loud. "You don't speak with an accent."

"We left when I was three."

They shared a small office. The room had sliver windows, facing the corridor on one side and a view of the street, trucks pulling up to loading bays, on the other. Mrs. Binder—Felice— showed Ronnie how to scan copy for quotes, how to make overseas telephone calls using various charge codes. Felice looked out at the men pushing racks of dresses down the street. "Rough characters," she said to Ronnie. "Watch your bag when you go to lunch." Ronnie noted her archaic turn of phrase as a sign Felice was a stickler, something of a fuddy-duddy, warnings that she might be difficult to work for. *A rough character, not,* Audrey would have said.

She had written *Berlin.* She wouldn't stay at the job long. If asked, she would have said that when she was still a baby, she was taken to live with her grandmother in Switzerland, and somehow a few years later, when her grandmother died, she was sent to a family in New York. The director of personnel had only looked at her application in a cursory way before sending her upstairs. For years she had filled in forms with place of birth, Brooklyn, then in the personnel office, she slowly drew a *B*, then turned the *r* into an *e*, and the rest followed, *r-l-i-n*, like a nonsense word which could scarcely evoke grainy goose-stepping newsreels or images of a split city. She tried it out for a while, *Berlin*. She dropped the *e* from her last name, saying her old name had been threatening, as if all it needed was the *n-s-t-e-i-n*.

There was a picture of Ronnie's mother holding her as an infant. The picture had been taken in Prospect Park, but from a distance. The baby could have been any baby. Birth records had been lost when they moved to California. The certificate had been in a box packed with bank statements, letters, a tin shaped like a submarine which was filled with foreign stamps, an ashtray from a motel in Los Angeles.

"The movers trekked up and down stairs for hours carrying boxes, so a few things were lost or accidentally left behind," Ronnie said.

Audrey turned the photograph over. Nothing had been written on the back. She thought the job checking quotes sounded like a rehearsal for a courtroom drama.

"Is that what you really said? Are you sure? Do you stand by the accuracy of your statements?" Audrey said into an imaginary telephone. Then she marched around the apartment singing Mrs. Binder's name to "Alouette." *Mrs. Binder. Mrs. Mrs. Binder. Mrs. Binder, je te plumerai!*

"It might be Mrs. Fast Binder," Ronnie said, "because she doesn't waste any time. You never know."

"It's Felice," said Audrey. "I looked at one of your forms. Who did you actually call today?"

"I read about a woman who had claimed to be Anastasia. She had been interviewed in Berlin many years ago. Actually, I had to speak to her grandson, who lives in Boston. Then I spoke to a man in Virginia who maintained he was the Lindbergh baby."

Audrey followed Ronnie into the kitchen and put her feet on the table. Ronnie gave her a small knife with melted chocolate sticking to it. Audrey licked the knife then held it as if it were a cigar, tapping imaginary ash to the floor. She had never heard of the Lindbergh baby and had only a vague idea of who Anastasia might be.

"He was the first man to fly across the Atlantic, but his baby was kidnapped and murdered. According to a man in Virginia, the child wasn't murdered. He claims to be the real Lindbergh, Jr. He offered to send his dental x-rays as proof."

"Did he send them?"

"Not to me."

"All these stories are about money and identity."

"And failure."

The television program droning in the background seemed to echo this theme. It was about a man who claimed to be the richest man in the world. He asserted that his money had been left to him by the last ruler of Ghana, and the billions were locked in something called the Ghana-Oman trust, sealed, inaccessible in a Swiss bank. He persuaded investors to give him money in order to conduct the legal process necessary to unlock the trust.

"*Unlock the trust,*" Ronnie repeated. It sounded mythological, not the language of legal suits. "There will probably be something written about this faker before the end of the week." The imposter promised them a return of ten times their initial investment. People turned up at his offices in droves. They couldn't write him checks fast enough. He was known as "The Fat Man," and he was filmed wearing African ceremonial robes in a townhouse in London. A businessman from Pennsylvania gave him seven million dollars. The Fat Man accepted the check, and the man from Pennsylvania never saw a dime, but he told the camera he was still hoping. He said he would hesitate to use the word swindle.

Audrey turned herself upside down on her chair so her legs were against the back and her head hung over the seat. She laughed at the floor. Ronnie found the program disturbing and turned off the television. Her daughter imitated the Fat Man. In a BBC accent, she asked her mother for twenty dollars, saying she was meeting friends and would certainly come back later with ten times that amount. Ronnie gave her the money, and Audrey disappeared.

Ronnie looked out a window and watched the old woman still sitting on the step babbling to Audrey, caught in her torrent of speech. *I don't know nothing. If anyone asks you, you don't know nothing.* Ronnie had seen condoms stuck under the woman's folding chair, sticky bits and pieces someone had used in the middle of the night. She would never notice them. With her masculine face and unwashed clothing, the concierge knew a lot about what went on in the street hour after hour, day after day, yet ignored what lay underfoot. What else could she do? Did Audrey hear the sounds from the street that kept Ronnie awake at night? Sometimes Ronnie looked in on her, opening the door only a crack, but she appeared to sleep through all of it.

A story about con artists, from the petty small-time cheats who circulate in train stations claiming to have lost their fare, to big-time crackpots, greeted Ronnie Friday morning. Crackpot was Felice's word. The writer of the story didn't make any judgments. These weren't really celebrity cons, and perhaps not cons at all. All denied invidious intent, they were only concerned with simple problems of identity. Ronnie felt overwhelmed by a deluge of facts, quotes, telephone numbers, and identities, broken-off chips of sentences, isolated tags of statements, often arriving at her desk without much of a context. Listening to others busy at their desks around her only contributed to the effect that nothing, all the references and allusions, was destined to stay in her conscience for long, but it was dizzying. She felt as if she had been assigned to work on some kind of conveyor belt on which fragments of stories and situations from popular culture to political intrigue zipped past her as she tried to assign meaning to each piece before they sped past her grasp.

As Felice moved papers from one side of her desk to other, Ronnie was reminded of an exhibit she had seen years ago in which a professor at an upstate New York college, an archaeologist, invented an ancient civilization and created all kinds of artifacts he claimed were made by these people. It wasn't a hoax, the objects and the invented people were openly just that, a fabrication on his part. If you looked closely at a series of votives, you would find they were made from parts of old blenders. Innards of toasters and irons had been fashioned into ritual ornaments. Pencil sharpeners turned into totems of questionable purpose. The original identity of the objects wasn't easy to spot. The people whose fragments of stories simultaneously disguised and unmasked themselves were like those objects she had spent a long time staring at until the game was figured out.

"They might be telling the truth," Ronnie said as she folded her newspaper.

Felice nodded, running her hand through newly garnet-colored hair. Ronnie began with the case of a woman who claimed to be a fraternal twin of Patty Hearst, her identity obfuscated by a deliberate mix-up at the hospital. She now lived in San Diego and, as a Hearst twin, felt she was entitled to part of their fortune. Same birthday, same hospital, a baby had been stillborn, a switch had been made with one of the twins. When a picture of Cathy Bell was placed next to a picture of Patty Hearst, they did look remarkably similar. Cathy Bell claimed her adoptive mother had been a nurse, and when her own baby died of sudden crib death, her best friend, a nurse on duty, made the switch. Both women were deceased, so Cathy's story ran into difficulty when it came to verification on her behalf. The Hearst family said Cathy was a lunatic. Her story was preposterous. Mrs. Hearst never had twins, and if she had, where was the bogus birth certificate of the snitched twin? Cathy had no answers but volunteered for a DNA test.

"They think I'm another kind of SLA, another Colonel Cinque or Squeaky Fromm trying to extort money," Cathy said, "and they're right to be suspicious, but really I'm not connected to any organization. I'm glad they're being careful with my money, at least."

Ronnie only needed to verify the quote but told her she did look remarkably like Patty Hearst.

"Of course I do," Cathy Bell said. "I'm her sister."

Cathy asked her how the air looked in New York; smog hung densely over Los Angeles. She had always wanted to see the Atlantic Ocean but had never been farther east than Tucson. She was bored at her job working in a small real estate office, and she was glad it was Friday. Ronnie felt complicitous with Cathy Bell, regardless of whether her claim was true or an invention. The sense of complicity was entirely false, and she knew it, but when she hung up, Ronnie felt alone in the room. She stared out the window in an unfocused way at the tiny heads and shoulders below. Felice was reading and looked up to ask Ronnie if she'd gotten her picture taken yet for her company ID.

Calls to secretaries in the State Department to verify quotes, and queries overseas, made Ronnie feel anonymous and important at the same time. She learned the various codes by heart, and rang foreign cities and statesmen's offices as if she were dialing the weather number. Translated quotes presented special problems.

"Sentences marked in green or red ink demand immediate attention," Felice explained. These were gateways to confusion. The foreign correspondent, in-house or freelance, had to be tracked down.

Ronnie skipped a story about a mathematical genius from MIT; instead she went on to a story about illegal aliens by a writer who worked in the building. She would be easy to call, four numbers, an extension which probably rang downstairs. As she waited she drew a little man standing in phone booth. Finally the writer picked up the line. Ronnie had been drawing slanting rain on the edge of a message pad and jumped when she heard a voice at the other end of the telephone.

"I'd like to repeat this quote," Ronnie said, but the woman on the other end of the line became angry, offended by an imagined suggestion of inaccuracy or fraud.

"Who do you think you are?" the writer asked.

"What do you mean, who am I? I'm a fact checker." Aware of Felice staring at her, Ronnie tried to sound more contentious but soon backed down.

"I'm sorry. I would just like to go over the translation with you. I'm not questioning your story."

Felice walked over to her desk and took the telephone from her hand.

"We're not saying you invented these people for the sake of a story." There was a pause while the other woman answered, probably defensively, and Felice looked upwards. "No, we don't think you made a mistake translating their words, we're only checking in the event that a slip-up might have occurred in the transcription."

Putting her hand over the receiver, Felice said, "She must be new. We do this all the time, and writers know it's standard procedure."

Ronnie reached for the telephone, but Felice waved her away, checked the quote, then hung up.

"That's just the way things are done," she explained.

"It could have been made up and true at the same time," Ronnie suggested with complete innocence.

"There's no need to be nasty."

"No, I mean it. The story, like many other stories, could easily have been made up and true at the same time." She tossed out half a cup of cold coffee, watching the sodden paper in the basket.

The story in question, written in short telegraphic sentences, was about illegal immigrants working invisibly throughout the city, and spoke of hidden injuries that remained or were incurred as a result of the aliens' seeming transparency in the city. They lived in fear and believed they had no legal redress from exploitative employers: sweatshop owners, pimps, thugs who kept them in near imprisonment or forced them to commit crimes, living under threats not just to themselves but to families back home. Ronnie looked out the window. Heads and shoulders congregated around one of the loading bays far below across the street, as if there might have been an accident. She imagined the stowaways and illegals the writer had interviewed, people terrified of doctors, afraid to give anyone their names. Inconspicuous dishwashers, hotel maids, gypsy cab drivers, seamstresses. Vital, the article had said, yet unknown and tax-free.

"*I can't verify their words. I don't even have their real names,*" the woman had said, as if Ronnie were some kind of naïve dolt. "*You read what I wrote. You must realize I can't put these people in greater danger than they're already in.*" She was angry, and Ronnie felt she had a right to be. It was the kind of anger that slid off Felice's back, but Ronnie took it home with her and lived with sharp particles of humiliation for days.

She looked forward to stories about dead people; there were fewer telephone calls to make when the main protagonists couldn't be reached. Felice warned her about what she called "smoking guns" and "stalking horses" in a piece of writing. It was four-thirty. She could make one more call, and so following Felice's advice, she scanned a story which appeared more about numbers, huge prices, millions of dollars, paid for nineteenth-century paintings. Ronnie called the auction house to verify a quote. It was simple.

"Could these be the correct prices?"

"We're seeing a lot of foreign interest, yes, that's what I said."

Felice, who had been listening again as she cleaned the top of her desk, pointed out the obvious irony in that the original artists may have died in the poorhouse, reaping no benefit from the inflated sums their paintings now commanded. It was Friday afternoon, and she threw pens and notepads into a drawer with gusto, a sign she was leaving early.

"All paths lead to Rome. See you Monday," she said, waving at Ronnie as she left, the office's glass doors swinging behind her. Ronnie waited twenty minutes after Felice could be seen getting into the elevator. She might become snarled in conversation with someone met on the way out or she might dawdle at the lobby kiosk, so Ronnie allowed time to avoid the possibility of running into her as she herself left for the day. She didn't want to talk to Felice for the few blocks they might walk in common together. She looked at the blue veins on the backs of her hands, smoothed the sleeves of an overly large black jacket, and watched. Unlike the cons, Ronnie usually felt at home in her body, although she recognized this feeling was in itself a kind of con she often put over on herself.

When Audrey moaned about having to write a paper about what she thought the future might look like, Ronnie suggested they go to Queens to see what was left of the 1964 World's Fair grounds. Because she had absolutely no ideas, Audrey thought this was a pretty good one.

They got out of the subway at Flushing Meadows–Corona Park, walked past the Perisphere and abandoned pavilions.

"Here was where we ate Belgium waffles, before you were born," Ronnie said. "Here was where the General Electric World of the Future was built." Ronnie wrapped her jacket around her more tightly against the chill wind. In the distance near the site of the former Vatican pavilion, a group of women and a few men stood aiming their cameras at the sky.

"I'm going to ask them what they were taking pictures of."

"Don't, Mom," said Audrey, backing off as Ronnie approached a woman in white gloves and a bell-shaped coat. Her mother smiled and didn't seem in the least embarrassed.

The woman explained that the Virgin Mary appeared in the

cloud formations on the site where the pope had visited the World's Fair in 1964. When the pictures were printed, her outline could be seen in the clouds, and she spoke to them through one of their number, a woman who called herself the Holy Voicebox. Audrey was far away, sitting on a park bench, pretending to dump a stone from her shoe. Although Ronnie looked into the sky and saw nothing but clouds, she appeared interested in the woman's description, nodding if no longer smiling. She walked back to Audrey's park bench.

"We should have brought a camera," she suggested.

"They wouldn't let us just take pictures of them while they have their cameras aimed at the clouds. They wouldn't like it," Audrey said. "They'd feel like animals in a zoo."

"No, not of them. We could take pictures of the sky, too. See what turns up."

Audrey thought her mother naïve. "You can't just take pictures of the sky. You have to be part of their group."

"Why?"

"Mom, please."

"You mean you have to be in touch with the Holy Voicebox first? I don't know why you feel you have to be so careful."

Audrey walked towards another pavilion so as to distance herself from her mother. Although still within eyesight, she wanted to give the impression they weren't necessarily together. She sat on a low swing she was too old for and not really interested in. A few yards away across cracked concrete, she made out a familiar shape, but she wasn't sure how she knew the man. As he straightened up briefly to stretch his back, she recognized the clerk who scared her, the one who told her off. He was eating from a plastic box, huddled over a bench, fork plunging into food, stabbing vegetables, shoving them into his mouth. He looked up again and squinted in her direction. Wiping his hands on his jacket, he angrily shoved the plastic container in a trash can, then walked over. Audrey froze. He was slight but had a presence of continual irritation and affront. She wanted to run away but didn't want to appear to have been so affected by the man that he could scare her off just by looking at her.

"So we are old friends, I think," he said.

"What?"

"I live near here. Within sight of the Soviet pavilion where the lights went out in 1939."

Audrey had no idea what he was talking about.

"I give you twenty dollars."

"What for?"

"What for? You're a smart girl. You know what is what for."

He reached for Audrey's arm, stroking it then pulling her by the sleeve. The wool of her baggy jacket made a kind of triangle shape as he yanked. It was an awkward move. He could have grabbed her whole arm but didn't. Audrey slowly pulled her arm away from him as if she were made of gum. She felt she had no will, and everyone she knew was impossibly far away. Responding to her gesture, he pushed her off the swing, causing her to fall to the concrete, but in the shove the swing swept high into the air from his blow and, jangling in its return, clipped him vengefully on the ear. It couldn't have caused him much pain, but caught by surprise, he turned red.

"You stupid girl. You don't know anything."

"No, you're the dip who doesn't know anything. Who do you think you're trying to be?"

"The King of Queens," he yelled at her as he moved off. His pants were short and tight, and despite the cold, he wore no jacket, only a thin sweater and no socks.

Audrey lay on the ground, knees in the air, stunned, afraid to move. She didn't know what to do and watched the man retreat farther into the park. This is what she observed: his legs were very white and slightly dirty. Achilles tendons stood out aggressively. A rolled-up magazine was stuck in his back pocket. At one point he turned back towards her. She got herself up without bothering to dust off her bruises and ran, colliding with the group aimed at the sky.

They had taken a break to load more film but were still gazing overhead. Wind blew someone's veiled hat off, but it was quickly retrieved with a kind smile towards Audrey. She grimaced in return, as if to acknowledge she knew she was an interloper. Wind blew leaves around benches, and the abandoned pavilions looked like architectural relics of a lost civilization, ancient, and modernist at the same time. Here was a church of commerce, here was a sort of archive of possibility; a trash can would be associated with the food ephemera of the tribe who had disappeared. There would be piles of things, utilitarian and vestigial, identified on a whim by a homesick anthropologist. It occurred to her that she might return alone just to see if the cloud formations would mystically align themselves on the film of a nonbeliever. They walked towards the former General Electric pavilion. The group posed, faces upturned, aiming towards the sky. Commissioned by the Holy Voicebox, they seemed to have confidence and a sense of purpose Ronnie envied. They looked like a photograph of a movie audience wearing 3-D glasses, staring mesmerized at the screen.

A gust of wind seemed to scatter the followers of the Holy Voicebox, as if they were a chorus unable to cohere.

"Why don't you take some notes?" Ronnie suggested. "Describe what you see."

But idea of the future rooted in these leftovers of a crumbling utopian projection eluded her. "I don't know how to begin."

"You always say that, but you always find something to say."

"This time I don't think I can." She hadn't seen any apartment buildings nearby and wondered for a moment where the clerk could possibly have lived. The monster, the untransformable frog, haunted the ruins of the future, nursing wounds he couldn't describe, inventing narratives inspired by obscene pictures, screamed in untranslatable dialects. She would write about him. She wasn't sure if describing the incident was a way of inducing more humiliation, or if relegating it to the future meant assigning the monster to the flimsy realm of possibility: rickety, a victim of the vagaries of fate, a man whose existence was as impermanent as a cloud formation. She took her mother's arm, even though she felt too old for such a gesture, clinging and hesitant.

"Tell me again about when you arrived in New York. Make up that story again."

"Why? Are you telling someone you were born somewhere else? Are you planning a brain transplant?"

Audrey didn't know exactly what to say. She wanted to tell a true story so that it would sound made-up. She would begin like the followers of the Holy Voicebox, aim her camera anywhere, see what turned up.

Resistance

A lvin Boudreaux had outlived his neighbors. His asbestos-siding house was part of a tiny subdivision built in the 1950's, when everybody had children, a single-lane driveway, a rotating TV antenna, and a picnic table out back. Nowadays he sat on his little porch and watched the next wave of families occupy the neighborhood, each taking over the old houses, driving up in their pairs of bug-shaped cars, one for each spouse to drive to work. Next door, Melvin Tillot had died, and his wife had sold the house to migrate up north with her daughter. Mr. Boudreaux used to watch her white puff of hair move through the yard as she snipped roses. Now she was gone, and there was no movement on his street that had consequence for him. Today he sat and watched the sky for sailing wedges of birds, or an army of ranked mackerel clouds, or the electric bruise of a thunderstorm rising from the molten heat of the Gulf. Sometimes he thought of his wife, dead now eight years. He was in that time of life when the past began coming around again, as if to reclaim him. Lately he thought about his father, the sugarcane farmer, who used to teach him about tractors and steam engines.

Two months before, Mr. Boudreaux had watched his new neighbors move in, a young blond woman, overweight, with thin hair, and raw, nervous eyes. The husband was small and mean, sat in a lawn chair in the backyard as though he was at the beach, and drank without stopping, every weekend. They had one ten-year-old, a plain, slow-moving daughter.

Mr. Boudreaux could not bear to look at these people. They let the rose bushes die of thirst and left the empty garbage cans sitting at the edge of the street until the grass under them forgot what the sun looked like, and died. They never sat on their porch, and they had no pets that he could see. But after a while, he tried to talk to the wife when she dragged out the garbage bag in the morning. Her voice was thin, like a little squeak against the thumb. She worked somewhere for six hours each day, she told him, running an electric coffee-grinding machine.

One mild afternoon, Mr. Boudreaux was going to visit the graveyard, and he rattled open a kitchen window to air the room out while he was gone. Next door, he saw the daughter come into the yard and show her father a sheet of paper. The father curled up his lip and took a swallow from a tall tumbler, looking away. Mr. Boudreaux felt sorry for the girl when she placed a hand on the father's shoulder and the man grabbed the sheet from her and balled it up. She put a forefinger to her glasses as if to bring the world into focus. The motion showed practice and patience. She was formless and looked overweight in her pleated skirt and baggy white blouse. Her carroty hair was gathered in a short tail above her neck, her lips were too big for her face, and two gray eyes hid behind glasses framed in pale blue plastic, the kind of glasses little girls wore thirty years before. She stepped next to her father's chair again, getting in his space, as Mr. Boudreaux's grandson would say. The father began to yell, something about a damned science project. He waved his arms, and his face grew red. Another child might have cried.

The next afternoon, Mr. Boudreaux was on his knees, pulling grass by the backyard fence when he heard the school bus grind up LeBoeuf Street. He was still pulling when the father came home at four-thirty and sat in the lawn chair, next to the back steps. The girl appeared behind the screen door, like a shadow.

"It's got to be turned in Monday," she said. Even her voice was ordinary, a plain voice with little music in it.

The father put his glass against his forehead. "I don't know anything about it," he said. "Do you know how tired I am?"

Her half-formed image shifted at the screen, then dispersed like smoke. In a moment the mother came out and stepped carefully past her husband, not looking at him until she was safely on the grass. "I'd help her," she said. "But I don't know anything about that. Electricity. It's something a man'll have to do."

The husband drained his drink and flung the ice cubes at the fence. Mr. Boudreaux felt a drop hit the back of his spotted hand. "Why can't she do something like a girl would do? Something *you* could help her with."

Mr. Boudreaux peered through the honeysuckle. The man was wearing jeans and a white button-down shirt with some sort of company emblem embroidered on the breast, a gay and meandering logo which suggested bowling alley or gas station.

The mother looked down and patted the grass in a semicircle with her left foot. "You're her parent, too," she said. It was a weak thing to say, Mr. Boudreaux thought.

The father stood up, and the flimsy chair turned over on its side. He turned around and looked at it for a moment, then kicked it across the yard.

After dark, Mr. Boudreaux went out on his front porch with a glass of iced tea and listened, wondering whether the girl's parents ever argued. He had never heard them, but then he remembered that since the coming of air conditioning, he'd heard little from inside anyone's house. When he first moved to the neighborhood, up and down LeBoeuf Street he could hear the tinny cheer of radios, the yelps of children chasing through the houses, a rare yelling match about money or relatives. But now there was only the aspirate hum of the heat pumps and the intermittent *ahhh* of an automobile's tires on the subdivision's ebony streets. He looked over at his fifteen-year-old Buick parked in the single drive. It embarrassed him to drive such a large old car through the neighborhood where everyone stood out and washed the dust from their Japanese-lantern compacts. Maybe it was time to trade it off for something that would fit in. Next door, the father came out and walked stiffly to his candy-apple car and drove away, dragging his tires at every shift of the gears, *irk, irk.*

The next morning, Mr. Boudreaux came out for the paper and saw Carmine sitting on her front steps waiting for the bus to appear out of the fog. Her eyes were red. He picked up the paper and began walking back toward the porch, telling himself, *Don't look.* But at his front steps he felt a little electrical tug at his neck muscles, a blank moment of indecision.

He turned his head. "Good morning, little miss," he called out, raising his paper.

"Morning, Mr. Boudreaux." Her low voice was small in the fog.

"How you doing in school?" He unfolded the paper and pretended to read the headline.

"Okay."

He bounced once on the balls of his feet. He could walk into the house and not look back. "It's springtime," he said. "My kids used to have to make their science projects this time of year."

She looked over at him, her eyebrows up in surprise. "You have kids?"

Mr. Boudreaux realized how impossibly old he must seem. "Sure. A long time ago. They're nurses and engineers and one's a policeman way up in Virginia. They all had their science projects. What about you?"

She looked down at a heavy brown shoe. "I want to do one, but no one can help me," she said.

He banged the paper against his leg several times before he said anything more. He closed his eyes. "Is your momma home? Let me talk to her a minute."

That's how it got started. After school, she rang his doorbell, and he led her into the kitchen where he fixed her a Coke float. Carmine smelled dusty and hot, and she finished her drink in less than a minute, placing the glass in the sink and sitting down again at Mr. Boudreaux's table, spreading open a spiral-bound tablet. She gave him a blank look of evaluation, an expression she might use on a strange dog.

Mr. Boudreaux sat down across from her. "Well, missy, what kind of project you interested in? Your momma said you needed a little push in the right direction."

"What did you do when you had a job?" she asked, pushing her hair out of her eyes.

He blinked. "I started as a millwright at LeBlanc Sugar Mill, and when I retired, I was a foreman over all the maintenance people."

She frowned. "Does that mean you don't know anything about electricity?"

Leaning back, he rubbed a spot over his eye. "I worked on a lot of motors in my time."

Carmine scooted her chair closer and showed him her notebook. In it were hundreds of O's drawn with legs, all running into a narrow cylinder and jumping one by one out of the other end of it. "These are electrons," she said. Some of the electrons were running through a bigger cylinder, and more of them seemed to be coming out the other side. "The tube shapes are resistors," she instructed. "Some let electrons through fast, some slow." Her short finger led his attention along the rows of exiting electrons, which had little smiles drawn on them, as though they had earned passage to a wonderful place. She told him how resistors control current and how without them no one could have ever made a television or computer.

Mr. Boudreaux nodded. "So what you going to call this project?"

"Resistance." She said the word as though it had another meaning.

"And we gotta figure out how to demonstrate it, right?" He closed his eyes and thought back to those late-night projects of his children. His son Sid, the state patrolman, had done friction. Friction, the old man thought. That was right up Sid's alley. "We have to state a problem and show how it's solved with resistors. Then we demonstrate how they work."

Carmine bobbed her head. "You *have* done this before."

The next afternoon, they sprawled on the rug in the den, drawing and brainstorming. When Mr. Boudreaux let the girl out at suppertime, he saw her father standing on the front walk, glowering. The next morning was Saturday, and he and Carmine got into his venerable Buick to go down to the electronics store at the mall. The girl hardly looked at her list. She spent her time browsing the tall pegboard sections hung with diodes and toggle switches, condensers and capacitors, fondling little transistors through the thin plastic bags. Mr. Boudreaux tended to business, buying a pack of foot-square circuit boards, little red push switches, eighteen-gauge wire. Carmine had brought him a dog-eared book, *Electricity for Children*, and from it he had memorized the banding codes for resistors. With this knowledge he selected an assortment of plastic cylinders which looked like tiny jelly beans decorated with red, black, and silver bands, an inch of silver wire coming out of each end.

Their purchases stowed in a loopy plastic bag, they walked the mall to the candy counter, where Mr. Boudreaux bought a quarter-pound of lime slices. Carmine took a green wedge from him, saying nothing, and they walked on through the strollers, teenagers, and senior citizens limping along in running shoes. Mr. Boudreaux looked at the children who were Carmine's age. They seemed stylish and energetic as they played video games or preened in the reflections of shop windows. Carmine was mechanical, earnest, and as communicative as a very old pet dog.

When they got back to Mr. Boudreaux's house, Carmine's father was standing in their way, wavering in the slim line of grass that ridged the middle of the driveway. The old man got out of the Buick and greeted him.

The other man had been drinking again. He pointed a chewed fingernail at Mr. Boudreaux. "You should have asked me before you took that girl off somewhere."

"I asked your wife. You weren't awake yet."

"Well, let me tell you, I was worried. I called up the police and checked you out." Carmine came around the car and stood between them, staring down the street as though she could see all the way to Texas.

Mr. Boudreaux passed his tongue along his bottom lip. "The police. You called the police about me? Why'd you do that?"

"You can't tell, nowadays. Old guys such as yourself and kids. You know?" The father stuck his pale hands into a pair of tight work pants.

The old man looked at the ground. He was embarrassed because he didn't know what to think, other than that nobody used to imagine such things. Not in a million years. "You think I'm gonna rob your kid or something?" he said at last. "Look." He held out the plastic bag. "I helped her pay for her stuff."

Carmine's father pointed a finger at Mr. Boudreaux. "She can pay for her own stuff. You keep your money in your pocket," he said. "I don't know why you think you got to do this." He gave the girl a wounded glance and then turned toward his steps.

Mr. Boudreaux looked at Carmine. She pushed her glasses up her nose and looked back at him. "Did you have a little girl back when you were a father?" she asked.

He looked at his house and then back at the child. "Yes, I did. Her name is Charlene. And I have another named Monica."

For the first time that day, her expression changed and showed surprise. "What would anybody need with two girls?"

That afternoon, he watched her write her report; he helped her decide where to put headings, and how to divide the information up. After supper she came over, and they planned the display. Carmine drew out a design on lined paper with an oversized pencil. "I want those little button switches that work like doorbells here," she said. "On the first circuit I want a straight wire to a flashlight bulb in one of those sockets we bought. On the second line I want a twenty-two-ohm resistor to the same size bulb. That'll make the bulb glow dimmer." She stuck out her tongue and bit it as she drew carbon ribbons of circuits. "The third button will turn on a line with two twenty-two-ohm resistors soldered together in series, and the bulb will glow dimmer." She went on to draw in the fourth circuit, which would be an ordinary pencil wired to show how current can pass through carbon, "which is what resistors are made of," she told him. A fifth circuit would have a rotary switch controlling a bulb. Carmine drew in the electrical symbol for a variable resistor at this point and put down her pencil.

"Now what?" Mr. Boudreaux asked, rubbing his eyes with his long forefingers. Since he'd reached his late seventies, he'd been going to bed around eight-thirty. At the moment, his knees were aching like great boils.

"Now we have to solder this together on the perforated circuit board."

"Ow. I don't know about that."

She didn't look up. "Don't you have a soldering iron?"

"I haven't seen it in years." They got up, and Carmine helped him down the back steps into the moonlit yard. Built onto the rear of the garage was a workshop. Mr. Boudreaux opened the door, and the glass in its top rattled. At one time he spent long hours here fixing the house's appliances or rebuilding bicycles and gas-powered airplanes. Now he came in once or twice a year to look for a screwdriver or to store a box. Carmine found the light switch.

"A workbench," she sang, going over to a vise and turning its handle around.

Mr. Boudreaux looked for the soldering gun while she dusted the maple counter with a rag and spread out the components. "Here it is," he said. But when he plugged the instrument in and pulled the trigger, a burst of sparks shot from the vents and a smell of melting Bakelite filled the shop. Holding it by its cord, he unplugged it and then threw it into the yard. The girl looked after the soldering iron sorrowfully.

"Do you have another one?"

"No, honey. And it's too late to go buy a new one. We'll have to finish tomorrow." He watched her look to the counter and purse her lips. "What you thinking?"

"Sundays are not good days," she told him.

He shook his head at the comment. "You'll be over here."

She stared at her blocky leather shoes. "Mom and I have got to be there, and we've got to stay quiet." She looked up at him, and her face showed that she was smarter than he ever was. "We've always got to be in the corner of his eye."

"What's that?" He bent a furry ear toward her.

"He wants us around, but kind of on the side. Never the main thing he looks at."

The old man looked up to a rusty sixteen-penny nail and took down his Turner gasoline blowtorch. "If this thing'll work, we'll try to get our soldering done the old-fashioned way."

She clapped her hands together once. "What is it?" She put a forefinger on the brass tank.

"Well, you open it up here," he told her, unscrewing a plug in the bottom and shaking out a few spoonfuls of stale, sweet-smelling gas. "Then you put some fresh lawn-mower gasoline in, turn it over, and use this little thumb pump on the side."

"To make pressure?"

"Yeah. Then you light the end of this horizontal tube and adjust the flame with these old knobs." He dug around in a deep drawer under the counter, coming up with an arrow-shaped tool with a wooden handle on one end and an iron rod running out of that into a pointed bar of copper. "You got to set this heavy point in the flame, and when it gets hot enough, you touch it to the solder, which melts onto the wires. That's what holds the wires together."

The girl grabbed the wooden handle and waved the tool like a weapon, stabbing the air.

In a few minutes the blowtorch was sputtering and surging, humming out a feathery yellow flame. It had been over thirty years since Mr. Boudreaux had used such a torch for soldering, and it took several tries before the first wires were trapped in melted silver. He and the girl strung wire and turned screws into a circuit board, and for a minute, he was a younger man, looking down on the head of one of his own daughters. He felt expert as he guided Carmine's short fingers and held the circuit board for her to thread the red wire through to the switch terminals. He felt back at work, almost as though he was getting things done at the mill.

The girl avoided his eyes, but did give him one glance before asking a question. "Why're you helping me with this?"

He guided her fingers as she threaded a wire under the board. "It just needed doing."

"Did you really help your children with their projects?"

"I don't remember. Maybe their momma did."

She was quiet as she turned in a stubby screw. "Did *you* ever have to do a science project?"

He looked out the workshop window and closed one eye. "I don't think science had been invented yet." He checked her face, but she wasn't smiling. Then he remembered something. "When I was in fifth grade I had to read a novel called *Great Expectations*. The teacher said we had to build something that was in the book, like an old house, or Miss Havisham's wedding cake or some such foolishness. I forgot all about it until the night before and knew I was going to really catch it the next day if I showed up without it."

Carmine took the hot copper away from the torch and soldered a connection herself. "What did you do?"

He rubbed his chin. "I think I cried, I was so scared. My mother would whack me with a belt if I ever failed a course, and I wasn't doing so good in English. Anyway, my daddy saw my long face and made me tell him what was wrong. He asked me what was in the book." Mr. Boudreaux laughed. "I thought that was strange, because he couldn't read hardly two words in a row. But I told him about Pip, and Pip's father, and the prison ship. That caught his ear, and he asked me about that ship, so I told him. Then he went outside. That night I went to bed and couldn't sleep hardly a wink. I remember that because I've always been a good sleeper. I go out like a light about nine, ten o'clock, you know?" The girl nodded, then turned a bulb into a socket. "When I got up for school, Daddy had left for work at the mill, and on the kitchen table was a foot-long sailing boat, painted black, three masts, deck hatches, gun ports, and a bowsprit, the rigging strung with black sewing thread. It was all done with a pocketknife, and it was warm to the touch because my momma said he had put it in the oven to dry the paint so it would be ready for school."

The girl seemed not to hear him. "I want the battery tied in with wire," she said.

"The old man was like that," Mr. Boudreaux told her. "He never asked me if I liked the boat, and I never said anything to him about it, even when I brought home a good grade for the project."

When they were finished, all the light bulbs lit up as she predicted. He built a hinged wooden frame for the two posters that held her report and drawings. They set everything up on the workbench and stepped back. Mr. Boudreaux pretended to be a judge and clamped his fingers thoughtfully around his chin. "That's a prize winner," he said in a mock-serious voice. Then he looked down at Carmine. Her lips were in a straight line, her eyes dark and round.

The next day was Sunday, and Mr. Boudreaux went to eleven o'clock Mass, visiting afterward with the men his age who were still able to come out. They sat on the rim of St. Anthony's fountain under the shade of a palm tree and told well-worn jokes in Cajun French, then told tales of who was sick, who was dead. Mr. Landry, who had worked under Mr. Boudreaux at the sugar mill, asked him what he was doing with his granddaughter at the mall.

"That was a neighbor child," Mr. Boudreaux told him. "My grandchildren live away."

"What was she doing? Asking you about the dinosaurs?" He laughed and hit the shoulder of the man next to him.

"She's doing a school thing, and I'm helping her with it."

Mr. Landry's face settled into a question. "She lives on the north side of you?"

"Yes."

Mr. Landry shook his head. "My son works with her daddy. She needs all the help she can get."

"He's a piece of work, all right."

The men broke up and moved away from each other, waving. Mr. Boudreaux drove the long way home, passing by the school, along the park, behind the ball field. He felt that by helping with the science project he had completed something important and that he and the girl had learned something. His old Buick hesitated in an intersection, and he looked at its faded upholstery, its dusty buttons and levers, thinking that he should buy a new car. He could cash in his insurance policy and finally use a little of his savings.

When he got home, even though he felt lightheaded, he began to clean out the glove compartment, search under the seats, empty the trunk of boots and old tools. He rested in the sun on his front steps, then decided to change into shorts, get the galvanized pail, and wash the car. He was standing in a pool of water from the hose, looking down at his white legs, when he heard the shouting begin next door. The mother's keening yell was washed away by the drunken father's roaring. The girl ran out as though she were escaping a fire and stood on the withering lawn, looking back into the house. Mr. Boudreaux saw a wink of something white at the front door, and then the science project posters flew out onto the walkway, followed by the circuit board display and the little platform they had made for it. The father lurched down the steps, his unbuttoned white shirt pulled from his pants, his eyes narrowed and sick. He kicked the poster frame apart, and Carmine ran to avoid a flying hinge. She turned in time to see the circuit board crackle under a black shoe.

"Hey," Mr. Boudreaux yelled. "Stop that."

The father looked around for the voice and spotted the old man. "You go to hell."

Mr. Boudreaux's back straightened. "Just because you can't handle your liquor don't give you the right to treat your little girl like that."

The father staggered toward him. "You old bastard, you got no right to try and make me look bad."

Mr. Boudreaux's heart misfired once. The walk was so slippery he couldn't even run away from the father, who was coming closer in a wobbly, stalking motion. He looked down at the father's doubled fists. "You stay in your yard. If you give me trouble, I'll call the cops." The father gave him a shove, and Mr. Boudreaux went down hard in a grassy puddle. "Ow. You drunk worm. I'm seventy-eight years old."

"Leave us alone," the father yelled. He raised a shoe, and for a moment the old man thought that he was going to kick him. Then the mother was at his side, pulling him away.

"Come back in the yard, Chet. Please," she begged. She was not a small woman, and she had two hands on his arm.

Mr. Boudreaux squeezed the lever on the hose nozzle and sprayed the father in the stomach, and he stumbled backward against the mother, cursing. He sprayed him in the forehead. "You rummy. You a big man with old guys and little kids."

"Screw you, old bastard." The father shook water from his hair and tried to pull out of his wife's hands.

"Aw, you a big man," Mr. Boudreaux shouted, trying to stand up. When he finally was able to see over the roof of his Buick, the mother was pulling her husband up the steps, and Carmine was standing under a wilting magnolia tree, looking over at the fragments of her science project scattered along the walk.

Mr. Boudreaux's lower back was sore. By eight o'clock he couldn't move without considerable pain. He looked through his living room window at the house next door. He went out onto his porch and watched the light in Carmine's bedroom window. Then he went in and watched television until nine. He adjusted the rabbit ears on his set and rolled the dial from station to station, not really paying attention to the images on his scuffed Zenith. He turned the machine off and looked at it a long time, felt the cabinet, and tapped it with his fingers. Then he got a screwdriver, unscrewed the back, and peered in. Mr. Boudreaux pulled off all the knobs on the front, slid the works out of the case, and carried it over to his dining room table, placing it under the bright drop fixture. When he turned the works over, he smiled into the nest of resistors. He read the band values, and with a pair of pointed wire snips, removed several that bore two red bands and one black. Behind the selectors were two light sockets, and he cut these out, noting with a grimace that the bulbs in them drew too much power.

In the living room was his wife's cabinet-model Magnavox Hi-Fi. He slowly ran a finger along its walnut top. Then he pulled the knobs off and opened it up with a screwdriver, removing several feet of red and black wire, as well as three light sockets which contained little bulbs of the correct voltage. The volume knob was a variable resistor, he now understood, and he removed that also. He went out to his workshop and took the little steel-tongued toggle switches off his old saber saw, his chain saw, his Moto-Tool. He needed one more and found that in the attic on a rusty set of barber's clippers that had been his brother's. Also in the attic he found his first daughter's Royal manual typewriter. Mr. Boudreaux could type. He'd learned in the army, so he brought down that, too. He emptied the new batteries out of a penlight he kept on his bedside table. They had bought extra sheets of poster board in case Carmine made a mistake while drawing the big resistors, but she had been careful. He dug the handwritten first draft of her report out of his trash can and penciled in the revisions he could remember. Then, on paper that was only slightly yellowed, he typed her report neatly, with proper headings.

Next he drew the images on the posters, big, color-coded resistors traversed by round electrons with faces drawn on. His lettering was like a child's, and this worried him, but he kept on, finishing up with instructions for operating the display. He drew in the last letter at two o'clock, then went out into the workshop to saw up a spruce two-by-four to make the poster frame again. He had no hinges, so he had to go to the cedar chest in his bedroom and remove the ones on the wooden box that held his family insurance policies. He mounted the posters with thumbtacks from an old corkboard which hung in the kitchen. The tacks' heads were rusty, so he painted them over with gummy white correction fluid he'd found in the box with the typewriter.

At four o'clock, he had to stop to take three aspirin for his back, and from the kitchen he looked across through the blue moonlight to the dark house next door, thinking maybe of all the dark houses in town where children endured the lack of light, fidgeting toward dawn.

In the garage he found that there was no more gasoline for the old torch, which had whispered itself empty on the first project. On the front lawn, he cut a short length out of his new garden hose and siphoned fuel from his Buick, getting a charge of gas in his mouth, where it burned his gums under his dentures. Later, as the soldering tool heated in the aspirate voice of the torch, he felt he could spit a tongue of flame.

He ran the wires as she had run them, set the switches, mounted the light sockets, soldered the resistors in little silvery tornadoes of smoke. He found the bulbs left over from the first project and placed them into the sockets, wired in the battery, checked everything, then stepped back. The posters and display were duplicates of those the father had destroyed. Though the workshop window showed a trace of dawn, and though Mr. Boudreaux's legs felt as though someone had shot them full of arrows, he allowed himself a faint smile.

He made a pot of coffee and sat out in the dew on the front porch, waiting for the father to come out in his hurting, hungover fog, and drive away. At seven-fifteen, he was gone, and Mr. Boudreaux loaded the project into the back seat of his car, started the engine, and sat in it, waiting for the school bus. Carmine came out and waited by the garbage cans, and when the bus arrived, its seats stippled with white poster boards, for everyone's project was due the same day, she looked up at the opened door, pushed her glasses up her nose, and got on. He followed the bus out of the neighborhood and down the long, oak-shaded avenue as the vehicle picked up kids in twos and threes, science projects at each stop. The farther he drove, the more fearful he became, thinking that maybe the girl wouldn't understand, or would think that he was doing this just to get back at her father, which in part, he admitted, he was. Several times he thought he'd better pass the bus, turn around, and head home. But then what would he do with the project? He wouldn't throw it away, and it would haunt him forever if he kept it.

The bus pulled into the school lot, and he followed it and parked. By the time he got to the covered walkway, children were pouring off, carrying jars of colored fluids, homemade generators, Styrofoam models of molecules. He had the bifold project in his arms, and when she came down the bus steps empty-handed, he spread it open for her. She stepped close and looked, lifted a page of the tacked-on report and checked the second, the third page.

"Where's the display?" she asked, not looking at him.

"It's in the car here," he said, sidling off to retrieve it. When he got back, he saw she had hitched her bookbag onto her shoulder and had the posters folded and under an arm.

"Give it here," she said, holding out her free hand, her face showing nothing.

He handed it to her. "You want me to help bring it in?"

"No. How do the switches work?"

He clicked one for her. "Up is on, down is off."

She nodded, then squinted up at him. "I'll be late."

"Go on, then." He watched her waddle off among her classmates, bearing her load, then he turned for his car. She could have called after him, smiled, and said thank you, but she didn't.

Because he was out so early, he decided to go shopping. He considered his options: the Buick lot, the appliance dealer's, the hardware. After half an hour of driving around town slowly, he went into a department store and bought two small masonry pots filled with plastic flowers. They looked like the jonquils that used to come up in the spring alongside his mother's cypress fence. He drove to the old city graveyard, and he walked among the brick tombs and carefully-made marble angels, placing a colorful pot on the sun-washed slab of his father's grave. His back pained him when he put down the flowers, and the bone-white tombs hurt his eyes as he turned completely around in this place where no one would say the things that could have been said, but that was all right with him.

PATRICIA HAMPL

The Bill Collector's Vacation

All week the heat has been killing. Foolish to walk the distance to the credit union even so early in the morning, imagining you can beat the worst of it. Think of the walk back, the pavement baking, not a tree for blocks. *Foolish*—a Kenneth word. *Don't be foolish, Marilyn, take the Volvo.*

This, as so often now, was her cue. The tiny, greased gear of her willfulness downshifted away from him, revving at the barest stroke of his control. Or his contempt. She wasn't free to do the sensible thing—drive the air-conditioned car out of the cool garage to the credit union two miles away. She had to fight. Fight what?

Anyway, it was good to walk. A recent article she had clipped made the point: walking was as good, even for cardiovascular, as jogging. Better, really, less threat to the joints. Kenneth was a runner—he didn't like the word jogger. She had put the clipping on the kitchen corkboard: *Jogging Benefits Questioned.* Not that Kenneth bothered to read the clippings she put up, though he could be annoyed by the sight of grocery coupons pinned there. "What are you wasting time clipping coupons for?" he would say, walking out the back door to the garage. That shrug of disdain as he passed by.

Get to the credit union by eight when it opens, home by nine-thirty, before the real heat of the day: this was her plan. She wasn't due at the bookstore until afternoon. But already the day's new heat was adding itself to the surplus still standing from yesterday. The night had left it all to simmer.

At the credit union, she pulled on the big glass door. It didn't budge. Her eye went to a white rectangle on the glass, above the handle: Weekdays 9 a.m.–4:30 p.m. An added judgment, another cluck of contempt. *Foolish, not to check the hours.*

She turned, was struck by the sun. A man was sitting on the low retaining wall in the shade, apparently having made the same mistake. He held a check and a green deposit slip in a meaty hand. He smiled at her in a way she recognized was harmless.

How could you tell that about strangers? Could you? Marilyn trusted her instinct on things like this. Strange, how she bristled at Kenneth, but she still trusted the world for no good reason.

"Plenty of room," the man said. He patted the low wall where he sat, and looked away, toward the state capitol and its immense greensward. She joined him on the retaining wall, ducking out of the sun.

She was annoyed by the hour wait—waste of time. Said so. Wasn't this something new, the nine o'clock opening hour? Were these temporary summer hours? Shouldn't the credit union have sent out notices of any change? "And in this heat," she added. She expected him to meet her on this. But he—beefy, younger than she, dressed in shorts and tee, stomach lazing over his waistband—veered away from the communion of resentment. "I'm on vacation," he said easily, gazing off. "Might as well wait."

Marilyn felt oddly annoyed, as if this fat stranger's contentment subtly betrayed her. *Foolish to be impatient.* She wished she hadn't settled in next to him, but it made no sense to walk back home (plus the question of facing Kenneth), and this was the only shaded place to sit.

A woman in cutoffs, her skimpy yellow hair raked high in a painful-looking ponytail, hurried to the door in flip-flops, her child trailing behind her. She took in the sign, sighed, squinted in the direction of the flower box. No room. Her feet smacked the steps as she rushed back to her car, the child's face impassive as a loan officer at her side.

Several others came by, mostly businessmen in suits too dark, too cruelly heavy, for the day. Sweating figures frowning theatrically at their watches. Each time the plot of discovery and disappointment looked stagier. Always, they walked off, got in their closed cars, drove away. People were becoming cartoons. Only she and the fat man sat there, waiting it out by the retaining wall, electric-blue lobelia rising from the flower boxes behind them.

The sharp edges of her annoyance melted, as she sat there regarding other people's irritation. What predictable animals we are. She was going to point this out to the heavy man sitting peacefully to her right. But her observation would seem to him, she sensed, mean-spirited. He wouldn't like it.

How did she know this—that he would be allergic to—to

what? Irony? The basic unkindness of reading people, observing them? He would not like judging people. That was it, he wasn't a judger. He was—she hadn't the slightest idea. But how interesting, anyway, to know he wouldn't like a smart observation. You know these things about people. It's the way you size up anyone, quick brush strokes of assessment you hardly know you're making. It's how we make our way through the day, down the street, she supposed. Glancing and judging, feinting to the left, dodging to the right.

She asked what he did for a living.

"I work for the Consolidated Bureaus," he said.

What was that?

A smile, sad smile: "I'm a nasty bill collector."

Was it a hard job?

"Well, only eight to ten percent of the bills sent to me ever get collected. Ever. Believe it. And of all the people I talk to—it's a phone job—only five percent show *any* willingness to work with me on the problem. Can you believe that?" He shook his head in mild wonder.

"Do they admit they owe the money?" Marilyn asked. His earnestness seemed to require the question.

"Sure."

"And?"

"They could care less."

"I suppose it makes you pretty cynical," Marilyn said. God, what a hopeless job.

"You don't trust *anybody*," he said richly. But his voice gave him away, no edge to it. He was a great unflexed wad of trust. Wasn't cynical, wasn't bruised. He was intact. Rare sight.

She should not believe, however, the people on *Oprah* and *20/20* who told outlandish tales about bill collectors. The part about threats. "There are rules and laws, we can't do any of that stuff," he said, repelled. The very idea he would menace anyone. He shifted slightly, a shiver of disgust.

Imagine being married to such a man. That sweet disgust at his own supposed power, rippling from the center of his soft pudding self—it was reliable, good. Something reassuring about disgust, less aggressive than contempt.

She had gone over this: it was contempt she had to contend

with from Kenneth, not just the grit of his practiced will sparking against her worn-out compliance. At first (thirty-six years!—their daughter was a mother twice already) his abruptness had struck her as certainty. Impatient, yes. But the good kind of impatient—eager, ambitious, hungry. Men should be hungry. The growl of love and work, lean and hungry. She used to think that way—men are, women are. Everybody did.

She had been proud, secretly, to recognize that hunger in Kenneth, willing to admit that's what she wanted. A twilight boat ride around the harbor, sponsored by their two Catholic colleges, spring, 1959. Holding a glass of shrimp-colored punch, feeling bold, though she did nothing illicit. Thinking, calculating about him—that was illicit. She shrugged off, in an instant, the domesticated male virtues so prized in Father Sullivan's Attributes of Catholic Marriage class. "Does he give you a champagne feeling of well-being, girls?" the priest rang out to his roomful of putative virgins. A nun, still wearing the Renaissance habit of the Order, sat at the back of the room grading papers, a sardonic eyebrow raised occasionally like a mordant punctuation mark to the old priest's blather. The sins he had in mind were corny, middle-aged fantasies. He warned them about wife-swapping, for God's sake.

The truth was, Kenneth *had* given her a champagne feeling, though not of well-being. Something grainier, like the dry sandiness of real champagne hitting the roof of your mouth. Even the faint sneer on Kenneth's face had not scared her off. Had there been a sneer, even then? She had looked up at his smooth face as he said something—what?—something funny, something a bit unkind, a circle of people around him, crewcuts and candy-colored sweater sets. Whatever he said, it gave her the chance to tilt her face up to him, a kiss-me angle, laughing, admiring. Oh, she wanted him. The big boat cut the water smoothly, then there was a shift as it turned. Her punch sloshed out of the glass, her hands got sticky. "Better watch that," he said, smiling. Had noticed her. They were married the weekend after graduation, to no one's surprise. They had become one of their campuses' solid "couples" since their sophomore year. Pre-law and el ed. "Great planning, Ken," an uncle whacked him on the back at the wedding, "she'll get you through law school."

Which Marilyn had, four years of second grade at Compton Elementary, using birth control without a qualm. *None of their business,* Kenneth said. He led them, with amazing nonchalance, away from the crafted certainties of their parochial background. He had no crisis of faith. It wasn't spiritual, not even intellectual. He simply saw that life was elsewhere. He began growing his hair long, not crazy long, just curling over his collar. They marched together downtown to the Federal Building, to protest the draft. But they threw nothing, not rocks, not blood. They did not get arrested. He was *Law Review,* clerked for a state supreme court justice. Good firm, some teaching. Then the children, just two, a girl, then a boy.

By the time the children were in school, Marilyn didn't want to go back to teaching, cramming down a damp sandwich in the staff room choked with smoke, the pent-up aura of captives in the corridors, mayhem roaring from the lunchroom. Motherhood spoiled her. It was orderly—to her surprise. Days alone, doing little things, one after another. Reading books to the children, their small fingers pointing: Train, elephant! Giraffe, giraffe, giraffe!

She opened a bookstore with the mother of another boy in her son's Montessori class. Children's books and educational games. Now the place, Charlotte's Web, was hers. She'd bought out her partner, who had moved to Florida. Business was good, really good. Kenneth was impressed. She had been approached about opening a second store in a mall, books, interactive multimedia products, a whole area devoted to hands-on computers. The computer stations for the new store reminded her of the hi-fi booths of her high-school years, where you could go and listen to a record to see if you wanted to buy it. Sit in the little confession-box-size glass booth, headset clamped on like earmuffs, melting into Johnny Mathis.

She stared off at the green shimmer of the capitol grounds across the avenue from the credit union. Was it Johnny Mathis who had sung "Moon River"? Audrey Hepburn was dead. Marilyn had cried, actually sobbed, alone, looking at the pictures in *People* magazine. My era.

"I was sitting here before you arrived," the bill collector said, as if they had been carrying on a conversation—had they? had she missed something?—"and I was watching that man on the mower on the capitol grounds across the street there, trying to figure out how he runs that thing."

Marilyn looked across at the figure on the mower.

"I've been watching him really close—no hand levers, nothing with his feet. I can't figure it out. He just sits on it, and it goes on its own." Fascinated by the likelihood of magic at work, voice rippling with awe. "Do you see anything?"

"No, I don't," Marilyn said. "He just seems to go."

"That's what I'm thinking," the man said.

This thought seemed to connect him to many other thoughts. There is absolutely no point, for example, he said, in attempting to collect a bill during the full moon: people are *nuts* during the full moon. Ditto during the twelve-year period when he managed a skating rink: he always hired extra security on full-moon nights. The kids were nuts then, too. Possessed. More murders on full moon nights, according to the police. More *everything.*

He expressed no irritation at the feckless and sometimes evil ways of the world. Apparently he lived in a state of astonishment.

From the full moon to astrology. He was a Taurus. Again the amazement of it all: most of his family were Gemini or Cancer—he had no *idea* why he was a Taurus. An unbidden mystery boring out of the core of his identity. There was meaning in all this. Believe it.

He also wondered why—as a Capitol Patrol car went by—there were city police and capitol police. Wasn't that a waste of money, an overlap? Marilyn mentioned the existence of the university police, another doubling of duty. Maybe there was a value in having this extra protection in sensitive areas? He thought that over, agreed. "There are lots of chemicals sitting around at the university," he said. "Things can blow up."

"The university," he repeated, as if pondering a thesis. It was a place he had come to know well in the last year. Wasn't it incredible, the labyrinth of corridors at University Hospital, the confusion of the place for the non-university person thrust suddenly into that maze? Take himself. He'd gone there every day for months and months. Never figured the place out. Pause. "My brother was a patient there."

They were turning a dark corner, she sensed.

The brother was big in astrology, Tarot, all that. He had come home from California for a family visit, had read their father's cards. He told his brother that the father would be dead before Christmas. But it was himself who was gone before Christmas. Just six months ago. "He read his own cards," the bill collector said, something like reverence in his voice. "The one thing you cannot do is read your own cards. But you can read your own fate in another person's cards. You don't even know it."

Oh yes, the cards had sometimes told him more than he wanted to know, too. He stayed away from the cards now.

He turned abruptly from the occult, steered them toward his *amazing* four-year-old. This boy liked *his* cooking better than his wife's. Why? Because it was spicier. Imagine: a four-year-old who loves spicy food, really spicy, like an adult. Incredible, but true.

So many amazing facts. Flowers can grow out of sheer rock, you saw that a lot along Lake Superior where he, the wife, and the boy were going for the week, as soon as he deposited his check. Or the oddity of sundogs, and the fact that a significant percentage of the population does not believe we ever landed on the moon. Some pretty interesting arguments, you know? His brother had a book on it. Also, he and his brother had once seen a funnel cloud twirling along 61 North. The amazing thing? It looked just the way you always heard they looked: absolutely a funnel, skidding around like a bad fast dancer, touching down, and then, for no reason, up and off again. He leaned back against the flower boxes. Weather was *really* weird.

Not to mention the host of unpaid bills all about us, the carelessness of people. "They say, 'Fuck you,' just like that, and slam the phone down," he said, marveling, not insulted.

Then there's the big one, Big D. The sudden disappearance of blood relatives, their unbelievable dematerialization. You keep seeing people who look just like them. Or rather, you *start* seeing people who look just like them, the backs of heads. You never noticed that before, not till he passed away, was gone. Then he seemed to be everywhere. "My brother was younger than me," he said, "but he goes first. They say, 'Expect the unexpected.' It's easy to forget that." Blue lobelia appeared to sprout from his shoulders where he leaned against the retaining wall.

The day was heating up. The humidity felt intentional, vicious, needling away at the air. It would be another heavy day to live through.

The bill collector wasn't looking at Marilyn. He just gazed out, kept talking, seeing things. Galena, Illinois, used to be located on the banks of the Mississippi River, but no longer is. You see, a river is not a straight line between banks. It's a whole system, and you don't know where it starts or stops, what space it really takes up. They make a big deal about finding the source of the Mississippi. That's dumb. The Indians laughed at that. There *isn't* really a source. It's a big muddle up there. They just choose this stream or that, call it "the source." You don't *know*. What you see is *not* what you got. Nor are you necessarily safe from earthquakes just because you live in the Midwest. Remember that little town in Missouri? Gone. And raisins are not a fruit, not a berry. Raisins are really former grapes, shriveled up—but he bet she knew that one already.

The bill collector's voice wheeled through the heat, his marvels believable and meaningless at once, lovely harmlessnesses making the world work, gears in a great engine carrying us over the rough patches. The grass across the avenue on the capitol greensward had been watered earlier in the morning from jets buried in the ground. Now the green gave off a low weather system, a minute fog just above itself, tiny rainbows evaporating by the minute as the heat burned them into the day.

The man on the riding mower worked the grass like a tidy quarter section of alfalfa, without lever or foot pedal, hands visible on the steering wheel, but no sign of where the energy came from. Something at the knee? Marilyn's eyes shut a quick instant against the disloyal thought. It was too far to see now, anyway. Who knows?

A gray Volvo wagon—their own, she realized—turned the corner. Kenneth coming to get her. He pulled up near the sidewalk, the tires making the watery sound of tires slowing on dry pavement. He leaned across the seat toward the passenger window so she could see him beckoning. His face was filmy behind the gleam of the rolled-up window. *And now you see darkly, but then face to face.* But when, when do you see someone face to face? Not in this life. Was he smiling?—she thought he was smiling. A good smile. Concern there. She could make out a hand, gesturing. He wanted her to be out of the heat. Oh, and safe. He worries. Always has. Sees trouble. It's what he thinks imagination is for—worrying. Remember the first time? "I'll always protect you"—the little patch of movie dialogue, the champagne of well-being, the two of them meeting the length of their pure bodies for the first time, crazy to touch. Some dumb motel on University Avenue, the *l* blanked out on the neon sign. *Star Mote.* Looking for trouble, the sweet, safe kind, a month before the wedding. *I'll always protect you.*

Soon, the big glass door will open. But not yet. Kenneth must wait, just a sec, honey. She must stay here in the shade, the lobelia gushing over the cinder blocks. The fat stranger keeps talking, listing all the unlikely things that happen, that just are. She doesn't move. She will go to the Volvo in a moment, explain it all. But for now, this extra instant, she stays put, here in the killing heat. She wants to look straight ahead at nothing for another minute, wants to keep listening to the bill collector, who, still in mourning, is describing the world as the wonder it must be.

ETHAN HAUSER

The Dream of Anonymous Hands

I am not ashamed to admit that I like being held with my back
to her—her hands on my stomach, arms arrowing down my
hips, fingers tracing the slightest underside of my jeans. I am not
ashamed to admit that the absence of a face, the surprise of not
being able to see, to predict motion, to prepare, is a charge. Eyes
closed, leaning backward, her body's bracing hold. When she
touches me like that, she could be anyone and we could be anywhere. And yet she is not anyone, and we are in the living room
or just inside the bedroom doorway or at the bathroom sink, and
I have just finished brushing my teeth. I'm dropping my tooth-
brush back into the porcelain holder; I'm recapping the tooth-
paste and thinking I'll risk the ire of the dental hygienist by not
flossing again, and her hand is on the small of my back. She could
be anyone and she is not anyone—she is Claire, my wife, her
hands, and we will find our way to the bed, trip over our shoes,
and ruin ourselves for the morning.

We have been married seven years, and I cling to these erotic
moments, make them larger events than they probably are,
because it's the little things that save us. Last week I stood at the
stove and heated up Chinese food, dumping white containers of
rice into kung pao chicken. Our son sat at the kitchen table, his
fingers working crayons deep into a coloring book. He sang a
song, too, and his endless verbal stream matched his chaos on the
page. Claire rested her chin on my shoulder and peered into the
pan. "Looks good," she said, and ran her toe along my calf. It was
only a second, an instant, a briefer time that it takes even to
remember, but it was important. I know it was because sometimes when I least expect it, when I'm hunting for my car in a
garage downtown, or pouring another tepid cup of coffee at
work, my body tightens for no reason at all. It's her touch. I know.
The imprint of a fingertip, a big toe, the bone in her ankle. She's
left traces on me, and they surface when I'm not ready, and this is
how I know things aren't so bad.

It's not even that things are so bad, really. We're just a little bored is what I keep telling myself. All my friends who would know and even my parents have told me that it's the first ten years which are the hardest. You make it through those, they say, and it's smooth sailing the rest of the way. Even if they're just telling me these things to make me feel better, I'm grateful. We're not having such a hard time. We haven't asked for shrink referrals or anything.

David is five. He's just started kindergarten, and he has Claire's green eyes and my chin. When he was a baby, after Claire could stand to be touched again, we looked for moments to steal. I'd wake up in the middle of the night to check on him, and Claire would tiptoe in behind me. When he stopped crying, we put him back beneath his covers and kissed under the paper-airplane mobile hanging from the ceiling. I'd whisper to him, to his unreadable and unflinching gaze, "I'm kissing Mommy...Uh-huh, I'm kissing your mom."

For the past three weeks, we've been driving out to the country. Claire holds the classified section of the Sunday paper in her lap, and we try to find all the chocolate Lab breeders she has high-lighted with a pink marker. David has a name already—Josie—so now it's just a matter of finding the right one. When we look at the puppies, David handles each one, getting down on the ground with them, barking right back at them, living out a fanta-sy life that only children are permitted to have.

The breeders are more surprised by his pickiness than Claire or I, and they do their best to convince him he has found the right dog. "Oh boy," they say, "looks like she really likes you," or "She'll follow you right home, probably just jump right into the car behind you." But David hasn't found the one he wants, and we don't press him.

I enjoy our drives into the country, the car dipping and sailing along tree-sheltered streets with names like Ridge Road or Gold-en Brook Avenue. Dappled sunlight streams into the car and yel-lows Claire's profile. Hair as fine as dust emerges along her earlobe. All three of us are mesmerized, and occasionally she lays her hand on my thigh, not even squeezing, really, just resting there. I acknowledge her gesture with one of my own, covering her fingers for a second, telling her I'm there, before returning my hand to the steering wheel. Often we don't make eye contact, staring instead out the window at a dilapidated farmhouse, or someone checking mail at the end of a long driveway. But we are connected, our hands tell us that, and to look at each other would only be redundant.

There are vegetable stands, too, with hand-painted signs advertising Silver Queen corn and cukes and new potatoes. Claire's favorites are the ones with fresh herbs, and we stop at these, and she holds the baggies of basil, thyme, and sage up to my nose and says, "Breathe." At home she sprinkles the herbs over a chicken and surrounds it with potatoes. We eat things which have been in the dirt only hours ago. They're pure, I think, and eating such fresh food is like an act of cleansing.

Our goal was to have the puppy by Halloween, but we have failed. David hardly notices because he is so preoccupied with the holiday. He announced weeks ago that he would be trick-or-treating as a Power Ranger, and ever since Claire has combed the aisles of what must be every toy store within a fifty-mile radius. She told me that she'd return home from each store and try to interest David in another costume, promising him that I would bring home some law volumes from the office and we'd dress him in a three-piece suit and he could go as a lawyer, just like Daddy. Or Michael Jordan, David's favorite sports hero. She called all her friends, too, to check what their children were going as. But everyone wanted Power Ranger costumes, and no one knew where to find them.

Last year he went as a Ninja Turtle, but when we suggested this costume David frowned at us.

"I'm sure we still have it," Claire said.

"I think it's just down in the basement," I added.

David scoffed at the idea, telling us, "Everyone knows Ninja Turtles aren't cool anymore."

I tried to help out in the search, using time between meetings to finger the yellow pages and call toy stores. The managers cut me off before I even finished the sentence.

"Hello, I'm calling to see if you have any Power—"

"No, sir, clean out. You're not going to find those anywhere."

I heard stories of fights in the aisles, mothers punching one another. One manager told me about the two women who each grabbed a leg and wouldn't let go. They ended up ripping the costume in two exact halves. "Now look what you've done," one said. "It's no good to either of us." And then, this was what really amazed the manager, the other mother said, "Well, I'm just glad your kid won't get to wear it."

At night, with David at a friend's house, Claire and I drove to the stores anyway and roamed the aisles of Toys "R" Us and Child World. We stared at the sky-high shelves, our senses assaulted and finally numbed by riots of dolls, chemistry sets, racetracks, play lawn mowers, more Legos than anyone could possibly ever need. You could probably build a whole other world with all those Legos, a green and red plastic replica of our own. Even after we knew there were no costumes, after we had seen the empty space in the shelf and traded tales of frustration with other parents, we continued on in a kind of trance. Like tourists, we gawked and paused by any particularly amazing display, as if it were a historical marker, or a famous painting. Claire even dipped a finger in the sample of neon-green edible slime. She tried to make me taste it, too, but I declined.

We love our son, but we wondered if we really needed to be contributing to all of this. It was just too much—too many toys, too much color, too much everything. In the parking lot we noticed the stars and the mist. Despite the infinite rows of cars, the sky stopped us. We talked about escaping to a place in the country, a rundown farmhouse we'd renovate, hammering and stripping and painting, dirtying old jeans, raising calluses on our hands, hard work we'd wear on our bodies. David could find excitement in living things—the metronomic crickets, or the improbably loud call of bullfrogs in a pond behind the house. We could have three dogs, and they'd have the run of our acres, and each of us would name one. Mine would be called Gus. David might miss the mall and the multiplex, but we'd stock our pond, and I'd take him fishing, and we'd cast our lines and reel in something for dinner. Undoubtedly we're not the first ones to dream of escape, but it didn't matter. Our lack of originality didn't make the fantasy any less appealing.

The week before Halloween, just when it was seeming hopeless and Claire had begun watching the Power Rangers TV show over David's shoulder, trying to memorize hemlines and collar sizes and the exact hue of the piping around the chest, I met with a new client. Claire had called that afternoon, before my meeting, and asked whether she should tell David she had sewn the costume herself or pretend it was from the store. Both of us agreed that things your mother made for you invariably were less cool than store-bought items, so we decided we wouldn't divulge the truth.

It never came to the lie. My new client worked for a toy distributor and in exchange for a slight discount in fees, he promised to "see what he could do." That same night a UPS truck squeaked to a stop outside our house, and the brown-uniformed man left a box on the doorstep. When Claire and I went to retrieve the package, she whispered that she felt like taking a match to it.

When I arrived home Halloween night, there was a note from Claire that said she had already taken David, before it got too dark. There was a chicken in the oven which I was supposed to keep an eye on. She signed the note the way she always does—a hastily scrawled heart, a comma, and her name. But there was one difference. In parentheses, under her name, she had written, "We'll talk later."

We had set that night aside for a talk. Not about any miscommunication or any such jargon, but a specific event. I had discovered recently, a week ago maybe, that before we were married, when Claire and I were dating, she had told her previous boyfriend to come to her apartment and act threatening. She engineered it so that we would be at her place—a railroad flat with hilly hardwood floors and a claw-foot tub in the kitchen— and he would demand to come in and speak to Claire. I would have to play the hero, and this would draw us closer.

We were on the sofa, falling asleep to the radio, when he started banging on the door. "Let me in," he yelled. "Claire, let me in." As he punched at the lock, I asked her whether he was ever violent, and she said no, but maybe if he got mad enough. "He can be sort of a live wire," she said. I remember that she looked scared, and every time he shook the door handle and rattled the door, her body tensed. She was clutching the arm of the couch hard enough that her skin turned white. I opened the door and told him to leave. He tried to push past me, but I stayed my ground, blocking the way to Claire. I was ready for a fight, but it never came to that, and he backed away, swearing liquor-stained frustrations while he clomped down the stairs in his heavy boots.

When she told me it was all a plan, I was furious, in that silent way that words can't reveal. A kind of rage bubbled in me, knotting in my stomach, crawling just under my skin, and we lay in silence for a long time. "It was so many years ago...It doesn't matter now," she said. "What are you thinking?" she kept asking, and all I could say was that she had lied and that I didn't want to talk about it right then. I needed more time to think, I needed the morning to come. She made me set a date when we could settle it, saying she didn't want it living inside me like a tumor. "It doesn't deserve that much attention," she told me. "Let's just have it out." So we decided on Halloween, and I was able to forget about it, to not let it gnaw at me. I suppose I thought it about it still, but when you schedule something, it's a way of shelving it, keeping it in view but not letting it rule your life.

Halloween night, I changed for dinner, laid my suit on the bed, searched for jeans and a T-shirt, and remembered last year's holiday. We had scattered packs of M&Ms in a basket by the door with a Post-it note that read, "Please take only one." We had both taken David trick-or-treating, flanking him like bodyguards while we passed parades of angels, presidents, cowboys, football players. We traded conspiratorial smiles with the parents and reminded David not to drag his plastic pumpkin pail on the ground. There were ghosts, too, and witches and pirates, and I couldn't help noticing David's disdain for these simple costumes: a sheet with two holes for eyes, a black cape and hook nose, a hoop earring and an eye patch from the medical-supply pharmacy.

At each house, David said, "Trick or treat," and was handed a piece of candy. He always said thank you, which made Claire and me proud, especially when we heard his quiet voice emerge from a passel of children elbowing each other to be first. Claire tried to look inside every house, check the furniture, glimpse the art hanging on the walls. She took deep breaths, figuring out what was for dinner. It's not that she's jealous, she's just curious. She cherished the chance to see what the other houses held, what lives hid behind the windows and stucco. I assume this is why she didn't complain this year when I told her I had a late meeting and she should go ahead with David. A couple times last year she lingered too long. David and I would arrive at the end of someone's shrubs and notice she was not with us. We looked back, only to see her still on the porch, chatting with the unsuspecting host, trying to steal one last look. "Mommm, come on," David would call, and she turned and walked toward us on the sidewalk, filing away the house in her mind.

For a few minutes, I wished that I had canceled my meeting and gone out with them. I sat on the edge of the bed and rubbed my weary eyes, picturing the two of them sharing moments, laughs, secrets. I guess, too, that I really didn't want to talk. I wanted the whole thing settled, but I had no idea how we'd get there.

The night before, we had spread newspaper over the kitchen floor and gutted a pumpkin, the largest one David could carry by himself. At the farm stands, when he kept pointing at the biggest pumpkins, we made a deal with him: if he could carry it, we'd buy it. Somehow "carry" became merely "lift," and we ended up with a pumpkin massive enough that David could brag, "We have the biggest jack-o'-lantern on the block." He had fidgeted all through dinner, urging us to hurry up and finish so we could carve the pumpkin. To satisfy him, we told him he could draw the face while we drank coffee, and so he used a black Magic Marker to sketch eyes, nose, and a mouth. Once we joined him on the floor, Claire guided his hand with hers, and they cut a thick disk from the top. David crinkled his nose in disgust while she removed handfuls of stringy interior. Later she separated out the seeds and roasted them on a cookie sheet.

After dinner, as we watched television, David fell asleep on Claire's lap. I took him and rested his head on my shoulder and went upstairs to put him to bed.

"Daddy," he said, his voice struggling against sleep, "why didn't you help us make the jack-o'-lantern?"

I had sat with them, but I had watched. I had watched my wife empty the pumpkin, saw through the shaky outlines of David's drawing, hold our son's hand around the paring knife. Sometimes I forget that he has eyes. Not that they are a part of his anatomy, but that they see things, little things, and would have noticed me sitting to the side, holding a cup of coffee, offering advice, my knees barely touching the outermost sheet of newspaper covering the floor.

"I guess I was tired, sweetie," I told him, rubbing his back with my free hand.

I nudged his bedroom door open with my knee and stepped carefully around his strewn toys. I lifted him off my shoulder and drew the sheets over his small body, stopping for a moment to admire his innocent face, as settled and content as a lake. "Next year, Daddy," he said without opening his eyes. I was at the light switch by the door. I turned it off. "Next year you'll help us," he said through the darkness.

I think I started smelling burnt chicken skin at the same time as I heard Claire's key in the front door. I rushed down toward the kitchen, taking the back stairs. The kitchen was already smoky. "Fuck," I muttered and turned on the fan.

"Honey?" Claire said from the front hall. Right on top of her greeting, with no tolerance for silence, David's own excitement: "Daddy, come see what I got."

David had already dumped all his candy onto the living room rug and pushed it into a mountain. He used his foot to rake the carpet for stray candy bars.

"Wow," I said, "look at your haul."

He had flung his mask on the couch but still wore the silver pants and shirt and boots and gloves. "Dad, we only saw one other Power Ranger, and his costume wasn't nearly as good as mine."

"Someone else went the homemade route, I guess," I said to Claire.

"All the true Rangers must be over in the Heights," she said as she left the room. Silver candy wrappers glinted from the pile. I heard the oven door open and then shut.

"Honey," Claire called.

The smell of burnt chicken grew stronger as I walked to the kitchen. Claire turned the fan to its highest setting, and I saw her face and arms behind a screen of smoke rising into the vent above the stove. She looked at me, her whole face a question.

"I'm sorry," I said, looking down at the seared chicken. "Is any of it still okay?"

Claire jabbed at it with a carving knife, and the crisp skin flaked off like confetti. "I don't think so," she said. She plunged the knife deep into the center. "Maybe down here, but it's probably too dry."

For a moment both of us stared at the smoke tunneling upward. I took a fork and poked at the bird. The bottom of the pan was blackened, too, along with the potatoes. "I guess I wasn't thinking," I said, but Claire didn't respond. She just kept looking at me through the smoke. "I mean, I guess I was thinking about something else," I said. I looked at my wife then and wondered if she regretted telling me the story. I wondered if she thought about it while she took David trick-or-treating, if it got in the way of her spying on other people's houses. I saw the clock on the stove, and I wanted to turn it forward, make it one in the morning, turn off my study light and join her in bed, have her body move drowsily toward me, her toes brush my foot, her fingers settle on my stomach, watch her chest fill and relent.

"I guess we should order takeout," I said.

Claire opened the drawer where we kept all the menus. She held them out like a fan. "Chinese, Indian, Thai... We haven't had Thai in a while," she said.

"How about pizza?" I said.

"Yeah, I want pizza, let's get pizza." David's voice surprised both of us. We hadn't noticed his entrance. "What smells?" he asked. "Who burned something?"

Claire started giggling, and I scooped up David. "Daddy burned dinner," I said and swung him onto my shoulders, feeling the shimmery material of his costume against my neck. "While you were out getting candy, Daddy burned the chicken so now we have to get pizza."

"Daddy, I'm glad you wrecked dinner," David said.

"And why is that?" I asked, though I knew.

"Because I love pizza. Can we get pepperoni?"

Through the last remaining wisps of smoke, I saw Claire pick up the phone. She ordered and took one more look at the ruined chicken before dumping it into the trash.

After we called for the pizza, there was a series of false alarms. Each time the doorbell rang, David ran to the door, only to be disappointed because it was another trick-or-treater. He lost interest rapidly in the costumes, and it made me think that hunger is as powerful as anything. When a woman with a live snake draped around her neck came to the door, David looked at her for a second, asked whether it was poisonous, and tossed a Snickers bar into her bag.

I was hoping the pizza would never come because I knew that after that there were no more distractions, nothing more to put off my talk with Claire. Several times, as we opened the door for more werewolves and movie stars, I thought of saying to her, "Fuck it, let's just forget about it." But I didn't want to forget it. Or I couldn't forget it. I wanted an explanation.

We ate in the living room, with plates balanced on our laps and beers on the coffee table, sweating rings on the glass surface. David sat on the floor, planted in front of the television, *The Lion King* humming along in the VCR for the umpteenth time. The heap of candy remained on the floor like some crazy altar.

"Is there any more beer?" I asked.

"In the kitchen," Claire said. "Will you get me one, too?"

I dropped the empties in the trash, watching them rest on top of the charred dinner. The room still smelled like smoke, and I cracked one of the windows. I grabbed two beers from the fridge, took a deep breath, and went back into the living room.

David had climbed onto the couch and into Claire's lap, nestled there perfectly, like a puzzle piece. She sifted her fingers through his soft brown hair, coaxing his eyes shut, occasionally resting her lips on the top of his head. She listened to his intermittent memories of the evening. "Remember the clown man? . . . He had a cherry for a nose . . . Godzilla was my second favorite . . ." She was daring me, asking, Do you want to shatter this?

"Maybe I should put him to bed," I said.

"I'll do it," Claire said without taking her eyes off of him. She stood and laid a hand on his neck, the way we used to make sure his head didn't fall when he was an infant. "Why don't you see if there's a movie on or something?" she said.

I looked through the TV guide while Claire climbed the stairs and readied David for bed. I heard him protest brushing his teeth, and then her gentle insistence. Their voices drizzled down the stairs like leaves, floating and slicing in the air, coming to rest, finding their own places. "Come on, sweetie, you promised me," she said.

The pipes went to work, and I knew that the bathroom faucet had just been turned on. I took a long pull of beer and then another. We don't usually drink during the week, and the derailed routine felt like we were getting away with something. While Claire took lazy steps down the stairway, I finished the last bit of my beer and went to the kitchen for another.

She caught me staring at the chicken again. "It's okay," she said. "I loved the pizza."

"I'm sorry. I guess I'm a little preoccupied." I felt warm from the beer, and I wanted Claire to feel warm, too. I handed her a cold bottle.

"Thanks." She took my hand and led me back to the living room. "Did you find anything?" she asked, her eyes motioning toward the television.

"Oh. No," I said. I sat down next to her on the couch. Claire finished the pizza on her plate and watched me watch her eat. The silence in the room reminded me of an awkward date, and I again wanted to set time ahead, slide the night into the past. We'd fall asleep to a lush breeze and wake to the heat of the sun, and nothing and everything would be the same, nothing and everything would matter.

The silence tugged at Claire, too, and she went to the stereo and slid an Al Green record from its jacket. I must have heard every click and pop as the needle stuttered toward the first song. It was one of those times when the world is waiting for you to say something. Rain suspends. Every traffic light is red. Claire came back to the couch and sat in the opposite corner. She picked at the corner of the beer label and studied the nearly empty pizza box, strands of cheese lining the bottom like wax.

"Mommy…" We heard David's voice from the top of the stairs. "Will you come up and read me a story?"

I looked at Claire and started to get off the couch, but she shook her head. "Go back to bed," she called. "It's late now."

"But I hear something… There's something scary."

Again I started to get up, but Claire palmed my knee and urged me back down. "There's nothing in your room, sweetie," she said. "I checked the closet."

"Under the bed, too?"

"Yes, under the bed also."

Both of our heads were cocked toward the ceiling. When we heard David's pajama feet pad over the floor, we let our shoulders fall back into the cushions. I went to the stereo to turn up the volume and on the way back crunched something beneath my feet. I saw a pack of Sweet Tarts ground into the rug. Claire was giggling. "I won't tell if you won't," she said.

I crouched down and gathered the pink powder in my hands and rubbed them together over the pizza box, watching the dust coat the lone cold slice. "Look at all his candy," I said. "This was one of a thousand."

"I don't know why you're making such a big deal of this," Claire said, and it took me a moment to realize what she was talking about. For a minute or so, I thought she was right. Her ex-boyfriend had banged on the door and demanded to talk to her. I protected her, or thought I was protecting her. Told him to leave, held her tight when we went to bed, caressed her back, and told her everything would be okay. I thought I was the hero. Turns out I was the only one who didn't know what was going on.

Claire continued, "So I told Philip to come over, have liquor on his breath, act like an asshole. So what?" She took a long swallow of beer. "Is it the end of the world?"

"It wasn't honest." My bluntness surprised me.

"You're being so moralistic. I was afraid you didn't like me enough. I was afraid you thought I was too independent, that I didn't need you, and I wanted to show you that wasn't true." She couldn't stop herself. "I was so afraid you would leave me and not marry me."

"So you play some trick on me?"

"It wasn't meant as a trick." She brushed a hair from her forehead. "What does it matter, anyway?"

"It matters because you lied."

"People are dishonest all the time. Just a minute ago we agreed that you wouldn't tell David you crushed his candy. What's the difference?"

"I don't know, but there is one." I felt buzzed from the beer. "You were dishonest, and it means the whole marriage is a lie."

"God, you're being ridiculous. That's not what it was about, and you know it. It wasn't about playing some trick on you for the hell of it."

"Then what does it mean?"

"It means I loved you a lot, and I was dying for you to ask me to marry you." Claire stared at the darkened TV screen. "That's the only thing it means. Don't try to make it something else."

"Loved?"

"Yes, loved. I loved you so much that it hurt when you left the room even for a few seconds, like to use the bathroom."

"So you don't love me anymore?" I was being a jerk, but I knew it, and somehow it made everything a little more bearable.

"Oh shit, Henry. Love, of course love. I didn't mean the past tense." Claire got up with a huff and went to the stereo. She flipped the record and with her back to me started talking again. "You know, I'm not going to apologize."

"Why?"

She turned to face me. "Because I don't think I need to. It brought us closer. Is there anything wrong with that?"

The doorbell rang, but neither of us made any motion to get it. A minute passed, and whoever it was walked down the steps, and I wanted to join them. I had been looking forward to Halloween, not this part but the earlier part. I remembered my own Halloweens, when my brother and I would empty all our candy onto the living room floor at the end of the night. Then we sorted it. And when we finished sorting, we traded—a Milky Way for a Three Musketeers, a Sky Bar for some candy corn—and this would continue until our father made us go to bed.

My mother warned us not to eat too much candy. "Remember your teeth," she admonished. "They're the only ones you've got." Every year she managed to schedule a dentist appointment the week before Halloween, and as we grew older, we began to recognize the logic behind what we had thought random coincidence. The dentist always ended the appointment with gruesome pictures of cavity-filled mouths, grotesque cartoons from a thin book called *The Story of Yuck-Mouth*. As if we needed anything more, Dr. Bennet added, "So be careful with the candy; wouldn't want you ending up like this fella."

What my mother never realized was that I was a hoarder and not a binger, and I derived far more pleasure from keeping candy around as long as possible, some years until Christmas, than from stuffing my mouth full of treats. My brother and I had an informal competition about who could make his stash last longest. I rationed myself—one piece after school every other day, and two on the weekends—and ended up winning each year. Around the middle of November, I would lord my remaining candy over him, bartering Hershey bars for household chores.

Claire moved closer to me on the couch, leaving her corner and the pillow she held in her lap. I wouldn't look at her. She took my hand, and I couldn't resist its insinuating warmth. "Are you still mad?" she asked.

"I don't know," I said. And it was true, I didn't know. Claire has always thought that you shouldn't apologize for anything, that you should move on, not dredge up the past, and this extremism is one of the reasons I love her. It's one of the things I idolize about her. "I'm going to put another record on," I said. But before I could get up, Claire grabbed my hand and clamped tight, both her hands around mine.

"Don't move," she said. "Let it repeat. Just sit here with me."

For the first time since we started talking, I looked into her eyes and noticed the hazel flecks within the green and the nervous flutter of her eyelashes. "I'll go get the rest of the beers," she said, "and we'll just stay and talk." She turned my hand over and opened my palm and followed its lines with her ring finger. "You can tell me anything." She brought my hand to her mouth, kissed it, and cradled it against her cheek. "Okay?"

I nodded and watched her walk out of the living room. When she was out of sight, I followed her and joined her at the open fridge. She turned around to face me, but I swiveled her body and held her with her back to my chest. "Once," I said to her ear, "I was purposely late for a movie so it would sell out and we'd have to go to my apartment instead."

She fished the last beers from the bottom shelf. We went back to the couch and laid down, her legs braiding mine. We drank beer and talked all night. We spilled our sins, handing each one out, dropping candy into bags.

L U C Y   H O N I G

Police Chief's Daughter

from Citizens Review

Then there was the police chief's daughter, always bad news.
Like tonight—another roasting summer night, air condition-
ers not quite keeping up—she sat alone at the bar, tapping her
chipped fingernails against a glass. She took a last drag on the cigarette the fag gave her, a lousy, tasteless, low-tar wimp of a cigarette. Drag on a fag. Fag in drag. She giggled. "They sure got that
right." She said it out loud in a deep voice. Then she said it again,
squeaky falsetto. "They sure got that right." Everybody said that
phrase these days, but what did it mean? You were always supposed to know these things but she was never sure she did. So kill
me, she thought. She tugged at the hem of her shirt, yanking the
plunging neckline into a deeper V.

She drummed her knuckles on the bar. Fidget, fidget, fidget.
Those had been her mother's words, a code meaning good children don't fidget, other children never fidget, fidgeting children
burn in hell. Like maybe she'd have rather had a cripple for a kid,
at least it wouldn't fuckin' fidget. "Fidget, fidget, fidget," she said
out loud, then she giggled. It was so weird to hear her mother's old
warning in here, with raunchy music blasting and couples neck-
ing, just the kind of place her mother would rather die than be in.
"Fidget, fidget, fidget." Even weirder to hear the words without her
father's inevitable retort. "*Who's* a fidget?" She mocked his voice, a
tight baritone swallowed down into her glass, doubling in on itself
in a liquidy echo. She giggled. "Not my little gi-*irl!*" By then she'd
have climbed up on his lap to start a long galloping horsy ride on
his knee, while her mother clucked her tongue and faded away.
That's how Francie Lou remembered it: her mother disappeared
from the scene like magic, the paltry substance of her becoming
wispier and wispier until she was transparent and, finally, invisible. But no, she must have simply walked off somewhere to pray,
to pray for Francie Lou's pathetic little soul. Nowadays she seemed
to have let up on prayer, thank God. Francie Lou giggled. "Thank

God." What a rip. "My little gi-*irl!*" She sang the words over the rim of the glass, which was empty now.

She turned and yelled to her boyfriend, who was down at the end of the bar. "Hey, Eddie, how about let's dance now!" In this lousy light, dwarfed by the guy next to him, Eddie looked washed-out and puny. She wished she hadn't noticed.

"Yeah, in a minute," he said, his voice not only flat but just this side of annoyed. Annoyed at *who*?

It pissed her off, him standing there, skinny and blank, talking with that hulk from New Jersey—a balding hulk with a paunch, ten years older than them at least, wearing an earring and tight jeans. He had to be a fag. Couldn't Eddie even see that? Nope. All he saw was a connection. Eddie and his fucking connections, like he'd just about stumble into an investor in this dive. He'd taken one lousy business course at the community college and figured himself a wheeler-dealer, as if there was anything there to wheel and deal except some half-baked idea he had about bungee jumping from the old railroad bridge. Who'd buy *that*? But this fag bragged about a weekend house somewhere out past Woodstock, and Eddie pictured bucks. Open your eyes, Eddie, Christ, the guy's cheap as sawdust, even she could tell. God, making such a production buying them a couple of drinks.

She slid sideways off the stool, wobbled, and steadied herself with one hand on the seat. She felt for the hem of her shirt, as if that was her way of orienting, taking stock, knowing her place in things. The shirt ended a couple of inches above the waistband of her little skirt, exposing a section of her midriff. She rubbed the slippery synthetic fabric between her thumb and forefinger, then patted her bare skin: firm, flat, cool. Her skin was always silky smooth and cool, even on the beach, even making love.

"Eddie, c'mon!" she called out to him. For a second he seemed to look toward her, but then he sideswiped eye contact, never breaking from the nodding assent with which he listened to the other guy.

Once she was on her feet, the thumping bass of the music took hold of her. With both palms flat against her cool belly, she dipped and swayed her shoulders and then her hips, took a step, then another, dipped and swayed, took a step, and undulated her way slowly toward the end of the bar, squeezing between couples who talked and danced, dancing sexy by herself. She slunk along and finally planted her backside right against the fag's, rolling it around there. He pushed and rolled right back. Well, what d'ya know, she thought, giggling. Then she moved on to Eddie, butt to butt, and did a slow rotation, hinging her hip to his, until she was in his face. "Take me in your arms," she warbled in no particular tune, "and dance with me-e-ee!"

"Goddamn it, Francie Lou, I'm *talking*!" He put a hand on each of her shoulders and pushed her away.

In a split second she knew that he had pushed her angrily, right here for anyone to see, so he could keep talking to a fucking fag rather than hold her and dance close to her and feel the dry coolness of her skin against him.

She started to shove back at him, reaching her arms out to slam into his chest, but he grabbed her by the wrists, rough and tight so it stung, and immobilized her.

"Quit it, Eddie, that *hurts*!"

"Hey, hey, you two, take it easy!" The guy from New Jersey put his big arm around her shoulder and with his eye on Eddie eased her slowly out from Eddie's grasp as Eddie let up and finally let go.

"Bastard," she muttered under her breath, massaging one wrist with the other hand.

The guy laughed and maneuvered her closer to the bar. "How about another drink, huh? You're ready for another. No point getting mad, we're all here to have a little fun, right?"

"Yeah, sure, right," she said, struggling up onto a stool. "Fun. Just loads and loads of fun." She stared sullenly at the whiskey sour in front of her, then lifted it, eyed it more closely, and put back half of it in one gulp. Next to her, Eddie and the guy nursed along their beers. Fags, she thought. Then she wished she hadn't thought it, but she couldn't unthink it now.

"Man, you gotta pay better attention to your lady friend," the guy from New Jersey chided Eddie.

Eddie snorted. "Believe me, I pay plenty. Pay through the goddamn nose."

Francie Lou scowled at him, but he wasn't even looking. She finished off the drink in a second gulp. "Hey," she tapped at the guy's shoulder, "you got another cigarette?"

He gave her a cigarette and lit it with a lighter that was trying to look like solid gold. Cheap, she thought. She took a deep drag, making sure the cigarette was lit okay, and blew the tasteless smoke up to the ceiling in perfect rings. "Thanks, buddy."

Then she slid off the stool, tugged her skirt down from where it had bunched around her ass, and stepped behind the guy and over to Eddie. "Hey, Eddie, find your own way home," she said. And in one quick move, sure at least that he was watching now, she held out her cigarette to focus his gaze, then shoved it down into his beer.

She turned and pushed through the crowd, past the dance floor, past the ladies' room, which God knows she could have used, out the door, and into the parking lot and the sweltering, thick moonless night. The dank heat stopped her. It encircled her totally, as Eddie had not; it licked her skin. She stood for a moment in the folds of humid air and peered through the murk in search of her car. Resting her hands against her cool midriff, she spotted the car, swayed, and goose-stepped her way to it.

Inside, she put the air conditioning on full blast, switched on the radio, turned up the volume, and peeled out of the driveway. Commercials blared, then oldies. An old Rolling Stones. Glimmers of distant lightning flashed above the Catskills. Now Beatles. She passed a truck, then turned off the highway to get to the old bridge into town, singing at the top of her lungs. *"Do you ne-ed anybody, I just need someone to love…"* She laughed. Right. Love. She cursed Eddie, she cursed the balding fag and his awful cigarettes, she cursed everyone she'd ever known who'd gotten in her way, which was everyone she'd ever known. *"Do you ne-ed anybody?"* she shrieked along with the Beatles on the bridge. It felt good, damn it, sealed up in her air-conditioned old Mustang, cursing and singing far above the inky ripples of the river. *"I get by with a little help from my friends, oh, I get high with a little help…"* Oh, but the words, for Chrissakes, she couldn't stand the words. She groped around on the floor for a tape, found one, it didn't matter what it was, she threw it in the slot. Then she looked up just in time to see herself drive into the rear end of a Chevy stopped at the red light at the end of the bridge.

The thwonking smash of metal was brief. "Shit," she hissed under her breath. She waited for the car to stop rocking before she inhaled. "Daddy is not gonna like this one bit," she said to the air. She felt for her extremities, stretched her limbs, rolled her neck all around, and decided she had not been hurt. But the car. Shit. Nothing smouldered or spurted, at least; there weren't any smells. But the front was shorter, its nose folded somewhere inside the back of the other car. The radio had stopped, the glove compartment had sprung open. She reached into it, felt around, and found a crumpled old cigarette pack with two flattened but whole cigarettes left in it. "My lucky day," she muttered.

Francie Lou lit a cigarette, rolled down the window to toss the match, and looked right into a face. A woman's face. A black woman's face. She jumped, startled and afraid, and rolled up the window fast. Then a hand *hit* the window, and close behind it menaced that angry face. How could all of this possibly be happening to her at the same time? Her heart thumped hard in her chest. Wake me up, she whispered, please wake me up. She stole a look back at the face, and as her glance traversed the scene, she took in the driver's door hanging open in the smashed car in front of her. And then it dawned on her: this person was the other driver.

She rolled the window back down. "Christ, you scared me."

The other woman spluttered. "*I* scared *you*! You damn near kill me, you come plowing into me and wreck my car and nearly kill me dead and you don't even *bother* to stir yourself and get out to see what you've done and if anybody's hurt and now you tell me I scared *you*! You *bitch*!"

"I'm sorry." Francie Lou forced herself to mumble the apology, not completely convinced yet that she was safe from harm here.

But the woman wasn't satisfied, oh no, she had to go on and on. "Just *look* at my car, will you? Will you please *look* at it!"

Francie Lou looked and thought it hadn't been much of a car to begin with but decided not to say so. "The insurance'll take care of it," she said. "Don't worry."

"I'm stopped at a red light, big as life, dammit, and you . . . you . . . what? What the hell is wrong with you? Are you *blind*?"

Francie Lou rolled her window up all but a crack. "I'm sorry, lady, Jesus, you'll get your money, it'll get fixed, that's what insurance is for, what the hell else do you want from me?"

The woman stomped off to the gas station on the corner, and

Francie Lou sat. All she had to do was wait for the cops to come, but waiting was hotter than hell. Still, she knew better than to start the car just for the air. She finished the first cigarette, which was stale but an improvement on those low-tar things she'd just had. She waited, tapping her fingers on the steering wheel. Her bladder was ready to burst. She squirmed. *Really* ready to burst. She looked around; the other driver was nowhere in sight. Nobody else either. So she opened the door carefully, got out, and scooted around to the curb. Then, hidden at least halfway by her own car, she squatted and peed onto the pavement. There was nothing else she could do but let go of a long gushing torrent that took forever. Damn good thing the streets were deserted in this God-forsaken neighborhood. Finished, she got back in the car and lit the second cigarette. She tapped her fingers on the dashboard. At last the cruiser pulled up, sirens blaring and lights flashing.

It was Sergeant Joe Schmidt, one of the old-timers. He looked in and smirked. "You again," he said. "Lookie here, Al," he called out to his partner. Albert Santino crouched down and clicked his tongue.

"Why, Francie Lou, you bad girl, you. It seems like just last month—"

"It *was* last month. Okay? Now will you just please call Daddy and let's get this over with?"

When the phone rang, he ran his hands through his headful of curls. To this very day, the chief's auburn ringlets still made the ladies in the church remember him fondly as the pudgy, impish little boy he used to be, so long ago. Back then, their desire to believe in—and believe—a child of such cherubic looks gave him license to pawn off on other kids the blame for the bullying assaults he himself inflicted on them all. He grew to count on it: the mothers would sooner jump to unforgiving conclusions about the guilt of their own sons than impugn those red ringlets, those rosy full cheeks. Frankie Hudgins, the angel.

Back then, he liked waylaying kids down by the creek, hammering with both his fists until they gave him the bike or the money or the BB gun. If it was a good day, they'd cry, too, and run home howling. Now, except for an occasional slug in the groin with someone really uncooperative, he generally talked his way through anything. A different sort of hammering, to be sure, but with basically the same results.

He was jowly now, his face broad and lumpy in the cheek. Any high color was from anger or surging blood pressure. Over the years his curls had become more brown, less red, and now they were flecked ever so slightly with gray, which the church ladies called distinguished. His poor little wife of twenty-some years, to cover up her own gray hair, endured periodic tortures that left burning red splotches on her forehead and scalp, a merciless itch that went on sometimes for weeks. She couldn't help be offended—resentful, even—that Frank got away with his gray. But what didn't he get away with? He got away with gray. He got away with jowls. He even got away with short-sleeved shirts, letting the TV crews tape him without a jacket as he gloated over the latest drug bust, his unashamed bare workingman elbows planted firmly on a cluttered desk, the extreme abundance of freckles and the pale, soft, almost womanly flesh above those elbows right out there for everyone to see. How many times had it run on the five o'clock news, that image of Frank the freckly good guy, the cherub who'd grown up to do his duty? How often had that image been juxtaposed against shots of grim muscular dark men in undershirts and sweatpants, arms raised to shield their faces from the camera, as they were led to the paddy wagon in a long, dismal line not so accidentally reminiscent of the chain gang?

"Again?" he asked into the phone. "Again?" he repeated. It was a word of confirmation rather than of questioning or shock or even anger. Chief Hudgins was never surprised to get a call about his daughter, though he was known to plunge his fingers deeper into his hair and clutch his temples in exasperation, especially if someone else in the department was in the room. In his line of work, of course, he had seen everything, but it was not just the hard reality of decades of police work that stole the surprise. No, in some strange way he actually looked forward to these calls: each new mishap only seemed to strengthen his grave and abiding disappointment in Francie Lou, a disappointment—unclouded by disapproval—that somehow satisfied him. The very dependability of its source, that inexhaustible spring of bad judgment, carelessness, lust, and self-preoccupation, fulfilled for him a certain pivotal expectation of family life. His other kids had not come half so close.

"Was anybody hurt?" he asked next. "Okay, good. Who was in the other car?"

He frowned as he listened. "Her? The one who got brought in the other night? Shit. No...No...Listen, forget it, we'll take care of that one later. Just get the information, call the wrecker, whatever, tell the lady to start making her wish list and send her home in a cab...Yes, right, a cab...Then write out a summons for Francie Lou...Yes, that's right...right...You got it. Yeah, yeah, sure, I'm sorry your Breathalyzer isn't working tonight." He laughed. "No...yes...a simple rear-end collision. And for Christ's sake, keep it off page six."

She had already waited while they called in to Daddy. She had watched them write out her ticket and make nice to the ranting raving woman in the other car—Christ, she *would* not let up, that one, until she went off, finally, in a taxi. Francie Lou thought it was over then. But just as the tow truck started to disengage the two cars, Sergeant Joe suddenly produced the Breathalyzer.

"No," she whispered, incredulous. "Daddy said do the test?"

Both officers nodded gravely.

"But he couldn't have! Why else..." She let her voice trail off. Something wasn't right. She tried to think. The wrecker, meanwhile, pulled slowly at the other car, which emitted a screech of grating metal, then yelped outright.

"Just like dogs," said Albert Santino, folding his arms across his chest as he watched. "Y'know, we shoulda tried a bucket of cold water."

Both men chortled.

The Chevy staggered forward with one last high-pitched groan. The Mustang rocked a bit, then stilled.

"You're trying to trick me," said Francie Lou.

Santino grinned slyly. "You wanna give Daddy a quick call and find out?"

She sighed. When the game got this weird, when it crossed over to that fuzzy place where things could not be said, she was out there on her own. Shit. She wasn't very good on her own. She pictured her father shaking his head at her in disgust. Daddy. She'd have to go back home to him, because that's where she lived. Even now, working off the DWI charge in the only way she knew how, she fought off the picture of him and the sound of his pissed-off whiny harangue.

Hurry up, hurry up, hurry up, she repeated to herself, sucking as hard as she could, bits of gravel piercing sharp into her bare knees. She grasped both of Joe's thighs for balance. Hurry up, hurry up. Al, the first one, had been so much quicker. A car went by, its lights flickering into the shadow she and Joe occupied behind the cruiser, and for a moment he stopped the frenzied pushing at the top of her head and checked that Al was waving the car on. But she kept going, faster, tighter, ignoring his gasping pleas to ease up. She worked her mouth in an urgent rhythm, aware of a staticky voice from the cruiser radio, then Al answering.

"Christ, take it easy," Joe hissed.

She did not take it easy, she did not slow down, she did not stop hurrying him up until Joe finally groaned and stumbled forward, almost knocking her over, and she counted the seconds in her mind, one-one-thousand, two-one-thousand, three-one-thousand, to keep from retching. Enough. She spat out the second mouthful.

He zipped and buckled, did not help her to her feet. Leaning against the cruiser, she picked out the gravel from her knees and shins. Al finished at the radio. "Trouble on Main Street," he called to Joe. "Backup." Not another word to her. She scrambled to get away from the car as it started up. And they were gone.

The Mustang moved okay, the steering worked, there were no fumes, no red lights or flashing signals on the dash. She drove slowly to Broadway, then stopped at Stewarts to buy cigarettes. If only she knew where she was going next. Not to Eddie's place, not after the way he treated her, she still had *that* much pride. But it was too late to barge in on Gloria or Deb, her only friends. And she was much too sober to go home and deal with her father, to listen to him rant at her or to hear him brush the whole thing off. Either way was disgusting. Icch. Like the bitter musty taste of cop still in her mouth. She needed something to get her through the rest of this.

She drove back down Broadway and parked by the riverfront, where places were still open and lots of people milled around, too hot to go home. On the deck at Annie J's, the partying roared full swing. She recognized guys she knew, but she had to lie low now, not get drawn in. From a pay phone she called Robert. His phone rang and rang and rang, and though she gave up hope, she let it keep ringing while she glanced around: Annie J's; Boat and Bottle; Wing Shu Garden. Uh-uh. No question of scoring in one of these places, three blocks from the police station.

And then, just as she was about to hang up, Robert answered, his voice thick with sleep and growly with impatience. "Whatdya want?"

"Robert, it's Francie Lou."

"Shit, I'm asleep, man, it's one fuckin' thirty in the morning."

"I need something fast," she said. "Whatever you got."

There was no answer, just the sound of a baby screaming in the back, his dumb wife hollering, a thunk of the receiver, and his voice shouting, then muffled, then silent. But she knew he was back on.

"Robert!" she called out. "Robert, I know you're listening. I know there was a bust and that you must've snitched first. I know they turn their backs when they let you in there." She didn't know any of this, but she was a pretty good guesser. He sure as hell didn't come by the stuff *honest.*

She waited through more screeching commotion in the background. Then he said, "You hear what's going on here, Francie Lou? I'm a family man, for God's sake. Christ, she argued with me for five fuckin' minutes before she'd let me even pick up the goddamn phone."

Francie Lou sighed as emphatically as she could. "Listen, Robert. I really don't have time for this. I'm down in a parking space in front of Annie J's. I just crashed up my car, I can't get to your place, you're gonna have to come here. But if you got something good, I got two hundred on me."

She took his silence as an answer.

"I'm waiting for you, Robert, I'm giving you fifteen minutes." She hung up. Then she got into her car, rolled down the windows, lit a cigarette, and waited.

What a pain, that Robert. Once he had been the kid in school who smelled. There always was one, here in the sticks. He'd lived on a farm where his father was the hired hand, and even when he wriggled out of helping in the barn or in the fields (and you always knew he wriggled out of anything he could), he'd still carry the not-so-faint whiff of cow manure with him wherever he went, a pungency that permeated his clothes and his skin, stuck in dry clumps to the bottoms of his shoes. You could tell with your eyes closed the second he got on the bus or walked into class. None of the kids liked him, anyway, so nothing held them back from heaping on the ridicule, not teachers, not school bus drivers, not common decency, and certainly not the meek presence of his mom or dad, who smelled, too; shrieks and taunts were hurled at him as soon as he got anywhere. Francie Lou remembered howling and pinching her nose along with the rest of them. She remembered how much fun it was, as she sat fidgeting in her car on this hot night.

He didn't smell anymore. He hadn't smelled of the farm for years. Probably right now she smelled even worse than him, sitting in this pool of sweat for God knows how long. But it still galled her to be indebted to someone who *used to* be the kid who smelled. Galled her more than being indebted to the snitching snake he had become. But really, who owed who? She and Robert were locked into this weird dance, a high-stakes game with rules they both understood but could never say: if she wanted to keep getting stuff, she couldn't tell Daddy any of the shit she had on Robert, but to make sure she didn't tell, he'd have to keep supplying, and on credit when that's all she had. But if she didn't pay up, he'd tell the chief she was his biggest customer; if he told on her, she'd tell Daddy he'd stolen the stuff from his own busts.

She thought she had the highest card, she had him nailed: Daddy would have to put Robert away if anything came out, but he'd never get rid of her. Leaning back in the car (and something did smell oily, after all, shit, maybe a leak?), she grinned to herself. Robert was the only game in town where she had clout.

But her smile faded. Deep down she sensed that Daddy knew everything. Must know Robert got paid off, this way and that. Must pay him off himself? Did he pay him off by letting him feed his daughter's habit, which he only pretended not to know about? She shuddered. No, impossible. She shuddered again. Yes, possible—as long as it was never said. Not a word. The ultimate collusion of hers and Robert's, their silence, somehow played right into her *father's* game, the *real* game. No, no, no, that was too far-fetched. She closed her eyes and shook her head, as if to empty it. She wanted to stop thinking. But a thought surfaced anyway: her father needed them to do just what they did. A dance for three, that's what it was. And not one of them could afford to have their cover blown.

"Hey, Francie Lou, wake up!"

Robert had pulled his car up next to hers. He got out and opened her door. "Let's take a little walk." He pointed to a bench facing the river, just past the gazebo.

After a few hits on a joint, she started to feel better and Robert started to seem okay, a long-lost friend.

"No arrest? Not even a DWI?" he asked as he folded up his money and she put the little bag of coke into her purse.

"Uh-uh. Anyway, there was no reason to suspect. I mean, do I look drunk to you?" Suddenly she sat up straight, crossed her ankles primly, frowned, and clutched her arms in front of her chest. It was as if a line of elastic running through all her muscles had been pulled tight.

Robert sniggered. "Right, sober as a judge."

"Hah! No judge in *this* town!" She let the elastic go, fell back so she was half-lying on the bench, and convulsed with laughter, clutching her bare midriff.

"That's one mean little stretch of road up there before the bridge," he said. "Not so long ago, remember? That lady got drunk at the Grove and ran over the two high school kids walking back from the skating rink. Remember? And come to think of it, ain't that where the off-duty trooper ran himself off and rolled over last month? They didn't do no test on him, either. And what a shitload of flak there was for *that*."

"So?"

"So, I woulda thought they'd be crackin' down along there about now. Crackin' down pretty hard."

"So? What are you trying to *say*, Robert?"

He laughed. "So, what I'm sayin' is that it must be nice, to have cops, like, so understanding."

"Oh, come off it, Robert." She burst into another long peal of laughter. "You got your ins more'n I do. Look at you. Christ, I have to do my daddy proud, I got this terrible, terrible weight on my shoulders, shit, while you're out dealin' dope right under their noses, I gotta be a fine upstanding citizen!"

He snorted. "Well, you're doin' one hell of a job, Francie Lou."

She laughed a string of long, dopey ripples. "Thank you *so* much. Y'know, that's what I like about you, Robby, you say such nice things, I mean, you know how to make a girl feel appreciated." Her voice dissolved again in giggles. She took another hit on the joint, then offered it to him.

He held up his hand, refusing. "You mean Eddie don't?"

"Oh, Christ. Eddie. Who brought *him* up?" She sat up straight, suddenly seething mad. "Hanging with fags. Did you know that? Over in Chick's hanging with a guy who wears an earring. What does that make *me,* I wanna know? What does that make me *look* like? The bastard. Two years we're together, and what do I have to show for it?"

Robert laughed. "A wrecked car. A lousy habit. For starters. Not to mention you're sittin' here with me on a Saturday night."

"Christ, sometimes I wish he was just out of my life. Out of my life for good."

Robert laughed again. "Hey, just say the word. It can be arranged."

She finished off the joint, then paused. "What can be arranged?"

He sniggered. "Now what was it you just said?"

She thought for a few seconds. "You mean 'out of my life.' "

" 'For good.' You said it. 'For good.' "

She rolled her eyes and scowled. "Shit. I didn't mean that like that."

"Hey, accidents happen all the time, Francie Lou. You know that."

"Robert, stop it. I didn't *mean* that, and you know it."

He raised an eyebrow. His lip curled in a sneer. "Then watch who you say things to."

She shuddered. "Christ, Robert." She breathed out a long sigh, looked away from him, then looked back. Now he was grinning. "Christ, you're weird."

He laughed. "I'm only joking, Francie Lou. Where's your fuckin' sense of humor?"

"Right, joking, sure."

"Lighten up, sweetheart."

She scowled, then giggled. The giggle picked up, took in air, blew itself into a full gale of laughter. She gasped as she tried to speak. "Is that better?"

"Yeah, that's better."

"Okay, then drive me home now, okay?"

It was as if she saw things through a telescope, as if they were brought closer from a great distance through long, narrow tubes: the driveway, the house, the front door, even the wrought-iron numbers, the one and the six and the four, and the lonely door-knocker figurine of a poodle's face right underneath. The real little dog who'd shared her childhood got run over years before. "Poor Noodles," she murmured, clutching the knob and bracing herself. Although every other house along this street of identical, well-manicured homes was wrapped in sleep and darkness, a pale orange light poured through gauzy drapes from every window of her parents' house.

And when Francie Lou stepped into the living room, there they sat, staring at the TV, which was not even on, a thick, tense silence already filling up the vast space between the two of them. Her father was fully dressed, his white shirt gleaming, as if he were at work. Well, really he *was* at work, he was always at work, always in control everywhere, even in his sleep. If he ever did sleep, which she doubted. Had she ever seen him sleeping? She tried to remember, but drew a blank. Anyway, three o'clock in the morning was nothing for old Frankie. But her mother—now *this* was a real occasion, her being awake at this hour. Her face drained to a total yellowish pallor, she was lost inside some awful ancient flowery housecoat that must have been the wrong size even years ago, and her hair was wrapped in a faded piece of cloth. A surge of disgust rose into Francie Lou's throat. Her mother looked like somebody's cleaning lady.

They sat on widely separate chairs, stewing in their own separate turmoil. At first they seemed tiny and far away, but now they appeared through those long telescopic tubes of Francie Lou's stoned vision and grew monstrously large. She squeezed her eyes shut. She'd die if either of them spoke first.

"I'm home," she announced. "I got a ride. I left the car parked down by the waterfront, in case you're interested."

They were silent, watching her.

She giggled, watching back, seeing them now as if at the end of that long telescopic tube, as if they were old birds, too dumb to fly, perched on chairs. Yes, birds, that fit them. Would they open their stupid beaks?

She took a big breath. "I thought the car was okay at first, when I started it up, but then it smelled funny. Oily, kinda."

Still they persisted in their separate, glum silences.

"Okay, then, great, we're all safe and sound? Fine. I'm going to bed." She kicked off her sandals and pushed them with her toes to the side of the kitchen doorway. (She repeated to herself her mother's first rule: no shoes in the house. Her second: no bare feet.) When she looked back around, her father was standing in the middle of the room, arms crossed, beak still closed. She noticed he was wearing his shiny black police oxfords, right there on her mother's carpet.

"Daddy, your shoes!" she exclaimed, then giggled again.

He slammed a magazine onto the coffee table. It was being stoned that made her notice: *Better Homes and Gardens.* Who was reading *that*? she wondered.

Then he spoke. "I just can't understand you, Francie Lou. Waltzing in here in the middle of the night, hours—*hours*—after—"

"And look at you!" her mother cut in. "Dressed like a—I can't even say it!"

Francie Lou laughed. "Yes you can, Mommy, c'mon, just once. Say 'ss-ll-uh-t.'"

"Shut up," said her father. "Shut *up*!"

"We were worried enough as is." Her mother was a crow now, beating her wings uselessly. "And then, where were you? Where did you go? Who knows? Having another drink? Having another accident? How many calls can we get in one night?"

"I did *not* drink after the accident. You did *not* get another call. Jesus, Mommy, have a little trust."

Her mother burst out with a loud squawk, a bird sound that started like nasty laughter but then petered out into a whimper.

"So where *were* you?" her father prodded. A seagull, she thought, pecking around, scavenging in the dump.

She clenched her jaw, then opened it. "I can't believe this. I'm shook up, y'know, I've been in a car accident, remember? And does anybody ask me am I all right? Did anybody offer to come pick me up? Jesus, Daddy, you left *me* to *my* own devices, and *I* did the best *I* fucking could."

"Your language, young lady!" shrilled her mother.

"We see you're all right," said her father. "The officers told me, believe me."

She snickered, tugging at the hem of her shirt. "I'm sure they did."

"You got yourself *into* the accident," said the crow, tucking loose feathers under her scarf. "Your father gets you *out* of trouble again. Again."

"Oh, he does, does he?"

"And you *did* manage to get yourself home. You're a big girl."

She sighed loudly. "If I'm such a big girl, then quit treating me like a child."

"Whatever your age, dammit," her father yelled, voice positively booming, "you live here in our house. You go by our rules. And you owe us, at *minimum,* some common courtesy!"

She threw him an angry look and raised her chin defiantly. "Yes sir! Yes ma'am! Is that common enough for you?"

"Oh, Francie Lou," said her mother in her low, resigned, there's-no-hope-for-you voice. She picked up a cup from the table, stood, turned slowly, and walked out of the room.

Francie Lou saw the movements as a beating of wings. "Take off, that's right!" she shouted after her. "Let Daddy do the big interrogation. After all, that's his *job.*" She threw herself down onto a dining room chair and glared at her father.

He stomped into the dining room. "Goddamn it, Francie Lou, I'm pissed as hell!" His grating voice was as angry and as domineering as it had been seconds before, but it had changed, as it always did when Margaret was out of hearing: not lowered, exactly, but loosened ever so slightly, a modulation only Francie Lou could detect, betraying a hint of relief. He yanked out a chair and sat down across from her. She watched him, his beak receding, as he became simply her angry father again. She could deal with that.

"You screw up!" the harangue began. "You screw up big time. At least have the goddamn sense to get out of the picture once it's taken care of!"

"Taken care of!" she hooted.

"How many times can you come running to Daddy to fix it?"

She sighed. "Fix *what*?"

"And keeping it outta the goddamn papers. Do you think that's easy for me? How many times, Francie Lou?"

"What do you mean, fix it, Daddy?" she asked. Hadn't she fixed it herself?

"Don't, for God's sake, ask me to spell it out for you, Francie Lou."

Suddenly she felt dizzy. "I don't think I get it, Daddy."

He blew out a long sigh of exasperation. "They treated you good, my men, right?"

She groaned. "Are you serious? Do you mean you think they did me some kind of favor out there?" She was utterly lost now. Of course she could not tell him how she got around the Breathalyzer. But what did he know? Or think he knew? That she'd been tested and found sober, or not tested at all? She tugged at the hem of her shirt, but it was no use: her bearings were gone.

"All they did was write out a ticket, right?" he asked gruffly.

"Yes, Daddy, that's all *they* did."

"No arrest, no talk of charges, right? And the other driver never got a chance to give you trouble?"

"Just some attitude."

"You don't think that other one had reason to be out for blood?"

She shrugged, dying for a cigarette.

He laughed. "So what does that mean, you're just lucky?"

She laughed, too. "I don't *know*, Daddy, there's still all the insurance stuff to get through, right?"

He sneered. "Drop the act, Francie Lou. You're faking it."

She suddenly felt a lump in her throat. For once she was really *not* faking. Instead she was floundering, in over her head and grasping for anything to hold on to.

"You're bluffing," he said, his tone utterly neutral.

Her voice shook. "And you're not?"

Their eyes met and locked. She was afraid he might actually answer her. But he said nothing, he didn't move at all, and the stare which they shared, maintained at first by an invisible but palpable tension from each of them, was usurped by his own hard glare, which pushed to hold and subdue her. She didn't breathe. The room was absolutely still, the heat more and more stifling. She struggled to glare back at him harder, unblinking, through an endless minute, while a videotape in her head spun silently out of control, racing back to the times when he'd beat his own small children at rummy and Go Fish, playing for real, Daddy triumphing again and again over a five-year-old, a seven-year-old, an eight-year-old; then to the giddyup horsy rides on his knee, those rapturous moments when she was encircled in his big strong arms and the entire sweep of his attention; then fast-forwarded through a long blur to this eternity of uncertainty, this tug-of-war of glares.

But then, as if in response to something, his look shifted. Had hers, without her knowing? Tiny smile lines began to crack first around his eyes, then at the corners of his mouth. Slowly he leaned forward, reached his arm all the way across the table and, with his thumb, blotted a tear from her cheek that she didn't know was there.

"Well, well, well," he said. That was how he declared himself the winner. "Well, well." Her tears—even just a single tear—automatically became his victory. Any show of feeling would have, but this hurt confusion of hers was like a gift to him, like throwing the game for him. She could read it now in his broadening smile: she couldn't have pleased him more if she had tried. Shit.

He pushed his chair back from the table and stood up. "I'm hungry. I'm gonna make some toast. Want some, Francie Lou?" Just like that, it was over. Balance was restored the way he liked it.

And she gathered herself together again. Grabbing at the hem of her shirt, she rose from her chair and followed him into the kitchen, where he seemed so large and clumsy, looming over those few, small, unimportant corners that were not his domain. He stared at the breadbox.

"I'll do it, Daddy," she said. She nudged him away, pulled out a bag, drew out six slices of white bread, and arranged them neatly on the toaster oven rack.

"So much?" he questioned.

She shrugged. "I'm famished."

He nodded and smiled again, as if she had presented him one more gift, another of her distorted appetites.

But he was the one who went to the refrigerator first and searched for the real butter instead of the imitation crap her mother would have used. And he was the one who pulled out the pale slices before the toasting even stopped. Standing side by side at the counter, wielding their knives, Francie Lou and her father worked fast but carefully, each letting the melting yellow swirls soak down into the web of tiny dry craters before they heaped on jam. They both ate standing up, side by side, slurping at the sticky mounds of strawberry that dripped down the edges of the bread. With their fingers, they both dabbed up the jam that ran onto the countertop, then licked their fingers clean. And when Margaret suddenly cleared her throat in the kitchen doorway, Francie Lou and her father exchanged the same quick, knowing look and smiled the same quick, knowing smile.

"Don't make a mess," her mother said, clutching the housecoat around her as if she were cold.

Francie Lou turned toward her. "Go to sleep, Mommy," she said.

"Go to sleep, Margaret," said the police chief over his shoulder as he shook the last four slices of bread out of the bag and opened the toaster door.

Votive: Vision

She draws. She draws a door. On the windowpane in breath. Breathes on the glass and draws. A door, an *O* spells polio. Six years old. She dreams. Walks with her father again. River of glass. To the river of glass collecting bits of this and that to examine later under the microscope. To hold. Insects, plants, stones. To draw. All is.

Votive: vision.

Drawn to the swirling. Live your life.

And her beloved papa photographs her and she makes love to the lens even then.

Live your life.

Embrace the life you've been given.

Your grave image. Even then.

Votive: vision.

And Tina Modotti will photograph you. And Lucienne Block will photograph you. Edward Weston. Nickolas Muray. Lola Alvarez Bravo.

And you make love freely to the lens and your life opens, and your life widens, like the river. Her grave reflection in the glass— small boats. And the air makes love to her—and the heat.

Listen: the drums. And you leave the frame.

Incessant. Your life—just a girl—opening.

She loves the sun clanging and she's drawn. Drawn to the swirling. The way color keeps coming and going. The way color.

Her teacher holds an orange and a flame—imagine—vast-ness—the planets—

Dreams the orange over—solar system—drawn—to the spin-ning—she stands in awe.

And the translucence. Beautiful. And she draws...Each mark a door.

She closes her eyes, just a child, and touches her dreamy thigh—before the accident—

With her finger in the dirt she makes a 3, a 7, a 9. She dreams...

You are the *alegría* girl, your lucky numbers are. And I am just trying to keep up.

Mischievous one. Cheeky. Cheeky one. Climbing trees. Prankster. Anarchic in the afternoon. Already her dark dares, her fierce pursuit of pleasure. Her refusal to refuse joy.

Votive: courage.

You are the *alegría* girl, ferocious child of fire, and I am standing next to your heat and light—for all these years. You leave the frame. Searching. *Fulang Chang!*

Childish pranks. Monkey business. Monkeys hanging. Clinging to your neck. *Fulang Chang!* you shout. Monkeys clinging Her sexual. Aura, halo, fire. Setting off firecrackers. Throwing sparklers—light, even then. Hanging from a tree upside down. Monkeys clinging to her neck, even then. She calls her monkey *Fulang Chang!* she shouts.

Irresistible one—taking, asking, begging—*answer me*—looking—looking harder—watching through the window just a child. She sees her face in the glass. Draws a picture on the glass—river of.

The sun clanging, *Fulang Chang!* the light. Drawn to the way color keeps coming and going, *Alejandro, venga.* The way color vibrates. In the public gardens in the whirling of her. Teenage Frida—*venga,* pink petals, the open fruit, giving up, soaked in its juices, juicy pulp and seed and pulsing. Need and lush.

Ambrosia. The soft dark nub.

Votive: cup.

Oh you are a curious one.

In a knapsack Frida carried a notebook with drawings, pinned butterflies, and dried flowers, colored pens, and philosophy books from her father's library.

And I am writing after her—incessant dreaming—just trying to keep up.

And she leaves the frame. And I am writing.

In the margins of her love letters she draws a woman with a long neck, pointed chin, enormous eyes. *Don't tear her, Alejandro, because she is very pretty—an ideal type.*

She draws a cat: *Another ideal type.*

Let's peel, let's peel back (twenty-four hours of incessant drumming on Good Friday) together gently—watch as I do it—a little bit of skin, my love, my love, just a—

little—to reveal (you tease) and later to paint. Fruit spread on the earth. Dripping. Fruit now opened, peeled back beneath an open sky. See how she.

Free. A little free.

Translucent, gleaming.

Sun-drenched.

Mischief-maker.

Incessant dreaming.

And she learns to swear. In the square on the days she skips school. Already her dark dares, her fierce pursuit of pleasure. She writes to Alejandro:

Answer me   Answer me   Answer me   Answer me
      "   "   "   "
      "   "   "   "

Her extracted heart in her hands. Her refusal to refuse pain, posing even then. Drawn to the swirling.

Unstoppable. Ribbons of light. Set me free. Answer me.

Answer me.

The girls say they are dying in your formal European. In your corridors of rules. In the diminutives, in the diminished.

In your regulations. The girls say. Bored with your pedestals.

Your Europe of thorns and decorums.

Looking. Harder. Looking harder.

Watching through the window the child sees her face in the glass and uses it as escape. Her face. Dream. Draws on the glass—

The two liked to loiter in the public gardens. Drawn. Drawn to the light. Green.

Eye and dream. Her aura—only a child—even then. The girls say. Watching him on a scaffold at the Preparatoria. Incessant dreaming. Painting. Drawn to the debilitating, the promise—and the fat man, painting, in the air *Creation*—can you feel it—color, shape. *Diego!*

Who's there? Soaping the stairs. And shouting from nowhere, insolent child, *Watch out, fat man, your wife is coming. You'll be caught, face of a dog, face of a frog* (a hundred clandestine affairs).

"My only ambition is to have a child by Diego Rivera, the painter. And I am going to tell him someday."

Frida, you are crazy. Just a girl at the Preparatoria.

Incessant dreaming: a fat man with a palette

on a scaffold casting
beauty, casting appalling
possibility on her—little one
childish pranks—to dispel the strangeness.
Her sexual halo even then. *You must have been an angel.* He
mutters. From the height.
Heat and light.
And one day she shall marry it.
Beauty is convulsive, as Breton will say. As your friend Breton
will say, or not at all.
But for now.
And you return to the frame. And posing is like freedom
some—sometimes.
Her dreamy, dreamboat, Alejandro—who will leave her—
sorry—loose, promiscuous one.
Incessant drumming.
Answer me.
Voracious in the afternoon.
The girls say they are dying—incessant dreaming—asked to
conform. In the thorned courtyard—exhausted by all the tired
forms.
Asked to believe those.
Assume those.
Revere those.
(Draw a blue door.)
Preposterous sexual stances of modesty and silence—
Voracious, irreverent—postures of I'm sorry and silence—curi-
ous, self-indulgent, mischief-maker. *Fulang Chang!* you shout
with glee.
Answer me.
Who's there?
Partially revealed. Voracious: microscope, lens, window, eye.
Reflected. Hold the pose a moment longer.
The girls say they are. We are. In those rooms of judgment and
pronouncements, dying. In the hedges. But the girls say they are.
Sparklers. And she draws a blue door. Dips her hands in the—
Votive: chalice.
Your charms and secret numbers. Fetish, altar, free a little. Just
a girl, your life opening...

Mischief-maker... "drinking tequila like a real mariachi."

The two girls loved to loiter in the public gardens of the university district where they would listen to the organ grinders and chat with truants and newsboys.

Sun-drenched. Incessant. *Answer me.*

She is the *alegría* girl—the way color keeps coming and going— the way color vibrates—drawn.

To the swirling.

Drawn.

To the light.

She is the *alegría* girl—sparkling—already on fire.

from *Beauty Is Convulsive*

The Wake

How many times since Elise's death had her husband, Mitch, said numbly, *Oh Christ, I can't believe she's gone, I don't know what to do.* And Joan replied helplessly, squeezing his hand, *I know! I know.*

Of course, there wouldn't be one—a wake. The deceased hadn't been Catholic. Hadn't been brought up in any church, though she'd been respectful (more or less, at least publicly) of religion.

At the time of death, at the time of the terrible starkness and finality of death, when you are staring into an abyss, and no bottom to the abyss, religion is a consolation, for some. If you can believe, if you can force yourself. *Yes, but we don't believe, and we can't force ourselves.*

Joan would date the hour, the very minute of Elise's death at the time she, Joan, received the news. At 8:40 a.m. in Baltimore, which was 7:40 a.m. in Milwaukee; in fact, Elise had died at 6:55 a.m. in Milwaukee General Hospital. But Joan had picked up the telephone in Baltimore, unguarded and innocent, and immediately she'd recognized the voice of Elise's husband, though some terrible change had occurred, Mitch's voice was quavering, broken. Joan thought, *Elise is dead. Elise is dead!* For never in the twelve years of their acquaintance had Mitch telephoned Joan, his wife's oldest friend.

So Joan heard the news from Mitch. "You're the first to know, except for Elise's older sister, who's going to break the news to her mother." Elise's mother had been ill for some time, in a nursing home; Joan hadn't seen her in years. "Elise wanted to call you herself. Sunday morning, she was going to try. But she couldn't, she was too weak. Joan, are you there?" Mitch asked anxiously, and Joan said, "Yes, of course, of course I'm here," thinking numbly, *Where else! Where else would I be!* and Mitch continued, "So she told me to tell you, Joan, she was thinking of you, and she's going to miss you, and—" There was a pause, some confusion at the other end of the line, possibly someone was speaking to Mitch, or Mitch had dropped the receiver, and Joan said, "Mitch? Mitch? Is something wrong?" and after a moment Mitch's voice returned, overly loud in her ear, agitated, "Elise is still—her body, I mean—in the hospital. And I'm here."

Joan said, "I'll come as quickly as I can."

Joan had forgotten how sick grief can make you. How like a physical blow it was—"grief." A fever, a nausea. Terrible raging anger.

So soon! She was so young—thirty-seven. I can't believe it.

Like my sister. My only sister.

My friend for life.

Always Joan had been just slightly jealous of Elise's other friends. Girls in high school, boyfriends; in time, lovers; one or two men Elise had come close to marrying; and the man she had married, Mitch—Mitchell Caleb Richards. Joan had been jealous of him, and, why not admit it, Joan had been, for years, a little in love with him. Since they'd been girls, Joan had been secretly drawn to Elise's men, and Elise had once flattered her by remarking that she, Elise, was drawn to Joan's men. This was a shock to Joan, and a pleasure: for Elise was a woman of striking looks, tall, golden-haired as a princess in a fairy tale, with an air of inward composure; in public, people turned to look at her; when she entered a room, people glanced up smiling, expectant. *Yes? Even my husband? Are you drawn to my husband, too?* Joan had laughed, and Elise had said, after a moment's hesitation, oddly shy, *Well—no. That's different.* But why, Joan wondered, was it different?

It was a fact not to be reduced to any other fact. Elise had died at 6:55 a.m. of April 15, 1996, in Milwaukee General Hospital.

It had been expected that Elise could not live beyond another eight months, the cancer had been metastasizing so rapidly; but it had not been expected that Elise would die so soon, of complications arising from kidney failure.

Joan couldn't help but feel cheated. Tricked. She and Elise had kept in contact by phone, and Joan averaged two or even three calls to Elise's one, and Elise had owed her a call, or two—the last time they'd spoken had been in mid-March. So Elise's abrupt death seemed to Joan impulsive, impetuous. For there was that side of her friend, too—making up her mind, then changing it; changing it again; leaving others behind.

Joan flew to Milwaukee on an early-evening flight, saying goodbye to her husband and her children, who were ten and seven, telling them she'd be back on Saturday evening, after the funeral. She believed herself to be, in their eyes, reasonably calm, contained.

Then, on the flight, she began to cry. Embarrassing herself, and others. And how strange, that crying should make her perspire inside her clothes, at an altitude of thirty thousand feet. A flight attendant tried to comfort her, but damned if Joan, any more than Elise would have done, would confess before strangers she was mourning a death, the death of her oldest, closest friend; she was a mature, unsentimental woman, the kind of woman who comforts others and does not break down herself. And thirty-seven years old—not young. She told the flight attendant, "It's hay fever. A virulent form of hay fever. That's all."

Then at the Milwaukee airport there was an awkward scene in which Joan seemed at first not to recognize Elise's husband, for whom she'd had vague romantic yearnings for twelve years, while Mitch, waiting at the gate, anxious, eager, seemed to fail to recognize, at first, his wife's friend Joan, though he'd driven to the airport expressly to meet her. Of course, they would laugh about it afterward.

Mitch was smelling of grief, too. Stronger and ranker than Joan's. Possibly he hadn't showered, changed his clothes, in some time.

Joan had seen a ravaged man who might have been any age between thirty and fifty (Mitch was in fact thirty-nine). With a thrown-together look—rumpled clothes, a soiled Milwaukee Brewers cap jammed onto his head and water-stained running shoes on his feet. His jaws covered in two days' gray-glinting stubble and his eyes red-veined, with a glassy sheen. He'd been drinking, but Joan hadn't known that at the time. His mouth looked as if it had been mashed. When he started for her, at last seeing her, to take her roughly in his arms in an anguished embrace, Joan felt a panicked impulse to lift her elbows in self-defense.

It was on the drive to the hotel that Mitch said, several times, as if he'd forgotten what he'd said only a few minutes before, *Oh Christ, I can't believe she's gone, I don't know what to do.* And Joan replied helplessly, *I know! I know.* These words were in acknowledgment of the impoverishment of all words, at such a time; yet, what choice had they, who'd loved Elise, except to repeat them? And repeat them.

Mitch announced to Joan that he couldn't do the obituary, please would she do the obituary? Elise would have wished that. And would she select a photograph of Elise from their photo album? And here was the number to call—Mitch's hand was visibly shaking—at *The Milwaukee Times-Ledger.*

Next day, Joan accompanied Mitch to Donovan Brothers Funeral Home, where Mitch made further arrangements for the funeral, signed a letter of agreement, and handed over a check, then they drove to a nearby Safeway since there was virtually no food in the house—Joan had checked the refrigerator on a hunch, the glaring white emptiness and a smell of something overripe and rancid had been a shock. Elise would have been embarrassed, upset. *Clearly, something has happened here! This would appear to be a refrigerator in a household in which something has happened.*

In the Safeway, Joan did most of the selecting, and Joan pushed the cart, one wheel of which had begun to stick. There was Mitch staring at pyramids of organic carrots, and satiny-purple eggplants that looked as if they'd been lacquered, and red-leaf lettuces arranged like works of art; he looked like a sleepwalker slow to awaken, by lights bright and unsparing as on a movie set. He turned to look for Joan, panic in his face, as if she'd left him; Joan smiled, for of course she hadn't left him. He was saying, "There's this terror I've had all my life, that I'll lose the names of things. Not just the things but what they *are.* Like a stroke victim. For instance, what the hell is this? Am I supposed to know?" Mitch lifted a pale squash shaped like an Indian club, gripping the stem. Was this meant to be a joke? Joan said, "I think it's a butternut squash. But we don't want it, we're sticking to essentials." "And what's this?" Mitch lifted a torpedo-shaped vegetable that resembled Chinese cabbage, glittering with moisture. "Fresh anise," Joan said. Mitch said, " 'Fresh anise'—how do you know?" Joan said, pointing, "Because it says so on the sign—'Fresh anise.' " "Right you are," Mitch said, with affable irony. "The sign explains everything."

Joan pushed on. She tried to ignore the wayward, lopsided motion of the shopping cart, but Mitch lost patience, saying, "Let me help you with that damned thing!" and would have wrested it from her except Joan quickly intervened. "No! It's fine. We're almost finished." She had a vision of Mitch shoving and jerking the cart, cursing, slamming it into a food display. He was flexing his fingers as if yearning to do violence; tears shone angrily in his eyes. Joan had been taking aspirin to dull her anxiety, and she guessed, smelling Mitch's breath, that he'd been drinking. She said pleasantly, "I noticed, Mitch—you're out of eggs." As if eggs were the only item Mitch was out of.

Mitch laughed. "Fuck eggs. I can live without eggs."

In the dairy products section of the store, steam lifted thinly from open refrigerated units. Joan began to shiver. Mitch said, "This place! Like a morgue." Joan said, not looking at Mitch's face, which she knew to be contorted, ugly, "Yes! But we're almost finished." Her eyes smarted from the overly bright colors, waxen containers, food packages stamped with the giddy-smiling faces of cartoon animals. How by quick degrees, during the course of her own lifetime, the world had become a place of cartoon animals, Disney creatures wanting us to buy, buy, buy. Mitch seemed to be reading her thoughts; as, when they were girls, Elise had sometimes seemed to read Joan's thoughts; he spoke with an edge to his voice that made other customers glance at him, "Joan, d'you think this is—all there is? The surfaces of things? Looks, smells? And there's nothing more?" Joan said brightly, "Butter? Skim milk? Cheddar cheese?" She was flinging items into the cart. Mitch hadn't been eating at home for days, perhaps hadn't been eating regularly at all. He'd lost weight recently, cruelly in his face. It was a young face, with an older face laid upon it like a gauze mask. His eyes had become starker, larger. And there was a new way he had of laughing without mirth, baring his teeth like a dog. Joan thought, *Without Elise between us, I don't know this man.* She would have liked to have left the shopping cart in the Safeway and returned to her hotel, but there seemed no way to negotiate such a maneuver. Mitch was saying, "Elise was a vegetarian, y'know. Helluva lot of good it did her, eh?" Joan said, incensed, "Elise was not a vegetarian! Since when?" "She'd quit smoking, and she'd quit 'red meat.' She was on some sort of desperate brown rice and greens diet. In addition to the chemotherapy. She didn't tell you? That's strange. I thought she told you everything." Joan said, disliking the tone of their conversation, "But Elise was never a vegetarian on principle. She'd have laughed at that. You know what Elise was like." Joan dropped a container of yogurt into the shopping cart, more carelessly than she intended.

Mitch said in a neutral voice, "What Elise was like—when? At the end, or when we knew her?"

Joan hadn't wanted to think about that. She hadn't seen Elise's body, of course. There wouldn't be an open casket at the funeral service on Saturday morning. There would be no wake—no "viewing."

Maybe death isn't real if you don't see the body. If you can't touch the body. If there isn't any body.

Joan had had a difficult time selecting a photograph of Elise to accompany the obituary. A smiling face, a radiantly happy face, is inappropriate for such circumstances, and nearly all of Elise's photographs depicted her smiling. She'd finally chosen a photograph that had been professionally taken, in which Elise, thirty-four at the time, appeared rather wooden, self-conscious; an attractive woman, yet not, somehow, "Elise"—not as they'd known her. When Joan showed the photo to Mitch, to ask his opinion of it, Mitch had glanced quickly at it, and away. Okay, yes, fine. That's fine.

While they'd been shopping in the Safeway, though it was only 5:30 p.m., the sky of massed storm clouds had darkened nearly to night. A harsh wind rose from the direction of Lake Michigan: Joan could imagine the lake whipped to a frenzy. On one of her early visits to Elise and Mitch, Elise had driven Joan along the lakefront at a time when a gale was rising; the lake had seemed an inland sea, immense, astonishing. Mitch suddenly began to shiver;

then, as if losing control, he began to shake with cold; his teeth were audibly chattering, panic shone in his eyes. Joan moved to him, to steady him. She tried to hold him, but he was too large and, holding grocery bags, too bulky; they stumbled together. Joan said quickly, "Get in the car, I'll start the heater." Mitch was trying to speak, but his jaws seemed locked. Joan took the bags from him, and Joan took his car keys out of his pocket, and Joan helped him, this stricken, near-convulsing man, into the passenger's seat. She started the motor, turned on the heater. "You'll be all right. You'll be fine. Just don't think about being cold. Try not to think about being cold. Here—here's the heat. Feel it? You'll be fine."

By degrees, Mitch's shivering began to subside. His lips were a ghastly purplish-blue, his face clammy-pale. Of course, he was deeply ashamed, humiliated, trying to explain or apologize, but Joan said for God's sake just be still, be calm, try to relax. She'd drive.

Lucky for them both, Joan would drive. Mitch's driving had been erratic, dangerous. The evening before, driving her back to the city from the airport, he'd talked, gestured, removing his hands from the wheel. He couldn't seem to comprehend the fact of Elise's death, let alone the fact he no longer had a wife. He hadn't been sleeping, he'd admitted, for several days. He'd been afraid that, if he slept, Elise might die; and something like that had happened. Joan had been terrified, several times, they'd have an accident—and at such a time.

How disruptive, death was. The death of someone powerfully loved. It simply could not be factored in.

When they returned to Mitch's house, it was to discover it darkened, and the rear door, leading from the garage into the house, unlocked.

Mitch muttered he must be losing his grip, forgetting to lock up. And he'd rushed out, to get to the funeral home on time for his appointment, without a coat.

Joan switched on lights, uncomfortable with the look of disorder, confusion in the house which, while Elise had been alive, had been spotless. And how strange to be in this house without Elise beside her, or calling to her from another room. Elise in the living room, Elise in the kitchen. Elise saying, *Joan! It's great to see you again, I've been missing you.* Elise had been a woman who'd liked to squeeze your hand, hug you, laugh with delight at her own happiness. How strange to think she would not be rushing into the room, surprised at Joan's visit. *Joan? Mitch? What's up? What's going on?*

Joan blinked in dismay, almost in a kind of vertigo, seeing the mess in which Mitch had been living. As if a storm had blown through the downstairs. In the living room with its wall of sliding glass doors and its elegant cathedral ceiling, there were scattered newspapers, magazines, books. Glasses, bottles. A ceramic vase which Joan recognized as an old gift of hers containing very dead, very blackened roses. A trail of dirt on the beige carpet. Tossed-down articles of clothing. And that sour odor of bodily grief.

Earlier, brought to the house by Mitch, Joan had done some hurried picking-up, but there was much more to do. How embarrassed, how angry Elise would be at the look of her beautiful house. As if it had begun to disintegrate, decay. As if all vigilance had been withdrawn from it. *Oh Christ, I miss her so,* Mitch was saying. *I want her back. I can't believe she's gone.*

In the kitchen, Mitch was banging about, setting a grocery bag down on a cluttered table, and immediately the bag overturned, items spilled out. Mitch cursed and kicked a grapefruit across the floor.

How strange, how unnatural to be alone in this house, Elise's house, in the company of Elise's husband, and no Elise, Joan thought. Joan was beginning to be frightened of Elise's husband.

Wondering, *How will we get through it! The days until the funeral. The nights. The next hour.*

Quickly Joan began to put things away—into the refrigerator, on cupboard shelves. Then she rinsed plates, glasses, cutlery; stacked the dishwasher and set it going, a high humming sound of consolation. Mitch hovered about, leaving the kitchen and returning, seeming to want to help but not knowing how, his hands clumsy. He offered Joan a drink, which she declined. He opened a can of lukewarm beer, foam dripped onto his knuckles. He'd been telling Joan a complicated tale of tenderness and irony about something that had occurred just before Elise had had to be hospitalized this last time, but he was interrupted by a ringing telephone; he let it ring, and ring; seeing the look of concern on

Joan's face (for certainly the call was an urgent one from a relative, a friend, the hospital, or the funeral home), he said carelessly
that the answering service would pick it up—"Like all the others."
Joan didn't want to ask how many others. Mitch hadn't removed
his baseball cap, which was twisted on his head. He wore a gray
pullover sweater damp beneath the arms and across the back. The
stubble on his jaws seemed to have grown sharper in the past
hour, and there was a fleck of something white, like dried tooth-
paste, in a corner of his mouth. He was staring at Joan contem-
platively. Joan suggested she might answer some of the calls, and
there was the obituary to finish and telephone in to the newspaper, but Mitch shook his head as if to clear it and said no, not
right now—"Let's relax right now." The phone had ceased ringing. The house thrummed with silence, but it was an uneasy
silence buffeted by wind, a high tolling sound above the roof;
there was a pressure against the windows like the soft slapping of
invisible hands. "I knew that Elise was dying, of course," Mitch
said slowly, bitterly, "but I didn't get it, she would actually *vanish.*
And just the body left behind. And that body not the one we
knew. All that—that hadn't sunk in, somehow. Though Elise isn't
the first person I've known who has died. Of course not. But—"
So Mitch talked, talked.

If they'd had children, Joan was thinking. *Maybe that would
make some difference, now.*

For the next forty minutes as Joan cleaned the downstairs of
Elise's house, too restless, too nervous to sit still, Mitch followed
her about, telling her a complicated story of how, thirteen years
and three months before, he'd met Elise on New Year's Day, in
Chicago; and how, the following year, they'd re-met on New
Year's Eve, in New York; how they'd obviously been fated to meet.
Joan knew the story well, it was one of Elise's favorite stories. For
what is a lifetime, what are friendships that stretch through life-
times, but the accumulation of favorite, much-repeated stories?
In fact, Joan had been a guest at the New Year's party in New
York, at the home of mutual college friends, and she'd been intro-
duced to Mitch, too, at that time; but Mitch wasn't remembering.

I might have fallen in love with you then. And you with me.
If that had happened, we'd call it "fate."

Mitch was on his second, possibly his third can of beer. He'd stopped shivering, though he was still shaky; his face had become ruddy, splotched. He spoke in a rapid, excited voice, and he moved his arms in wide and exaggerated gestures. Mania, Joan thought. She wondered if it was contagious. Certainly there was something erotic, sexual in it—such energy, certainty. Mitch was smiling peculiarly. It was a beat or two before Joan understood what he was saying. "This time before Elise and I moved in together, in Hyde Park, my last year of law school—we gave each other a lot of grief, those days. I always wondered, if she'd been completely faithful to me."

Joan was shocked. "Mitch, for God's sake."

"What? 'For God's sake'—what? Just tell me." Mitch was smiling harder with his mouth, but his eyes stared, red-veined and glassy.

Evasively Joan said, "That was—a long time ago, Mitch."

"No. Hardly twelve years. A flash." He snapped his fingers, and the sound was loud, jarring as something broken. "Just tell me was Elise completely faithful to me, or was she involved with that guy, that French economist at the university, remember? The one who—"

"If you wanted to know, you should have asked Elise."

Mitch screwed up his face in pain. He'd never been able to ask Elise.

Cruelly Joan thought, *Because Elise would have told you, yes?*

She said, meaning to comfort him, this warm, despairing man who was crowding her, "Mitch, you're exhausted. You haven't eaten all day, and you haven't been sleeping, and you aren't thinking coherently. Let me make us something to eat, and I'll go back to the hotel, and you can sleep, and in the morning—"

Mitch said, miserably, "It can't wait until morning. How can I get through it—to morning. Joan, help me, I'm just trying to know what I should feel."

The dishwasher was still humming, clicking; going through its cycle. And the wind. And a telephone ringing, unless it was a ringing in Joan's head. She felt dazed, dizzy. A terrible sensation of exhaustion swept over her, but she would not give in to it.

Years ago Elise had confided in Joan, *I love Mitch more than I've loved any man, but I've loved other men I might have been happy with, too. Is that a terrible thing to admit?*

Elise had confided in Joan, *If you don't have children, like Mitch and me, you're in danger of remaining a child yourself all your life.*

"What should you feel?" Joan said. "Exactly what you feel."

Impulsively—for this was a gesture of Elise's—Joan took hold of Mitch's trembling hands, and briskly rubbed them, and steadied them. She removed the sweat-stained baseball cap from his head. His graying brown hair stood up in short spikes. His forehead was creased in wavering horizontal lines. Joan said firmly, "You'll get through it, Mitch. Of course you will." The phone rang, and this time Joan went to answer it; it was a Milwaukee friend of Elise's, a woman not known to Joan, who'd just heard the news.

Elise said, *The saddest thing about someone you love dying, Joan,* when the girls were fifteen, when Elise's father died unexpectedly of a heart attack, *isn't just the person is gone forever and you'll never see him again, but time keeps going, like nothing special happened after all. It just keeps…going.*

Here was a shocking thing, which Joan didn't intend to tell Mitch—*The Milwaukee Times-Ledger* charged for obituaries unless the deceased was a person of prominence; a "newsworthy person already in our files."

Joan had worked at the obituary for over an hour, composing it painstakingly, by hand; less than three hundred words, and her eyes smarted, her head throbbed, her fingers were stiff and clumsy as if arthritic. Mitch had provided her with the facts of Elise's life, birth date, birthplace, parents' names, lists of schools Elise had attended and degrees earned, jobs, activities, affiliations, the exact title of Elise's most recent position (in a well-known Milwaukee private school); other facts Joan herself had provided; but it was the organization of these facts that gave her difficulty. She could not seem to think. She transposed and misspelled words. She had to stop several times to walk about, nearly overcome by sorrow, dread, nausea. Bright, vivid Elise! Beautiful Elise! Joan's friend of nearly thirty years, closer to her than any sister, reduced to a brief column of newsprint and a small photo in the back pages of a daily newspaper.

No wonder Mitch had been too upset to compose the obituary himself. When Joan asked him to check it for errors, he glanced through it quickly, told her it was fine, and handed it back.

So Joan called in the obituary, to learn that there was a charge for obituaries. As the bored-sounding, youngish woman at the other end of the line said, tactlessly, it seemed to Joan, the rate was the same as for classified ads. Unless the deceased was "newsworthy." Joan's heart beat quickly in mortification and anger. "I think that's a cruel policy. I think it's selfish. I don't understand it at all." The woman at the other end of the line said mechanically, as if she'd recited the words countless times, "Because there are so many deaths, ma'am. Every day. Not just in the city but in this part of Wisconsin. The paper has to charge."

So Joan paid for Elise's obituary with her Visa card, two hundred eighty-eight dollars, reading the numbers over the phone with barely controlled emotion. At least, Mitch would never know.

Somehow it was late, almost nine o'clock by the time Joan finally prepared a meal, scrambled eggs and Canadian bacon, sourdough bread, Campbell's minestrone soup and cheddar cheese and Rye-Crisp crackers, which Mitch and she ate at the kitchen table. Joan was both dazed with hunger and mildly nauseated; Mitch was ravenous, but now drinking wine, glass after glass. Joan agreed to a glass, though she could see it wasn't a good idea, not in the condition they were in. It wasn't a good idea, but there she was drinking. Mitch had hurriedly shaved, and might have washed, a bit; he'd changed his soiled sweater for another sweater. Small patches of stubble remained on his jaws amid tiny razor nicks and scratches. His eyes were badly bloodshot but bright, alert. He finished the food on his plate and continued to eat compulsively, chunks of cheddar cheese, crackers, and bread, without seeming to taste what he was chewing. When Joan suggested that he go to bed, she'd call a cab and return to the hotel and see him in the morning, he panicked, grabbed her arm— "No! Don't leave, Joan. You can't leave." Joan managed to extricate her arm from Mitch's fingers, which were strong, blunt fingers, leaving dull marks on her skin. Carefully she said, "You have to sleep, Mitch. You'll be hallucinating if you don't sleep."

Joan would have risen to carry plates to the sink, but Mitch prevented her. He said, "We used to talk sometimes, Elise and me, about dying together. I don't mean suicide, I mean—dying, together. We said we wouldn't want to live without each other. We—" Under other circumstances, Joan would have been embarrassed to be told such a confidence; she would not have wished to be told such a confidence; now she said, laying a steadying hand on Mitch's arm, "Mitch, you don't want to be thinking that way. Not now." She recalled how in the aftermath of passion, many years ago, she and her young husband had uttered such things to each other; had seemed to be making vows; and how touching, how sad and silly such words now seemed, like the utterances of children. Mitch said, "I don't want to think that way. But it's hard not to."

Mitch poured the remainder of a second bottle of wine into his glass, and into Joan's.

With a part of her mind, Joan was calculating how she'd get up from the table and telephone a taxi, because Mitch wasn't in any condition to drive her home; nor was she in any condition to drive Elise's car to the hotel. But Mitch kept her there, talking urgently, anxiously. It was clear he was terrified of being alone. Outside, the wind was stronger; tiny pellets of ice were being flung against the windows. Joan was in fact on her feet, but Mitch was holding her; he was embracing her, and groaning; clutching at her for his very life. Joan couldn't breathe. She pushed at him, gently. But then she was leading him out of the kitchen, and upstairs. In the bedroom that had been Elise and Mitch's, there was that same air of disorder, of something gone wrong. Scattered clothes, towels. A stale smell. A smell of soiled bedclothes. Joan said, "Maybe if you took a bath, Mitch. A hot bath. Maybe you could sleep, then."

So they prepared a bath for Mitch, running noisy hot water into a tub. Joan was reminded of her children's baths, when they were younger: the playful comfort, the ritual: the safe conclusion of a day. Mitch insisted upon keeping the bathroom door ajar so that they could talk. Joan agreed; Joan was quickly changing the bedclothes on the large double bed that had been Elise and Mitch's; as Mitch called out to her, Joan responded as she might have responded to one of her children—"Yes, that's right. Oh yes.

Yes—" She pushed soiled sheets, pillowcases, towels and underwear and socks of Mitch's into an already stuffed clothes hamper.
Who would be doing this laundry? she wondered. Elise had had a
cleaning woman, of course. Though maybe Joan would do the
laundry herself, tomorrow. Though people died agonizing deaths,
though they died before they were ready to die, and though others were deranged with grief, though grief was bitter and unexpected as bile in the mouth, yet laundry must be done, dishes
must be washed, clothes shaken and hung up neatly on hangers.
On a chair amid layers of tossed-down clothing, Joan discovered a
white cotton knit sweater of Elise's. She snatched it up to her
chest with a little cry of pain—"Oh. God." The appalling realiza-
tion swept upon her as if for the first time, she would never see
Elise again.

The bedroom was fragrant and warm with steam. Mitch was
out of his bath, in a terry-cloth robe, barefoot. His hair was
damp-combed, and his face flushed with a look of being out of
focus, like melting wax. Joan said goodnight, but Mitch gripped
her begging her, not to leave just yet—"Please! Please." They were
sitting together on the edge of the bed. Joan had put fresh sheets
and pillowcases on the bed, crisp clean bedclothes in a floral pattern resembling bedclothes of her own; she'd folded a downy
comforter neatly at the foot of the bed. Joan said, "I won't leave
you, Mitch, but you have to sleep. Will you try to sleep?" It
seemed that they were lying together on top of the bed, awkwardly. Mitch was groaning, pulling at clothing; he tried to kiss her;
pressed his damp, hungry mouth against her, groaning. *He thinks
I'm Elise,* Joan thought. *There's no harm to it to it.* At first she neither resisted the man nor did she respond; she was apprehensive,
excited; sexually excited; as in a confusing dream, she experienced
emotions that seemed not entirely her own, arising from a source
she could not have identified. With a thrill of guilt, she recalled
that she hadn't telephoned her husband and her children that
evening, as she'd promised. She had meant to call them from the
hotel. She'd last spoken with her husband that morning; hours
ago; she could scarcely recall their conversation; she could scarcely recall her husband; there was a sense in which all husbands
were interchangeable, as bodies may be interchangeable, considered as anatomical specimens. Mitch was saying what sounded

like *I can't make it, I can't make it,* and again Joan assured him she wouldn't leave him. Mitch's body was heavy, and very warm; his skin burned, touching hers; he'd pulled at Joan's clothes, and Joan had pulled at her clothes, until they were naked together, and one of them, it must have been Joan, had drawn a sheet over them. Joan was breathing quickly, she felt the man's penis against her thighs, she felt him begin to pump his groin against her; felt him getting hard, or nearly; he was sobbing, groaning as if in pain. His weight on her collarbone was considerable. She was having difficulty breathing. She thought, *I will have to go through with it.* She was kissing him as one might speak to him, reassuring him, comforting him. His mouth, his tongue. As Elise would have done. He was saying, *I love you! Love you,* and she was saying, *I love you, I won't leave you.* He nudged his knee between hers; she stroked his muscular back, his thighs; she held his penis, which was warm, and soft; their faces were damp with perspiration. Mitch was sobbing quietly, and Joan held him as by quick degrees sleep overtook him; his limbs began to twitch; several times he kicked, as if he were tripping; but she held him tight, he didn't fall. Icy rain continued to be blown against the window almost in a rhythm, a discernible rhythm. Joan recalled how when the biopsy had come back from the laboratory, this would have been more than a year ago, Elise had called her, *I'm calling you first, you're the first to know. Oh Joan!* Yet she could not remember what she'd said to Elise. She tried, but she was slipping down a steep incline. She fell into a heavy exhausted sleep like one at the bottom of a pit. Waking open-mouthed as a drowning fish, her throat parched, at two a.m., not knowing where she was; her right arm aching and numbed from the weight of a man close beside her, his limbs entwined with hers; too exhausted to move from the bed except to detach herself carefully from the heavy perspiring man who slept beside her, breathing in harsh, arhythmic swaths of air; she knew this man was Elise's husband, yet she seemed not to recall his name, nor could she recall why she was with him, the two of them naked; though understanding *This is a man I once loved.* Yet simultaneously she was sitting in warm sunshine, and her young husband was bringing her a baby snugly wrapped in a sky-blue blanket, to set in her lap; they were outdoors, on a flagstone terrace; the sight of her young husband's smiling face, the tenderness of his gesture—she thought her heart would break; yet she couldn't remember which of her children this baby was, and really she couldn't see her husband's face. For it might have been Elise's husband who brought her the baby. It might have been Elise herself, for as girls they'd talked about babies, having babies, would you be brave enough to have a baby, I don't think I would be, I'm afraid, yes, but—if you were in love? Maybe that makes a difference?

Joan woke for a second time at 5:38 a.m. And the light in the bedroom still burning. Her head was throbbing violently from the red wine, her throat so dry she could scarcely swallow. She was sweaty, exhausted. Yet what relief—that it was morning; at last, it was morning; and Elise's husband still sleep beside her, rolled onto his back now, in a deep stuporous sleep, mouth slack, snoring. Joan slipped from the bed and drew the comforter up around his shoulders, gathered her fallen clothing and switched off the bedside lamp and went downstairs to quickly dress, and call a taxi to take her to the hotel; and when at 6:15 a.m. the taxi's headlights turned ghostly and silent into the driveway, out of a pale, predawn twilight thick with mist, Joan quietly left the darkened and locked house, left the sleeping man—what relief! what happiness! They'd gotten through the night. This was their achievement, Mitch's and hers, and they'd done it together— they'd gotten through the night. And never would they need to speak of it, even to each other. They'd gotten through the night.

Permanent

Betty doesn't know how much longer she can stall Mrs. Beatrice. For more than a month, the poor thing has tried to schedule an appointment. She phones and chats as if nothing is the matter, as if she hasn't a care in the world, and Betty hopes that just this once she won't ask, but she always does. And then Betty has to tell Mrs. Beatrice how sorry she is, but right now she simply doesn't have the time.

"I don't know where it goes," Betty says. "Time, I mean."

"I don't, either," Mrs. Beatrice says.

"Oh," says Betty. "Oh, I'm so sorry."

"Don't be. If you don't have the time, you don't have the time."

"Well, that's true."

"I'll just call back next week. How's that? Maybe you can squeeze me in somewhere. Would that be all right?"

"Of course, of course," says Betty. She says, "Call back next week," but Betty hopes she won't. The truth is, Betty has too much time. The house is empty. Her son is in college out west, and her daughter is backpacking with a gentleman across Italy or Ireland, Betty can never remember which for sure. When her husband offers to take early retirement so they can go traveling, Betty just worries more. Too often she's heard of men who stop working, can't adjust, and die. She imagines being stranded at the Grand Canyon or Disney World with a corpse, and then she has to ask herself, Who needs to see new places?

"You're lucky," her husband says, "to have so much time." They are lying in bed. He is hugging her from behind, while Betty stares out the window. When she doesn't answer, he says, "This is what you've worked for."

"I guess," she says.

"You always said you wouldn't mind if a few of your ladies went to a beauty shop instead."

"No, you're right."

"And now you say you wouldn't mind if more of them came here."

"No, I know."

He laughs in the dark. He kisses her hand. He brushes the hair back off her forehead and rubs her skin with a thumb until the furrows of worry fade. He says, "I don't know why I married you," and then she laughs, too.

But even after he's long asleep, Betty lies awake. The last time she saw Mrs. Beatrice must have been a year ago. She had a head of healthy hair then, shiny and obedient, hair that made Betty's job easy, hair that couldn't help but look pretty. What she has now is anybody's guess. In the darkness of her house, with her husband breathing against her back, Betty imagines reaching into the tangle on Mrs. Beatrice's head and coming away with a clump. She's heard about the treatments. She knows what they do. There are people, she thinks, there must be people whose job this is.

Betty squirms closer to her husband. Outside the bedroom window are the stars she's begun to watch. She can't see the heavens change from night to night, but now she knows they do. She's noticed the difference from week to week, and she can't believe how much they've moved since last month, when she first found herself staring out the window at night instead of sleeping. Betty flushes hot with confusion. She never knew the heavens change. She shuts her eyes and forces herself to keep them shut, and she tells herself that in the morning she will call Mrs. Beatrice and schedule the appointment. Then she backs up until her husband's chest hairs brush against her skin, and they bristle, but the rhythm of his breath soothes her, and soon they breathe as one.

But Betty doesn't call. If it were anyone but Mrs. Beatrice, she would welcome the appointment. More and more, Betty finds herself filling the days between customers in front of the mirror in the basement, testing a new style on herself, or a change in shade. Her favorite time is under the dryer. The roar makes her deaf, the dome makes her blind, the heat makes her numb. She imagines herself inside a cocoon. She might emerge as anything, she thinks, or maybe she won't emerge at all. But recently she's been thinking instead about Mrs. Beatrice. She thinks how she could be using this time on Mrs. Beatrice's appointment, and then the ammonia in the solution sickens her and she has to raise the dome before she suffocates. She sits in front of the mirror then, working her hair over, pulling it and pricking it and jabbing it and teasing it until it's back the way it was, until it's back to Betty.

She thinks about quitting. It used to be she had so many customers she didn't have time to think. She could spend five mornings a week, most of Saturday, and any number of evenings on her ladies, abandoning the dishes in the sink or the dust rag in the bedroom at the sound of the doorbell. The new beauty shop in the neighborhood is only part of the problem. Some of her ladies have taken their business there, and others have moved, but most have simply grown less attentive to their appearance over the years, saving their visits to Betty for special occasions, a daughter's wedding or a son's graduation or, maybe, the morning they wake up and look in the mirror and realize how long it's been since they treated themselves to a permanent. Still, Betty can't bring herself to retire. She knows her ladies depend on her. She knows they need her, even the ones who stray to the beauty salon but return to Betty without apology or explanation. No stranger in some five-chair beauty salon could ever make the ladies pretty the way Betty in her basement can make them pretty because Betty knows their hair: the exact mixture of tint to keep this one looking five years younger, the gray on that one nobody else ever sees, the little curl on the forehead that makes Mr. Beatrice hunger for his wife.

And she knows more than hair. There is something about being ugly that brings out the sadness in people, and Betty has seen them at their ugliest. She has seen them, each of her ladies, with conditioner caking in wrinkles, with sheep placenta streaking the makeup on their eyes and cheeks, with pink plastic rods sticking straight away from pink scalps. At precisely these moments, Betty always swivels the chair, guiding her ladies away from the mirror. But still they talk. And when they talk, they are beyond Betty's grasp, past the point where any amount of scalp massage or tint magic will help. Betty works her fingers as fast as she can. Her ears fill with their hopes and sins. The blood inside her head pounds so hard she barely hears the rumors of adultery, the confessions of coveting a neighbor's house or husband, the fantasies of health and happiness for their own husbands, their children, themselves, each other, Betty. She closes her eyes to steady herself.

But she must open her eyes to keep her fingers working, and so she does, and so they do, until they're done. And when she has restored the ladies, when she has returned to them their beauty, she tells them to close their eyes. Then she swivels the chair back toward the mirror. In that moment, with their eyes shut, their faces free of makeup, their hair styled to perfection, their mouths and maybe their minds closed against all their ills—in that moment Betty always wonders whether they'd be better off this way forever. Then they open their eyes, and they are, again, themselves. Betty turns her back and replaces the caps on the bottles and dips the brushes into the disinfectant, so that her ladies might inspect themselves in private. But Betty looks, too. She wants to marvel with them at their resurrection. Their eyes uncloud. The color rises in their faces. Smiles crease their cheeks as they realize that they need never worry as long as they can call Betty. But then, their smiles waver.

"What I said," they say, searching for Betty's eyes in the mirror, "just now, what I was saying—"

"Pretty is as pretty does," Betty says. Besides, she adds to herself, it's only hair, and what is hair, anyway, except tissue that's dead?

When she's made her way back upstairs, Betty is always grateful that she's not one of the ladies.

What finally prompts her to schedule an appointment with Mrs. Beatrice is when several weeks pass without hearing from her. Betty thinks about consulting with a customer to make sure Mrs. Beatrice hasn't taken a turn, but when she opens her book of appointments, she sees she has none. Nothing. Nobody. This happens, and then it always passes, the calls coming in, the familiar names materializing on this page or that, the days and weeks beginning to assume a life of their own. Still, for now, her book is blank. Quickly, before she has a chance to change her mind, Betty phones Mrs. Beatrice to say she's got good news, she can squeeze her in that evening. Then Betty goes alone to the basement.

Sitting in the chair before the mirror, she sees no reason why she shouldn't keep the appointment as brief as possible. She sets out the exact number and sizes of curling rods. She selects the brushes. She checks the bottles of solution and neutralizer. When she's done, she stares at the digital clock on the wall. Its numbers fade and focus with an electronic flutter that Betty's never noticed before. She goes back to the brushes. She picks out some stray strands of hair and shakes them from her fingertips into the garbage pail. Watching the fuzz disappear into the darkness of the bag, it occurs to her that whatever is inside Mrs. Beatrice now, eating her alive, was probably there a year ago, during her last permanent.

Betty goes upstairs to the living room and starts to strip the plastic coverings from the furniture. Her husband lowers his road map and watches for a while. Finally he says, "Company?"

"I have a customer."

She squashes the sofa cover against her stomach.

"It's Mrs. Beatrice," she says.

"Oh."

He stands up and fumbles with the road map until it's folded. He sets it on the end table with the other maps and the tourist brochures that have been arriving in the mail lately from all over the country. Then he removes the plastic from his chair.

"How is she handling things these days?" he says, following Betty into the bedroom. Elbow to elbow, they stand in the closet, stacking the packages of plastic on a shelf. "How's she doing? How is she looking?"

"I don't know. But the least we can do is make her feel at home."

Her husband stays in the bedroom to put on a fresh shirt, and a tie.

Mrs. Beatrice arrives by car, even though she lives in the next block. Her husband waits for her to make it inside the front door before he drives away.

"I told him to pick me up in two hours," Mrs. Beatrice says.

"There's no rush," says Betty. "You should have told him to come on in."

"Why?"

"Well," says Betty, "coffee. And cake."

They join Betty's husband in the living room. They sit on the furniture, still good as new.

"It's funny," says Mrs. Beatrice, "but I don't think I've ever seen your living room before. It's very nice. Did you redecorate?"

"Oh," says Betty, "these old things."

Mrs. Beatrice looks fine in this light. She's smaller than Betty remembers her, in the face and in the waist. And her clothes hang loose. But she's always been on the delicate side, and other than that, everything is just fine. Betty wonders what the worry was.

"I'm so glad you could fit me into your schedule," Mrs. Beatrice says.

Betty's husband has been sitting with his hands between his knees, staring at his fingers. Now he looks up at his wife.

Betty says to him, "You told a funny joke yesterday. Why don't you tell it for Mrs. Beatrice?"

Her husband says, "I don't remember making any jokes yesterday," and he goes back to studying his hands.

After a moment, Mrs. Beatrice says, "Oh, I see you're going away."

Betty has to stare at her a moment before realizing that she's referring to the maps and brochures on the end table. Betty turns to her husband, who is himself looking at the pile of literature as if he's never seen it before.

Betty says, "We're thinking about it. It should be nice. It's what we've worked for, don't you think?" She keeps staring at her husband, but he's gone back to examining his hands. "Would anybody care for some coffee?" she says to Mrs. Beatrice.

"Maybe I didn't make myself clear on the phone," says Mrs. Beatrice. "I've been getting more forgetful lately. I should have said that I wanted to make an appointment for my hair."

"Well, yes," says Betty. "Of course. So we'll skip the coffee, then. We can go right downstairs."

Once they're alone in the basement, Mrs. Beatrice suddenly says, "Betty, do I make you nervous?"

"No, no, of course not, no." Betty slips into her pink smock. She pulls the belt tight, and the hem balloons away from her waist, like a little girl's dress. She slaps at her sides to make them behave.

"Because if I do," Mrs. Beatrice says, "that's all right, I don't mind, I can go to a beauty shop instead."

"Oh, no, please sit down." Betty stations herself next to the chair by the sink. "Please."

"It's just that you do know my hair so well."

"Of course I do," says Betty. "I understand. Please. You're looking just lovely. Really you are. How are you?"

Mrs. Beatrice winces as she lowers herself into the chair, and she winces again when she leans her head back. She cranes her neck all the way back, so that her head lolls over the basin, but her hair just barely clears the collar on her smock. The hair is shorter than Betty remembers. That would be the treatment, she tells herself. Or, maybe, the new beauty salon.

"Now you did say a permanent," Betty starts, then catches herself. She's never noticed before what a silly word it is, for something that's not. It should be called something else, like temporary.

"Betty, would you mind if maybe I didn't talk too much? Sometimes it's difficult for me. The doctors say I should save my strength."

"Of course, of course." Betty takes the hose from the bottom of the basin and runs water over the hair. It is mostly gray now. She reaches for it. She takes her hand back. She has jerked her hand back, but Mrs. Beatrice doesn't notice. Her eyes are closed. Betty tries again to touch the hair. Her fingers are tingling, her skin is rippling all over, even her own scalp is prickling. In a while, she tells herself, this won't happen. In a while she'll be able to touch Mrs. Beatrice and it won't bother her a bit. If she had to do this all the time, it would be just a job.

She touches the hair. It is thin. It is brittle. That would be the treatment, too. In some places, Betty sees patches of scalp. It, too, is gray. Much of her skin is gray. Up close, Betty sees where skin sags, below the ears, at the neck, under the eyes. Betty closes her own eyes to catch her breath.

"Just because I don't talk doesn't mean you can't," says Mrs. Beatrice.

"Oh. Well, of course. What should I say?"

"I don't know." Mrs. Beatrice laughs. "I don't care. You don't have to talk, Betty."

"No, I'll talk. It's just that I don't, usually. Usually I just listen. But I can talk. Sure."

"So tell me. You sound so busy lately. That's good, isn't it?"

"Oh, yes," says Betty. "It makes the time pass." She asks Mrs.

Beatrice to sit up so that she can set the rods. "It's not just that it makes the time pass, of course. I mean, nobody really wants time to pass. But you know how it is. You go and go, and you never seem to be able to do half the things you want to do, and you keep saying you can't wait for the day you can actually have a moment to catch your breath. And then one day, you wake up, and you've got all the time in the world. Your children are raised." Betty has set the first curl before she knows it, then moved on to the next. "They're gone. Then what? They're off at school, or falling in love in Italy or somewhere. They have their own lives ahead of them, which is fine and all, but where does that leave us? Oh, we can travel. We talk about traveling. We talk about taking an early retirement and going off I don't even know where. Just off, I suppose. It doesn't matter, does it? I mean, I've seen pictures of the Grand Canyon, I don't need to go there to know I've never been there. One place is just like the next, only the rocks are piled different. My mother used to say that, and she should know, she was from the old country. I remember the teacher telling us once in school about how people used to travel by the stars, and that always made sense to me until now, because do you know what I've noticed lately? Lately, I don't know why, but lately I've noticed the sky at night. When I'm in bed. When I'm in bed and I can't sleep. I look out the window sometimes, and I've noticed that the stars move. Oh, not just when the earth turns, I don't mean that. I mean from night to night, the same time, you look at it, and you'll see, the stars won't be in quite the same place. I never knew that before. Does everybody know that? I always thought they stayed still up there. Otherwise how could people travel by them? It just doesn't add up to me. Do you know anything about this? What do you think?"

She looks down. Somehow she has set all the curls. She pulls her hands away, to herself, and turns them over and back and over again.

"Oh," Betty says, "don't pay any attention to me."

"Well, I really shouldn't talk much. But I do know I've always wanted to see the Grand Canyon."

Without another word, Betty squirts solution all over Mrs. Beatrice's hair, places a cap over her head, and sets her under the dryer. Almost at once Mrs. Beatrice is dozing.

147

It is then that Betty sees the toll the evening is taking on Mrs. Beatrice. Her head is puny inside the dome. Her face is white, her sockets shadows. The smock swallows everything else. All that shows from beneath it are her arms and legs, four sticks with skin.

Betty retreats up the stairs. She finds her husband at the kitchen table, hunched over a road map. He's tracing a line across it with a red marker. Over his shoulder she sees hundreds of little circles that must be cities, a thousand pinpoints, and the thick red line that connects the dots. She has no idea what state this might be. Betty goes into the bedroom, sits on their bed, and wonders why she had to go and tell Mrs. Beatrice that she has trouble getting to sleep.

"What's happening?" her husband says. He's standing in the bedroom doorway. He starts to reach for the light switch on the wall.

"Don't." He drops his hand to his side. "Nothing's happening."

"Downstairs?"

"She's there." Betty is silent for a moment. Her husband waits. A breeze from the open window at her back sends a shudder along her spine. "She's frail. You could have said something to her. She's very frail. It's so terrible, really. I can see her get tired right before my eyes. You could have acted like she was there."

"It gives me the creeps," he says, "for you."

"Someone has to do it." She shrugs. "It's the least I could do for her."

The shadow in the doorway nods its head.

"You going to be late?" he says.

She springs off the bed and rubs her arms up and down, hugging herself. "Don't worry," and she brushes past her husband, "if you don't want to see her leave, just hide in the bedroom."

In the basement, Betty watches Mrs. Beatrice until she wakens.

"I must have dozed," Mrs. Beatrice says. She stretches the hem of the smock to cover herself. "Have you been watching me?"

"No," says Betty, pointing a finger toward the ceiling, "no." She is trying to make sense above the drone of the dryer. Mrs. Beatrice nods, nods, nearly drops off. Betty considers letting her sleep several more minutes. Maybe she needs it, she tells herself. Maybe I need it. But she shuts off the dryer and helps Mrs. Beatrice to her feet. Soon, Betty reminds herself, this evening will be over.

She guides Mrs. Beatrice by the elbow to the sink, where she rinses her hair, then to the mirror. Mrs. Beatrice has to hold on to the back of the chair as she eases herself down to the hard cushion. Once she's settled herself, Betty swivels the chair slightly, and Mrs. Beatrice gazes away from the mirror.

Mrs. Beatrice, really, has hardly enough hair for Betty to work with. The layer of skin that separates her skull from the rest of the world is so thin in spots that Betty can see the white right through it. She can count the ridges. She can feel bone.

"This has been a difficult evening for you," Mrs. Beatrice says.

"You don't have to talk."

"I want to talk."

"Don't talk." You are ugly now, Betty thinks, but soon you will be pretty. "I mean, shouldn't you be saving your strength?"

"I napped. Really, I want to talk. I want to tell you how much this evening has meant to me. You don't know what it's like. All the time, people not looking at you."

Betty takes a rod in her hand and gently unfurls it. She rolls it away from Mrs. Beatrice's scalp. This first curl—this creation of beauty that Betty has fashioned with her own fingers from a tangle of dead tissues—unravels, springs once, and stays. Betty stifles a sigh and moves on to the next rod.

"All the time," Mrs. Beatrice continues, "people not talking to you. I know what the experts say, that it's not me people are afraid of. It's themselves. I know all that. But it doesn't do you any good to know it when every time you step out of the house, you're treated like something that's not human. It's not the pain. I can live with the pain. And it's not death. I can live with that, too. I've made my peace. What it is, is the people. They don't mean to hurt. But they do. In a million ways. It's them. They're the ones who can't live with the pain. They're the ones who haven't made their peace. They're the ones who make my life a hell."

"I'm sorry." Betty has stopped unrolling the rods. She is staring into a tiny bald spot. "I'm so sorry."

"Why should you be sorry?" ·

"For tonight."

"Don't be silly. You've been wonderful."

"You don't know."

"Yes I do. I do know. That's what I wanted to say. I know how difficult this must be for you, and you've been wonderful. You fit me into your schedule."

Betty doesn't know what to say. She says, "Close your eyes."

But she sees in the mirror that Mrs. Beatrice already has them closed. In silence, Betty sets to work. She unravels the last few rods, and when she gets to the final curl, Betty lowers it over the forehead, just the way Mrs. Beatrice would want to be remembered by her husband. Then Betty swivels Mrs. Beatrice toward the mirror. Betty steadies the chair, removes the smock, and waits.

Slowly Mrs. Beatrice opens her eyes. If they show anything, Betty can't see it. They are filmy. Betty figures that Mrs. Beatrice is simply studying her work, so Betty does the same.

She has done, she supposes, the best job she could. But for what? Tomorrow, next week, a year from now, what will it matter? Whatever it is that Mrs. Beatrice is, under the hair that's gray and thin, inside this skin that's already leaving her, will be gone. Betty has done the best job she could, and she has done nothing.

"You remembered," Mrs. Beatrice finally says. She is caressing the curl over her forehead. "You remembered."

Betty waits for Mrs. Beatrice to say something else, or to struggle from the chair, but Mrs. Beatrice doesn't move. She just sits there, staring into the mirror. When Betty looks up at the mirror, into Mrs. Beatrice's eyes, they are meeting her own.

"Do you think I'm pretty?" Mrs. Beatrice says.

Pretty, Betty wants to tell her, pretty? Pretty isn't important. Pretty doesn't matter. Pretty doesn't count.

"Pretty is as pretty does," Betty finally says, but she is too late. Mrs. Beatrice has turned away. The color has left her cheeks.

"Thank you," she says, anyway, glancing up at the digital clock. "My husband should be here any minute now. Thank you for the permanent, Betty. Thank you for your time."

Betty stays awhile in the basement, alone, combing strands of gray hair from the brushes she's used tonight. Then she dips the brushes into the disinfectant. Then she dips the comb in the disinfectant. Then she dips the rods. When she's done, she collects the hair and the brushes and the comb and the rods inside the garbage pail and twists the seal on the bag and carries it outside to the alley and dumps it all in a trash can.

In the backyard, she pauses and watches as the light in the bedroom window winks out. When she goes inside, she knows the house will be dark and empty, and she knows she will not be able to sleep. She turns in the direction that the bedroom window faces and searches until she finds her section of the heavens. She wonders if her son or daughter can see those same stars from where they are. She wonders if her children ever look at the night sky and ask the same question about her. She wonders if Mrs. Beatrice, one block away, is staring at this same square of stars. Then she goes inside.

Still in her smock, Betty climbs into bed and says, "She told me she really doesn't mind the pain."

"I tried," her husband says.

"She told me she's made her peace."

"I did my best."

The lights are out. The house is empty. The only surprise is a crinkle from the closet, where the plastic covers are slowly unfolding.

"I know," she says. "It's not you." Her husband pulls her close. "She told me I'm wonderful."

How does she do it? Betty can't believe what Mrs. Beatrice told her is true. Surely she has her moments of doubt. Surely she's not as peaceful as she seems. She must be lying awake now, Betty thinks. She must be staring out her bedroom window, maybe not at these same stars, but at her own section of the heavens. Betty imagines Mrs. Beatrice straining for sleep, aching for it, actually hurting with the need, in the shoulders and the neck and the eyes, and the more she strains the more she can't sleep. But then she realizes that Mrs. Beatrice must already be asleep. No matter how worried she is, she must be even more exhausted. But how can she sleep? But how can she not sleep? And why does she waken? How does Mrs. Beatrice do it?

Betty's husband is whispering something into the back of her neck. He's saying that Mrs. Beatrice is right, that Betty really is wonderful, but she doesn't answer. Betty is saving her strength.

The Tent in the Wind

On his way home from the Holland Park Underground Station, James Briggs had a curious sense of event in the windless, autumn evening. The house in which he lived with his wife and their one-and-a-half-year-old son was in a square, and in the garden of the square a fire was burning, the high, cracking flames illuminating the smoke as it rose up among the dark bushes and casting the shadows of these bushes through a faint mist and against the flickering housefronts. The still, misty air was filled with the scent of burning leaves. Before he went into the house, James Briggs stood on the pavement for a while and looked at the fire burning in the garden.

He found his wife, Diane, in the kitchen of their flat watching the baby in the highchair eat, and he kissed her and kissed the top of his son's head. He retained that sense of event, and it seemed to him that the by now familiar scene of arriving home was somehow curious. He felt, a little, that he was playing a part in the event, and he was aware of playing the part. The baby picked up food from his bowl, put it in his mouth, chewed, took the mess out, looked at it, and put it back into his mouth and swallowed.

"I'll watch him," James said to Diane.

Smiling in the quiet way she always did, even at a funny joke, she went out, and after James had wiped the baby's hands and face and lifted him up from the highchair to bounce him in his arms so he laughed, Diane returned, her hair brushed and her blond face delicately touched with makeup.

"You'll give him hiccups," she said.

"Let me bathe him and put him to bed," James said.

Bathing the baby, getting him ready for bed, sitting by him in his cot while he read him a story about a blue balloon, James thought, why did the sense of event he had make him feel he was holding something down with ropes and stakes that was about to fly apart?

At supper, Diane said, "Joanna rang today."

Joanna was James's ex-wife. He had no idea what Diane's reactions to her ringing was, because Diane, as if Joanna were a person about whom she had no right to have any thoughts or feelings, never expressed any about Joanna.

"How did she sound?" James asked.

"Confused."

James put a hand to his forehead.

"She didn't know what time it was, and said she thought you'd be home. It was around noon. She did apologize."

"I had a feeling she would ring."

"I'm sorry I had to tell you," Diane said and smiled a little. "I should have waited."

"But I did already know," James said.

Joanna was American. After their divorce, she had not moved back to New York from London, but had stayed on in a service flat in Mayfair which he had helped her move into, but where James never went to visit her.

All evening, he expected her to ring.

In the deep night the telephone rang, and Diane answered it, as she slept on that side of the bed. She said the call was for him. He didn't turn on a light to reach for the receiver, because he knew where her hand was in the dark. He heard "Hello," and an echo, "Hello." When James recognized the voice of Joanna's mother in New York asking, "Is that James there?" he answered, "Yes," and the answer sounded as though it had come before the question.

"I'm sorry, I'm so sorry," Joanna's mother said. "I don't know what time it is there."

James waited.

"James?"

"Yes, Mrs. Clermont."

"I'm so sorry. I know how difficult Joanna is. I know you did everything that you could do. I've tried, too, I've done everything I could do, but I know she can't be helped, as she knows, she knows she can't be helped. She telephoned to say goodbye, and I'm telephoning you—"

James wasn't listening to the voice, he was listening to the echo.

Diane switched on the lamp by the telephone on the bedside table after she hung up the receiver. James couldn't recall Joanna's telephone number, and he got out of bed for it. Diane lay with her eyes shut and the sheet drawn up to her chin. James stood by the bed and dialed and listened to the telephone on the other end of the line ring a long time. He was about to hang up and dress and rush out just when it was lifted and a voice said "Yes" without inflection.

"I'm coming over now," James said.

"No."

"I'm coming over, and you'd better open the door, or I'll go get the police and come back with them."

He didn't have enough cash for a taxi, and he thought he shouldn't ask Diane, but then he thought, of course he would ask her. "You've got to lend me ten pounds," he said. Without opening her eyes, she drew out an arm from under the sheet and pointed towards the bureau, where he found her small purse, from which he took the money.

He got a taxi outside the Holland Park Station. The dawn was level above the still-lit streetlamps, and there was no traffic.

He asked the driver to wait in the deserted Mayfair street. Through the glass doors, he saw into the illuminated foyer. The porter was not there, and the door was locked. There were rows of little metal buttons beside numbers on a metal plaque at the side of the entrance, but James couldn't recall the number of Joanna's flat. Then he thought he had forgotten the telephone number at home. He hadn't. It was in his wallet with the ten pounds. Back in the taxi, he asked the driver to find a telephone box. As the driver went round the streets, James looked from right to left, thinking, I should have told her to light all the lights and walk about and not lie down or even sit. Before the taxi came to a stop, James opened the door when he saw a telephone box on a corner under a streetlamp. Now, he didn't have ten pence. His disorganization angered him: the disorganization of the world angered him. The taxi driver gave him ten pence. He dialed the number by looking carefully at each numeral in turn, and even then he thought he made mistakes; once, his finger slipped, and he didn't know if he formed the number. Sweat broke out all over him as he waited for the ring to be answered. The air in the box smelled of cigarettes and urine. Outside, the driver was leaning against the taxi door. He was wearing a black, baggy jacket. James wondered if ten pounds would be enough. Sweat dripped down his back, his chest, under his arms. The telephone receiver was picked up.

"Give me the number of your flat," James said.

He heard breathing.

"Give me your flat number," James insisted.

"Fourteen," Joanna said.

"You'd better be ready to leave when I arrive."

"Please."

"At least put on shoes." He added, "Don't lie down. Keep walking about. And turn on all the lights." He didn't wait for her to speak, but hung up and thrust his body against the door of the box to get out.

"Back to the same place?" the driver asked.

Joanna let James into the foyer as soon as he buzzed. Upstairs, the door to the flat was ajar. Joanna was leaning against a wall. She had one shoe on, one held in her hand, and she was wearing a raincoat. James knelt and put on her shoe. He stood and, taking her by an arm, started to guide her, then stopped.

"Do you have the keys to the flat with you?" he asked.

She shook her head. In her bedroom, he found her purse. The keys were inside, and a sheaf of folded twenty-pound notes. He was not going to allow any more disorganization. He was not going to let the extravagance of the situation undo him; he was going to fix the situation down to the little facts. He guided Joanna out to the landing and double-locked the door, then put the key into his pocket. As they went down in the lift, he told her to button her raincoat against the morning air, which she did without fumbling. She did not appear vague, but totally withdrawn.

The driver knew which hospital to go to. In the taxi, Joanna sat up straight and looked ahead of her. James kept his eyes on her.

He wanted to fix what was happening onto the practicalities of dealing with it all, but, at the same time, he wanted to let it go, let what was happening billow out and, as if in a high wind, pull up the pegs of the practicalities and send the whole tent flying, allowing the acrobats, the clowns, the trainers, even the animals, the sudden freedom to do everything they'd always wanted, which was to give up the whole fucking circus, with the excuse of the wind, the exceptional wind.

When Joanna closed her eyes, he said to open them. She did.

The taxi stopped before the casualty entrance of the hospital.

James helped Joanna out, and the driver came out, too, to help, but simply looked at James walk Joanna past him. James thanked him and gave him the ten-pound note, which was almost twice as much as the fare, even with the tip. The driver turned away, but as James and Joanna got to the hospital door, he returned, put five pounds in James's jacket pocket, and, before leaving, said, "I'm glad I could help."

There were benches around the walls of the waiting room. James brought Joanna to one. Across the room was a couple, a man and woman, sitting silently. They looked middle-class and were middle-aged. The moment Joanna sat, the neon ceiling lights went out and the room filled with morning light. James went to look for a sister. He was not playing a part, he kept telling himself; he was only doing what was strictly necessary, and nothing more. He made his voice expressionless when he told a sister his close friend had tried to kill herself. The sister, who seemed very tired, came with him to Joanna. She sat beside Joanna and in a notepad wrote down her name and address and age and asked her what she'd taken, which Joanna told her with long pauses, but with precision: sleeping pills, tranquilizers, antidepressants, aspirins. The sister stood and said to Joanna, "Can you follow me on your own?" and Joanna got up, un-buttoned her raincoat, took it off, but held it by one hand as she followed the sister, dragging the coat along the floor. Before she went behind a hospital screen, the sister turned back and asked James please to wait. He watched Joanna's raincoat being pulled around the bottom of the screen.

On a bench, James looked at the couple across from him, turned away from one another.

The neon lights came on again, then, after a flickering moment, went off again.

Whatever part he was playing, James knew it was a small one, and it would make no difference to anyone if he gave it up.

He looked at the woman's shoes, the man's haircut, and what he saw—those shoes, that haircut—filled him with despair.

The couple stood when a blond young woman came from behind the hospital screen. She walked unsteadily towards, surely, her father and mother, one hand out to touch the wall. Her face was white. She looked at the floor. A sister was behind her.

Her father said, "Well, you're going to live, I see."

The girl tried to smile.

A sister came to James and asked him if he'd follow her behind the screen into a bare room where Joanna was sitting on a trolley, one of the straps of her nightgown fallen off a shoulder and her raincoat across her knees. Under her wild hair, her face was pale and stark.

"Will you be able to stay with her awhile?" the sister asked James.

He nodded.

The sister asked Joanna to lie on the trolley, and she wheeled her out of the room. James walked alongside. They went down dim corridors, up in a lift, and along more corridors, and met no one. Then they went through metal double doors, which James held open, and through a ward, where all the beds were behind white curtains. Joanna lay with her eyes open. On the bottom shelf of the trolley was an oxygen tank; its tube trailed on the floor. James wondered if he should offer to push the trolley. He wanted to do something. He held the doors open to another ward for the sister to push the trolley through. This ward was filled with old women in narrow beds, most of them asleep, a few sitting up. They were toothless, and their thin hair was loose about their skulls.

Pity twisted James's throat, and he just managed to say, "Joanna, close your eyes," then his throat convulsed. She closed her eyes, and her eyelids twitched.

In the next ward, James stood back while the sister helped Joanna stagger from the trolley onto a bed, about which the sister drew the curtains. In the other beds, women lay flat with their eyes closed.

A young doctor came into the ward and went behind the curtain. When he came out, he said to James, "She'll have to stay a few days." The doctor smelled of body odor.

The sister opened the curtain, and James went to Joanna, who, in a white hospital gown, was sitting, her back straight. She looked at James as though he was going to do something to her. He sat sideways on the very edge of the bed. Her body jumped with a sudden spasm. She pulled the thumb of one hand with her other hand, and pulled, in turn, each finger, trying, it seemed, to pull them off. She changed her hand and seemed to try to pull the thumb and the fingers off the other. Again, her body jumped. She tried to pull her hand off, her arm. Then she tried to pull her breasts from her body.

James did not know what he could do for her. He prayed for a great wind to come and release her.

My Best Friend

I met my best pal, Phil, about ten years ago through our mutual
wife. I was a young actor on the rise then, a couple of years out
of Julliard, I'd done two seasons of *Biloxi Blues* (Broadway and a
touring company) and although I was raised as a nice Jewish boy,
I kept getting cast as a grunt in a series of Oliver Stone flicks
because of my Irish tough-guy mug—courtesy of a converted
Catholic mother. So the phone was ringing, and the lunches were
getting paid for, and the money was pouring in. I mean, I was
feeling pretty good about myself back in those days. For a brief
while, anyway, I was golden.

At the time, I figured those Vietnam movies were going to be
my big break, or actually a series of little ones, running like frac-
tures across a brittle tibia, chipping away at the bone of the business until I was *in;* but something happened to change all that
during my last leg of boot camp in a remote Thai jungle. Oliver
had us all go through two weeks of basic training with his own
imported drill sergeant; he'd picked the guy up during his much
chronicled tour in the Marines. The theory behind all this effort
was *verisimilitude,* but it felt more like a frat initiation; he wanted
his pretty-boy actors to suffer as much as he had. Me, I went
through that whole routine twice—twice a studio flew me first-
class to Asia in a skybed—which back then I thought was pretty
cool, but now I see the entire episode as a fulcrum in my life, and
if I had my choice of a chapter to reenact from Oliver's nutty
autobiography, I'd prefer some dumb love story taking place at
Yale.

See, I sailed though basic training on the first picture like a real
Zen warrior—Oliver called me "Iron Man," and the rest of the
guys looked on me with awe—but what always happens when a
guy dares to display a little confidence? Punishment. I got dysen-
tery: chills, fever, hallucinations, the whole nine yards. And then
when *that* was over, I got paranoid. The terrain in the jungle was
leafy and thick, and the vine-covered trees were full of screaming

monkeys. I'd taken to constantly looking over my shoulder when I walked back and forth from the trailers to the latrine and brushing the ground before me with a stick. I think I was hunting for land mines.

By the time rehearsals were over and we were into the shoot, I was ten pounds lighter and smoking so much Thai-stick I really began to believe the set and script were real. I mean I *really* did. I believed that I was a bonafide member of Charlie Company. I guess that was Oliver's aim. At night, back in the barracks, I had nightmare after nightmare of battle. Bombs blowing up, torched thatched huts, massacres of innocent villagers, skinny dogs. All that Nam via Hollywood stuff. Post-traumatic stress by proxy, the doctor on the set had called it. So much for method acting. But if I do say so myself, it made for one of hell of a great performance.

Nevertheless, when I finally got home to New York, all I wanted was a musical here in the city, or a romantic comedy shot on the safety of a lot in Southern California. Jeannie, my best pal Phil's ex and my current, then a casting agent, picked me up at a casting call. She says I had this great romantic, beat-up look back then, she says I looked like I needed someone to save me, but at the time I think she just wanted out of her marriage, and I was moderately successful, and if I may say so, a pretty sexy guy.

I'm Scott Kaminsky. I grew up as Scott Kamins, son of Dr. David Kamins, a preeminent OB-GYN on Park Avenue, New York City, New York, a child of the Upper East Side, but when I joined the Screen Actors Guild, there was another Scott Kamins, so I went back to my roots. Took the name of my grandfather, a Russian peasant, one of nine barefoot but scholarly children working a grain mill in a shtetl somewhere in the hard-bitten Latvian fields. Kaminsky. It had a nice European ring to it, and in the early eighties, I thought it leant me a certain air of attractive hunger, a provocative ethnic panache.

Jeannie was scouting for an NBC sitcom, looking for a cop. She called me back three times to read; I performed in a cold, empty studio stripped down to my skivvies. It was a locker-room sequence, broad and humiliating, and she strung me along shamelessly, Jeannie, so I was pretty pissed off, after a month of that tease, when my agent called to tell me I didn't get the part.

That is, I was pissed off enough (and intrigued enough) to take matters into my own hands. I marched myself down to Jeannie's office to give her a piece of my mind.

After I'd finished ranting and raving—an impassioned speech about the toll of warfare, Oliver, and the jungle, and how after all I'd been through for my country, I was entitled to a job—I still didn't get the work, but I certainly got the prize. Jeannie and I went out for beers at The White Horse Tavern, and then I wound up back at her brownstone apartment.

Upstairs, we mixed our liquors as quickly as we could in order to get the particulars on the table and out of the way as soon as possible. Jeannie was at the tail end of a marriage (Phil!) and on her way to Southern California, where she wanted to make it big. She said, "I have impeccable taste." Then she assessed me, professionally speaking, with a practiced eye. She said, "You're a wreck, a sexy wreck, which I think should become increasingly marketable, as soon as you grow out of that dopey GI Joe phase. In fact," she went on, "if my instincts are right—and they're always right—you just *might* become a star."

It's probably no surprise to you that I didn't.

Jeannie was pretentious and overblown and overly dramatic back then—now she's pretentious and overblown and wound tight—and I liked it, especially the star business, I liked hearing her go on and on about me. But it would be wrong to pretend I actually *listened*, I didn't listen to anything Jeannie said that night, including the married part, I just liked to watch her pace and strut and wiggle around her tiny apartment while I built up the nerve to take her to bed.

I may have only been twenty-eight, but that first night spent with Jeannie harkened back to a wilder, mythical time, it made me nostalgic for the teenaged sex I never had—high school girls were loathe to do anything with the son of an OB-GYN, and much of my senior class was made up of my father's patients. By two a.m. Jeannie had me coming and going in all sorts of directions, and by morning I was so slippery and wet that when she went to hug me, I swear I started to slide. After a shower in the bathroom down the hall, we dressed, me in my same khakis and white shirt, Jeannie in a polka-dotted mini and one of those fuzzy sweaters. And then we sat at her little scarred wooden table, and we drank our moldy old orange juice and ate our freezer-burned English muffins gazing into each other's eyes.

At around eight o'clock a.m., the key turned in the lock, and Phil walked in. Jeannie didn't even bat an eye. "Sweetheart," she said *to me* ("Sweetheart"!), "this is Phil, my husband."

We were fast friends, me and Phil. I mean, we hit it off that morning. I don't know what possessed me to stick around when he first came home, plaid shirt untucked, black jeans stained, biker boots and a soul patch, for God's sake, *and* a gold band encircling his left ring finger—maybe it was because I already knew that I wanted this girl—but I did stay.

"Hey, sweetheart," said Phil first to me with irony, and then to Jeannie in gentle, sweet defeat.

He was an embattled young novelist, coming home from a night shift as a proofreader at the law firm Sullivan & Cromwell. They had met in a poetry seminar five years earlier at Sarah Lawrence. "He wrote me love poems," said Jeannie, making a face, a hand over the phone receiver as she called the local deli to see if she could get them to deliver coffee and bagels—we'd given up on the English muffins—which she could. Jeannie could get anyone to deliver anything, except Phil. He was thirty-two years old, he'd gone back to college as an old guy after kicking around for ten years playing backup bass in a band and waiting tables. "I'm a loser," he said to me, looking for attention. "It's true," said Jeannie. "Ask him what he does all day. Go ahead," my love said cruelly, "ask him what it's like to be a bum."

I nodded in Phil's direction, and Phil confessed, as was his way. In those days he was a beaten man. After the law firm he would usually just strip down to his underwear and lie on the futon couch for a few hours trying to catch a snooze, while Jeannie went to work. Then in the afternoons he'd get up, make spaghetti, and watch *thirtysomething* reruns. Most of his day was spent, he said, actively *not* writing his book, not doing much of anything.

So we got to talking, me and Phil, because I liked *thirtysomething* and I liked to read a lot and, let's face it, I'd just poked his wife, so I owed him. We spent the rest of the day together stretched out on the same futon couch, now folded up, that Jeannie and I had spent the better part of the night rolling around on. By the time she came home for dinner, we had moved out to a local bar and back again, and when Jeannie came in the door, we were both already three sheets to the wind and into it—Phil was going to write a screenplay, a star vehicle for me—so we all ended up arguing plot points and story arcs and ordering Chinese take-out until Phil left for his nine o'clock shift and Jeannie and I unfolded the futon couch again.

It was only a matter of months of this before Jeannie moved Phil out and me in, only a matter of months after that that she got me to sport the last of my Oliver money on a diamond ring. Phil was my best man. We got married at Phil's mother's country cottage in Connecticut—she was, thank God, away that weekend, or even for us it would have been too weird. And after that, and a honeymoon in Paris (they had gone to Rome) Phil and I still spent most of our weekdays together, meeting for an afternoon movie after a morning audition, sitting in cafés discussing poetry over biscotti and bitter black coffees. He was a good man, Phil. He accepted his defeat easily. He hadn't deserved his wife, and so he'd lost her, period. Most of the time we shot the breeze, we drank or smoked a lot of pot, and waxed on and on about our dreams. I was still going to a lot of auditions back then, but I was coming up empty. It took about another three or four years before it became clear that I was permanently unemployed; that, my total collapse as an actor, coupled with Jeannie's first pregnancy, made our three-way marriage suddenly untenable. That's when Phil wrote the letter.

Scott, dear Scott,
You're my best friend and all that, but now you've gone and impregnated my wife. There's so much a man can stand. (Ha! Ha!) I've decided to borrow some money from my mother and head out to the beach. Start over, live by the sand and the sea and do what I was meant to do, be who I was meant to be. If I can manage to eke out one halfway respectable novel, even if it's not publishable, I'll figure my time on earth was well-spent. But for now, the two of you are probably better off without me—I mean maybe now you'll get a job. (Ha! Ha!)
Yours in friendship always,
Phil

He left the note hanging on the mirror above my dresser—he still had his old set of keys. Jeannie was glad to see him go. "That

goddamned good-for-nothing, he's infected you, you bastard."
Not that she didn't believe in me and my career—some nights
when she couldn't sleep, I'd catch her in the living room watching
my reel, trying to suss out what went wrong with me—but she
was getting hard-edged and bitter, my wife. Impending motherhood, being broke, two washouts as her husband, it was all too
much for her. She was a frustrated woman, and she showed it.
Little frown lines played around her eyes.

I did carpentry and urban gardening to avoid them.

Our baby was born in May, two weeks late. We named her
April, because that's what we'd been calling her for nine months
already and we were used to it. Two years later we had Ethan, her
little brother. At this point we had to have a larger apartment,
health benefits, and a baby-sitter. So I got a day job. That is, my
dad got one for me. I performed high-resolution sonograms at
the neonatal clinic at Mt. Sinai Hospital. All those tiny legs and
arms, the baby-bracelet of a spine. After the second kid, Jeannie
had gone half-time.

We had not heard from Phil since he left town, save for a post-
card or two from Mexico that waxed on rather awkwardly about
the cruelty of poverty and the beauty of the sunsets. Aside from
his rather pedestrian letter, these were the only examples I had
ever seen of his strained and awkward prose, which resulted in
some delicious schadenfreude—I went around the house quoting
"the blushing bruise of evening" and "the paper-thin quality of
money." One horrible winter evening, there was a drunken rambling phone call when he asked me for a loan, and then begged
Jeannie to come back to him. It did sting a bit to hear her say:
"Thanks for reminding me that I could be worse off than I am."
After that, shame must have taken hold, because Phil did not even
respond to Ethan's birth announcement, and we soon lost track
of him altogether, which by that time was fine with me. He had
angled for my wife. I didn't miss the guy. In fact, I started associ-
ating him with my downfall, a bad influence and all that, contagious lousy karma. I mean, before we'd started hanging out, I'd
been riding high.

Sort of.

I was at work one day, reading *People* magazine. Tom Cruise,
who I'd worked with on *Born on the Fourth of July*, was on the

cover. Johnny Depp and Charlie Sheen (my bunkmates in *Platoon*) were featured on the inside. A girl who had given me a blowjob in a closet at a party in 1985 had just gotten her very own prime-time soap. It was a slow day at the hospital. We'd done four amnios that morning and then nothing. Nothing but coffee from the machine and torn-up, booger-stained magazines. I flipped through the pages with a pencil. Decided to call my agent and was put on hold. I did this from time to time, called in in desperation. I held the line and read the story about the actress, Dallas Merchant. She was starring in this new show—the world was fashion magazines and it was shooting out on the West Coast. She'd been found at a giant casting call by the show's producer and creator, Felipe Elbazz, who she was now engaged to.

Phil. Our Phil! Jeannie's and my mutual husband.

There was an accompanying photo of him, bearded now (all those guys are bearded—there's a direct correlation, I'm sure of it, between driving ambition and a weakness in chin), holding hands with Dallas. The caption said he had two other pilots in the can and three more series in development. The happy couple were rebuilding his house in Malibu that just last winter had been hit by a mudslide and fallen into the sea. "A mixed blessing," said *Felipe,* the producer and creator. "Now there's an excuse to buy all new art and all new furniture."

I wanted to watch him bleed.

And for the first time in my life, I understood the saying "jumped out of his skin," for I jumped out of mine. That is, I jumped out of my lab coat. Just jumped out of it, out of my seat, out of my job (for the afternoon). I told the big-haired receptionist in the lobby that I was coming down with something sniffly— the last thing all those pregnant women wanted was a technician with a cold—locked up the lab, and split. And then I walked home, all ninety-nine blocks, to our apartment on First Street and First Avenue. And with every middle-aged step I took, I hated myself a little more.

Nothing had turned out the way I'd planned. I had no career, no dignity, no money. My wife was getting pinched. My kids were virtually underprivileged—April said: "Look, Daddy, the country!" every time she saw a vacant lot. There I was, thirty-eight, practically forty, and I was not a homeowner or a car owner, I possessed no bonds nor stocks. And like many a loser before me, I'd retreated into the family business—spreading ladies' legs—that is, I was pretty much working for my father. Almost a decade had gone by, and I had accomplished almost nothing. What had I been doing with myself during that squandered, precious time?

When I finally arrived at our apartment, footsore and blistered and halfway out of my mind, Jeannie took one look at me and ran the bath. I'm not ashamed to say that after I stripped down and got naked, after she brought me a beer, I soaked in that hot water and cried my eyes out. Jeannie sat on the toilet waiting for the faucets to dry. She'd never seen me like this, but later on she said it hadn't frightened her. In fact, she said, even a nervous break-down at that moment felt like a ray of hope.

So when I finished crying, I leaned over and pulled the *People* magazine out of my pants pocket off the floor. I covered my eyes while my wife read the article sitting on the closed lid of our toi-let. Jeannie got up then, I heard her, I felt the breeze of her mov-ing body and the palpable release of tension that came in those days whenever she left a room. And then a moment or two later, Jeannie and all her accompanying anxiety came back inside again—you could sense it, rippling across the bathwater. She peeled my hands back with her hands, stuck the cordless phone into my fist.

"Call him," she said. "He owes us."

She said, "I don't care if you have to suck his dick."

And then she sat there and monitored my efforts as naked and shivering and pitiful, I tried to track Phil down. She sat there as I rang up *his* mother, *his* office, a string of *his* personal assistants; she sat there as my skin shriveled to the consistency of a prune. And I do believe she was having a rather good time of it, bearing witness, as I prostrated myself to the altar of her ex, for there was a hard, cool light enlivening her eyes and a nasty smile playing around her lips.

It had been years since I'd made her so happy.

Within three weeks I had quit neonate at Sinai and I was safely ensconced in the Shangri-la Hotel in Santa Monica on a modest but adequate per diem. Phil had been delighted to hear from me, "delighted." He'd just written a part into the show *with me in mind,* he said, so we were "fated," and the timing of my phone call couldn't have been more "divine."

I thanked him profusely for his largesse, and wondered what it was about L.A. that made everyone sound like a drag queen.

Then I packed my bags.

"Write, don't call," said Jeannie. "Get in the habit of sending child support checks."

Phil sent his personal assistant to pick me up at the airport in a limo when I arrived, and a basket full of very large fruit—berries the size of quail eggs, a grapefruit that rivaled a melon—was waiting in my hotel room. But it wasn't until the next day on the set that I got a chance to see him. I waited forty-five minutes in his outer office. Finally some D-girl ushered me in. Phil was on the phone, sipping a hot latte, but he waved me inside with a wide grin, pointing broadly at his cup to see if I wanted my own coffee.

I mimed back no, I was fine, then instantly regretted it.

Even with his face bisected by a phone cord, Phil looked better than I remembered. Gone was that wan, hunched-over, defeated look that he'd worn like a badge in the eighties. The beard, of course, helped give him definition, but his hair was nicely silvered and faded jeans hung just so from his slim hips.

Phil's phone call lasted another fifteen minutes. So I awkwardly wandered the office, past the potted palm, perused stacks and stacks of scripts, studied his few framed art prints, and then sunk into his couch and stared at my feet on the floor. I was still wearing my hospital loafers.

Phil was wearing hand-stitched Italian moccasins.

Finally, he got off the phone.

"Hey, sweetheart," said Phil, walking around the island of his desk to vigorously shake my hand.

"Thanks, Phil," I said, a little too heartfeltly. "I'm really grateful for the opportunity to work."

We both looked away then, I suppose to avoid my further humiliation.

"How's Jeannie?" said Phil.

"Good," I said.

An awkward silence.

Then, "Glad to hear it. And the kids?"

"The kids are fine, Phil."

"Dynamite," said Phil. "Terrific."

Thank God, at that moment, the phone rang, the D-girl barged in, and with a half-blown kiss and another wave of his hand, I was soon shuffled out of Phil's office. After that brief, tortuous encounter, I rarely saw my old best friend again. He was always away in Hawaii or Aspen or holed up at his Montana ranch, and the few times he came into the studio, he was breezy and light and avoided me like the plague; which was fine with me. In his absence, it was easier to pretend I had gotten this gig on my own merits.

My part was small, more of an accent, and less than a role, but it was job, a Guild job, a Guild job with benefits. It had been years since I'd been before a camera, years since I'd been on a set. It had been years since I ate hot Danish and cold coffee and stuffed my coat pockets with bagels from the catering table and sat around all day waiting for my three lines. I played Dallas Merchant's ex-husband. I'd come to town as a threat to her present love interest, Chip, a conflicted but good-looking editor at the magazine where she was editor-in-chief. I started off the season with a series of idle threats. My name was Spencer Klein—another half-breed like myself—and I'd swooped in, ostensibly to buy the company out from under them, but really to reclaim Dallas. A cocaine habit on my part had done the marriage in. Dallas was a good girl, if a little overly ambitious, and she favored short, tight suits with slits. Now that I was sober, I wanted a second chance.

A second chance. Isn't that what I'd prayed for and gotten in my real life? The weeks passed into months. The show shot up in the ratings. Phil, according to Dallas, apparently flew home on weekends, but he was busy running the world then, and except for a couple of quick phone conversations where he was sure to compliment my work—laying it on thick enough to make me feel like a jerk—I never really spoke to the guy. Meanwhile, my part grew—Spencer was a real prick, but also, oddly enough, a growing hit with the ladies. He took the network (and Phil) by surprise. So my hours on the set got longer. I'd been away from home for a while, and in some weird way my life in New York began to feel like it belonged to someone else. While I still spoke to the kids on the phone each night, Jeannie was avoiding me. But at the time I felt my career had to be my first priority. If I failed again, the only fallback was that lubricant-slicked sonogram wand and the small sadistic pleasures it afforded me. So I got more and more caught up with my life in L.A. I even rented a little apartment. And when I closed my eyes at night in my little beach bungalow, when I was driving with the top down and my shades up on the 405, and increasingly when I was rehearsing a scene with Dallas, I was a single guy.

A young single guy. *Under* forty. Trim. Going to the gym. Running on the sand. Drinking bottled water. Receiving fan mail and making money. Massaging Dallas's feet with peppermint foot lotion in the private confines of her trailer.

Spencer was full of dirty tricks. In one episode, while masked and coming up from behind, he'd even pushed Chip out a plate glass window of a steely thirty-five-story building. "Thank God," Spencer comforted an innocent and grieving Dallas, "the fountain and pool were there to break his fall." Chip was in a coma, and Dallas and I were in a clinch. On any other show, this would have made a grand season finale, but Phil was a trashmeister of the first degree, and he and his team whipped this crap up on a weekly basis. What was shocking was that the worse Spencer got, the more completely he won over the female audience. He was mean and duplicitous and *sexy.* "Masterful," a mother of five from Tulsa wrote me. I even got a note from one of my former patients. "I wish I'd known who you were when you were conducting my sonography," she said. "Does that count as having sex?" And Dallas herself, one afternoon as we were reading lines, said. "You're blowing Chip out of the water, babe."

She was a good-looking woman, Dallas. Polished with the blond, gold sheen of a prime-time diva. And she took a healthy pleasure in her own reflection, which, after years of a tight-lipped, frown-lined Jeannie, had its own appeal. While Chip was in a coma, Dallas and I had to do a couple of steamy love scenes. We rehearsed a lot. On and off the set. One evening she even invited me out to their house at the beach. She said, "We've got to crack that damn shower sequence." But before I could drive out on the PCH that night, ready and eager to break my marriage vows, Dallas called me back. Her voice sounded a little shaky. *Felipe* had just rung her from New York, and after learning of our rehearsal plans, he'd decided to work out of his office in L.A. She'd see me Monday on the set.

I took Phil's imminent arrival as a celestial reprieve from the heinous act I had only moments ago been eager to commit. Jeannie and I may have had our problems then—we *always* have our problems—but I love the girl. That night I called home, eager to make amends, but the kids were left with a sitter and Jeannie was out to dinner with a "friend."

"How do I spell your last name again?" asked the sitter.

I hung up, went out, and got so drunk at a popular dive bar in Hollywood that in the wee hours of the morning, the bartender folded me into a taxi.

Phil had rewritten the next episode. When I arrived on the set, the director took one look, shoved the new script under my arm, and sent me directly into makeup. I learned my new lines as a cosmetician did her best to "even out my tone." Spencer and Dallas were still in the shower, but just when they were about to make use of all that steam, Spencer was to *grab his ears* and fall down to the floor moaning. A cerebral hemorrhage? Multiple personality disorder? Dallas, naked, would rush out of the water to call an ambulance—the late-night adult audience would be fortunate enough to see her butt. We'd find out what happened to me in the next episode.

And so it went. It seemed that Spencer suffered from post-traumatic stress disorder, thanks to the horror, the horror, of the time he'd spent as a soldier in the jungle—the miniature palm trees and lush bougainvillea in Dallas's solarium triggering his most brutal recollections. Over the next few weeks, Spencer went into a shocking decline. He was reduced to a sweaty, trembling wreck (I wasn't allowed to shave, they oiled my scalp and painted gray streaks around my temples), he was afraid to get off his couch, afraid to do much of anything. And let me tell you, fear like that can be contagious. For the first time in years, Oliver Stone peopled my dreams. So I was in trouble, but Spencer was worse off. First he lost his business, and then, of course, without money, he lost Dallas. Somehow she'd gotten wind of the fact that he'd thrown Chip out the window—Chip had come out of his coma and was now president of the magazine's parent company—and she'd finally seen Spencer for the bum he was.

I didn't like going to work anymore. My nights were sleepless, lonely, and damp, and I'd show up in the morning all twisty and exhausted. My fan mail changed to hate mail, and the other actors seemed to avoid me. Even Dallas. I carried the stench of a canceled contract, I could even smell it on myself. Sour, rancid, cheesy. Each Monday morning when the script girl handed me my pages, I took a deep breath and readied myself for my own demise. A suicide, perhaps? A car accident? Dallas and the sexy silver pistol she carried strapped to her left thigh? But there was no easy out for me. Instead, Spencer went back on coke, had hallucinations, lost his apartment, lived in a car, ate out of the garbage pails of fancy restaurants while Dallas and Chip dined royally inside. There was even a proposed episode where I was to be gang-raped by a posse of teenage Latinos, but thankfully the top brass at the network put a stop to it, something to do with public relations.

Feeling all alone, I called home and whined to Jeannie. She had been watching the series with apparent glee. The closest she got to sympathy was to say, "I keep telling Phil to either have Spencer buried alive in a coffin or saddled with cement shoes and thrown off the Santa Monica Pier."

"You've talked to Phil?" I said.

"Oh, we had dinner a couple of times."

"Honey," I said, "don't you think it's time that you and the kids moved out here?"

"Why?" said my wife. "You're going to be out of a job in another week."

I let this sink in. "Did Phil say something?"

"God," she said. "What a narcissist. We never talk about you." And then Jeannie hung up on me.

That's when I went into my desk and dug out Phil's old letter—which I'd kept as a souvenir. In the past, whenever I felt especially lousy about myself, the letter gave me solace. But now as I read and reread it, the opposite happened for me. The letter was the same old melodramatic mess, overwritten and self-deprecating. "And if I can manage to eke out one halfway respectable novel, even if it's not publishable, I'll figure my time on earth was well-spent." But Phil was practically running an entire network! How could such a loser turn into such a huge success? And on my watch. Off my back. Engaged to my crush. Eating dinner with my wife and actively *not* discussing me.

I talked to Dallas. That is, I took the opportunity to barge into her trailer. I came bearing that stupid letter, now crumpled and sweaty in my fist. I wanted her to see the evidence, to *know* Phil, the man she was engaged to. A failed novelist. A thirty-five-year-old who'd borrowed money from his mother. A cuckold who befriended the guy who was sleeping with his wife. This was the *real* Phil, I was going to say with dignity, and here is the written proof. But Dallas allowed me no time for such theatrics. With my mouth barely open, I only got to flap the wrinkled paper before her like a fan.

"Darling," said Dallas.

I flapped the letter limply.

Dallas was sitting at her dressing table in a blue kimono with no makeup on, her hair in a ponytail, looking washed-out and a little aged. She was reading the next week's script. But before I got a chance to say a word, she gazed up at me with pity. She handed me the pages and said quietly, "I'll go get you a cup of tea." Then Dallas exited her trailer, half-dressed, without the comfort of her war paint, onto the bustling set and into the crowded commissary, so I knew in my bones that disaster was probably imminent.

The next episode chilled my blood. According to the script, while freebasing coke—after prostituting myself on Hollywood and Vine to a cruising male pornographer—I had a little accident with the lighter. That is, I was scheduled that Monday to go up in flames, "flames flickering across his face, filling all four corners of the frame" (Phil was a sucker for alliteration). I'd wake up in the hospital with burns over ninety percent of my body. The scene notes suggested that after a week or two of touch and go and moan and scream, when no one in the cast would deign to visit me—"What goes around comes around," was Dallas's line, directed to be delivered "tearfully"—I would survive, hideously scarred and completely crippled. At this point I would come to Chip literally on my hands and knees—the directions said I was to "crawl" up the walkway of his and Dallas's house out at the beach—and beg for a job as a stockboy at a women's health magazine. Chip, out of the goodness of his heart, was to stroke his beard and agree to hire me if I really could change my ways. A close-up on what used to be my face made it clear that for the life of me, I couldn't. Change, that is. The directions said to focus in on my "evil eyes."

"Red-streaked and unrepentant." "Surrounded by foamy, blistered skin hanging off in strips."

My hands were shaking. Enough was enough, I was going to confront my maker. I left the set and drove out to the beach.

When I arrived in Malibu, Phil was sitting at his desk on a deck hanging over a dune with a heart-stopping view of the water. It was a gorgeous day, the air was dry, pressed by the sun into fragrant, soft sheets of breeze. Seagulls lounged about the sky and the ocean did a cancan across the shore, teasing and retreating, flashing a little ankle. I walked up the beachside entrance. Phil's head was bent, and as I noted competitively, he still had a full head of hair. The bastard was typing away furiously. Quadriplegia. Colostomies. Who knows what evils he was designing for my future.

It must have been the roar of the waves, or the low, distant rumble of the Pacific Coast Highway, or even perhaps the dynamic state of flow he probably experienced whenever he was destroying me, but Phil did not hear me approach until I was halfway up his stairs. And so unobserved, I leaned over and picked up a decorative piece of driftwood and held it behind my back. In the other hand I carried that stupid letter. Thus armed, I continued my ascent, until Phil looked up, and rose from his seat.

"Sweetheart," said Phil.

I handed him the letter.

Phil read it slowly, smiling, I suppose, when he hit the line about the novel. Then he folded it up and put it in his pocket.

He said, "Do you think I should have it framed?"

That's when I took the driftwood and smashed him over the head.

I still don't know what possessed me. I was never a violent boy, and I'm not a violent man. But that day at the beach, I looked at my wife's ex-husband, a handsome, rich, successful motherfucker, positively glowing in the sun on his beachfront property, and I smashed him with a piece of his own decorative driftwood. I smashed him so hard, blood oozed out and stained his silver head.

For a while it was quiet. Neither of us knew what to do or say. We were shy with one another. Phil slowly brought his hand to his hair, touching blood.

I scuffed the wooden deck with my sneaker.

"I guess I need a towel," said Phil. "And probably some ice." He started into the house, then turned around politely. "You're welcome to come inside."

"No," I said. "I mean, no thanks." I said, "I think I'd better go."

"You're sure?" said Phil.

"Yeah," I said. "I'm sure." And then I said sincerely, "Thanks. Thanks again, Phil, for hiring me."

Phil nodded generously in my direction.

A dribble of blood plopped down on the deck.

"I guess I better tend to this," said Phil, apologetically.

I nodded. And then I turned and started walking toward the staircase.

That's when Phil dove, he literally dove on top of me, when my back was turned and I was walking away. The whole attack took me by surprise, but of course I should have been ready. He was a stealth bomber, Phil. This was his M.O.

We fell against the wood railing of his deck, which sighed and gave, then splintered and crashed, and then in a clinch we flew off the deck and through the air and down into the dunes. Rolling around, one on top of the other, like tangled pant legs in a dryer, we tumbled onto the beach.

We were beating the shit out of each other.

What can I say? That I'm proud of how I behaved? I grabbed a fistful of sand and ground it against Phil's teeth, until something cracked. I pulled back, and he spat a phlegmy, crunchy mess into my face, and then he sunk his molars into my shoulder. I howled and elbowed him so hard, later we found out I'd broken three of his ribs and even ruptured his spleen. He kicked my shin until the bone chipped, and when I bent over to grab my injured limb, Phil pummeled my back, lightly bruising my left kidney. Next my elbow fractured his eye socket.

We were trying our damnedest to kill each other.

It was a beautiful day. The sun beat down, but there was just enough wind to keep it cool, so our sweat dried faster than our blood and our skin stretched taut and cracked as if with paint. As we rolled end over end, sand glommed onto our wounds. We were bloody and wet and caked. But as I remember it now, we weren't in pain. Etherized by adrenaline, by competition, by our mutual hate, Phil and I were a tangle of braided muscle rolling toward the sea, so twisted and intertwined we were almost one man.

The water was at low tide, foamy and blue. It lapped around our edges. And there at the shore, we lay still, so close to one another I could feel Phil's heart beating inside my chest, lending a rhythm to mine; perhaps this alone is what saved me, because when the rescue team finally came and pulled us apart, my heart stopped, and I needed resuscitation.

God, did the tabloids have a field day! And the publicity did wonders for our careers. We sued and counter-sued each other. And then about a year and a half later, after Jeannie had left and come back to me, after Dallas ran off with her new co-star and Phil got a quickie marriage to one of his PAs, we called a truce. We met at a bar on the beach, had a couple of beers, and agreed to sell the rights to our story—Phil was to write and to produce, and I was guaranteed a lead. Pay or play. We were once again a team of sorts, although, of course, by then both of us had production companies and families and egos to support, and, true to form, we were each out only for ourselves.

But before, on that glorious day in Malibu, when we were both twisting weakly like a couple of fish on the same hook, it was Phil alone who sustained me. His breath was warm against my neck, his blood salty on my lips, or perhaps it was the brine of the ocean that I tasted, for the waves crashed close and closer still, wetting us now with sea spray. Then it was Phil and I and no one else, and I have to admit I kind of liked it that way. For we were lying half-dead in each other's arms when the waves began to break over us, like lovers, curled up in the warm, damp bed of the sand.

Flower Children

They're free to run anywhere they like whenever they like, so they do. The land falls away from their small house on the hill along a prickly path; there's a dirt road, a pasture where the steer are kept, swamps, a gully, groves of fruit trees, and then the creek from whose far bank a wooded mountain surges—they climb it. At the top, they step out to catch their breaths in the light. The mountain gives way into fields as far as their eyes can see—alfalfa, soybean, corn, wheat. They aren't sure where their own land stops and someone else's begins, but it doesn't matter, they're told. It doesn't matter! Go where you please!

They spend their whole lives in trees, young apple trees and old tired ones, red oaks, walnuts, the dogwood when it flowers in May. They hold leaves up to the light and peer through them. They close their eyes and press their faces into showers of leaves and wait for that feeling of darkness to come and make their whole bodies stir. They discover locust shells, tree frogs, a gypsy moth's cocoon. Now they know what that sound is in the night when the tree frogs sing out at the tops of their lungs. In the fields, they collect groundhog bones. They make desert piles and bless them with flowers and leaves. They wish they could be plants and lie very still near the ground all night and in the morning be covered with tears of dew. They wish they could be Robin Hood, Indians. In the summer, they rub mud all over their bodies and sit out in the sun to let it dry. When it dries, they stand up slowly like old men and women with wrinkled skin and walk stiff-limbed through the trees towards the creek.

Their parents don't care what they do. They're the luckiest children alive! They run out naked in storms. They go riding on ponies with the boys up the road who're on perpetual suspension from school. They take baths with their father, five bodies in one tub. In the pasture, they stretch out flat on their backs and wait for the buzzards to come. When the buzzards start circling, they lie very still, breathless with fear, and imagine what it would be like to be eaten alive. That one's diving! they say, and they leap to their feet. No, we're alive! We're alive!

The children all sleep in one room. Their parents built the house themselves, four rooms and four stories high, one small room on top of the next. With their first child, a girl, they lived out in a tent in the yard beneath the apple trees. In the children's room, there are three beds. The girls sleep together and the youngest boy in a wooden crib which their mother made. A toilet stands out in the open near the stairwell. Their parents sleep on the highest floor underneath the eaves in a room with skylights and silver-papered walls. In the living room, a swing hangs in the center from the ceiling. There's a woodstove to one side with a bathtub beside it; both the bathtub and the stove stand on lion's feet. There are bookshelves all along the walls and an atlas, too, which the children pore through, and a set of encyclopedias from which they copy fish. The kitchen, the lowest room, is built into a hill. The floor is made of dirt and gravel, and the stone walls are damp. Blacksnakes come in sometimes to shed their skins. When the children aren't outside, they spend most of their time here; they play with the stones on the floor, making pyramids or round piles and then knocking them down. There's a showerhouse out-side down a steep, narrow path and a round stone well in the woods behind.

There's nowhere to hide in the house, no cellars or closets, so the children go outside to do that, too. They spend hours stand-ing waist-high in the creek. They watch the crayfish have battles and tear off each other's claws. They catch the weak ones later, off-guard and from behind, as they crouch in the dark under shelves of stone. And they catch minnows, too, and salamanders with the soft skin of frogs, and they try to catch snakes, although they're never quite sure that they really want to. It maddens them how the water changes things before their eyes, turning the min-nows into darting chips of green light and making the dirty stones on the bottom shine. Once they found a snapping turtle frozen in the ice, and their father cut it out with an axe to make soup. The children dunk their heads under and breathe out bub-bles. They keep their heads down as long as they can. They like how their hair looks underneath the water, the way it spreads out around their faces in wavering fans. And their voices sound different, too, like the voices of strange people from a foreign place. They put their heads down and carry on conversations, they scream and laugh, testing out these strange voices that bloom from their mouths and then swell outwards, endlessly, like no other sound they have ever heard.

The children get stung by nettles, ants, poison ivy, poison oak, and bees. They go out into the swamp and come back, their whole heads crawling with ticks and burrs. They pick each other's scalps outside the house, then lay the ticks on a ledge and grind their bodies to dust with a pointed stone.

They watch the pigs get butchered and the chickens killed. They learn that people have teeth inside their heads. One evening, their father takes his shirt off and lies out on the kitchen table to show them where their organs are. He moves his hand over the freckled skin, cupping different places—heart, stomach, lung, lung, kidneys, gall bladder, liver here. And suddenly they want to know what's inside everything, so they tear apart everything they find, flowers, pods, bugs, shells, seeds, they shred up the whole yard in search of something; and they want to know about everything they see or can't see, frost and earthworms, and who will decide when it rains, and are there ghosts and are there fairies, and how many drops and how many stars, and although they kill things themselves, they want to know why anything dies and where the dead go and where they were waiting before they were born. In the hazelnut grove? Behind the goathouse? And how did they know when it was time to come?

Their parents are delighted by the snowlady they build with huge breasts and a penis and rock-necklace hair. Their parents are delighted by these children in every way, these children who will be like no children ever were. In this house with their children, they'll create a new world—that has no relation to the world they have known—in which nothing is lied about, whispered about, and nothing is ever concealed. There will be no petty lessons for these children about how a fork is held or a hand shaken or what is best to be said and what shouldn't be spoken of or seen. Nor will these children's minds be restricted to sets and subsets of rules, rules for children, about when to be quiet or go to bed, the causes and effects of various punishments which increase in gravity on a gradated scale. No, not these children! These children will be different. They'll learn only the large things. Here in this house, the world will be revealed in a fresh, new light, and this light will fall over everything. Even those shady forbidden zones through which they themselves wandered as children, panicked and alone, these, too, will be illuminated—their children will walk through with torches held high! Yes, everything should be spoken of in this house, everything, and everything seen.

*   *   *

Their father holds them on his lap when he's going to the bathroom, he lights his farts with matches on the stairs, he likes to talk about shit and examine each shit he takes, its texture and smell, and the children's shits, too, he has theories about shit that unwind for hours—he has theories about everything. He has a study in the toolshed near the house where he sits for hours and is visited regularly by ideas, which he comes in to explain to their mother and the children. When their mother's busy or not listening, he explains them to the children or to only one child in a language that they don't understand, but certain words or combinations of words bore themselves into their brains, where they will remain, but the children don't know this yet, ringing in their ears for the rest of their lives—repression, Nixon, wind power, nuclear power, Vietnam, fecal patterns, sea thermal energy, civil rights. And one day these words will bear all sorts of meaning, but now they mean nothing to the children—they live the lives of ghosts, outlines with no form, wandering inside their minds. The children listen attentively. They nod, nod, nod.

Their parents grow pot in the garden, which they keep under the kitchen sink in a large tin. When the baby-sitter comes, their mother shows her where it is. The baby-sitter plays with the children, a game where you turn the music up very loud, Waylon Jennings, "The Outlaws," and run around the living room leaping from the couch to the chairs to the swing, trying never to touch the floor. She shows them the tattoo between her legs, a bright rose with thorns, and then she calls up all her friends. When the children come down later to get juice in the kitchen, they see ten naked bodies through a cloud of smoke sitting around the table, playing cards. The children are invited, but they'd rather not play.

Their parents take them to protests in different cities and to concerts sometimes. The children wear T-shirts and hold posters and then the whole crowd lets off balloons. Their parents have peach parties and invite all their friends. There's music, dancing, skinny-dipping in the creek. Everyone takes off their clothes and rubs peach flesh all over each other's skin. The children are free to join in, but they don't feel like it. They sit in a row on the hill in all their clothes. But they memorize the sizes of the breasts and the shapes of the penises of all their parents' friends and discuss this later amongst themselves.

One day, at the end of winter, a woman begins to come to their house. She has gray eyes and a huge mound of wheat-colored hair. She laughs quickly, showing small white teeth. From certain angles, she looks ugly, but from others she seems very nice. She comes in the mornings and picks things in the garden. She's there again at dinner, at birthdays. She brings presents. She arrives dressed as a rabbit for Easter in a bright yellow pajama suit. She's very kind to their mother and chatters to her for hours in the kitchen as they cook. Their father goes away on weekends with her; he spends the night at her house. Sometimes he takes the children with him to see her. She lives in a gray house by the river that's much larger than the children's house. She has six Siamese cats. She has a piano and many records and piles of soft clay for the children to play with, but they don't want to. They go outside and stand by the concrete frog pond near the road. Algae covers it like a hairy, green blanket. They stare down, trying to spot frogs. They chuck rocks in, candy, pennies, or whatever else they can find.

In the gray spring mornings, there's a man either coming or going from their mother's room. He leaves the door open. Did you hear them? I heard them. Did you see them? Yes. But they don't talk about it. They no longer talk about things amongst themselves. But they answer their father's questions when he asks.

And here again they nod. When their father has gone away for good and then comes back to visit or takes them out on trips in his car and tells them about the women he's been with, how they make love, what he prefers or doesn't like, gestures or movements of the arms, neck, or legs described in the most detailed terms— And what do they think? And what would they suggest? When a woman stands with a cigarette between her breasts at the end of the bed and you suddenly lose all hope— And he talks about their mother, too, the way she makes love. He'd much rather talk to them than to anyone else. These children, they're amazing! They rise to all occasions, stoop carefully to any sorrow—and their minds! Their minds are wide open and flow with no stops, like damless streams. And the children nod also when one of their mother's boyfriends comes by to see her—she's not there— they're often heartbroken, occasionally drunk, they want to talk about her. The children stand with them underneath the trees. They can't see for the sun in their eyes, but they look up, anyway, and nod, smile politely, nod.

The children play with their mother's boyfriends out in the snow. They go to school. They're sure they'll never learn to read. They stare at the letters. They lose all hope. They worry that they don't know the Lord's Prayer. They realize that they don't know God or anything about him, so they ask the other children shy questions in the schoolyard and receive answers that baffle them, and then God fills their minds like a guest who's moved in, but keeps his distance, and worries them to distraction at night when they're alone. They imagine they hear his movements through the house, his footsteps and the rustling of his clothes. They grow frightened for their parents, who seem to have learned nothing about God's laws. They feel that they should warn them, but they don't know how. They become convinced one night that their mother is a robber. They hear her creeping through the house alone, lifting and rattling things.

At school, they learn to read and spell. They learn penmanship and multiplication. They're surprised at first by all the rules, but then they learn them too quickly and observe them all carefully. They learn not to swear. They get prizes for obedience, for following the rules down to the last detail. They're delighted by these rules, these arbitrary lines that regulate behavior and mark off forbidden things, and they examine them closely and exhaust their teachers with questions about the mechanical functioning and the hidden intricacies of these beings, the rules: If at naptime, you're very quiet with your eyes shut tight and your arms and legs so still you barely breathe, but really you're not sleeping, underneath your arms and beneath your eyelids you're wide awake and thinking very hard about how to be still, but you get the prize anyway for sleeping because you were the stillest child in the room, but actually that's wrong, you shouldn't get the prize or should you, because the prize is really for sleeping and not being still, or is it also for being still…?

When the other children in the schoolyard are whispering themselves into wild confusion about their bodies and sex and babies being born, these children stay quiet and stand to one side. They're mortified by what they know and have seen. They're sure that if they mention one word, the other children will go home and tell their parents who will tell their teachers who will be horrified and disgusted and push them away. But they also think they should be punished. They should be shaken, beaten, for what they've seen. These children don't touch themselves. They grow hesitant with worry. At home, they wander out into the yard alone and stand there at a terrible loss. One day, when the teacher calls on them, they're no longer able to speak. But then they speak again a few days later, although now and then they'll have periods in their lives when their voices disappear utterly or else become very thin and quavering like ghosts or old people lost in their throats.

But the children love to read. They suddenly discover the use of all these books in the house and turn the living room into a lending library. Each book has a card and a due date and is stamped when it's borrowed or returned. They play card games and backgammon. They go over to friends' houses and learn about junk food and how to watch TV. But mostly they read. They read about anything, love stories, the lives of inventors and famous Indians, blights that affect hybrid plants. They try to read books they can't read at all and skip words and whole paragraphs and sit like this for hours lost in a stunning blur.

They take violin lessons at school and piano lessons and then stop one day when their hands begin to shake so badly they can no longer hold to the keys. What is wrong? Nothing! They get dressed up in costumes and put on plays. They're kings and queens. They're witches. They put on a whole production of *The Wizard of Oz*. They play detectives with identity cards and go searching for the kittens who have just been born in some dark, hidden place on their land. They store away money to give to their father when he comes. They spend whole afternoons at the edge of the yard waiting for him to come. They don't understand why their father behaves so strangely now, why he sleeps in their mother's bed when she's gone in the afternoon and then gets up and slinks around the house, like a criminal, chuckling, especially when she's angry and has told him to leave. They don't know why their father seems laughed at now and unloved, why he needs money from them to drive home in his car, why he seems to need something from them that they cannot give him—everything— but they'll try to give him—everything—whatever it is he needs, they'll try to do this as hard as they can.

Their father comes and waits for their mother in the house. He comes and takes them away on trips in his car. They go to quarries, where they line up and leap off cliffs. They go looking for caves up in the hills in Virginia. There are bears here, he tells them, but if you ever come face to face with one, just swear your heart out and he'll run. He takes them to dances in the city where only old people go. Don't they know how to fox-trot? Don't they know how to waltz? They sit at tables and order sodas, waiting for their turn to be picked up and whirled around by him. Or they watch him going around to other tables, greeting husbands and inviting their wives, women much older than his mother, to dance. These woman have blue or white hair. They either get up laughing or refuse. He comes back to the children to report how they were—like dancing with milk, he says, or water, or molasses. He takes them to see the pro-wrestling championship match. He takes them up north for a week to meditate inside a hotel with a guru from Bombay. He takes them running down the up-escalators in stores and up Totem Mountain at night in a storm. He talks his head off. He gets speeding tickets left and right. He holds them on his lap when he's driving and between his legs when they ski. When he begins to fall asleep at the wheel, they rack their brains, trying to think of ways to keep him awake. They rub his shoulders and pull his hair. They sing rounds. They ask him questions to try to make him talk. They do interviews in the back seat, saying things they know will amuse him. And when their efforts are exhausted, he tells them that the only way he'll ever stay awake is if they insult him in the cruelest way they can. He says their mother is the only person who can do this really well. He tells them that they have to say mean things about her, about her boyfriends and lovers and what they do, or about how much she hates him, thinks he's stupid, an asshole, a failure, how much she doesn't want him around. And so they do. They force themselves to invent insults or say things that are terrible but true. And as they speak, they feel their mouths turn chalky and their stomachs begin to harden as if with each word they had swallowed a stone. But he seems delighted. He laughs and encourages them, turning around in his seat to look at their faces, his eyes now completely off the road.

He wants them to meet everyone he knows. They show up on people's doorsteps with him in the middle of the day or late at night. He can hardly contain himself. These are my kids! he says. They're smarter than anyone I know, and ten times smarter than me! Do you have any idea what it's like when your kids turn out smarter than you?! He teaches them how to play bridge and to ski backwards. At dinner with him, you have to eat with your eyes closed. When you go through a stoplight, you have to hold on to your balls. But the girls? Oh yes, the girls—well, just improvise! He's experiencing flatulence, withdrawal from wheat. He's on a new diet that will ruthlessly clean out his bowels. There are turkeys and assholes everywhere in the world. Do they know this? Do they know? But he himself is probably the biggest asshole here. Still, women find him handsome—they do! They actually do! And funny. But he *is* funny, he actually is, not witty but funny, they don't realize this because they see him all the time, they're used to it, but other people—like that waitress! Did they see that waitress? She was laughing so hard she could barely see straight! Do they know how you get to be a waitress? Big breasts. But he himself is not a breast man. Think of Mom—he calls their mother Mom—she has no breasts at all! But her taste in men is mind-boggling. Don't they think? Mind-boggling! Think about it too long, and you'll lose your mind. Why do they think she picks these guys? What is it? And why are women almost always so much smarter than men? And more dignified? Dignity for men is a completely lost cause! And why does anyone have kids, anyway? Come on, why?! Because they like you? Because they laugh at you? No! Because they're fun! Exactly! They're fun!

* * *

Around the house there are briar patches with berries and thorns. There are gnarled apple trees with puckered gray skins. The windows are all open—the wasps are flying in. The clothes on the line are jumping like children with no heads but hysterical limbs. Who will drown the fresh new kitties? Who will chain-saw the trees and cut the firewood in winter and haul that firewood in? Who will do away with all these animals, or tend them, or sell them, kill them one by one? Who will say to her in the evening that it all means nothing, that tomorrow will be different, that the heart gets tired after all? And where are the children? When will they come home? She has burnt all her diaries. She has told the man in the barn to go away. Who will remind her again that the heart has its own misunderstandings? And the heart often loses its way and can be found hours later wandering down passage-ways with unexplained bruises on its skin. On the roof, there was a child standing one day years ago, his arms waving free, but one foot turned inward, weakly— When will it be evening? When will it be night? The tree frogs are beginning to sing. She has seen the way their toes clutch at the bark. Some of them are spotted, and their hearts beat madly against the skin of their throats. There may be a storm. It may rain. That cloud there looks dark—but no, it's a wisp of burnt paper, too thin. In the woods above, there's a house that burnt down to the ground, but then a grove of lilac bushes burst up from the char. A wind is coming up. There are dark purple clouds now. There are red-coned sumacs hovering along the edge of the drive. Poisonous raw, but fine for tea. The leaves on the apple trees are all turning blue. The sunflowers in the garden are quivering, heads bowed—empty of seed now. And the heart gets watered and recovers itself. There is hope, every-where there's hope. Light approaches from the back. Between the dry, gnarled branches, it's impossible to see. There are the first few drops. There are the oak trees shuddering. There's a flicker of bright gray, the underside of one leaf. There was once a child standing at the edge of the yard at a terrible loss. Did she know this? Yes. The children! (They have her arms, his ears, his voice, his smell, her soft features, her movements of the hand and head, her stiffness, his confusion, his humor, her ambition, his daring, his eyelids, their failure, their hope, their freckled skin—)

Goodbye, Tinker Bell, Hello, God

When we were children, my brother, Frank, and I handled our mother's danger signals differently.

Mama could pluck a word from a simple statement, then snap it back covered with ice. Her very blue eyes could deepen from midday sky-blue to late-afternoon darkening blue, or worse, to night-charged-with-lightning blue. Her normal alto-toned voice could rise to middle (command tone), or worse, the high pitch of fear.

My way of coping with these shifting moods was to initiate very little conversation. I grew more and more skillful at reading the many blues of my mother's eyes, and the three main levels of her voice. Her face became my barometer, my instrument for peace, especially when the three of us were together.

Frank, whose life burst forth in dramatic gestures and a big voice, would pull down the curtain at the first sign of trouble and turn the spotlight on me. Pushed to center stage, I would be furious and fearful, but I loved him fiercely and protectively, and so would attempt to change the subject or take one aspect of it and develop it so that it looked as though we had both misunderstood him. Maybe that is how I learned to make up stories.

But there was something else. In spite of my fear of my mother's mood swings, I craved both expression and adventure—especially at the time of this memory.

In April of 1928, I was just past twelve and Frank almost ten. My restlessness was at a high, and had no place to go. Sex education in the schools did not exist, nor did we have it at home. Sensations were puzzled over, kept secret, like finding out about death, or that your grandfather had a mistress. Once I found neatly folded oblong pieces of flannel in my mother's dresser. At nine, I paid no attention. But I had found them again recently and wondered. I thought the objects had something to do with being a woman, in the sense that they had nothing to do with being a man. But I did not ask. And was not told.

All of these things were on my mind that Thursday night in April when the three of us were at the supper table. My brother, with wild gestures of arms and hands, was describing a branch, fallen from a dead tree, that he and his friend Donald had found in the park. Mama's eyes were a lovely afternoon blue. The branch, he narrated, stretched down into a shallow ravine. Interlacing branches and dead leaves made a roof. By breaking through some of the branches, the boys had made a hidden cave.

"We're having a club there," he said. "No girls."

A faint alarm interrupted my thoughts. Frank was headed toward dangerous ground—a hidden cave!—but before I could alert him with a discreet kick, Mama spoke. Low voice, but her eyes were approaching evening. "I don't want you sneaking into hidden places, Frank." Two ominous words: sneaking, hidden. Both were coated with ice.

Frank delved into mashed potatoes. I got a not too discreet kick.

I delved into a deep breath to calm my annoyance and find my lines. "It's not a good cave at all," I exhaled. "It's only a dead branch. You can see right through it. Anyhow, the park men are going to lug it away."

I had never seen the fallen branch. I knew nothing about carting away dead trees. I was uneasy. My legs wanted to stretch to ease sensations higher up that embarrassed me. I was mad. It was like somebody giving me information I needed to save my life, but the tone was so muffled I couldn't hear it.

After a tense interval, I looked up. Mama looked ill, not angry, not quite fearful. Why? Did she know that I had never seen Frank's branch? If so, why didn't she accuse me in her top voice—storyteller—as she had done many times before?

Later, with rare intimacy, Mama said, "I worry about Frank. He needs his father." The retort *What about me?* died in my throat as she concluded her concern: "It's hard to raise a boy alone. You will have to help."

Before I went to sleep, I tried to sink into my pirate chest, my inner treasury of memories. I wanted my father, but all I could bring up was a picture of my mother without any face, just a long skirt and hands wrapped around a tray, noiselessly climbing the stairs that led to my dying father.

When we came home from school at lunchtime the next day, Mama told Frank that he was having lunch at Donald's house and then going back to school with him. "Mrs. Hopkins is waiting for you," she said.

She stood at the door of the dining room just off the landing of our third-floor flat. Still breathless from the race up the two flights, we simply stared. Donald was Frank's best friend and classmate. He lived two houses away, and we had just left him. We never ate in other people's houses unless they were our relatives.

Mama had moved aside, indicating that I should go in.

Inside, I faced the table. On the far side, fastidiously wrapped in white tissue, lay several neatly folded pieces of the mysterious white flannel. Next to them was a small duplicate of the odd-shaped belt.

She must have seen me rummaging through her drawers. The sound of my own heart almost drowned out Frank's first *Why?* to his startling invitation.

"Your sister is staying home this afternoon," she was saying. Over my fear and guilt, I felt another emotion. My face was hot. A strange rebellion propelled me around just in time to see Frank's hurt look as he voiced his second *Why?*

Mama's middle voice. The command voice. "She isn't feeling well." The signal passed between us, stronger than his bewilderment, stronger than my fear, but not stronger than my rebellion. I listened to my brother clumping down the stairs. I felt as though our fragile unit had been sliced into three parts.

"I'm not sick," I said, but now I wasn't sure. She took my arm and led me to her chair by the window. If you looked sideways, you could see the Statue of Liberty from there, and at night, when it was dark, the partying lights of luxury liners lit up the sky. I had often seen her sitting there alone. Perhaps, looking outward, she found the same escape in the lights of a passing ship that I found, looking inward, at the lights of jewels in my pirate chest. I wished I could talk about it, but I didn't know how. Intimacies must have beginnings. Ours did not. From the past, memories of the constantly moving caretaker with no face had moved to a caretaker who could change signals like a storm-beaten lighthouse fighting for lives she did not know.

She took my hand and looked embarrassed. I felt embarrassed. I said again, quieter this time, "I'm not sick."

Matter-of-factly, she said, "I saw a little blood on your pajamas this morning. Your monthly periods have begun."

I didn't know what she meant, but I looked at the package on the table. She nodded and then demonstrated how to put on the strange equipment. I got up and, awkwardly, over my school uniform, mimicked her actions. She told me to go into the bathroom so that I could see what she was talking about. "Do you want me to come with you?"

I said no, but when I came out, frightened and near tears, she was close by the door. We went back into the dining room. For the first time, I noticed the smell of strong beef tea and saw the cups of custard cooling by the kitchen window. I remembered the nourishment being carried up to my father. This terrible thing must be something like tuberculosis.

Mama handed me a little calendar. She placed it on my lap, and while I watched, she marked the date with a tiny dot, then counted four weeks beyond and made a check. "About every twenty-eight days," she said.

"What's twenty-eight days?"

"This."

"You mean this will happen again!"

"Every month, dear." Mama was holding both my arms, as though to anchor me into a reality that wasn't. Not my body. Not her voice. For a moment I closed my eyes. From inside, I wanted to hear the new voice, store it in a safe place, but there didn't seem to be room, and now she was speaking from outside. I opened my eyes.

"It happens to every woman, Eileen. It's a beautiful thing, really. It makes it possible to have a baby."

"I'm going to have a baby!"

"Someday. Not now. You have to get married first."

"If I don't, will this thing go away?"

I saw her smile. Really smile. She said, "No. Not till you're much older."

"How old?"

"Late forties, fifties, maybe."

"Fifty!" My face was hot again. "Will this happen to Frank?"

"No." Voice and eyes darkened. Neither signaled danger, but when she brought me the beef broth on a tray, she used her middle voice, the command voice. "You are not to tell Frank anything about this. Nothing. He is only a child. I'll tell him what he needs to know."

When Frank came home, a little past three, Mama had just finished instructions on how to care for the flannel. Salt. Cold water. Overnight soak. Pail under sink. Kirkmann's Soap. Washboard and hot water.

Frank said, "Are you all better?"

Mama's eyes signaled. "I'm not allowed to talk about it."

He turned to Mama. "Is she going to school Monday?"

"Yes." Mama's answer was crisp.

"She didn't have to go today."

I couldn't look at him. I picked up the Frank Merriwell I had been reading, a Frank who was tied up and buried up to his neck in the desert sand, standing upright and facing a wild beast just a few yards away.

Later, Mama went down to Kellbeck's to buy milk, and Frank stole back in. "How long are you going to have this sickness you can't tell me about," he demanded.

"Fifty years," I said.

"Fifty years! We'll all be dead."

Then over the silence he asked, "If our daddy hadn't died, would it be a sin for him to talk about it, too?"

"Sin! Who said anything about sin!"

"Well, if you've got it, and you can't even tell me, then it must be a sin to tell me, and if it's a sin to tell me, you've got a real big one, not the kind we make up to go to confession with."

Sin. Napkins. Blood. Mostly, I wanted Mama to stay away so that I could tell him. I hadn't promised. But my excited brother was still talking.

"Donald has a *real* dad. Maybe I'll ask him."

Merriwell crashed to the floor, and my tears, hidden for hours like the salted flannel under the sink, flowed. I grabbed him by the shoulders. "My daddy is real," I screamed. His lip quivered, and he ran out.

The next day, Saturday, I was allowed to go by myself to Woolworth's to buy more flannel. On the way back I got caught in a sudden cloudburst. Within seconds, visibility disappeared, and my old winter coat was soaked through into my Saturday blouse and skirt. I was within a half block of Our Lady of Angels church. One arm held the package under my coat, while the other flailed the stinging curtain until I felt the bars of the iron fence, then I stumbled my way to the entrance, up the steps, and into the silent vestibule. It was dark but dry. I pushed open the heavy red doors and stood at the back of the long middle aisle of the church.

The sanctuary lamp was flickering gently in the draft so that rippled images played upon the red carpet. Even the still air was alive and moving. I remembered my young experience of thinking that the burning lamp was Tinker Bell making her eternal plea, all that kept her alive, "Do you believe?"

The church was empty. Carefully, I let my eyes wander up and down the aisles to make sure. No one. I had never been alone in my church before. The silence was kind. I was welcome. I wanted to respond with an embrace. Wrapped only in the outside sounds of cascading water, I felt majestic. I took a few steps down the aisle, leaving footsteps on the polished floor. Mama said I could not have a baby until I was married. I saw myself in a wedding gown walking down that aisle. The image was suddenly broken by the unpleasant smell of my drenched coat. And something else. I sniffed the faint odor of my new womanhood. Frank had said "sin." I wondered if it were a sin to walk down the church aisle without a wedding gown, leaking water from one end and, ever so faintly, blood from the other.

A new excitement began to overwhelm me. It was like the unexpected power in my voice yesterday when I said I was not sick. I processed slowly down the aisle toward the altar rail, looking around nervously to be sure I was alone. No visitors while the storm lasted. I removed my coat, put the package on the kneeling part of the communion rail, then draped my coat across the rail, near the votive lights, hoping for some warmth. After I removed my sandals, I walked up and down the kneeler, holding out my arms to balance, the way Frank and I used to balance on a fence. The carpet tickled my feet. They began to feel warm. Then in sheer exuberance, I leapfrogged over the altar rail and into the sanctuary. I stopped and smiled up at the sanctuary lamp. Tinker Bell had gone, and God did not strike me dead. I danced after the shadow of the flickering light as it leaped across the rich red of the rug. Nobody had ever told me that God laughed and wanted me that close. Nobody had ever told me that He loved to dance.

When I reached home, Frank was on the front steps, his head slumped over his fists.

"Why don't you go upstairs?"

"I'm scared."

I sat beside him. "What did you do?"

"Mama will kill me," he said.

"Why?"

"Donald's mother came to see Mama. She just left a little while ago." He repeated, "I'm scared."

"Me, too." I could only guess. "You told Donald about what happened to me."

In two days he had gone from best friend and companion to little brother. Now his little boy voice rose a pitch. "I didn't *know* what happened to you." He was crying. I could never bear to see him cry.

"Is that why Mrs. Hopkins came to see Mama?"

He sat up. "I was on Donald's porch telling him about how you didn't have to go to school because you had something wrong with you that you were going to have almost forever and you couldn't even tell me."

I wished I were back on the red carpet.

Frank continued, "Mr. Hopkins heard us talking and he came out and Donald told him and then Mr. Hopkins asked me when Daddy died and lots of things like that. Then..."

"Then, then what?"

"Then he told us, Donald and me, about girls, you and all girls, and he talked about us."

"Us?"

"Yeah, boys. Things happen to us, too. He said it was all very wonderful."

"Mama said that, too." I came to her defense.

"Then Donald's mother came out. She gave us milk and cookies, and that's when she said that all of this happened by accident."

"It isn't an accident. It's supposed to happen."

"No. No!" I had never seen him so agitated. "She meant me now knowing and asking Donald and Donald asking his father, and so *I* got all of that big secret stuff explained to me *there*." As he belched out the *there*, he waved his arms in the direction of the Hopkinses' house. "She said it was Mama's right to tell me all that, and so that's why she came to see Mama. To tell her how I got to find out."

I thought of Mama's rules about family business.

He was crying again. "I'm glad you're not really sick, but Mama must be awful mad!"

I remembered Mama's awkward tenderness in telling me what she should have told me long ago. And I thought about my horror at hearing it, not even wanting her calendar.

But this?

"Frank," I said, "I think we should both go in." My laughing God was far away.

The too quiet flat had a wonderful aroma of beef stew. Frank's favorite. A lemon meringue pie was on a plate from our good china. My favorite. Intimate smells of treats prepared before Mrs. Hopkins's visit.

Where was Mama? I took Frank's hand. We tiptoed through the small hall bedroom and into the front room.

We did not see her at first. She was molded into the rocking chair. It was almost dark. Multi-shades of gray clouds coaxed the lace curtains to touch my mother's thumbs. Those thumbs were wrestling each other, playing like kittens in her hands. Except for the thumbs, she looked as though she would never move again.

We stood together. Stunned. After a moment, I let go of his hand. "Go to her," I said. And he did. I saw him drop onto her lap, neither caring nor watching for danger signals. Her long dry sob crunched the frozen river of my childhood like an icebreaker on the Great Bay. I did not know if the broken chunks were coming up through my throat or down between my legs.

For a moment, I longed to join them, but I knew that once

again I was outside. Instead, I went into the kitchen to light the light under the stew.

Matches were forbidden to me. But those rules were a long time ago, long before I saw that my mother had a face, and long, long before I danced with God on His own red carpet, smelling of early womanhood and a spring storm.

from *What Mattered We Left Out*

Part Two
Section One

1.

Not far from here, at the end of River Run, is a group of streets named by the Mave brothers for the members of their family: John, the father; Marguerite; and her brothers, Charles and James. At the end of the main road was the house where John Joseph Mave, the father of Celia's mother and two uncles, lived for only a year before his death. After Celia's own father died, Celia and her mother moved into the house.

From the front steps of the house, you could see the Ohio River as it flowed past the Kentucky foothills to the southeast. In the afternoon, alone in her room, Celia sat by the window. Her view was of the trees in the yard; a dense cluster of leaves hid the river from sight. Close against the side of the building was a warm shadow. By late day there was no shade and the trees were bright green. It was very hot, and the curtains, made of white cloth, never moved.

The riverbanks were lined with trees. The water carried the reflections of trees and the occasional boat floating by. If she was very still, she could hear the beating wings of large birds looking for fish in the river, or leaves rustling on the branches. If she waited long enough, she heard the sound the water made, soft, then getting louder, a rush of force without meaning; her thoughts idle, swift, also without meaning.

Now the river is lined with buildings, old docks and ferry launches turned into restaurants and bars. The water is brown, the boats are industrial. On sunny days Celia played along the water's edge. It's different now, everything's changed. Factories, warehouses crouch under overpasses, highways connecting places that used to be reached on foot, or on dirt roads along the river where the Indian trail used to run.

* * *

The house was named Lookout and stood at an elevation and at the angles of north and south, east and west. Built from materials taken from the Blessed Sacrament parish house when the church was razed in 1899, it was a rambling three-story structure of brick and stone with a mansard roof, wood and stone porches on the sides.

The wings at each side were added later. One of the wings housed a chapel with a high-pitched roof and early English lancet windows. Under the altar were the sacred bones of St. Felicitas, presented to the Mave brothers by an envoy from Rome in 1910, the year that Celia was born.

Beyond the main hallway, the house opened out onto the backyard and a patio, a floor of baked mud and the dandelions which miraculously grew out of the parched soil. The house became dilapidated, the roof sagged, and there were leaks in it. Inside, the furnishings varied in relation to their function. Personal quarters were modest. Upstairs in rooms with dormer windows, the family slept on camp beds. Celia slept in a room at the side of the house.

As time went on, Celia's mother developed a fear of the dark. At night she walked across the porch below Celia's open window, back and forth. Celia listened to her footsteps. Her mother stood looking at the trees, down the road, maybe at nothing at all. When the wood began to rot, it was harder to walk across the porch. Celia's uncle kept promising to fix the boards but never did. He said if they rotted away completely, she'd stop walking.

Each year, in the springtime, the dullness of the falling-down house was lifted by the bright flowering trees and beds of wild myrtle. Each spring the magnolias and dogwoods blossomed early, their buds coaxed open by a few warm days in March then killed by a frost soon after. By summer the trees had lost their flowers, the dogwood petals making a carpet under the trees.

2.

Blood Run Boulevard was the name of the old valley trail that ran behind their house. According to the map of 1812, the road was named in 1789 after a group of travelers were tomahawked in an Indian ambush. The valley, too, was named Blood Run. In 1929, the town council decided to rename the road. Though people resisted the loss of the historic name, the council won. Now it's Victory Parkway that runs through Blood Run Valley, and not even the wooded hillsides and meadows that flank the road are called by that name any longer.

On a ridge above Blood Run Valley, far from the city traffic, was the Northern County Tuberculosis Sanatorium. A map from 1921 shows the layout. The main hospital looked out over one hundred and fifty acres of land above Lick Run Valley and the Ohio River. The buildings, made of stucco and brick, were grouped on a hill near the center of the grounds; a main hospital building, a nurses' home, garage, preventorium, occupational therapy building, and dormitories for the medical staff. The hospital had five hundred and eighty-three beds, plus a hundred additional beds in the preventorium. A short distance from the rest of the buildings, the preventorium was where children from families with tuberculosis were sent. It was where they treated those who'd been exposed to the disease and were at risk from tuberculosis, and it housed a children's school run by the state.

Celia had lived in the house with her uncles and her mother for twelve years when her mother died, upstairs on a cot in a room with no screens in the windows. She remembered how the flies and mosquitos had swarmed the kerosene lamp every night until her mother passed away. After that, her uncles raised her, a strict upbringing. When she was old enough, Celia worked in the sanatorium, keeping minds and hands busy with embroidery frames, balls of wool, painting. At first, when they'd just arrived, the patients weren't allowed to read. They could only listen to the radio. No games, no crossword puzzles. The mildest game, if it excites you, exhausts you, the nurses said.

Just after she'd turned sixteen, Celia started showing signs of consumption. She grew thin and tired. She had spells of nausea. By her next birthday, she had contracted TB, and for the next four years, spent time in and out of the various wards.

The last time she stayed at the hospital, she was placed in the same room where her father had died. The windows along the hall outside her room looked out across the sanatorium grounds, the new St. Joseph Cemetery, a one-hundred-and-seventy-five-acre burial ground bounded on the north by Rapid Run Pike, on the east by Nebraska and Pedretti Avenues. The eastern half of the cemetery, bordering directly on Nebraska Avenue, was known officially as Cathedral Cemetery. The old St. Joseph cemetery still occupies both sides of West Eighth Street, west of Enright Avenue. The nine-and-a-half-acre plot on the north is the Irish Catholic section.

3.

It was always dark outside when they came to wake her. Someone came to the door and banged loudly. She put the pillow over her head when they came in. Underneath the covers, she closed her eyes and imagined she was running away. She was meeting Francisco at the railroad tracks, behind the neighbors' fence. She pushed through the tall grass that grew along the tracks, knee-deep in weeds, and tripped on a root, fell onto her hands. Then he was standing there, behind her.

It had been years now since the day they'd made that plan; two years before she'd gotten sick, while her mother was still alive. Francisco was a boy in her school, but her uncles had long ago forbidden them to meet. He'd said he'd come for her soon, that they'd go somewhere together where he had friends. That was at least three years ago now. He must have gone without her.

4.

To see outside, she had to look through the wire mesh that kept the flies out. The screen made a mosaic on the buildings across the way, the pieces of the mosaic were red; the buildings were made of brick, strong and impervious. The planes of light that shimmered on the colored areas were diffused by the screen. Sometimes squinting, she saw the wire mesh as a thin covering, a veil that she might slip through and then she'd be on the other side.

In the morning, the aide came in at six with a pint of milk and a raw egg, then again at seven, again at eight. Next she went to the porch and sat outside for an hour. Then breakfast was served in a large room in the basement, where the patients who could walk met three times a day for feedings; the undernourished nourishing themselves. Watching the mortal parts waste away while the spirit grows lighter, after desire has died away. Never as lovely as on that day when the last traces of earthly degradation are gone forever.

When she returned she noticed the room was filled with flies.

She wondered, out loud, how the flies got in so quickly.

Because it's summer, a voice answered her. There was a new bed in the room with a woman sitting up in it, beautiful like Celia, white pallor and red flush.

Because you lifted the screen and insisted on leaving the windows open, the voice added.

She liked the air, she said, and besides, she only left it open that morning when she went to breakfast. She forgot, and when she came back, she found the flies swarming. Celia went over to the window. She walked with a slight stoop.

From her bed, through the screen, she saw the tops of other buildings, red brick towers, and she watched the sun move across them. Her hands were so thin, folded in her lap.

It's dangerous, being so careless—Eleanor Grymes introduced herself. She leaned forward slowly and handed Celia a copy of *Cheerio*, the newsletter for the people who never went beyond the grounds of the sanatorium. For the period of November 21 to December 25, there were forty-five new names under the heading Admissions and at least thirty names under the heading Discharges. What it didn't say was that fifty-six percent of the men, that sixty-eight percent of the women, survived, or that in 1931, 21,930 people would die from TB.

The January issue of *Cheerio* was a dozen typed pages of patients' contributions, including poems, and a section called News Flashes. Celia read the News Flashes.

Greetings, Fellow San Mates!

The fat boy in the elevator playing a red ukelele. And what about the boys in A-3? Singing "everybody knows you left me" since their girlfriends were discharged. Everyone says they better hurry up and get out themselves or their girls will have new boyfriends. Annie and Stella were transferred to the D-Building.

By late morning, sunlight fell across the yard, and she watched the workmen outside. They work so hard out there . . . she thought about them a lot. As a child she'd been accused of having an inexhaustible supply of energy. Now, she was always tired, and time seemed to hang suspended in some middle distance, nearer to eternity, so infinitesimally slow in its progress, like a drop of water that wouldn't fall.

Everyone's asking who was that boy in the elevator playing the red ukelele? Well Happy New Year to all and here's to our new colleagues, welcome Minnie and Josie. A note for the girls: Lonely Romeos temporarily laid up with jupe desire company. Come down and look them over some evening.

Welcome Harriet. We hope the newcomers like us and that their stays are pleasant and short.

Boys in the East Wing are talking again. Trips to the country, husking corn, splitting wood, shooing the chickens out of the pen. Shooting pool and playing poker—one has to be a Chicago gangster to keep in the running with these boys.

Since RH has had the pneumothorax he can't go up the stairs so he's asking folks to stop by and visit him in A-3. And has anyone seen Mr. Becker? You can't touch him since he's been promoted to a wheel chair. He was last seen on the West Porch. The girls on the West Porch want to thank Miss Rose for serving real coffee with the lovely Thanksgiving dinner. And we've got the cutest baby on the West Porch. She plays with stuffed rabbits and wears a blue checkered cap with a strap tied under her chin on cold days. (Hey—where does she tie it on hot days?)

5.

Celia was pale and lovely with a beautiful wide mouth, fleshy lips. Subject to spells of hyperactivity, then languor.

God hath not called us into uncleanliness but into holiness. Mrs. Grymes recited her prayers in the morning. Mrs. Grymes was only there because they threatened to put a red quarantine tag on her family's house if she stayed.

It may or may not have been your fault, she told Celia, but it's certainly someone's fault you got sick.

Celia's collapsed lung was bad. Beanbags on the chest weren't working. Four hours a day, she lay there with the bags on her chest, looking at the ceiling. They decided to operate, first remove a few ribs and part of the lung. Then in a few weeks they planned to remove the rest of the lung.

Under ether, the nerves and muscles were cut, ribs snapped and removed. A crescent-shaped scar from the base of her neck to her armpit, another long line below that. The lung, collapsed, forever out of commission. The flesh had fallen in beneath the collarbone.

Calcified cavities can rupture, causing sudden death. That's what happened to Miss Parks. They were all sitting on her bed telling jokes, and when she stopped laughing, she started coughing up blood. An hour later she was dead. Everyone had said she was getting better.

Emaciated. Sunken chests, claw-like hands. Night sweats, fever, burning up from within, and the brightness that comes in the morning, the clarity of vision. Celia dreams of a prairie fire, of cows and pigs consumed in flames, and the disease moving through the air, infecting her lungs.

Dr. Good said repressed desire always returned in the form of disease. Sleeplessness, permanent diarrhea, ceaseless coughing, spitting up yellow phlegm then blood.

Adulteresses with lung trouble. Quarantined there. The suffering they'd caused they can't imagine.

Celia was in bed for six months after the surgery. Couldn't hold up her head, no support for her spine, since they took out all the ribs on her left side.

On her twenty-first birthday, Celia was given Extreme Unction for the seventh time. At night she lay awake; listened to groans and sleeptalking. The voices ask Mary Magdalene, Woman, why weepest thou? Death row, the isolation ward, was occupied by outpatients. Putting them in tubs of crushed ice to slow the internal bleeding. In the dawn light Celia counted the frozen bodies of those who'd died the night before, laid out on the lawn, waiting to be removed.

6.

Celia recalls her life before she came here. She imagines all sorts of things, all day, while other people, people she can't see, are free to come and go, their migratory passings to and from places she could only guess at. She closes her eyes and pictures a thin line of gray asphalt, a road she might have traveled. They're riding on an empty road, a smell of freshly cut grass comes in with the warm air. She keeps the picture in her mind, the picture is of him. She watches his hands.

The doctor said it was a matter of months before she could leave. She writes a letter. She pretends she's back in the town, that she's still in the school where she met him, that she's still a young girl, with two lungs and a healthy body.

I've been sitting here in this room afraid I might die of boredom or loneliness until I saw you down there in the street. I hope you'll let me know if you want to see me, leave me a note. Tomorrow I can slip out for a minute and check to see if you've left anything on the ledge above the ivy. I promise I'll write back if you tell me what you'd like me to do.

Celia tore the note into pieces. No one was waiting for her. She looked over at the empty bed next to hers and tried to imagine the next roommate. She picked up *Cheerio* and studied the list of admissions for a name that sounded nice to her.

Just a little longer, Dr. Good said. There was a great deal of discharge from the sinus and violent pains. Nothing serious.

Outside, the green had given way to brown, after seventeen months in the hospital; the same yellow walls, gray curtains.

Annie and Stella were transferred to the D-Building. The preventorium is full. They listen to the radio constantly, keeping up on local news, hoping it won't be long until they'll resume normal life on the outside. The patients of C-11 are losing one of their finest, Nurse Bradly. She will surely be missed. Congratulations to you Mary Moon on leaving your bed twice a day. And a welcome to our new colleagues this month, Minnie and Josie. The girls on the West porch say hello.

Note: The newsletter Cheerio *is based on a newsletter of the same name which the author found in Ohio—an issue dated January 1934.*

Tea at the House

I was born on the grounds of the Mount Mohonk Hospital for the Insane, where my father was Chief of Psychiatry, and because of this I grew accustomed to the sounds of misery before I went to sleep at night. I would lie in bed upstairs in my family's house, which was situated one hundred yards from the main building, and after lights out, I would hear shrieking and weeping as though animals were being slaughtered. No, no, it was nothing like that, my father assured me, coming into the bedroom. These patients were in psychic anguish, he said, and no one was laying a hand on them.

Now it has been nearly fifty years since I lived there, and while the hospital still exists, its nurses now wear street clothes, the bars have been sandblasted off all its windows, and "Insane" has long been extinguished from its name. But back when I lived on the grounds of the hospital with my father and mother, the gates were padlocked at dusk by an aging groundskeeper, and those night-time shrieks echoed through the surrounding hills, frightening the locals and waking the deer.

"Is anyone being beaten?" I asked my father before bed.

"No one is being beaten," he answered.

"Is anyone being whipped?"

"No one is being whipped."

"Slapped?"

"No one is being slapped."

"Throttled?"

"Where did you learn *that* word?" asked my father. And so it went, this bedtime ritual, and though many of the patients stayed up weeping and howling throughout the long night, I was able to sleep the fluent sleep of children. To the patients, this place was a hospital, a prison, but to me it was home.

It was my father who decided that I would become a doctor. He had read in one of his medical journals that an unprecedented number of girls were entering the field of medicine, and there were even photographs accompanying the article, as if anyone needed proof: a fleet of bulky young women in white coats and harlequin glasses, standing behind an autoclave. The idea of me, a seven-year-old girl who pasted pictures of iceboxes and hairstyles into scrapbooks, eventually transforming into one of these women, seemed a reach. But my mother had been told she could bear no more children. This meant that there would never be a son, so one morning my father walked into my room, sighed, then stretched the jaws of a stethoscope around my neck. For a brief moment, thinking it was jewelry, I picked up the silver disk at the bottom and held it between my fingers like a religious medal. My father tried to smile encouragingly, for this was clearly a big moment for him, a rite of passage. His stethoscope and his trays of equipment and his vast library with titles such as *The Hysterical Female* and *Sexual Normality and Abnormality: Twelve Case Studies*—all of this would be turned over to me at some appropriate point in my life.

By the time I grew up, most of the authors were long dead, as were their tormented patients. Even the publishing houses—with names like Pingry & Seagrove, Burroway Bros., Smollett and Sons—no longer existed. The entire world, as I knew it then, no longer existed, but seemed to have been snuffed out like some ancient star. Back when my father decided I would become a doctor, the Depression had settled in over the whole country. Nurses had been "let go," as my father said, and I pictured packs of women in white scattering across the lawn, their fluted cupcake-paper nurses' caps sent sailing. Week after week, families yanked seriously ill patients out of the hospital. A schizophrenic man might be shipped off to distant cousins in Iowa or Nebraska, doomed to spend his days with an American Gothic couple who had agreed, for a fee, to take in this peculiar relative who never spoke. The farm couple would stare in perplexity at their boarder and wonder what in the world to do with him: sit him down on a thresher and put him to work? Wrap his hands around the swollen udders of a cow? Or just let him sit on the porch and rock? Other patients were pulled out of the hospital and deposited on the streets of New York City, which swallowed them effortlessly. Many of these men and women drank themselves sick or froze during the long winter.

A small, elite population remained at Mount Mohonk through-out the Depression, and these patients were my father's bread and butter. They were an unlikely assortment of men and women whose families had secret, inexplicable reservoirs of money, and who seemed untouched by dark times. Here was the nucleus of unassailably rich America: shrewd bankers who could afford to keep unbalanced, yammering wives confined to the mountaintop for as long as it took. And sometimes it took forever.

Over the years, seeing the same faces in the windows of the hospital, the same figures in soft robes lumbering down the gravel footpath, I became comforted by how little anything changed. The faces were as familiar as those of relatives seen year after year at holiday dinners. There was Harry Beeman, a financier who had jumped from his fifteenth-floor office in the Bankers' Equity Building, only to bounce twice on the striped tarp of the build-ing's awning, crushing several ribs and both legs. Now he limped through the halls of Mount Mohonk with a copy of *The Financial Times* in front of his face, muttering about figures as though any of it still mattered to him. There was Mildred Vell, a society matron with milky cataracts and a delusion about being Eleanor Roosevelt, which none of the nurses really minded, because it made Mildred a great help on the ward, always volunteering for some project or other. The core group of patients never grew worse, never seemed to get better, and never asked when they could leave. The world wasn't going to open up for these people; it stayed stubbornly shut, an aperture that let in no outside light.

The same was true, in a way, for my family. We seemed separat-ed from the world, at least the world as it revealed itself through the large rosewood radio that sat in the living room. The Depres-sion touched the edges of our lives, fraying them, certainly, but leaving everyone intact. What I did learn about the world came largely from a source that had been available to me for years, but which I had never thought to consult. One morning, when I was twelve years old, with my mother in the kitchen downstairs and my father at the hospital across the lawn, I entered my father's study, mounted a rolling ladder that was attached to the floor-to-ceiling bookshelves, and brought down the copy of *Sexual Nor-mality and Abnormality: Twelve Case Studies.*

What did I know about these matters? All morning I sat with

the book heavy in my lap, struggling to make out the tiny type-face. I sat with legs crossed, chewing a piece of hair, shocked but caught up in the tide of words and their meanings. All winter my father kept the thermostat in his study at a constant fifty-eight degrees, and I imagined that the temperature had to be kept so low or else the books might self-destruct. It was as though I were holding the original Gutenberg Bible in my hands, and that this room served as some special emergency vacuum in case of fire or apocalypse. But even if there was an apocalypse, these words would float over the wreckage of the world, so deep were they embedded in me, so deep already at twelve.

And all my father had done was drape a stethoscope around my neck. But somehow he had crowned me some twisted version of Miss America: Miss Toilet Mouth, Miss Disgusting Secrets, *Little Miss Disgusting Secrets*. I could hardly get through the week without dipping into my new fund of knowledge. Images scrolled by in pornographic frescoes, and I realized that I could have become rich in the playground of my day school, had I sold my classified information. Any single page torn from *Sexual Normality and Abnormality: Twelve Case Studies* would have fetched a good price at school, and since the volume was over five hundred pages long, my father would have never known the difference. But I couldn't tear anything out of that book; it would have been like ripping "Letters to the Romans" out of the Gutenberg Bible. Entire sections stayed in my mind, eventually memorized as thoroughly as the Pledge of Allegiance:

"Miss H.," began the case study on p. 348, "was born in a rural home in Norway to illiterate farming parents. Because she did not attend school, but instead worked the fields alongside her brothers, she had no official medical records. It was not until many years later, when she was working as a cook in the village of S___ and was subsequently hospitalized for acute appendicitis at the regional clinic in that village, that physicians discovered the truth about Miss H. She was a rarity, a true hermaphrodite, equipped with both phallus and vagina, the former being no bigger than a pea pod, the latter equally undeveloped. The doctors at the clinic in S___ allowed a small group of visiting medical students to view their patient's deformity, and she was thusly paid a wage to appear regularly at lectures at the medical college in nearby O___. Miss

H.'s life, while spent alone, proved far more satisfying than the lives of other such individuals, many of whom attempt to join in sexual relations, and who find their advances rebuffed, often by a horrified individual who has just realized the True Nature of this creature. Sometimes, the hermaphrodite can find a peaceful home among the denizens of a carny troupe or travelling sideshow." [1]

The story of Miss H. was as riveting as it was appalling; I could imagine the woman's wide Nordic face, and even, if I tried hard enough, her collision of sex organs. Sometimes I would forego the text entirely and just read the index, my finger skittering along the stunning list of words. Every body part was in this list, and every perverse activity; nothing was excluded. All the shameful words from the school bathroom walls were here, printed neatly on heavy-bond paper, not gouged into plaster by a twelve-year-old's erratic penknife. No janitor had tried to paint over them, to refinish the surface with some virginal gloss. No, these words were *actually meant to be understood.*

So this was my future, this world where people with contorted minds and bodies coupled blindly in assorted ways. I couldn't bear to believe it, yet I knew it was true. I knew it because of my parents, could see it in their eyes and their easy posture when they were together. My father was always touching my mother; there was rarely a moment when they were in the same room and their limbs did not lightly connect. Since my mother could not conceive, what they did in their bedroom was done for the pleasure of it. They were a good fit, my father with his red mustache and rimless glasses and thick arms, my mother with her black hair swept off her neck with a silver comb.

They had met and fallen in love one summer when both of their families were staying at a bungalow colony in the Catskills called Lustig's. My father, David Welner, was a young medical student at the time, which gave him a certain clout. Whenever anyone approached him that summer, he would cheerfully agree to listen to a litany of complaints, to inspect what someone called, under his breath, a "suspicious" mole. In reality, he had no clinical experience yet; at City College's medical school, his class was still enmeshed in the fundamentals of biology and chemistry, spending afternoons drawing diagrams of the Krebs Cycle, or becoming familiar with the respiratory systems of fish. When he lifted the ribbed undershirt of a sixty-year-old man on vacation and peered at a dark brown disk the size of a quarter, he was simply using a combination of common sense and bits of knowledge he had gathered from the weekly "Ask Dr. Colin Sylvester" column in *The New York Herald*. But he charmed everyone, and no one was worse off for his diagnosis.

"Avoid the sun like the plague, Mrs. Kimmel," he told a woman with parchment skin. "Get some rest," he told a nervous young newlywed husband. All around the colony, men and women followed David Welner's instructions, lying in the shade for naps, swigging plenty of fresh water, eating roughage. Everyone was happy, mosquitoes dotted the surface of the lake, the summer slowly unrolled.

Toward the end of the season, my parents became engaged. My father had been chosen to judge the bungalow colony's annual beauty pageant. Of the twelve Brooklyn and Bronx girls who paraded along the dock, making their way across the scarred planks in their stiletto heels, my mother was the one he chose, hands down. At eighteen, Justine Fogel was tall, with a head of jet hair and high, impressive breasts. She was planning on studying voice in Manhattan in September. A neighbor knew of a vocal coach named Oskar Mennen who would instruct her once a week for a low fee. His slogan was "If *you've* got a sliding scale, I've got one, too."

But my mother never went to see Oskar Mennen. Instead, she married David Welner shortly after Labor Day, and the couple moved to a tenement apartment on Chrystie Street in Lower Manhattan. During the day, my father went to classes and my mother sat at home practicing scales; at night they cooked a plain dinner on their stove and went to bed. Sometimes in the middle of the night, he woke up and sat in the living room studying; she could see a tiny yellow bulb burning in the living room, and his silhouette curved in concentration under the light.

Slowly, my father became noticed in his classes. One day he attracted the attention of a visiting professor of psychiatry named Fox Mendelson, and over the years the two men kept up a correspondence. Later, when my father was looking for a position, Mendelson recommended him to the board of trustees at a private hospital called Mount Mohonk. The job paid poorly, but my father was willing. He was a Jew, and had noticed a distinct strain of anti-Semitism among psychiatrists, despite the fact that their god was a Jew himself. In the hospitals and clinics of New York City, he encountered psychiatrists with names like Warner Graves and Loren St. John, men with silver-threaded hair and deep, uninflected voices and degrees from Amherst and Harvard. What my father had going for himself was wit, dexterity, and the ability to leap from bed at four in the morning to subdue a schizophrenic who was smacking a nurse over the head with a cast-iron bedpan. He was handsome and didn't seem too ambitious, and he raised interesting points during grand rounds. At age thirty-two, he became the youngest chief psychiatrist in the brief and undistinguished history of the Mount Mohonk Hospital for the Insane.

He and my mother inhabited the large house across the lawn from the hospital, taking as their bedroom the room that overlooked the road out front. It was almost possible for them to lie in their four-poster and imagine that they lived in a normal home, on a real street, like any other young couple. But at night, when the howling started, they remembered.

My father was a hit with the nurses and orderlies. He strode the shining halls of the hospital as though he had been running the place since birth. Even his memos were praised. ("Re: hospital gowns. It has come to my attention that the dung-colored gowns worn by our patients are perhaps no good for morale. Might we find something with a bit more dash—perhaps peach or sky-blue?")

My mother fell quickly, but less gracefully, into her role as the chief psychiatrist's wife. Before the Depression, her job largely entailed standing in the middle of her kitchen, conferring with a mute Negro hospital cook about upcoming dinner parties at the house. She would wave her pale hands vaguely, opening drawers and pointing to spoons and knives, saying, "Now, there are the spoons. Oh, and the knives." She was hesitant in this role; no one had ever waited on her before except her grandmother, who used to section her grapefruit for her with a serrated knife. But that was different. That was family. This was help. *Help;* the word itself was so strong, something you would call out when you were drowning. Her whole life was becoming unrecognizable.

They were aimless, both of my parents, rolling around in this huge house together, anxious to populate the rooms with children. By the time I was born, they were ready, tired of seeing only mentally ill people, eager for an infant's simple and understandable cry. But when the obstetrician told my mother that she could bear no more children, my father let his only daughter into his life in a way that no one, not even his wife, had been allowed.

Every few months he took me on a whirlwind tour of the hospital: the dining room, which smelled perennially of fried flounder, the Occupational Therapy room, where dead-eyed patients pressed images of dogs and presidents onto copper sheeting, the solarium, the visitors' lounge. We breezed past doors with doctors' names stenciled onto the grain, and past doors with signs that read WARNING: ELECTRICITY IN USE. These doors were always shut, and I longed to see what electricity looked like when it was "in use." And I also longed to see where the patients actually lived, where they showered and dressed and bathed. But the wards themselves, with their heavy doors with chicken wire laced into the glass, were off-limits. I was allowed to see hospital life only from a distance, watching as patients slogged through the halls in their dung-colored gowns and flannel robes. I often stood staring at them, and once I made prolonged eye contact with an obese man whose face was blue with stubble, until I was whisked off into the nurses' lounge, where big band music emanated from the radio, and I was given a handful of sourballs by a trio of fussing women. And then the tour was over.

Although I was allowed into the hospital only at my father's invitation, I was free to explore the grounds whenever I liked. With the sun sinking and the air aromatic with pine and earth and Salisbury steak, the whole place smelled like a summer camp. One day, at the rear entrance of the building, I saw delivery men unloading drums of institutional disinfectant. As they rolled them up a ramp and into the service entrance, I could read the words "Whispering Pines," and even though the name referred to nothing more than a rancid fluid that would be swabbed across the floors and walls at dawn, it sounded like the perfect alias for the hospital, the ideal name for a splendid summer camp.

Whispering Pines, I whispered to myself as I stepped into the thicket that continued until the edges of the grounds, where it was held back by the iron fence. Vines flourished along that fence, wound around the spokes like a cat winding around a human leg. Just as the patients often seemed to want out, so did the vegetation. Everything grew frantically at the farthest reaches of the property. The most tangible signs of the times could be found there, at the edges of the land, where nobody had bothered to prune or clip or chop away at the excess. Sometimes a group of patients would sit on Adirondack chairs on the lawn, taking in a chilly hour of sun, and sometimes a nurse would take a patient on a supervised stroll, but only along the circular path closest to the hospital, and never into the woods. The woods were mine, at least for a while.

The summer I turned fourteen, my father implemented a program he called "Tea at the House." This involved inviting a promising patient to join him and my mother for afternoon tea in our living room. The patient was always someone at least a little bit appealing, someone who wouldn't make any sudden moves. Someone very close to health, who needed a bit of encouragement to topple him or her completely onto the other side.

The first person invited to Tea at the House was a woman named Grace Allenby, a young mother who had had a nervous breakdown and was unable to complete any action, even dressing herself in the morning, without dissolving into hysterical, gulping sobs. At the hospital she had made a slow but admirable recovery. She came to tea on the Friday before her husband was to bring her home, and I sat watching at the top of the stairs. Both Mrs. Allenby and my mother were lovely-looking and uncertain, like the deer that occasionally made a wrong turn in the woods and wound up stunned and confused and frightened on the hospital lawn. The women shyly traded recipes, while my father sat between them, nodding with benevolence.

"What you want to do is *this*," Mrs. Allenby kept saying, and as she spoke she blinked rapidly, as if to remove a speck from her eye. "You take an egg and you beat it very hard in a bowl with a whisk. Then what you want to do is *this*..." The living room smelled strongly of Oolong tea, my father's favorite. He liked it because it was the closest thing to drinking pipe tobacco.

I eavesdropped on several Teas at the House over the year, and I came to understand that mental patients could be divided into two groups: those who wore their affliction outright like a bold political stance, and those who hid it so actively that that became their trademark, grinning until their teeth might splinter, wanting so badly to hold themselves together.

Warren Keyes was of the second variety. He was a nineteen-year-old Harvard undergraduate who had tried to kill himself in his dormitory room eight months earlier, and who was close to leaving Mount Mohonk to return to school. Over dinner, my parents discussed this boy, who would be coming to Tea at the House the following day. "He's young," my father said, "and good-looking, in that Harvard way."

Warren Keyes registered in my mind in that moment, was locked into place even before I had met him. Here was a Harvard man. That went over well with my father, who often fantasized about a privileged upbringing, complete with long walks along the Charles River and various racquet sports. And it went over well with me, too, for even before I met Warren Keyes, I had sculpted his features and his limbs into some crude rendering of attractiveness.

The next afternoon at four o'clock, Warren sat in the living room gripping the fragile handle of a teacup. He had trooped across the lawn with a squat nurse, who now sat in the foyer, dully knitting like Madame Du Farge. I knew that he had been invited to the house as a reward for getting well, but casting a critical, fourteen-year-old eye on him from the top of the stairs, even I could see that he was not well.

"Warren plans on returning to Harvard next semester," my father said. My mother hummed a response. "Leverett House, isn't it?" my father went on, he who had studied at City College, yet who knew the names of all the houses at Harvard. He, who had ascended to Chief of Psychiatry at Mount Mohonk and yet who was, irrevocably, a Jew.

"No, Adams House," said Warren. His voice was relaxed, although his cup jitterbugged in its saucer.

Conversation pushed on about Harvard in general, football season, and New England weather. My mother didn't add much, and my father kept plying Warren with questions, which he politely, if wearily, answered. At the end of the hour, Warren Keyes looked exhausted. I imagined that he would go back to his hospital bed and sleep for thirty-six hours straight, regaining his strength.

Breaking his own tradition but questioned by no one, Dr. Welner invited Warren Keyes back for a second Tea at the House, and then a third. On his fourth tea, he was unaccompanied by the dour-faced nurse. Instead, he made a solo flight across the lawn, his coattails floating out behind him. That afternoon, I had been strategically sitting on the porch doing my homework before taking a walk in the woods. My hair was sloppily bound up behind my head with elastic, and there was ink on my fingers, for I had not yet mastered the fountain pen. But even so, Warren Keyes climbed onto the porch and gave me a good hard look. Although it was not the first time I had seen Warren Keyes, it was the first time he saw me.

"I'm the daughter," I said. He nodded. "They're inside," I told him, inclining my head toward the screen door. Deep in the house, the tea kettle shrilled.

"Do you like tea?" Warren asked. It was the kind of question that my father's colleagues often asked me when they came to dinner: well-meaning and uninteresting probings from people who had no idea of what to say to children, yet somehow, maddeningly, meant to be answered.

"I like it okay," I said.

"Your mother makes good tea," Warren said. "It's Chinese, you know."

I slid off the railing. "I have to go," I said.

His eyes widened slightly. "Where are you going?" he asked.

And for some reason, I told him. I told him where I went every afternoon; I practically drew him a treasure map with an X. Later, I sat in the woods reading *The Red Badge of Courage,* and suddenly there was a parting of branches. Warren Keyes came through, stooped and stumbling in. He had in his hand a familiar folded linen napkin with scalloped edges. He squatted down beside me, this handsome, ruined Harvard sophomore, and he opened the napkin, which contained three golden circles: my mother's Belgian butter cookies. I took them silently, and ate them just as silently, while Warren watched.

"So what's it like to live here?" he asked.

What it was like, I thought, was like anything else. Like going to the day school seven miles away. Like owning arms. I shrugged. How I wanted to ask him a similar question: What was it like to live *there*, inside a hospital for the insane? What was it like to be insane? Was it like a long and particularly vivid nightmare? Did you know you were insane? Did you long to crawl out of your body? Did you actually see things—shapes and animals and flames dancing across the walls of your room at night? But I couldn't bring myself to ask him anything at all. Light was draining from the patch of woods, and suddenly Warren said, "May I ask you something?"

"Yes," I said.

"Could I maybe touch you?" the boy asked.

I nodded solemnly, really believing, in that moment, that he was referring to my hand, or my arm. He wanted to touch me to see if I was real, the way, years earlier, I myself had surreptitiously touched the bloodless face of my cousin's beloved china doll. He wanted to touch me in order to have the experience of touching someone who wasn't insane—someone who had a normal life and lived with her parents in a real house without bars on the windows. He wanted to touch me to see what I was like.

Warren came closer, sliding across the dirt floor to where I sat with my book. "I won't hurt you," he said.

"I know," I said. When his hand came down on one of my breasts, those recent arrivals, I could not have been more shocked. I did not know how to stop this, and I felt at once hurled out of my own realm and into his. "Now wait," I said, but his hands were already moving freely above my clothes. He seemed not to have heard me. He sat in front of me, touching my breasts, my neck, my shoulders, and in fact he wasn't hurting me. So what was I upset about? I didn't know what to call it, this thing he was doing, this casual exploration. It was his face that frightened me—the intense and worshipful expression on his features, as though he were kneeling and lighting candles. His mouth hung open, his eyes were focused.

"I'm not hurting you," he kept repeating. "I'm not hurting you." And all I could answer was, "No. You're not."

I closed my eyes so I wouldn't have to see his face. I closed them as if to block out a strong sunlight. I felt myself grow dizzy, but I thought it would be worse if I fainted, because who knew what would happen then? When I came to, I could never be sure of what had taken place. So I made myself stay conscious, and I felt each motion he made, the starfish movements of his fingers as they slipped beneath my blouse and headed downward. I knew the names of all the parts he was touching, and in my panic I recited them under my breath. His hands toured a living index from the back of my father's book, and as they did, I summoned up all the words I knew. But what good did it do me to know these things, to know what they meant when I couldn't even *manage* them?

He moved against me as if in a trance, and I felt like a wall, something for others to rub against; I was a cat-scratching post, a solid block. I felt his large hand inside my underwear, so out of place, so wrong. The elastic waistband with its row of rosettes was pulled taut against his knuckles. Just that morning I had chosen the underwear from a drawer, where it lay with the others, ironed, white, floral, and touched only by me and by Estella, who did our family's laundry. No one else was meant to touch it. Warren's hand was trapped inside it, like an animal that had run into a tent and was now caught. It seemed there against its will, if that were possible, if hands had a will of their own.

Now one of Warren's fingers was separating itself from the other fingers and pushing into me, sliding up into my body. I felt a shiver of pain, and then something that wasn't pain at all, but surprise. I sat straight up, and started to cry. His big finger, which had held on to my mother's teacup, which probably wore a Harvard ring sometimes, which had a flat fingernail that he trimmed in his cubicle in the hospital for the insane, if they let him have nail scissors, was deeply embedded in me, like something drilled into the ground to test for water or crude oil. Like a machine, a spike, testing the earth for vibrations or for moisture. The finger felt all these things, but I felt nothing.

After some endless time, Warren Keyes made a small sound like a lamb bleating or a hinge groaning open, and I knew that it was over. I sank back onto the surface of leaves, my body returning to itself: small, flexible, a skater's body, while Warren turned away from me, wiping his face and the front of his trousers with my mother's napkin.

In a gentle, quaking voice, he told me it was better if we left the woods separately and, of course, if I told no one about what had happened. "There's nothing to tell, anyway," he added. "I didn't hurt you." And it was true; he hadn't hurt me.

I left first, walking slowly with book in hand as though nothing had happened, like a dreamy teenaged girl leaving an afternoon of reading, but when I reached the edge of the woods, where the lawn began, I broke into a run toward the lights of my parents' house. Inside, I walked straight up the stairs, claiming I was ill and didn't want dinner. My mother pressed a cool hand to my forehead, but I shrugged it off. There would be no more touching today; even the back of a familiar hand, prospecting for fever, was too much.

That night, before going to sleep, I pushed up the window by the bed and poked my head out. From the hospital across the lawn, I heard the familiar crying and baying, and without thinking, I opened my mouth and softly joined the chorus. The sound came naturally, and I hung out that window in the warm spring night, howling quietly in a low, effortless voice, as though I had been doing it since I was born, as though it was natural to my species.

Weeks passed, and I noticed my own shift in feeling almost as though I were charting the progress of a bruise, watching it go from black to blue to brown to yellow, until finally it was only a smudge, a small trace memory. I didn't understand whether what had happened was something that Warren Keyes had actually wanted to have happen, or whether he been unable to stop himself because he was, as the name of the hospital announced, insane. Should I have felt furious, or should I have felt compassion, as my father would have? I was lost, not knowing, and after a while it became too late to ask anyone. Time separated me from the memory, and other things rose to replace it—real things, much more important than a young man touching a girl in the woods of a mental hospital somewhere in the mountains of New York State.

Arching over everything was the war in Europe. It had come into our lives through the large rosewood cabinet that my father kept in the living room beneath a Winslow Homer print, and now during dinner parties, when the meal was through, my father and his colleagues gathered around it. The maid moved through the rooms emptying ashtrays, while the doctors' wives sat quietly, sipping brandy and looking concerned, and the men out-shouted the broadcast with a running commentary of their own. They argued about invasions and strategies, and I was confused. How much would the war in Europe affect any of us? After all, the Depression had touched only the edges of our lives. The hospital had far fewer patients and a much smaller staff than it once had, but still it stayed intact, a neutral duchy in the middle of a rapidly dividing world. I decided that a war on another continent could not really touch anybody here, not these psychiatrists with their identical little mustaches, or these wives who sat listening to the barbershop quartet of male voices around them, or even me. For a while I was actually able to sustain this feeling; for a while I hung suspended in it.

But then eventually we were in the war, too; *we,* my father had said, and the word referred to some of the hospital's staff. Dr. Rogovin, Dr. Sammler, young Dr. Herd, and several of the orderlies had all enlisted. Nurses, too, left that winter to work for the Red Cross. Whispering Pines had actually gone to war.

Then one night at dinner late that January, my father slipped a letter from his breast pocket. It was written on Harvard stationery. "You remember Warren Keyes," my father said to my mother. "That Harvard boy." When I heard this, my hand sent a butter knife involuntarily crashing against a glass. After the chime subsided, my father began to read the letter aloud:

Dear Dr. Welner,

I hope you still remember me. You helped me a great deal not too long ago, and after leaving the hospital I returned to school where I gave my attention to Classics and found great pleasure in my work. Last year I took first prize here for my translations of Catullus. I wanted to let you know that I have enlisted in the Navy, and, despite my psychiatric record, have been accepted. Before I go overseas, I thought I should write you a short note to thank you for everything you have done. My regards to your wife.

Respectfully,
Warren Keyes

I sat very still at the table while my father finished reading. As he held the page up toward the light, I could see the silhouette of a small, perfect crimson seal shining through.

---

[1] Dr. Lucian Hargreaves, *Sexual Normality and Abnormality: Twelve Case Studies* (New York: Eppler and Keeney, 1919).

ABOUT MARY GORDON

A Profile by Don Lee

Earlier in her literary career, Mary Gordon was fond of quoting Flannery O'Connor, who'd once said that writers learned everything they needed to know before the age of eight. What does Gordon—the celebrated, bestselling author of four novels, three collections, and a memoir—believe she had learned? "I think I learned the importance of story," she says. "I think I learned the pleasure-bearing aspect of language. I think I had experiences of real formal beauty in Catholic liturgy. I think I knew about secrets and lies, although I didn't know that I knew it. And I think I didn't expect that human life was about happiness."

Such knowledge might seem overly profound for a mere child, but Gordon was, to say the least, precocious. Born in Far Rockaway, Long Island, in 1948, Mary Catherine Gordon grew up in Valley Stream, New York, a few towns southeast of Queens. It was a working-class neighborhood, predominantly Irish Catholic, and intellectual ambitions were actively discouraged. Yet Gordon's father, David, taught her to read when she was three years old. He took her to the library every Saturday, and he wrote her poems and love letters in German, French, Greek, and Latin. She idolized her father. A Jew who had converted to Catholicism in 1937, he passed himself off as an erudite writer and publisher who had graduated from Harvard and bandied about Oxford and the Left Bank in his youth. To his daughter, his only child, he was charismatic, handsome, fun-loving, brilliant. Decades later, Gordon would discover that he had fabricated much of his biography, but there is no denying that her father had impelled her, even at that nascent stage, to become the writer she is today.

It is no surprise, then, that Gordon was doubly shattered when her father died of a heart attack. She was seven years old. She and her mother, Anna Gagliano, the daughter of Italian and Irish immigrants who never went past the eighth grade, moved into her grandmother's Valley Stream home. Her aunt lived with them as well, and Gordon grew up with these pious, cloistered women,

Joyce Ravid

feeling utterly alone and miserable. Her mother, a legal secretary, and her aunt, a key-punch operator, had been polio victims as children and were crippled, and her grandmother was seventy-eight and ill. Gordon was the only able body in the house, one who was dreamy and artistically inclined—traits her family tried to knock out of her. "When my father died," Gordon remembers, "it was like all lights went out. I was really isolated, and really an odd duck. I think I was quite numb until adolescence, and my only real life, I would say, was reading, and I was quite prayerful. I didn't have many human relations." She attended parochial school and knew no non-Catholics. Owing to her Jewish heritage, she was made to feel like an outsider. Her family referred to Jews as "Hebes" or, in private code, as "the Persians," and, as Gordon writes in her memoir *The Shadow Man,* occasionally "they spoke the sentence that was most horrible to me, one I would hear from time to time, the tone of which gave me the only clue I have ever needed to the timbre of real hate. 'That's the *Jew* in you,' they would say whenever I did something they didn't like. Even now the memory of their emphasis on the word 'Jew' frightens me like the reports of the noise of Kristall-nacht."

Throughout her childhood, Gordon was convinced she would become a nun, albeit one who wrote poetry on the side. Her rebellion evolved slowly, coincident with her interest in boys, and was manifested by small acts of anarchy. She had always been smart, but she also caught on that she could be funny, the class clown, and therefore popular. So at fourteen, she organized an uprising. A nun was phobic about bubble gum. Gordon bought and distributed enough gum so all the students in the classroom, fifty-six insurgents, could chew and smack and blow at the same time. Real revolt soon followed. Instead of going to Jesuit-run Fordham University, as her family insisted, Gordon chose to accept a scholarship to Barnard, the women's college associated with Columbia. She had been fascinated by J. D. Salinger's books, particularly *Franny and Zooey*, and she wanted to go to New York City and meet Jewish intellectuals like Seymour Glass.

It was the late sixties when she entered the college, and she was elated by her newfound freedom in the permissive climate of the counterculture. She promptly lost her virginity, experimented a little with drugs, participated in sit-ins, went on marches to Washington, D.C., and joined the women's movement. "There was such a sense of possibility—that you could change the world, and that the poor were important and were your concern, and that others were your concern, and you had a vested interest in making the world better. It was very exciting. On the other hand, it was also a very *dark* period because the Vietnam War darkened everything. We couldn't believe anyone in authority. And we believed that our country was doing something absolutely heinous and lying about it. At the same time, there was a kind of faith that we could change it."

What she lost faith in, however, was Catholicism, alienated by its attitude toward women and its censures about sex. Even though she has since returned to the church, ultimately comforted by its role as "a caretaker of a kind of spirituality that matters a lot to me," certain doctrines deeply troubled her as a college student, and remain a conflict. "I think that the tragedy of the Catholic Church in the twentieth century is that it has put so much energy into forbidding sexual freedom," she says. "It turned itself into a kind of very perverse sexual policeman, and it's eroded its own moral authority for that reason."

Political and religious concerns notwithstanding, Gordon's main preoccupation was always her writing. After Barnard, she pursued graduate studies in literature at Syracuse University, where she took workshops with the poet W. D. Snodgrass. Disappointed by the lack of female faculty at the school, she joined a women's writers' collective that had Julia Alvarez among its members. Gradually, Gordon found that her poems were becoming more narrative, and she switched her concentration to short stories, one of which was taken by *The Virginia Quarterly Review* in 1975. Over the next three years, she published in a flurry—at least seven stories in magazines ranging from *Redbook* to *Ms.* to *The Atlantic Monthly.* And in the midst of working on her dissertation on Virginia Woolf, she started a novel, *Final Payments.* Without question, Woolf was a major influence. Gordon used to copy passages from Woolf's books onto index cards, tucking them away to support points in her thesis, and in doing so, she gained an understanding of prose rhythms: "She was the person who gave me the courage to move from poetry to prose, because she gave me the belief that you could have that poetic and imagistic intensity in a novel, that it wouldn't be lost. And I think I was very moved by the incantatory and repetitive nature of her prose and the complexity of her sentences, which were tied to a kind of velocity that made the prose move very fast."

Gordon was living in London (her first husband was an Englishman), researching Woolf at the British Museum, when, on a whim, she wrote a letter to the novelist Margaret Drabble. "I was so lonely in England," Gordon recalls, "and I loved Margaret Drabble, and I saw her on the BBC, and I wrote her a letter, a complete stranger, nobody—I hadn't been published—and I described my day. She called me up and invited me to dinner." Drabble read the manuscript for *Final Payments* and then introduced Gordon to her American agent, Peter Matson, who signed her immediately.

Final Payments went through several revisions, the most significant of which—going from third- to first-person—was suggested by Elizabeth Hardwick, Gordon's former teacher at Barnard. Random House brought out the novel in 1978, and Gordon, at twenty-nine, became an overnight sensation. The critics gushed, comparing her to Jane Austen, Doris Lessing, and

Flannery O'Connor. *Final Payments* sold sixty thousand hard-cover copies and well over a million in paperback.

The novel opens with the funeral of Joseph Moore, a conserva-tive Catholic who had been a literature professor in Queens. His daughter, Isabel, now thirty, had lived at home for the past eleven years, nursing him through a series of strokes: "I gave up my life for him; only if you understand my father will you understand that I make that statement not with self-pity but with extreme pride.... This strikes everyone in our decade as unusual, bar-barous, cruel. To me, it was not only inevitable but natural. The Church exists and has endured for this, not only to preserve itself but to keep certain scenes intact: My father and me living by our-selves in a one-family house in Queens." Isabel then sets out to develop a new life for herself, and along the way, she must ques-tion the nature of devotion and sacrifice, and make choices between the pull of the flesh and the claim of the spirit.

Gordon—who was teaching composition and living in Poughkeepsie, New York, at the time—reacted surprisingly to the tremendous fuss over her novel. "I was completely miserable because I was getting divorced," she says. "So that whole year just seems to me like a completely dislocating blur. I went from earning $11,000 a year as an instructor at a community college to suddenly being in *People* magazine. It just seemed almost to have nothing to do with me. And in that way, I didn't take it very seriously."

She dove back into her writing, and published her second novel, *The Company of Women,* in 1981. But then she noticed a disturbing pattern to her work's reception. She was being pegged—and perhaps dismissed or diminished—as a religious writer. In an interview during that period, she tried to appear cavalier about the issue. She declared that the function of novels was pleasure, to be beautiful and true, and if they were acciden-tally instructive, that was all well and good. "I'm interested in the novel as a form of high gossip," she said. These days, when asked if writers have any moral imperatives, Gordon acknowledges the difficulty and complexity of the proposition: "I think writers have a moral obligation to do the thing as beautifully as it possibly can be. Let me turn the question around and say that I think the interdiction against a moral perspective is so much in the air that writers have a responsibility not automatically to *exclude* the moral perspective." As to the matter of labels, she says, "I guess when they start calling John Updike 'the Protestant writer,' then they can start calling me 'the Catholic writer.' Again, in the way that it assumes that white male Protestant is the norm, and anything else is an 'other,' I don't want to be looked at as an exotic. Which is not to say that I don't think the experience of Catholicism has been extremely formative, but I think if you say 'Catholic writer,' you give people an excuse not to read you, and I don't like that kind of foreclosure."

Nonetheless, her books after *The Company of Women* have focused less overtly on religion. Her 1985 novel *Men and Angels* portrays an art historian who hires a psychotic religious fanatic as a mother's helper, but the book examines the more universal struggles of domesticity and human fellowship: "She wept and wept. People were so weak, and life would raise its whip and bring it down again and again on the bare tender flesh of the most vulnerable. Love was what they needed, and most often it was not there. It was abundant, love, but it could not be called. It was won by chance; it was a monstrous game of luck." Gordon's next novel in 1989 was a multi-generational immigrant saga, *The Other Side.* On a single day, the entire MacNamara family gathers at the deathbed of the matriarch, who has slipped into memory and dementia: "Within the nearly visible skull, the brain, disintegrating fast, reaches back past houses, curtains, out to ships and over oceans, down to the sea's bottom, back down to the bog's soaked floor, to mud, then to the oozing beds of ancient ill will, prehistoric rage, vengeance, punishment in blood."

Gordon also came out with a collection of short stories, *Temporary Shelter,* in 1987, as well as a volume of essays, *Good Boys and Dead Girls,* in 1992, and a book of novellas, *The Rest of Life,* in 1993, but her most personal work to date has been her 1996 memoir, *The Shadow Man: A Daughter's Search for Her Father.* She does not know what led her to investigate her father's history, but in the early nineties, she began delving into library archives, census reports, immigration records, yearbooks, and microfilm reels, and she confirmed what she had always suspected: her father was not the man he purported to be.

He was the author of a few poems and essays that appeared in

The Nation, The New Republic, and *Harper's,* and he was the publisher of *The Children's Hour* and *Hot Dog,* a men's humor magazine, but he lied about nearly everything else. He was not a
descendent of French aristocrats. He was born in Vilna, Lithuania,
and his immigrant family spoke only Yiddish. He never went to
Harvard or Oxford or Paris—he didn't even have a passport. He
had dropped out of high school at sixteen and worked as a stenog-
rapher for the Baltimore and Ohio Railroad. And, most horribly,
he was a virulent anti-Semite. In print, he called Einstein a "Jew-
boy" and Max Baer a "ham-hater," and he thought Hitler's worst
sin was closing the Catholic schools in Bavaria. Gordon writes in
the memoir: "I learned less than what I'd hoped, but enough so
that I understood that his life had been made up of lies, some trag-
ic, some pathetic, all of them leaving me with the feeling that I'd
been stolen from. I had lost him as the figure in history I thought
he was; I had lost my place in America."

As traumatic as unearthing these facts was, the truth was oddly
cathartic. "I no longer had to be afraid of the ghost jumping out
of the closet," Gordon says. "I have confronted that ghost, and he
was both more terrible than I had thought and not as terrible as I
had feared. And I think in giving up an idealized father, I stopped
being, most importantly, a daughter."

Today, Gordon considers being a mother to her two children—
Anna, sixteen, and David, thirteen—as her most important role.
She and her children and her second husband, Arthur Cash, who
teaches at SUNY at New Paltz and who is Laurence Sterne's biog-
rapher, live in Manhattan, and Gordon insists she will never leave
the city: "I think I'll be buried in this apartment, yes, I'm so
happy here." She has museums and galleries to satisfy her appetite
for art. She can hop on the bus to Broadway: "If I'm ever sad, I go
to Broadway. What I think is so wonderful about living in this city
is remembering how many other ways there are to live besides
your own. I find that endlessly hopeful and endlessly interesting."
She has frequent opportunities to indulge in a surprising passion,
dancing: "I've done tap, I've done tango. I really love dancing."
And she has a little study in her apartment for her writing, where
she sequesters herself early in the morning, scrawling drafts with
a Waterman fountain pen on Middlesex notebooks, which she
specially orders from England.

Three days a week during the academic year, Gordon teaches at her alma mater, Barnard College, where she is Millicent C. McIntosh Professor of English. "I teach very intensely," Gordon says, though it's abundantly clear that she invests herself fully into everything she does. "What my students give me is hope, and a sense of not being alone, and not being at the end of the road. There's so much talk about the end of literacy, that what comes after us is just a wasteland, vulgar, and cheap, and it's of no value, and when I meet these wonderful students who are as in love with literature as I was at eighteen and nineteen, it gives me great hope that the parade is still going on. It's not going to end with me."

DON'T ERASE ME *Stories by Carolyn Ferrell. Houghton Mifflin, $20.00
cloth. Reviewed by Elizabeth Searle.*

"You ain't no Body," a young girl is told in Carolyn Ferrell's
powerfully compassionate first collection, *Don't Erase Me*. With a
rich variety of voices, Ferrell lets her characters—most of them
African-American girls and women—answer back resoundingly.
Ferrell focuses on their struggle to survive, to avoid being
"erased," and she inhabits her characters fully, body and soul.

Many stories begin with the most basic forms of hunger. "Gain
some weight," the HIV-positive heroine of the title story advises
herself. "... Make plantains. Molasses-fried pork chops. Cherry
dump cake. Corncob supreme. Get rid of the diet pills. You were
born fat and now the sickness makes you want more fat, more all
over so you'll stay longer." Correspondingly, characters in other
stories feel all but invisible in their harsh urban worlds, and sometimes seek attention through sex. A gay teenager meeting his first
lover is told: "This is where your real world begins, man." With
similar intensity, the narrator of "Don't Erase Me" recalls her need
for her own first love: "When he wakes me up, it is all I can do not
to squeeze him to death in love."

Though most of the women and girls in the collection wind up
disappointed by men, Ferrell never reduces her characters to victims and villains. In "Country of the Spread-Out God," she adroit-
ly shifts between the points of view of a teenage mother and her
baby's embittered young father. "You realize that you really are in
the armpit of hell when you are waiting in Family Court," he com-
plains. Yet he adds, "Don't misbelieve me. I love my kid. When I'm
not with Sleepy, my kid's on my mind like a crown. But the rule in
life that I am busy learning right now is: Don't let them see you
sweat. Don't let them in on your goodness." His girlfriend sees that
"goodness." Still, she tells her side of their story with the matter-
of-fact lack of illusions that characterizes Ferrell's street-wise narratives: "And me, I have all these people in my house acting like

animals, because everybody is selfish about their own something and they are all pissed to see all the other somethings that live in the world today... and I think it's a miracle that I can remember *good* at all in the face of all this. Don't you?"

To create such fully realized voices, Ferrell capitalizes on her keen ear and her playful sense of speech rhythms. Her characters come to life in dead-on dialogue ("Thanks Lorrie man I got a favor to ask you please don't tell me no please man") and intense inner monologues that often center on the frustration they feel at trying to express themselves ("I am in silent love in a loud body").

Ferrell renders this frustration most painfully in the wrenching stories that close the collection, centering on daughters struggling with their white mothers. One daughter concludes, as she and her mother fight, "... and I knew it didn't make any kind of sense... and you realized the dead fact that your mouth was really too small to allow the sentences to break out proper that belonged together."

Despite the multiple odds against them, many of Ferrell's characters do find ways to express themselves, often in secret. In the poignant and mordantly funny "Tiger-Frame Glasses," an outcast girl tormented by bullies creates in her private notebook a "Stupendous" group of girls who form a "Helper Squad" and spend their days deciding "Who Should Benefit from Our Good Deeds?"

And, again, in the unforgettable "Don't Erase Me," the narrator faces down her mortality and her sense of worthlessness ("Am I invisible? And why you start walking faster every time you see me?") with a new resolve, telling herself: "Rebirth yourself." Working her way back from the day she receives her HIV diagnosis, she creates a searing chronicle of her life so far. Like many of Ferrell's characters, she finds comfort among other women. She is especially drawn to a woman named Melody who lives on the street, telling historic stories "about black people, *her* people." Marveling at how Melody "doesn't let nothing get in her way," the narrator comes to this conclusion: "Maybe she knows she'll always be in people's minds, and maybe that keeps her going."

In *Don't Erase Me,* Carolyn Ferrell has indelibly drawn vivid and compelling characters who will always be in the minds of her readers.

Elizabeth Searle is the author of My Body to You, *which won the Iowa Short Fiction Prize. Next February, Graywolf Press will publish her first novel,* A Four-Sided Bed.

THE HOUR BETWEEN DOG AND WOLF *Poems by Laure-Anne Bosselaar. BOA Editions, $12.50 paper. Reviewed by Wyn Cooper.*

It is obvious from the first poem in Laure-Anne Bosselaar's debut book of poetry in English that her concerns will be large: "while my grandfather, a prisoner of war / in Holland, sewed perfect, eighteen-buttoned / booties for his wife with the skin of a dead / dog found in a trench, shrapnel slit / Apollinaire's skull, Jesuits brandished / crucifixes in Ouagadougou, and the Parthenon / was already in ruins." The poem, and the book's first section, is called "The Worlds in This World," an apt name for a poem—and a poetry—so inclusive.

Bosselaar, whose first book, *Artemis,* was published in French, grew up in Belgium. The poems in her new book, particularly in the first section, do more than address life there—they evoke it in every color, smell, texture, and taste. It's more bitter than sweet: life in a convent of nuns devoted to God in shocking ways: "We knew what to do: kneel by the empty bottle pile, slip on the gloves, / grab a bottle by its neck, and wait for the signal. It never took long: / with a wail, her half-empty bottle split the air over our heads / / and shattered against the wall." These narrative poems have so much to say, the lines tend to be long, but Bosselaar's ear is never far from the lyric.

One of the book's strongest points is its variety. The second section, "Lost Souls Roaming," is a series of short lyric meditations on place, from the Rockies to Europe, that bring us to the present. I wondered at first why I found these poems as powerful as the not-for-the-timid narratives that preceded them, until I looked more closely at how Bosselaar makes the land come to life, even stand for the lives of those in the poems: "and the landscape opens like a naked body, / trembles with skin-colored hills, bone-pale / rocks, coppery shadows and deep / crevices, dark." It is from under those shadows that the power of these poems makes its way into "every branch, / every twig, every single waving leaf."

"Inventory," the book's final section, is just that. The first poem, "Fallen," takes the idea of a found poem in a new direction: the narrator receives dahlia tubers in the mail, wrapped in shredded paper which, it turns out, is a losing manuscript from a poetry contest. Bosselaar includes two memorable lines, saves them for posterity from the shredder, and in the process makes a comment about the state of poetry, something also addressed by Charles Simic in his excellent introduction. Other poems in this section explore Bosselaar's love of language (she's fluent in four), love of the natural world, and love for her adopted country, but the real love—romantic love—poems are ultimately the most moving. Without the slightest hint of sentimentality or confession, they are unabashed and unequaled, startling in their impact and, like this book, unforgettable.

Wyn Cooper recently completed his second book of poems, The Way Back. *His poems, stories, reviews, and essays have appeared widely. He lives in Vermont.*

BREATHE SOMETHING NICE *Stories by Emily Hammond. Univ. of Nevada, $13.00 paper. Reviewed by Fred Leebron.*

There are no quiet stories in *Breathe Something Nice,* Emily Hammond's first collection of fiction. In a series of ambitious evocations, Hammond demonstrates fresh wit and a fine irony. Most remarkable, though, is her willingness to keep opening up the stories to further possibilities, rather than shutting them down through resolution. These nine stories will linger in the reader's mind long after the last page has been turned.

In the title story, Wanda is a twenty-year-old college student stuck with her classmates in volunteering at a youth detention facility. But unlike the other students, Wanda allows herself to be taken in by John, an ominous and ultimately evil inmate. Wanda's perceptions are interlaced by a kind of testimony from Helena, a classmate, who concludes, "if I had to be stuck in a drainpipe with one of these guys, it'd be any one of them and not him." Wanda and John engage in public sex, in a scene that wonderfully reveals the naïveté and politeness of both the inmates and the classmates, and then Wanda helps John break out in violent fashion. The story doesn't stop there, but pursues Wanda's future long after John has left her by the side of the road with his final instructions: "Breathe in through your nose and out through your mouth. Again. Keep breathing, faster now. Imagine something—something nice." Like most of the stories in the collection, "Breathe Something Nice" hinges on the sexual promiscuity and social precocity of a young woman brash enough to do what she wants and say what she thinks.

In "Wicked," the complexity of the dysfunctional family dynamic is captured precisely in the opening line: "My stepsister is my older brother's ex-girlfriend." Frances, the fifteen-year-old narrator, is on her parents' Hawaiian honeymoon with her two brothers and her new stepsister and stepbrother. The stepmother, Margaret Ann, thinks "housekeeping was on par with running the country: full of important lessons about morality and inge-nuity and good old-fashioned sense." Frances gets into hot water by hooking up with Roger, "the first cute boy who ever talked to me of his own volition...I had a neck like a water heater." When her father confronts her, all that is submerged comes to the sur-face. "Tell Margaret Ann," Frances says, "that her own son hates her. It's all he talks about, how he hates his mother. Another thing: do you know the walls in your room are too thin? Every night we have to listen to you." The story seems it will end with the breakdown of this honeymoon, but it then continues to embrace the lives of the characters long after the failure of the marriage.

Other stories also focus on vacations doomed to failure. "The San Juans Are Beautiful" follows Nance, a thirty-year-old woman, on a Pacific Northwest geriatric cruise with Ellie, her eighty-five-year-old benefactor, "amid the bald-pated gentlemen, age spots on their heads like maps of the Old World, and their scarved wives, tiny and dressed in white jackets with gold buttons, and Keds that looked too large." Throughout the voyage, Nance awaits some kind of truth or epiphany, be it refrigerator sex with the cruise MC, or facts about Ellie's sister's mysterious death. In "Polaroid," Melissa, a nastily thin eighteen-year-old girl trapped on a trip to Solvang, California, with her overweight mother and father and brother, must decide exactly how much her blubbery mother means to her: "When I was younger I believed my real parents were dark and handsome foreigners who...left me with those people, in the care of this big waddling woman who some-how got it in her head that she was my mother. She fed and clothed me and enrolled me in Brownies and Girl Scouts and clapped over every miserable little thing I did."

Breathe Something Nice is populated by such conflicted charac-ters, witnessing and helping to worsen a kind of misery, only to find that what awaits them at the end is a better understanding of what it is that they have been through and survived. It is a compelling and remarkably complete collection.

Fred Leebron's first novel, Out West, *was recently released in paperback by Harcourt Brace/Harvest. He is the co-editor of the forthcoming* Postmodern American Fiction: A Norton Anthology. *He teaches at Gettysburg College.*

SKY OPEN AGAIN *Poems by Gian Lombardo. Dolphin-Moon, $10.00 paper. Reviewed by Priscilla Sneff.*

The prose poem, constructed of sentences rather than lines, is a more liquid sort of solid than other poems. More like glass—that is, molten, mobile, globby—than crystal, the prose poem makes do without enjambment, relying instead on gelatinous processes internal to and constitutive of the sentences and paragraphs, including the control of syllogistic movement, to organize and energize it. In this collection of prose poems by Gian Lombardo, the result is an intense eddy of language, a substantially lyrical thing. Look, for example, at the poem "Satisfaction Not Required": "Animals have always been wary of snares, especially of ones set in mid-air, ostensibly to catch light, or maybe a breeze. Children have always been determined to misspell a word when it is convenient for them to do so. On the mesa, it's all too frequently the 'sun's in the sky' being the same as 'the page is in the book' being not the same."

Here rhyme (wary/snares/mid-air; snares/ones/breeze) and parallelism (animals/children; always been/always been/all too frequently...being; being the same/being not the same) organize the paragraph into sonic units that interweave to construct a larger and quite complex sonic unit that "makes sense" to the ear quite apart from its semantic meaning. Yet the poem itself critiques or at least complicates this sort of reading: voice or image—"breeze" or "light"—are clues that we are in the presence of snares; they are but the *ostensible* intention of the window in the poem and of the poem. What is the real intent?

The poem I've just quoted is from the first, and my favorite, section of the book, called "Under the Tongue," set in a Southwestern desert landscape. Here, in the words of the poem "Warm," "there are lush worlds and there are burnt worlds...And when it is dark you have the grace of not seeing which world you step into." In another poem, Lombardo writes, "I don't want to look too closely." These poems deliberately dispense partial views, tolerate cloudinesses, thwart an easy and automatic forward movement—they are compositions of "the new sentence," to use Ron Silliman's term—and while the poems work together and collectively resonate to form a retroactive narrative, they also always force the reader to shift back from that narrative into an awareness of the language that composes it—that is, back and forth between the burnt world of desert and the lush world of language.

Priscilla Sneff *has published poems in* Ploughshares, The Yale Review, Sulfur, *and other magazines. She teaches at Tufts University.*

EDITORS' CORNER

New Books by
Our Advisory Editors

EDITORS' SHELF

Books Recommended by
Our Advisory Editors

Ann Beattie, *My Life, Starring Dara Falcon,* a novel: Beattie's sixth novel is narrated, with soaring irony and comic verve, by Jean Warner, a young bride in New England whose life and marriage are spun helter-skelter by the arrival of Dara Falcon, a brilliant, pathological liar. (Knopf)

Richard Ford, *Women with Men,* three stories: Three long stories which once again demonstrate Ford's mastery. Two of the stories are set in contemporary Paris, the third in Montana—all about men trying to fathom the women they love. (Knopf)

Maxine Kumin, *Telling the Barn Swallow,* essays edited by Emily Grosholz: Lively analyses by twelve fellow poets of Kumin's diction and prosody, her literary forebears, and characteristic thematic patterns. Also included here are provocative poems, some published here for the first time, to or about Maxine Kumin. (New England)

Robert Boswell recommends *Breathe Something Nice,* stories by Emily Hammond: "This is an extraordinary collection of stories—beautifully written, artfully crafted, and utterly haunting. It should be required reading in every workshop in the country." Reviewed in "Bookshelf" on page 229. (Nevada)

George Garrett recommends *Narrative Design: A Writer's Guide to Structure,* a textbook by Madison Smartt Bell: "A remarkable textbook with an unusual point of view, in which the structural design is primary in the writing of fiction. With excellent examples and analyses." (Norton)

Marilyn Hacker recommends *Naming the Light: A Week of Years,* essays by Rosemary Deen: "These essays mostly begin with the natural world near at hand: the author's rambling garden in Ulster County, New York. But they range and reach out the way a brilliantly polymath mind does: to Florentine painting, American rural architecture, medieval polyphony, the origins of words, the Elgin marbles, the varieties of human love—and they're everywhere made fresh and surprising by the author's deft, lyrical, accurate prose, a virtuoso performance on a lovingly crafted instrument." (Illinois)

Maxine Kumin recommends *Invisible Horses,* poems by Patricia Goedicke: "These poems are about subjective and objective realities of the hidden impulses we live by—very powerful and innovative: '. . . wondering / what strings us together, self / and self-image, and the words for it . . .'" (Milkweed)

Philip Levine recommends *Believers,* stories and a novella by Charles Baxter: "This is a superb collection; the stories are unusually daring and imaginative—

'Time Exposure' and 'The Lures for Love' are two not to be forgotten. The novella 'Believers' demonstrates an extraordinary ability to deal with and invoke a past era and to show how sex, power, money, and class determine the lives of ordinary as well as exceptional Americans. 'Believers' is so subtle, potent, and authoritative, it recalls that other Midwestern master of fiction, F. Scott Fitzgerald. To my way of reading it is the best of Baxter, as well as the best novella I've read in years." (Pantheon)

James Alan McPherson recommends *Life in Double Time: Confessions of an American Drummer,* a memoir by Mike Lankford: "A very unpretentious account of the riff-style lifestyle of dedicated musicians. This is an excellent, humorous account of rock and roll." (Chronicle)

POSTSCRIPTS

Miscellaneous Notes · Fall 1997

COHEN AWARDS Each year, we honor the best short story and poem published in *Ploughshares* with the Cohen Awards, which are wholly sponsored by our longtime patrons Denise and Mel Cohen. Finalists are nominated by staff editors, and the winners—each of whom receives a cash prize of $600—are selected by our advisory editors. The 1997 Cohen Awards for work published in *Ploughshares* in 1996, Volume 22, go to Andrew Sean Greer and Campbell McGrath:

ANDREW SEAN GREER *for his story "Come Live with Me and Be My Love" in Fall 1996, edited by Richard Ford.*

Andrew Sean Greer was born the son of chemists in Washington, D.C., in 1970 and was raised in the Maryland suburbs. He received his undergraduate degree from Brown University, where he won awards as a playwright and studied with Edmund White and Robert Coover. He was also chosen as commencement speaker for his class, and unexpectedly caused a semi-riot with his unrehearsed remarks, which critiqued Brown's admissions policies. ("I recently went to my college reunion," Greer says, "and my classmates had still not forgiven me.") He lived in New York City for two years, and after one paid writing assignment for a design magazine, which was killed for being "too flip," he supported himself with odd jobs: being a chauffeur for a television writer, driving boys to prep-school interviews in New England and posing as their ESL teacher, and running lights and sound for a downtown theater, "a job I had no qualifications for and, as was discovered on opening night, no talent." Last spring, Greer graduated from the M.F.A. program in creative writing at the University of Montana, and now lives in Seattle. "Come Live with Me and Be My Love" was his first published story; his second appears in the August 1997 issue of *Esquire.* He is currently at work on a novel.

About his story, Greer writes: "For years I'd been fascinated by stories I'd heard of gay men and lesbians in the fifties in marriages of convenience, with secret tunnels under their houses so their lovers could sneak into hidden bedrooms, a suburban facade where next-door neighbors mowing lawns were all part of this literally underground society. Surely these were urban legends of the gay community—subterranean tunnels?—but they intrigued me. I couldn't, however, think of a way to portray them that wouldn't seem creepy or utterly dated. I also had always had a problem writing about love, since that's what I saw it as—some kind of tacky *Romeo and Juliet* tale, meeting through tunnels at night. No, that kind of love story had been seen before. And then much later, in one of those awful moments writers have at the keyboard, dreaming up ideas, I ranged through my memory for the saddest things I'd known, and I thought of the time I sat in the highest window of my empty apartment in Providence, watching my best friend sneak off into a cab, my roommate for years, tossing her bags into the back seat without a goodbye, and riding off away from me. She must have known I was up there watching. I'd never understood quite what I felt at that moment, why it felt like my fault, why you can't have romantic farewells with friends the way you can with lovers—as if friends couldn't break your heart, too. Somehow I thought again of those marriages of convenience, and how, as terrible as they were, there must have been something so touching about them, these barely acquainted spouses trapped together, like war buddies in a trench, so after everything, after all my frequent dismissals of romance, I ended up writing a love story after all."

CAMPBELL MCGRATH *for his poem "Praia dos Orixas" in Winter 1996–97, edited by Robert Boswell & Ellen Bryant Voigt.*

Campbell McGrath was born in Chicago in 1962, and grew up in Washington, D.C. He attended the University of Chicago, where he received his bachelor's degree in 1984, and he graduated from Columbia University's M.F.A. program in 1988. McGrath—along with wife, Elizabeth—then returned to Chicago, where he served as Visiting Poet at the University of Chicago in 1991. He has also taught at Northwestern, Columbia College, North Park College, and, he quips, "anywhere else that would have me." His son Sam was born in Chicago in 1988, and his son Jackson was born last November in Miami Beach, the McGraths' current home. For the last four years, McGrath has taught in the M.F.A. program at Florida International University. His three books are *Capitalism* (Wesleyan, 1990), *American Noise* (Ecco, 1994), and *Spring Comes to Chicago* (Ecco, 1996), which won the Kingsley Tufts Prize. His poems have appeared in *Ploughshares* several times, as well as in *The New Yorker, Harper's, The New York Times,* and *Antaeus.* He has new work forthcoming in *The Paris Review, TriQuarterly,* and *The Kenyon Review.*

" 'Praia dos Orixas,' " McGrath writes, "is one of a series of travelogue-like prose poems I've been writing over the last two or three years, part of a soon-to-be-completed (I hope) manuscript called *Road Atlas.* So, on the one hand, the poem is part of an exploration of the form of the prose poem, specifically the notion of moving the prose poem beyond closed-off, block-like paragraphs. In general I wanted to see what happened when one broke the prose apart on the page in a sculptural way, not as lines, in a prosodic sense, but as fragments of varying lengths and types. This idea seemed to me to open up a hidden world of spatial possibility and great textural range, constrained by neither poetic nor prose notions of propriety—the world between the line and the paragraph. As I look at it now, 'Praia dos Orixas' seems pretty conventional on the page, its divisions predictably ordered by syntax and narrative; but the notion of prose/poetic hybridization and formal freedom was central to its original intent.

"The idea to work with open-ended prose forms was suggested to me by Robert Hass's poems, especially the beautiful sequence of 'strophic' poems at the beginning of his book *Human Wishes.* This was one good reason to dedicate 'Praia dos Orixas' to Hass. Another was the poem's interest in language as subject as well as medium, and in the disjunction or collision between the symbolic world of language and the not-quite-expressible *thingness*—or erotics, to use one of Hass's terms—of the natural world. This is a long-winded way of saying that one of the poem's concerns is the so-called mind/body dilemma, a frequent subject of contemporary American poetry. Thus 'Praia dos Orixas' ironically embodies the idea of the limits of language in its roadside encounter, another amusing anecdote from the great epistemological road trip of life.

"And it's a true story, for the most part—a composite of several different excursions we undertook into the backwoods of Bahia, in northeastern Brazil, about ten years ago, when Elizabeth and I went to visit her brother, Joshua, who was conducting anthropological fieldwork in one of the larger shantytowns outside the city of Salvador. The incident of the broken fan belt, as I recall, took place somewhere on the island of Itaparica, where we saw the sign for Praia dos Orixas, which translates as 'Beach of the Gods' or 'Beach of the Spirits.' (More specifically, the *orixas* are the gods and goddesses of Candomble, the Brazilian folk religion descended through generations of African slavery from animist religions of West Africa—an exact counterpart to Spanish-Caribbean Santeria, where the *orixas* become the *orishas,* and to Haitian Voodoo, where they are known as *loas.*) What did the sign mean, in that weird, beachless backwater? Who knows. Is there really a place called 'Praia dos Orixas'? I think so. If not, there should be.

Steve Satterwhite

"Lastly, upon completing this poem, I was particularly delighted with its final line, which seemed a stunningly concise and clever conclusion to both its narrative and intellectual concerns, resolving the mind/body duality by playing off the suggested meanings of 'speaking in tongues.' It was a lyrical enactment of the poem's conceit, the forging of a kind of erotics of language. It was also my third and most important reason for dedicating the poem to Robert Hass, since it is in fact his line that ends 'Praia dos Orixas'—stolen almost verbatim from the poem 'Spring,' in *Field Guide*—a fact I realized with some chagrin several weeks after completing the final draft of the poem. While I thought I had been engaged in a critical dialogue with Hass's work, it turned out I had been plagiarizing it—which is an entirely different kind of glossolalia. Oh well. It still seems like a great line, and a great ending for this poem. For which I am thankful to Robert Hass and the rest of the *orixas.*"

ANNUAL PRIZES Mary Gordon's story "City Life," which appeared in the Spring 1996 issue of *Ploughshares,* edited by Marilyn Hacker, has been selected as the winner of *Prize Stories 1997: The*

O. Henry Awards. The anthology, edited by Larry Dark, will be published this October by Doubleday/Anchor.

Alyson Hagy's story "Search Bay," which was included in the Fall 1996 issue, edited by Richard Ford, has been picked for *The Best American Short Stories 1997*. This year's volume, which has E. Annie Proulx as the guest editor and Katrina Kenison as the series editor, will be published this November by Houghton Mifflin.

Three pieces from *Ploughshares* have been selected for the annual *Pushcart Prize XXII: Best of the Small Presses:* Andrea Barrett's story "The Forest," from the Winter 1996–97 issue, edited by Robert Boswell & Ellen Bryant Voigt; and Rane Arroyo's "Breathing Lessons" and Thomas Sayers Ellis's "Atomic Bride," both poems from the Spring 1996 issue, edited by Marilyn Hacker.

Finally, Gina Berriault, whose stories first began appearing in *Ploughshares* in 1979, was named the winner of the 1997 Rea Award for the Short Story. The $30,000 award, sponsored by the Dungannon Foundation, annually honors a writer who has made a significant contribution to the short story form. Berriault's most recent collection, *Women in Their Beds* (Counterpoint), her first book in twelve years, won the PEN/Faulkner Award and the National Book Critics Circle Award.

CONTRIBUTORS' NOTES

Fall 1997

ALICE ADAMS was born in Virginia, grew up in Chapel Hill, North Carolina, and graduated from Radcliffe. Since then, she has lived mostly in San Francisco. She has published one travel book about Mexico, four short story collections, and ten novels, the most recent of which is *Medicine Men*, which was published this spring by Knopf. Another novel and a new story collection are due out next year.

E. M. BRONER is the author of nine books, including *A Weave of Women*, *The Telling*, *The Women's Haggadah*, *Ghost Stories*, and *Mornings & Mourning*. She has received two fellowships from the National Endowment for the Arts, as well as a Wonder Woman Award. She lives in Manhattan with her artist husband, Robert Broner.

BLISS BROYARD was a Henry Hoyns Fellow at the University of Virginia's creative writing program. Her fiction has appeared in *Grand Street* and *The Pushcart Prize*. Her first collection of short stories is scheduled to be published by Knopf in the spring of 1998. At that time, an essay of hers will also appear in the anthology *Twenties in the Nineties* (Houghton Mifflin). She lives in Brooklyn, New York.

SUSAN DAITCH is the author of a collection of short stories, *Storytown*, and two novels, *L.C.* and *The Colorist*. Her work has appeared or is forthcoming in *The Voice Literary Supplement*, *Bomb*, *The Iowa Anthology of Transgressive Fiction*, *Avant-Pop*, an anthology edited by Larry McCaffery, *The Pushcart Prize*, and *The Norton Anthology of Postmodern Literature*. Her work was the subject of the Fall 1993 issue of *The Review of Contemporary Fiction*.

TIM GAUTREAUX's fiction has appeared in *The Atlantic Monthly*, *Harper's*, *GQ*, *Best American Short Stories*, and *New Stories from the South*. He has taught at Southeastern Louisiana University since 1972. The recipient of a National Endowment for the Arts fellowship and a National Magazine Award for fiction, he was selected to be the John and Renee Grisham Visiting Southern Writer in Residence at the University of Mississippi in 1996. *Same Place, Same Things*, his collection of stories, was published last year by St. Martin's Press, which will also release his forthcoming novel and another collection of stories.

PATRICIA HAMPL is the author of the memoirs *A Romantic Education* and *Virgin Time*. She has also published two volumes of poetry, and short stories in various magazines. She has written a screenplay based on *Spillville*, her book about Dvorak in America, and is finishing *I Could Tell You Stories*, essays on memory and imagination. She is Regents' Professor at the University of Minnesota.

ETHAN HAUSER was born and raised outside of Boston. He now lives in New York City, where he is writing a novel and a collection of short stories. His fiction has appeared previously in *Confrontation* and is forthcoming in *Esquire.*

LUCY HONIG's short stories have appeared recently in *DoubleTake, The Gettysburg Review,* and *Prize Stories 1996: The O. Henry Awards.* For a number of years, she was the director of a local human rights commission in upstate New York. Currently, she teaches in the graduate program in international health in Boston University's School of Public Health. "Police Chief's Daughter" is from *Citizens Review,* a novel in progress.

CAROLE MASO is the author of *Ghost Dance, The Art Lover, Ava, The American Woman in the Chinese Hat,* and *Aureole.* She teaches at Brown University.

JOYCE CAROL OATES is the author, most recently, of the novel *We Were the Mulvaneys* and the story collection *Will You Always Love Me?* Her forthcoming novel is *Man Crazy,* a chapter of which, "Easy Lay," appeared in *Ploughshares.* She lives and teaches in Princeton, New Jersey.

RICHARD PANEK's short fiction has won a PEN Award and been broadcast on National Public Radio. He is the author of two nonfiction books: a cultural history of the telescope, to be published in 1998, and *Waterloo Diamonds,* a social history of an Iowa factory town and its minor league baseball club. He often writes for *The New York Times* and is a contributing writer at *Elle* and *Mirabella.* He lives in New York City.

DAVID PLANTE was born in a working-class, French-speaking parish in Providence, Rhode Island, in 1940. Though he has now lived abroad in England, Italy, and Greece for much longer than half his life, he feels he still resides spiritually in that small parish, where his principal work—the Francoeur novels—is centered.

HELEN SCHULMAN is the author of a collection of stories, *Not a Free Show* (Knopf), and a novel, *Out of Time* (Atheneum). Her new novel, *The Revisionist,* will be published by Crown in May 1998. She is the co-editor, with Jill Bialosky, of *Wanting a Child,* an anthology of essays that will be published next year by Farrar, Straus & Giroux. She has written or co-written five commissioned screenplays. She currently teaches in the Graduate Writing Division of Columbia University.

MAXINE SWANN lives in Paris, where she is completing her graduate studies in French literature at the Sorbonne and writing her first novel.

EILEEN TOBIN's last published story was in 1943, when she was a student in a writing seminar taught by the late novelist Millen Brand. In 1994, Tobin began writing again under the tutelage of another novelist, Mary Gordon, who, while fulfilling a public service condition of a grant from the Lila Wallace–Reader's Digest Fund, conducted a writing workshop for elders in New York City's Upper West Side. "Goodbye, Tinker Bell, Hello, God" is from Tobin's memoir in progress, *Bog Oak.* She is eighty-one years old.

NOLA TULLY spent several years as a photojournalist based in New York. She has worked with the Sygma picture agency, and her photos have appeared in *Newsweek, Time, Life, Paris Match,* and *Stern;* in exhibits; and in a book on the Gulf War. She studied photography at the Rhode Island School of Design and painting and art history at Hunter College, and she received her master's in writing from Columbia University. She is currently finishing her first novel. This is her first fiction publication.

MEG WOLITZER is a novelist whose books include *Sleepwalking* and *This Is Your Life.* A recipient of a 1994 fellowship in fiction from the National Endowment for the Arts, she has taught at the Iowa Writers' Workshop, Skidmore College, and Boston University. Her upcoming novel, *Surrender, Dorothy,* will be published next year. She lives in New York City.

～

SUBSCRIBERS Please feel free to contact us via e-mail with address changes (the post office usually will not forward journals) or any problems with your subscription. Our e-mail address is: pshares@emerson.edu. Also, please note that on occasion we exchange mailing lists with other literary magazines and organizations. If you would like your name excluded from these exchanges, simply send us an e-mail message or a letter stating so.

SUBMISSION POLICIES *Ploughshares* is published three times a year: usually mixed issues of poetry and fiction in the Spring and Winter and a fiction issue in the Fall, with each guest-edited by a different writer. We welcome unsolicited manuscripts from August 1 to March 31 (postmark dates). All submissions sent from April to July are returned unread. In the past, guest editors often announced specific themes for issues, but we have revised our editorial policies and no longer restrict submissions to thematic topics. Submit your work at any time during our reading period; if a manuscript is not timely for one issue, it will be considered for another. Send one prose piece and/or one to three poems at a time (mail genres separately). Poems should be individually typed either single- or double-spaced on one side of the page. Prose should be typed double-spaced on one side and be no longer than twenty-five pages. Although we look primarily for short stories, we occasionally publish personal essays/memoirs. Novel excerpts are acceptable if self-contained. Unsolicited book reviews and criticism are not considered. Please do not send multiple submissions of the same genre, and do not send another manuscript until you hear about the first. Additional submissions will be returned unread. Mail your manuscript in a page-size manila envelope, your full name and address written on the outside, to the "Fiction Editor," "Poetry Editor," or "Nonfiction Editor." Unsolicited work sent directly to a guest editor's home or office will be ignored and discarded; guest editors are formally instructed not to read such work. All manuscripts and correspondence regarding submissions should be accompanied by a self-addressed, stamped envelope (S.A.S.E.) for a response. Expect three to five months for a decision. Do not query us until five months have passed, and if you do, please write to us, including an s.a.s.e. and indicating the postmark date of submission, instead of calling. Simultaneous submissions are amenable as long as they are indicated as such and we are notified immediately upon acceptance elsewhere. We cannot accommodate revisions, changes of return address, or forgotten s.a.s.e.'s after the fact. We do not reprint previously published work. Translations are welcome if permission has been granted. We cannot be responsible for delay, loss, or damage. Payment is upon publication: $25/printed page, $50 minimum per title, $250 maximum per author, with two copies of the issue and a one-year subscription.

THE NAME *Ploughshares* 1. The sharp edge of a plough that cuts a furrow in the earth. 2 a. A variation of the name of the pub, the Plough and Stars, in Cambridge, Massachusetts, where a journal was founded. 2 b. The pub's name was inspired by the Sean O'Casey play about the Easter Rising of the Irish "citizen army." The army's flag contained a plough, representing the things of the earth, hence practicality; and stars, the ideals by which the plough is steered. 3. A shared, collaborative, community effort that has endured for twenty-six years. 4. A literary journal that has been energized by a desire for harmony, peace, and reform. Once, that spirit motivated civil rights marches, war protests, and student activism. Today, it still inspirits a desire for beating swords into ploughshares, but through the power and the beauty of the written word.

DIRT ANGEL
Stories by Jeanne Wilmot

An electrifying debut, *Dirt Angel* is informed by an original voice from the urban landscape of cross-over culture. The negotiations between lovers, cultures, races, siblings find their place on these pages in highly charged and yet authentic ways. Passionate, sensual, violent, and tender, *Dirt Angel* is a striking collection by a bold new talent.

"A strong, original work with a vivid flow of language and landscape. Altogether a striking and memorable performance." —Elizabeth Hardwick

"With her first book, Jeanne Wilmot, like her fast-talking, fast-walking protagonists, has hip-hopped onto fiction's center stage, and she nails our attention there from the first page to the last. A remarkable debut." —Russell Banks

"Wilmot's stories are fierce, exacting, often dazzlingly smart and penetrating. They regularly mimic life's elusiveness, and in those moments of evanescence and clarity they are actually breathtaking." —Richard Ford

Ontario Review Press
Distributed by George Braziller, Inc.
(212) 889-0909 • Fax (212) 689-5405

BENNINGTON WRITING SEMINARS

MFA in Writing and Literature
Two-Year Low-Residency Program

A. BLAKE GARDNER

FICTION
NONFICTION
POETRY

For more information contact:
Writing Seminars
Box PL
Bennington College
Bennington, VT 05201
802-442-5401, ext. 160
Fax 802-442-6164

the modern writer as witness

MFA
CREATIVE WRITING
UNIVERSITY OF MARYLAND, COLLEGE PARK

FACULTY – 1997-1998

Poetry

Michael Collier Phillis Levin
Stanley Plumly

Fiction

Merle Collins Joyce Kornblatt
Reginald McKnight Howard Norman

RECENT VISITING WRITERS

Russell Banks	Marita Golden	Philip Levine	Mary Robison
Henri Cole	Robert Hass	Peter Matthiessen	Marilynne Robinson
Rita Dove	Seamus Heaney	William Maxwell	C.D. Wright
Louise Glück	June Jordan	C.E. Poverman	Charles Wright

For more information:

Michael Collier, Stanley Plumly, Directors
Department of English
University of Maryland, College Park, MD 20742
(301) 405-3820

Boston Review's *5th Annual*

SHORT STORY CONTEST

Boston Review is pleased to announce its 5th Annual Short Story Contest. The winning entry will be published in the *Review*'s December 1997 issue. Stories should not exceed four thousand words and must be previously unpublished. The author's name, address, and phone should be on the first page of each entry; do not send a cover letter. A $10 processing fee, payable to *Boston Review* in the form of a check or money order, must accompany all entries. Entrants will receive a one-year subscription to the *Review* beginning with the December issue. Submissions must be postmarked by October 1, 1997. Stories will not be returned. Send entries to: Short Story Contest, *Boston Review*, E53-407 MIT, Cambridge, MA 02139.

First Prize: $1,000

Ploughshares

a literary adventure

Known for its compelling fiction and poetry, *Ploughshares* is widely regarded as one of America's most influential literary journals. Each issue is guest-edited by a different writer for a fresh, provocative slant—exploring personal visions, aesthetics, and literary circles—and contributors include both well-known and emerging writers. In fact, *Ploughshares* has become a premier proving ground for new talent, showcasing the early works of Sue Miller, Mona Simpson, Robert Pinsky, and countless others. Past guest editors include Richard Ford, Derek Walcott, Tobias Wolff, Carolyn Forché, and Rosellen Brown. This unique editorial format has made *Ploughshares*, in effect, into a dynamic anthology series—one that has established a tradition of quality and prescience. *Ploughshares* is published in quality trade paperback in April, August, and December: usually a fiction issue in the Fall and mixed issues of poetry and fiction in the Spring and Winter. Inside each issue, you'll find not only great new stories and poems, but also a profile on the guest editor, book reviews, and miscellaneous notes about *Ploughshares*, its writers, and the literary world. Subscribe today.

Sample *Ploughshares* on the Web: http://www.emerson.edu/ploughshares

---

❑ **Send me a one-year subscription for $21.**
I save $8.85 off the cover price (3 issues).

❑ **Send me a two-year subscription for $40.**
I save $19.70 off the cover price (6 issues).

Start with: ❑ Spring ❑ Fall ❑ Winter

Add $5 per year for international. Institutions: $24.

Name _____

Address _____

_____

Mail with check to: Ploughshares · Emerson College
100 Beacon St. · Boston, MA 02116